Dead Man's Handle

Peter O'Donnell began writing at the age of sixteen, when he sold his first story. He has lost count since then but thinks the tally reaches over a thousand short stories and novels. He also writes television and film scripts.

Born in 1921, he spent two years working on juvenile periodicals and served in the Royal Corps Signals during World War II. He began writing strip cartoons – the best known are probably 'Garth' in the *Daily Mirror* and 'Tug Transom' in the *Daily Sketch*. 'Modesty Blaise' took him a year to create and in 1962 she was presented as a strip-cartoon character in the *Evening Standard*. The cartoon was an immediate success, soon syndicating in over forty countries, and the 'Modesty Blaise' series of novels followed.

Dead Man's Handle

Peter O'Donnell

Pan Books
London and Sydney

First published 1985 by Souvenir Press Ltd
This edition published 1986 by Pan Books Ltd,
Cavaye Place, London SW10 9PG
9 8 7 6 5 4 3 2 1
© Peter O'Donnell 1985
ISBN 0 330 29452 0
Printed and bound in Great Britain by
Cox & Wyman Ltd, Reading

1

Her name was Molly Chen, she was nineteen, and she was frightened. An aircraft coming in low to land at Kai Tak airport gave her an excuse to say nothing until the noise had faded. She stood up, moved across the small office to close the window that looked out from Kowloon across Victoria Harbour to the island of Hong Kong, then returned to her seat at the cluttered desk.

The Englishman who sat facing her was also afraid. He did not fidget, or show any outward sign of nerves, but the tension in him was so great that she could feel its resonance within herself. Trying to keep her voice steady she said, "My grandfather is not available at the moment, Mr Garvin."

Blue eyes studied her suspiciously. "When will 'e be?" the man demanded. His voice was uncultured, and she thought the accent was what the English called Cockney.

Uncertain how to answer him, she countered with a question of her own. "What proof do you have that you represent Modesty Blaise, please? I have been secretary to my grandfather, Wei Lu, for two years now, and I have not seen you before, neither have I heard your name."

The big fair man with the somewhat rough-hewn face said, "It's the first time I've worked for Modesty Blaise. She sort of . . . picked me up in Thailand a week or two ago. Gave me this job to do before she flew back to Tangier. I'm 'ere to collect fifty thousand sterling in Royal Dutch Shell bearer stocks from Wei Lu for services rendered." He felt in his pocket and laid a small ivory plaque on the desk. "That says Modesty Blaise sent me."

Molly Chen leaned forward and studied the Chinese characters engraved on the plaque, then nodded. "Yes, that is her chop. Nobody but her representative would have such a credential, Mr. Garvin."

Willie Garvin put the plaque away and relaxed slightly. "Then when do I get to collect the certificates from Wei Lu?" he demanded.

The girl's hands fluttered in distress. "I am sorry," she said, and now her voice faltered. "It is impossible. Three days ago my grandfather's yacht was stopped by a gunboat of the Chinese Navy while returning from Macau, and he was taken off. There is a grapevine, you understand, and from this we know that he is now in the Republic, in the hands of Chinese Army Intelligence."

In the silence that followed she saw the colour fade slowly from the Englishman's face, and wondered why he should be so deeply shaken. Modesty Blaise was a reasonable person who had a good relationship with Wei Lu, and would know that this was not a piece of trickery. Besides, it was no fault of this man Willie Garvin that he would have to go away empty handed. At last he said in a hoarse voice, "Can you get 'old of the bearer certificates on Wei Lu's be'alf?"

She shook her head apologetically. "If I could do so I would, Mr. Garvin, for I know the transaction is agreed, but I do not even know which bank holds the documents, or if my grandfather has them in private safe-custody somewhere. In my duties as secretary I deal with only certain parts of his business."

Willie Garvin closed his eyes and muttered, "Oh, Christ . . ." After a moment he opened them again and said with quiet desperation, "D'you know where they've got Wei Lu?"

She dipped her head in answer, fingers twining together nervously, and said, "According to the grapevine my grandfather is being held for interrogation at the headquarters of Tenth Corps Intelligence Section, which is based at Kui-tan." She hesitated, then went on, "You must understand that to a great extent this is a personal matter, Mr. Garvin. Many years ago my grandfather was an officer in the Army of the Chinese Republic under Mao. He deserted and fled to Hong Kong. His superior at the time was disgraced and imprisoned for two years. Since his release he has been rehabilitated and now he is a Colonel in charge of the Intelligence Section at Kui-tan. I think his purpose is revenge. My grandfather will be brainwashed into making a detailed confession of many crimes, and will then be executed."

She saw that Willie Garvin had listened with ferocious attention to every word. Now he said, "Where's Kui-tan?"

"A hundred miles or so up the coast and five miles inland."

She went to a cupboard, produced a map, unfolded it, and spread it on the desk. When he stood beside her she was again conscious of the huge tension in him. For three silent minutes he studied the map with frightening concentration. Then: "I'll 'ave to get your grandfather out of there, Molly, and I'll need more funds than I've got, so 'ow much can you raise?"

She turned her head to stare at him. "Out of Red China? That is madness, Mr. Garvin. It cannot be done. Please believe that I love my grandfather and would do anything to help him, but I know what is possible and what is not. I do not understand why you should even think of something so hopeless. For me this is a great sorrow, but for you it is only a matter of making a telephone call to Modesty Blaise in Tangier, and telling her what has happened—"

"No!" His voice almost cracked on the word. He swallowed, and continued quietly. "No, Molly. She sent me to do a job, first I've ever done for 'er, and there's no way I'm going to ring up and start whining about problems."

She moved to sit down limply in her grandfather's chair. "You . . . you seriously mean to enter Red China and try to bring him out, Mr. Garvin?"

He shrugged impatiently. "I got no other option." Abruptly he stood up and began to pace the small office, eyes blank with thought. She sensed the tension in him being converted to furious thought, the brain behind the blank eyes humming like a dynamo. A small, wary hope was born within her. There was something curiously potent in the big man's aura, and on top of this he came with the chop of Modesty Blaise herself, which gave added potency.

"I'll need a boatman," he muttered as if speaking his thoughts aloud. "Someone reliable. Need a few things from a doctor, too. Then there'll be scuba gear, field glasses . . ." His voice faded but his lips continued to move slightly. She watched him halt by the window for a while, gazing blindly out, then he resumed his pacing and muttering. "No small arms . . . just me knives and a few skittles. If it comes to a shoot-out I've lost anyway. Grenades, maybe? A diversion . . . ? It's all going to cost." He stopped in his stride and said, "Can you raise a bit of cash, Molly?"

She lifted her hands, palms up. "Mr. Garvin, I am a young Chinese girl. I have a few hundred Hong Kong dollars of my own, and you are welcome to them, but—"

He cut her short with a gesture and said, "D'you know which bank Modesty Blaise uses 'ere?"

She nodded. "Yes. The Hong Kong and Macau Fidelity Bank."

"Right. I'll use 'er chop to get funds there." Molly Chen saw sweat spring out on his brow as he spoke those words. Then: "You reckon they'll play?"

"I think so, Mr. Garvin. The chop of Modesty Blaise is much respected. If the bank refuses, I know several private persons who will certainly lend you money against it."

He wiped his brow with a handkerchief and said, "I'll need a boat, Molly, a cruiser with a decent turn of speed, and a good man to handle 'er. All I'll want 'im to do is drop me off in an inflatable about three miles off-shore at night, then come back each night for the next four nights and stand by for a couple of hours, say from two a.m. to four a.m., pushing out a radio beam for me to home in on."

She said, "For four nights?"

"If I'm not back then I won't be coming back. That's when you phone Modesty Blaise and tell 'er. Not before."

She came from behind the desk and stood looking up at him. "Mr. Garvin, it is very difficult to keep anything secret in Hong Kong. If one other person knows what you intend, there is a chance that it will reach the grapevine. But my grandfather owns a Seahound. It cruises at twenty knots with a range of three hundred nautical miles, and I have handled it often. I know that I am only a female, but—"

He cut her short with an almost irritable shake of his head. "Have 'er thoroughly checked, and be ready to sail at seven p.m. the day after tomorrow. I'll need that much time to get everything together." For a moment his taut anxiety faded and he looked at her as if recognising another human being. Then he put a hand on her shoulder and said gently, "Thanks, Molly. We'll do fine together, just fine."

His gaze lost focus again and he turned away. "Now . . . radio equipment, scuba gear, weapons, a doctor. You got good contacts?"

"Yes, Mr. Garvin."

"Right. In a minute I'll start listing everything we'll need. There'll be nothing to give any of these people a clue about what I'm doing. They'll just think I'm setting up some kind of scam for Modesty Blaise. You got a thousand scams going on this island, so one more won't attract much interest." He pulled a chair up to the desk and took a ballpoint pen from his pocket. "Let's 'ave a pad to write on, Molly. I'll do that list now, and I'd better get it right."

She took a lined pad from a drawer and put it in front of him. "Mr. Garvin . . . do you really believe that you can bring my grandfather safely home?"

He sat still for a moment, then slowly raised his head to look at her, and in his eyes she saw a deep grey weariness, a soul-weariness born of the despair that might come to possess a man who had never found himself. "I reckon there's 'alf a chance," he said quietly. "It's surprising what you can get away with when people aren't expecting anything. Main problem's going to be locating 'im. If I can do that, the odds get a lot better." He paused, and for a moment she glimpsed another man within him as humorous resignation touched his eyes. "But you can count on me 'aving a good try, Molly, even if there isn't 'alf a chance, because if I don't get Wei Lu back, I'd just as soon not come back meself."

✳ ✳ ✳ ✳

Five days later, an hour before sunset, Willie Garvin lowered the field glasses from his eyes and looked at his watch. He lay in a fold of ground near the rounded crest of a hill overlooking Kui-tan from the south, with a few square feet of camouflage netting spread in front of him. Behind him lay a backpack weighing well over a hundred pounds.

He had lain here for almost two days now, having paddled ashore from the Seahound soon after midnight forty-four hours ago in a black fourteen-foot single canoe. This now lay on the sea bed, weighed down by rocks. Apart from his backpack the canoe had carried a heavy duty battery, a deflated rubber dinghy, and a small but efficient battery-driven outboard motor he had spent six hours adapting in Wei Lu's garage. These items were now hidden in a crevice of the low cliff that hemmed a narrow rock-strewn beach on the deserted stretch of coast.

Moving across country under fitful moonlight he had reached the hills south of Kui-tan by three a.m. and established his position before first light. Throughout that day he had studied every detail of the little town with unfaltering concentration. The map had told him that it straddled a river and that on the north side the ground rose steeply. For this reason he had chosen to place himself on the south side first, and his choice was good, for it was here that a dozen large huts formed a barracks standing clear of the town.

Throughout the long hours of daylight he had been able to make a close estimate of the number of men. There were fewer than three hundred, a Corps Headquarters cadre, he decided, consisting mainly of Signals and Administration personnel. On the west side of the barracks were the transport lines, a mixture of lorries and small vehicles. Soldiers moving between barracks and town either walked or used bicycles. He had seen no motor-cycles. South of the barracks was a fuel store. The familiar jerricans, which had served so many armies so well, were neatly stacked and surrounded by a fence of barbed wire. East of the barracks were a few fields where the army was presumably growing some vegetables for itself. The main area of agriculture lay west of the town proper, along the river.

The feature that had held the larger part of Willie Garvin's attention for two days now was a small brick building. This stood between the fuel store and a hut from which most authority seemed to be exerted – presumably the Commanding Officer's domain. Only the front and one end of the brick building were visible to him. The end was a blank wall, and he suspected that this was also true of the back and far end. In the front were set ten solid wooden doors, each with a very small grille at about head height in the wall beside it. This, he now knew, was the barracks prison, with each door opening into a narrow cell.

Three of the cells were empty, he assumed, for he had seen no coming or going from them. Five held men in uniform, one to a cell, who were brought out and drilled arduously three times a day. Both the remaining cells held a man in civilian clothes who was kept handcuffed and whom Willie had seen only once a day, at different times, when each was taken from his cell and marched across to the headquarters hut. One was a youngish man in drab Chinese trousers and jacket. The other was in his sixties and wore no jacket, but his grubby shirt, his rumpled trousers, and his shoes were all of western style.

Willie Garvin had concluded that the two civilians were undergoing interrogation by the Intelligence Section under the colonel whose disgrace Wei Lu had caused so many years ago. The older of the two civilians was Wei Lu, of that he was now certain. He had been able to study the face for a few seconds through the powerful field glasses, and though it was ravaged by fear and whatever had been inflicted during interrogation, he was able to match it satisfactorily against his mental picture of the photographs Molly Chen had shown him.

Willie Garvin put down the glasses, scratched the stubble of beard on his chin, then slowly ate some chocolate and a handful of raisins before sipping from the second of his water bottles, still almost full.

Last night, after dark, he had risen from his cramped hiding place and exercised steadily for two hours, then slept soundly for four. Throughout the day he had again patiently studied every inch of the barrack layout, and every movement that took place.

Now, resting his head on his arms, he closed his eyes and pondered. Would it be foolish to make the attempt tonight? Whenever he thought of Modesty Blaise a lump of apprehension came into his throat, but he knew he must not allow that to push him into acting too soon. Was there any more of value to be learned from another day's study of the situation? Struggling to be objective, he thought not.

Last night he had spent an hour moving silently down to the perimeter of the camp, and another two assessing the situation there. A sentry was posted at the point where the road from the town entered the barracks, another by the fuel store, another by the prison. They were relieved every two hours, on the even hour. If he took action after the midnight relief, he would have, say, an hour and a half to get clear before the alarm was raised. Not enough to get a man in his sixties across five miles of rough country to the coast. A diversion would be needed and he had plans for that.

Sudden bitterness flared within him, a searing resentment towards whatever powers of heaven or earth or malignant fate had decreed that Wei Lu should have made an enemy long years ago and that the enemy had sought revenge on him *now* . . . just at the time when Willie Garvin had a commission to perform which required Wei Lu's presence. The commission was simple enough, but to Willie Garvin it was the most important thing he had ever tried to do in his whole life.

A thousand miles away but not many days ago, he had seen a dark-haired girl in a white linen dress watching from a ringside seat when he was fighting Thai-style against the local champion, Chit Leng, trying to earn enough *baht* to get out of the country. Moments after he had won, the police had come for him as he was pulling on his shirt, to arrest him for the brawl he had been involved in the night before. He had caught her eye as they took him away, had seen the speculative curiosity in her gaze, and had roused from his sullen bitterness long enough to acknowledge her with a shrug and a grin.

When they released him after an hour, informing him that Modesty Blaise had paid sufficient money to cover his estimated fine, he knew this must be the girl he had seen at the stadium, and he was stunned. The name Modesty Blaise was being spoken increasingly throughout

13

the underworld of late. She was head of an organisation called *The Network*, based in Tangier, and of fairly recent origin, but growing fast, and pulling off some astonishingly clever coups in various fields.

Willie Garvin had never dreamt that she would prove to be a girl barely out of her teens. When he found she had left the gaol after buying his freedom he chased down the street after her, then stood thanking her with stumbling words while she looked at him with that level gaze of midnight blue eyes. It was in those eyes, he realised vaguely, that you could see the will, the intelligence, and above all the depths of experience more suited to one twice her age, which now caused her name to be spoken with awe in circles where men were not easily impressed.

When he fell awkwardly silent at last she said, "They tell me you're a dangerous rat, Willie Garvin. I've no use for rats, but I've got a hunch there's some sort of man inside you trying to get out. If you work for me, he might get a chance." She took a wad of notes from her bag and gave them to him. "Set yourself up decently, and come to see me at the Amarin Hotel in Ploenchit Road at ten tomorrow morning."

Willie Garvin watched her walk away, feeling that his whole world had suddenly been unmade, dazed by emotions utterly strange to him. He had known many women and many kinds of women, but never one like this, who despite her youth made him feel adolescent, and for whom he would have done anything simply to win a smile of approval. As he gazed after her a deep and almost painful hunger was born in him, yet it was a hunger that contained no element of sexual desire, and this was truly strange, for she was of striking good looks with a superb body and that particular beauty of movement which speaks of rare physical potential.

He was in the lobby of the Amarin Hotel half an hour early, freshly bathed and shaved, wearing a dark ready-made suit that fitted his big frame reasonably well. The meeting in her hotel room was short. She gave him a valise containing a small case holding gold coins worth ten thousand American dollars, to be delivered to a man in Hong Kong called Fenton. She also gave him an ivory plaque with Chinese characters engraved on it. This was her chop, and would give him authority while in Hong Kong to collect bearer documents from a man called Wei Lu. Neither man was to know about the other transaction. There was nothing sinister in this, it was simply her way of doing business. Both transactions were legal, and should involve no danger other than the natural risk that went with carrying valuables. There was an envelope with a thousand American dollars in twenties, an airline ticket for Hong Kong, and an open ticket to bring him from Hong Kong to Tangier via Rome when his task was completed.

Willie Garvin stood looking at all the items she had laid on the table and rubbed his mouth nervously. "You're *trusting* me with this lot?" he asked.

She looked at him steadily. "Is there any reason why I shouldn't?"

He gave an uneasy laugh. "Well, plenty. Nobody's ever done it before."

"Then let's give it a try." Her manner was neutral, with neither threat nor warmth.

He drew in a long breath and said softly, "You're a princess, lady. A real princess. I won't let you down."

She folded her arms and said, "How long have you trained in Thai-style combat?"

He looked vaguely puzzled. "I never trained. Just picked it up. It's . . . sort of an interesting combat form."

Surprise touched her eyes for a moment, then was gone. "Do you always use Thai-style?"

"Well, I've picked up a few other combat disciplines 'ere and there."

"Which is best?"

He shook his head slowly, "None of 'em. If you're in a fight for real, you use whatever mixture works best. I mean, according to the opposition." He hesitated, then went on uncertainly, "I asked the police about you, Princess. They said you'd been 'ere six months studying under Saragam."

She lifted an eyebrow. "So?"

"No offence," he said quickly. "It's just I worked at Saragam's *dojo* for a while a couple of years back till I mucked things up and got chucked out. Saragam's the best, I reckon, but he never goes beyond what's strictly manual, and the way I see it, a lady like you wants to keep 'er 'ands nice if she can, even if she gets in a rumble sometimes, so I made this for you last night."

He took something from his pocket and held it out to her, his eyes anxious as if from fear of giving offence. On his palm lay a short spindle of polished wood, its ends rounded out bulbously like mushrooms. She stared, then took it from him, her fingers closing round the stem so that the hardwood knobs protruded from each side of her fist.

"Called a kongo," he said. "I dunno why. It's fast, though. You can strike from standstill with it in any direction, and you go for the nerve-centres–" he broke off with a grimace. "Sorry. I don't 'ave to spell it out for you."

She stood gazing at the object in her fist with absorbed interest, moving her hand tentatively this way and that as if appraising the potential of the unlikely little weapon. "I like it," she said at last. "Thank you, Garvin." Still examining the kongo, she added, "You'd better go along now. I'll expect to see you at my office in Tangier about a week from today. Any questions?"

He picked up the valise. "No questions."

She looked up and said quietly, "It's a simple task, Garvin. I want it done quietly and without fuss. If you meet a snag, deal with it. I expect results, not excuses. Is that understood?"

He did not answer at once. He was studying her soberly and with great intensity, as if committing every nuance of her face and body to his memory. After a few seconds he gave a little start, made a gesture of apology, then smiled for the first time. It was a remarkably engaging smile.

"Understood," he agreed in his deep gravelly voice. "Like you say, Princess, it's simple."

*　　*　　*　　*

But it was not simple after all.

Just his luck to cop a total mess like this. It was all so unfair, so *bloody* unfair! He lay in his hidey-hole on the hill overlooking Kui-tan, clenched fists pressed to his eyes, body rigid with the venomous resentment that surged through him as he mentally raved at god and devil, man and beast, all things in creation, seen and unseen, raved at them for hating him and inflicting this new persecution on him.

Then in his mind's eye he conjured up the image of the dark-haired girl with the quiet manner and serene eyes who had trusted him. The spasm passed, and he emerged from it sweating and shaking, filled with self contempt. "Oh, you whingeing, whining, miserable bastard, Garvin," he whispered softly. "You want to go back to the way it's always been . . . ?"

He lay letting strange new thoughts drift gently through his mind, eyes on an insect a few inches from his nose, yet somehow seeing the whole of his life in a new way, perhaps in the way he felt it might be seen by two cool midnight-blue eyes. After a while he turned on his back, relaxed to a degree he had never before experienced. Life was as it was, and neither god nor man hated him . . . he was not important enough for that (what a marvellously liberating piece of knowledge this was) . . . and the task before him *was* simple, after all. It called for the exercise of certain small skills, but so would any task worth doing. Of course, if something unforeseen went badly wrong, he might fail, and die. That would be a pity, but hardly a tragedy. Nobody would miss him. He grinned quite cheerfully at the thought.

On the other hand, the chance of success was good. He had got here safely, remained undetected, and had located Wei Lu. The rest was straightforward, and if he made it . . . if he made it . . . ah, then she might put her trust in him again, and yet again. There might even come a day when he would win her smile.

He set his mental alarm for two hours and slept. At half an hour before midnight he was at the camp perimeter. The pack on his back was lighter now. He wore webbing equipment adapted to his particular needs, with four pouches. Four grenades were carried in two of the pouches. Each of the other two carried three skittles. These were short wooden clubs shaped like miniature skittles, their large ends hollow and weighted with lead. He had spent two hours making them in Wei Lu's garage and they were quite crudely fashioned, but it was his particular gift that he could throw any missile with quite extraordinary accuracy, including the two handmade knives he carried.

At five minutes past twelve, when the sentries had been changed, he watched the man posted by the prison building prop his rifle against the wall and settle down with a cigarette on the low bunker outside. At ten minutes past twelve Willie Garvin felled the man with a thrown skittle to the side of the head from twenty paces. Wei Lu's doctor in Hong Kong, asked for means of ensuring unconsciousness for a few hours, had provided a hypodermic, a box of ampoules each containing three grains of phenobarbitone, and a demonstration of how an injection should be made.

Two minutes later, leaving his pack by the bunker, wearing the sentry's peaked cap, cigarette dangling from his lips, and slumping to reduce his height, Willie Garvin strolled across the compound towards

17

the fuel store, pausing to hawk and spit noisily when he was close enough to make out the figure of the sentry there. No challenge came, only a few casual words in Chinese, perhaps asking a comrade soldier for a cigarette or a light. Willie Garvin grunted a wordless reply, moved on, and threw his second skittle underhand at short range, following up swiftly enough to catch the unconscious man's rifle before it hit the sandy ground.

The last of the guards was in the sentry box at the gate, sitting on a stool, awake but not alert. He knew one brief instant of shock when an arm darted round the edge of the box and took him by the throat, then he slept. Willie Garvin used his third ampoule, propped the man in the corner of the box, and made his way back to the fuel store. There he clamped a small incendiary device to one of the stacked jerricans, setting the detonator to operate at five minutes after two a.m.

The cell doors of the prison were furnished with mortice locks. Selecting a lockpick from a slim wallet of tools, he unlocked the door of Wei Lu's cell in thirty seconds without a sound. Inside, he closed the door before switching on a flashlamp masked with coarse black cloth to give a dim and diffused light. A man lay on the bunk against the wall. His eyes were open and full of fear. Willie Garvin put the light on his own face and whispered, "I'm an English friend. Are you Wei Lu?"

The man nodded warily, his pain-racked eyes still fearful and suspicious. The light was switched off and the whispering voice from the darkness said, "Modesty Blaise sent me to fetch you out. Come on, let's go."

Long seconds passed. The bunk creaked. Then came a stifled sob as Wei Lu breathed, "I . . . cannot. My feet."

Willie Garvin put the flashlamp on again and knelt by the bunk. The elderly Chinese was sitting up now, shivering, gazing down at his feet on the floor. They were bare, horribly swollen, and encrusted with dried blood. Still on one knee, Willie Garvin switched off the flashlamp. He had seen Wei Lu walk with his escort to the interrogation hut and back at mid afternoon, and the man had not been crippled then. They must have subjected him to another session later, after dark, and had now begun to use the element of torture in their treatment. This was unexpected and not typical, but Willie Garvin told himself bleakly that he should have anticipated the possibility. Wei Lu's old enemy wanted revenge. It was hardly surprising that he had varied his brainwashing techniques with a touch of old-fashioned torture.

Wei Lu was slightly built, and it would be easy enough to provide him with socks and boots from one of the sentries; but there was no way, no way at all even with help and support, that he could make his way across five miles of rugged country to the coast in the next few hours. Not on those mangled feet. In the darkness of the cell, Willie Garvin stood up and braced himself for the surge of bitter hatred and fury that would now possess him at this cruel trick of fate.

It did not come. Somewhere in his head was the image of quiet eyes in a calm face appraising him, assessing, making a judgment, making a decision. He heard again the mellow timbre of her voice as she said, "*If you meet a snag, deal with it . . .*"

As simple as that. You concentrated on the answers, not the problems. His pleasure at this revelation was so great it almost hurt. As if falling into step with some shadowy companion, Willie Garvin put himself to examining the situation without emotion, and to considering with a fully flexible mind the objective of escape in the light of whatever external facilities might be bent to his purpose.

Thirty seconds later he groped for Wei Lu's arm and whispered, "All right, gran'dad. Let's 'ave that blanket to pad your feet, then you get on my back and 'old tight. I'm taking you 'ome."

* * * *

The office above the casino was beautifully and expensively furnished. Garcia stood by the window, watching the girl at the big Finn Juhl designed desk as she studied the latest report from the South of France area. As her chief lieutenant in *The Network*, Garcia was mightily thankful that she was back now. It had been a severe test of the organisation for Mam'selle to spend six months away in the Far East, even though she had maintained control by daily phone-calls and cables.

Just as well she had delayed no longer, Garcia told himself. The vicious Kadiri mob had been pushing, pushing, and were on the verge of a full scale challenge to *The Network*, which would have meant a bloody battle. But with Krolli and two men from his section she had taken Kadiri out within four days of her return in a typically skilful operation. Kadiri was now an unwilling guest of the nomad Arab tribe she had lived with for a time during her childhood, and his gang had dispersed. One of Krolli's men had a broken wrist, and Mam'selle herself had needed two stitches for a minor knife-cut in her upper arm. A cheap victory indeed.

It was a pity, thought Garcia, that she had misjudged this man Garvin so badly. Surprising, too. Her instinct for reading men was usually very sound. He glanced at Danny Chavasse, seated on the couch by the wall to her right, masculinely elegant as ever. Danny was watching her soberly, respectfully. In his gaze was that hint of curiosity Garcia had seen in the eyes of so many men when they looked at her. He shrugged mentally. Even to him, Garcia, she was still an enigma, and he knew her better than anyone.

She laid the report aside and said, "Danny, do you think La Roche's wife now realises you seduced her so you could pump her for information on the bank security system?"

He nodded. "Yes, Mam'selle. She is an intelligent woman."

"Might there be any come-back from her in that respect?"

"No, Mam'selle. She knew before we parted, and still we parted with affection. She will not wish to harm me."

"They never do," said Modesty Blaise reflectively.

Garcia chuckled. "Danny has magic," he said.

It was true that Danny Chavasse had magic for women, young and old. Their heads would not turn in the street when he passed, but given a target he could make himself irresistible on a one-to-one basis. His greater magic was that he could end an affair without undue pain or acrimony. These powers were his special attribute, and of untold value to *The Network*.

Modesty Blaise crossed off a note on her pad and said, "Is there anything else to report this morning, Garcia?"

"Only the Hong Kong situation, Mam'selle," he said diffidently. "Garvin should have been here six days ago now, at the latest, and there has been no word from him. I think we must assume that he has defaulted. Do you wish me to call Wei Lu in Hong Kong and start inquiries?"

She sat frowning down at the desk for a few moments, then shook her head. "We'll give him ten days. Don't ask me why, because I don't know. Maybe I'm playing a hunch, but I don't even know what hunch, so–" She broke off as one of the phones on her desk rang.

Garcia moved to pick it up and said, "Yes?" He listened, and his eyebrows jerked up in surprise. "You mean he is with you now?" He listened again, then lowered the phone and said, "Garvin has arrived, Mam'selle. He is downstairs now, asking to see you."

She sat up straight in her chair, eyes narrowed. "Then let's have him up," she said curtly. "I want to know just what the hell he's been doing for the last six days."

Danny Chavasse said, "You wish me to leave, Mam'selle?"

She considered, then said, "No. I'd like you to have a look at him, Danny."

Two minutes later he tapped on the door and entered at her call, carrying a small briefcase. The suit he had bought in Thailand was newly pressed, he wore a clean white shirt, well polished shoes, and was freshly shaven, but the tension in him seemed to fill the room as he said, "Good morning, Princess," and stood waiting.

Garcia gestured towards a chair. Willie Garvin moved forward and sat down facing her across the desk. She studied him for a few moments, then said, "Have you brought the bearer documents?"

"Yes, Princess." As he opened the briefcase on his knees she saw that his big hands were trembling. He took out a large envelope, leaned forward and laid it on the desk. She unfolded the flap, drew out the certificates, examined them carefully, then passed them to Garcia.

Looking across the desk again, she was puzzled by the fear this man was clearly struggling to conceal, but she took care not to let her puzzlement show. "You delivered the gold?" she asked.

"Yes, Princess. I got a receipt 'ere from Fenton." His shaking hand passed a smaller envelope across the desk. She studied the receipt, then laid it aside. He put the ivory plaque bearing her chop on the desk and said, "There's this, too."

She waited a few seconds for him to speak, but when he sat staring down at his hands in silence she leaned forward with her folded arms on the desk and said, "Why are you six days late, Garvin?"

He looked up, distressed. "I'm sorry about that, Princess. I ran into a bit of a snag and it took a few extra days to sort it out."

"What kind of snag?"

He ran a finger round his collar and said uneasily, "You told me you didn't want any excuses."

She shrugged. "I don't. But I'm interested in reasons, so tell me about this snag."

"Well . . . I got to Hong Kong and made the delivery to Fenton, but Wei Lu wasn't at 'is office. Just 'is granddaughter, Molly Chen. She told me he'd been grabbed by some old enemy of 'is, an army colonel, and they'd got 'im in Kui-tan in Red China." He glanced at Garcia·and Danny Chavasse with a hunted look, then at Modesty Blaise again. "So I 'ad to go and fetch 'im out," he said apologetically, "and it took a bit of time."

There was absolute silence in the room for long seconds. Then Garcia breathed, "Get him *out*? Holy God!"

Modesty Blaise blinked, then said slowly, "Wei Lu was a prisoner of the army in the Chinese Republic, and you went in there and brought him out? Is that what you're saying?"

Willie Garvin nodded unhappily. "There was no other way to get 'old of the bearer certificates, Princess. You can check with Wei Lu and Molly Chen. I'm sorry it took so long, but I was a bit slow in working it all out."

She glanced at Garcia, met his stunned gaze, then relaxed and said, "I think you'd better tell us the whole story, Willie Garvin. From the top, please."

It was an occasion Danny Chavasse would never forget. He listened entranced as the story haltingly emerged, his eyes moving from Willie Garvin to Modesty Blaise, fascinated by the intensity of her interest. Several times she had to prompt the big man with a question, and once he ground to a complete halt with sweat breaking out on his brow as he told how he had raised funds for his task by using her chop to borrow from the bank. When she simply nodded and said, "All right, go on," he seemed to breathe more easily.

Garcia stood by the window, arms folded, face impassive until Willie Garvin came to the moment of the shattering discovery that Wei Lu was unable to walk; then Garcia winced and drew in his breath sharply. Modesty Blaise said quietly, "So then what?"

For a moment something like a grin broke through the anxiety on Willie Garvin's face. 'Well, then it got a bit comical, Princess. I cut strips from a blanket to wrap 'is feet in, then carried 'im out to where the bicycles were lined up in a rack. A lot of the soldiers used 'em locally. There wasn't one with a pillion, and I didn't fancy 'aving Wei Lu on the crossbar, so in the end I cycled out with 'im perched on me back. It was like a couple of clowns doing a circus turn. The road wasn't good, and every time we 'it a pot-hole he kept praying in Chinese. Well, I think it was praying, and in between he kept backseat driving in English. This was after we'd cleared the town, and there wasn't a soul about. We quarrelled all the way to the coast, and I got so mad I put the price up. It only took an hour to get there, but . . ." he scowled and shook his head. "It made me realise I'd been dead stupid to plan on bringing 'im out the way I'd gone in. Once I saw the bicycles I ought to 'ave realised they were the best bet anyway."

Danny Chavasse glanced at Modesty Blaise, and was startled to see a sparkle of amusement in her eyes. It was almost a smile, and he had never seen that before. A moment later it was gone, and she said, "You had no more problems?"

"Not really, Princess. When we got to the estuary I 'ad to carry Wei Lu 'alf a mile along the rocks to where I'd left the inflatable, but there was a bit of moonlight to 'elp. Then when I came to blow it up I found the compressed air cylinder 'ad leaked, but I'd taken a footpump along, just in case, and we got the dinghy launched by two a.m., earlier than I'd 'oped. Needn't 'ave left the incendiary to fire their fuel store, as it turned out, but I'd reckoned I might need a diversion round about then. Anyway, we homed in on Molly Chen with the Seahound, she picked us up about two-thirty, and next day in Hong Kong – no, it was the same day really – old Wei Lu handed over the bearer certificates."

There was a brief silence, then she said, "What did you mean when you spoke of putting the price up while you were quarrelling with Wei Lu on the bicycle?"

"Ah, I was coming to that, Princess." He opened the briefcase again, took out a thick envelope, laid it on the desk, and eyed her anxiously. "I told 'im *The Network* wasn't going to save 'is skin for nothing, and I was making a provisional charge of twenty thousand American dollars plus expenses to the tune of five thousand, subject to Miss Blaise's approval. I'd 'ad ten grand in mind, but then I doubled it, and told 'im it was a knock-down bargain. He must 'ave agreed, because when we got to Hong Kong I didn't even 'ave to ask again." He nodded at the envelope. "It's in hundred-dollar bills, Princess. I 'ope I did right."

Garcia exhaled a long slow breath and muttered, "Jesus!" Danny Chavasse made no attempt to restrain a laugh. Modesty Blaise looked across the desk at Willie Garvin and said, "You don't feel that this should be your own money?"

He looked startled. "Blimey, no. I was acting on your be'alf, Princess. Your be'alf."

"I see." There was a longer silence. After a while she got up, paced slowly to the window, stood gazing out for several moments, then turned to study the big man again with puzzled eyes. "What is it you haven't told me, Garvin?" she said brusquely.

He blinked, then moistened his lips. "Well, nothing, Princess. I mean, only small details that don't matter—"

"You're scared," she broke in. "You've been scared ever since you walked into this room, so there must be something you're holding back. I want to know what it is."

He rubbed a hand nervously over his face, then said with quiet desperation, "I'm scared all right, but it's not something I'm 'olding back. I'm scared you might not let me work for you, Princess, that's all. I've felt . . . different since you trusted me to do that job. I can't explain. I just know that if you give me the elbow I'll end up worse than the way I was before . . . and that scares me stupid."

She looked at him for long seconds, then moved back to the desk and sat down. "You're working for me on six months probation, Willie Garvin," she said. "You take orders from me or from Garcia here, nobody else. You'll be provided with good accommodation and reasonable funds, paid monthly in advance. Garcia will explain the system we use and anything else you need to know. Just for the record, I'm more than pleased with the way you handled the Wei Lu affair. Have you any questions at the moment?"

He shook his head slowly, drawing in a long breath and letting it out in a sigh of relief. The tension that had gripped him like a strait-jacket seemed to drain from his limbs, and the briefcase almost slid from his grasp as the muscles went slack with reaction. "No questions, Princess," he said almost sleepily. "You've told me all I wanted to 'ear. Just . . . thanks. I won't let you down."

"Good. Now go and wait downstairs at reception, please. Garcia will be with you in a few minutes."

He stood up, smiling now, an element of wonder in his eyes, acknowledging Garcia and then Danny Chavasse with a polite nod before turning and going quietly from the room. Modesty Blaise leaned back in her chair and looked from Danny Chavasse to Garcia, letting her astonishment show now. "What in God's name do we make of this one?" she said.

Danny Chavasse smiled. "I think *you* can make whatever you wish to of him, Mam'selle. He is raw material for you to mould."

Garcia paced the office, hands on hips, shaking his head in bewilderment. "But what material! He is mad, of course. A freak. Any man must be, who goes alone into Red China to take a prisoner from an army camp."

"The point is, he made it," Modesty Blaise said softly. "Who else have we got in *The Network* who could pull off a stroke like that?"

Garcia shrugged. "There is no other man, Mam'selle. To find one who is able to work solo on a task such as that is rare indeed. By God, what an operator."

She said as if to herself, "I'd like to have seen him arguing the toss with Wei Lu when they were on that bicycle." Again Danny Chavasse saw something that was almost a smile in her eyes, and again he marvelled. She picked up the thick envelope, slit it open and riffled through the hundred-dollar bills. "Expenses apart, this is his by right, Garcia," she said. "Open a local bank account with it for him."

Danny Chavasse cleared his throat unnecessarily, and she glanced at him with a lifted eyebrow. "Yes?"

"I think it would be wise to reconsider, Mam'selle," he said respectfully. "It is plain that to work for you is this man's heart's desire. He brings you that money not as a gift, but as belonging to you, and I think it would be wrong to throw it back at him. Better perhaps, at the end of six months, and if he does well, to give him a bonus of . . . say, half that amount?"

She dropped the money on the desk and said, "God damn it."

"I'm sorry, Mam'selle —"

"No, it's not you, Danny. You're right. But I should have seen it for myself." She looked at Garcia. "So we'll play it that way. I shall want an assessment of Garvin's skills as soon as possible, and I've a hunch you may find them quite extensive." She turned to Danny Chavasse again. "I also want him to spend time with you, Danny, learning how to handle himself in any company and any circumstances. The whole idea is to build self-confidence into him, so he can walk tall. Seeing that he pulled off the Wei Lu business only a few days after I'd taken him out of the gutter, God knows what he'll be capable of once he's able to realise his full potential. There's risk in it . . . if he gets big headed in the process, I'll throw him out. But it's a risk worth taking. He just might be the best investment *The Network* has ever made. Any comment?"

Danny Chavasse said thoughtfully, "I don't think he will get above himself. The way he handled this mission indicates that he has style. It is a rare quality, and it does not go with a big head."

Garcia grinned. "Mam'selle has style. You have style, Danny. After

25

that, *The Network* is much lacking in this quality. It will be good to have a man with style in our active service department." He gestured. "No offence, Danny, but you are a boudoir warrior."

Danny Chavasse laughed. "Agreed, Rafael. To each his own speciality."

"There is another thing," said Garcia, and looked at the girl behind the desk with a crooked smile of apology. "I am fifty-one years old, Mam'selle, and I have been with you from the beginning, but perhaps in a year or two you will feel that I am getting too old for my job. I know of nobody who would be exactly right for you to appoint in my place." He gestured vaguely. "A special understanding is necessary. But if this crazy freak Garvin comes good, I say *if* he comes good, then he may be the very man."

She shrugged. "We'll see, but that's all a long way off, and you're not too old yet, Garcia. Now, is there anything else concerning Garvin? If not, I want to discuss an industrial espionage contract we've been offered, and an approach for a freelance mission that's come from a British intelligence bigwig named Tarrant."

Garcia said, "I have no further comment on Garvin – oh, except that I will instruct him that he is not to address you as Princess. He must address you as Mam'selle, like everybody else."

Modesty Blaise picked up the ivory plaque bearing her chop and studied it absently. "No, don't do that," she said at last. "God knows he's done enough to earn something of a *cachet* in the organisation, so let him go on calling me Princess . . . but just make sure nobody else does."

2

When the Chinese girl in the skimpy bikini of soft leather was a hundred yards away along the shore she halted and turned, leaning her head to one side and extending a spread hand in an attitude of query. Willie Garvin responded by thrusting a thumb skywards several times in an exaggerated gesture of approval, then he concentrated on the frisbee he held, a blue plastic disc a foot across, raised in the centre to form a shallow cone.

Carefully he weighed it in his hand once again, sensing it in all its aspects, considering the weight, the shape and the aerodynamic properties, seeking an intuitive understanding of its whole nature. The shore was a broad strip of golden limestone thirty yards wide, worn smooth from millennia of weathering by wind and sea. To his right the great cliffs of Malta's south-western coast reflected the afternoon sun and also caused a slight deflection of the small breeze blowing obliquely towards him from a little to seaward of where the Chinese girl had halted. To his left the flat limestone fell sharply away at the sea's edge in a tangle of jagged rock.

Except by climbing there was no access to this stretch of shore from the land, for it was cut off at each end by sheer cliffs thrusting out into the sea. They had come here in a motorboat that now lay moored in a small natural inlet piercing the rocks near the eastern end of the beach, and had picnicked in solitude except for sight of a sailing dinghy passing well off-shore.

A big man, Willie Garvin, with untidy fair hair and cheerful blue eyes. There had been a time when they were rarely cheerful, but that was long ago; for many a year now they had looked upon the world with an air of serene enjoyment and pleasurable anticipation. At the moment he wore only faded denim shorts, revealing a tanned body without surplus fat but not obtrusively muscled. Dangerous men had died from misjudging his strength and speed.

When satisfied that he had established rapport with the frisbee, he looked up and began to assess the external factors that would influence its flight; the strength and direction of the slight breeze, the cooler air the disc would encounter when curving out over the sea, the warmer air rising from the limestone shore.

Without losing concentration, he noted and was amused by the sight of Molly Chen walking about on her hands while she waited, slender legs waving in the air. This was a new trick she had acquired in pursuit of her ambition. A little over five feet tall, Molly weighed less than a hundred and ten pounds. Her body was small-boned but nicely fleshed, and Willie Garvin had found great delight in it. Her dark hair was cropped short, and it seemed to Willie that her face had scarcely aged at all in the nine years since he had first met her in Hong Kong. It was a broad face, rather plain, with large happy eyes, and Willie was very fond of it.

He folded his tongue between his teeth and emitted a shrill whistle. She came to her feet, stood to attention, gave an exaggerated salute, then lifted both hands above her head and waited. Eyes fixed on her hands, Willie Garvin let his subconscious take over and threw the frisbee with a long swing of his arm. It soared sweetly, spinning fast, curving in a shallow loop out over the sea, starting to slant down, then curving in again and steadying to descend at a slower rate as it met the warmer air.

It would have passed a foot above Molly's hands and a little to one side of her if she had not jumped slightly to catch it. She made an elaborate bow, then dropped the frisbee and strutted with hands clasped above her head in a mime of boxing ring victory. It hadn't been that good, thought Willie, but it hadn't been too bad either. Not that it mattered anyway —

When the shot sounded he felt no immediate alarm, for this was the season when many Maltese lay in wait to shoot the quail migrating from North Africa, and his first thought was that somebody had used a shotgun on the flat cliff-top. Then he saw that Molly Chen had started to run towards him, very fast, and in the same moment he realised that the report had not been that of a shotgun but of a smaller calibre weapon.

She was calling something as she ran, and signalled urgently for him to stop when he started towards her. He ignored her signal, and saw a man appear from beyond where Molly had stood, clambering up from the rocks fringing the sea, wearing jeans, a grey shirt and a jockey cap.

Another man appeared behind him, this one in navy slacks and shirt, bare-headed. The first man carried something in his right hand, something that glinted metallically in the sun. As Willie reached the Chinese girl the man stopped, rested the barrel of the gun on his forearm, and fired again.

Willie said, "Keep going," and swung round behind Molly to cover her as they ran. A handgun with a long barrel, then; perhaps a Ruger Blackhawk or something of that sort. But the shots had gone well wide, as was to be expected. Sixty yards was an absurd range for the average gunman with an average gun. The big trouble was, Willie told himself grimly, that the range would not remain at sixty yards. The end of this rocky beach was not far off, and beyond that there was nowhere to go except up the cliff face or into the sea, either of which would be fatal.

The man with the gun would arrive before they were twenty feet up the cliff. And close by, along the shore, would be the boat that had brought the man with the gun. There was no way they could hope to out-swim it. Molly was veering right, towards the tiny inlet where Willie had moored their own boat, but he knew there was no chance of escape that way. The inlet was dogleg in shape, and it would take a full minute to manoeuvre the boat out and start the engine. By then they would be sitting targets.

He glanced over his shoulder and saw that the man with the gun had not bothered to run but was walking at a steady pace, the gun hanging from his hand. There was an air of easy confidence about him now, and it was well justified. He had a gun, his quarry had gained ground but could not escape, and they were unarmed. A good situation for a simple risk-free killing.

Willie Garvin assessed all that was available to him. It was very little. A few pebbles here and there, thrown up by the sea, nothing big enough to do real damage as a thrown missile before the man came close enough to start shooting. Now if only –

He called sharply, "Hold it, Molly! Stand still!" She halted after a pace or two, breathless with running, turning with fear in her eyes as he came up to her. "The boat, Willie – we must get to the boat," she panted.

"No use, love." He was staring about him, bending to pick something up. "Let's 'ave your bikini, *quick*."

"My . . . ?" She was uncomprehending, but his coolness steadied her and she snatched at the thongs of her bikini top.

"Jesus, no. The bottom," he said, and looked back along the shore. The man with the gun was fifty yards away.

The Chinese girl said in a shaking voice, "Here, Willie," and put the small leather pouch in his hand, an elongated triangle with a thin leather thong at each corner. His hands moved with the ease of long practice as he wound the ends of two of the thongs round his third and fourth fingers, slipped a smooth pebble into the pouch, and clipped the third thong between his thumb and index finger.

The man was forty yards away . . . now thirty-five and raising his gun. The improvised sling spun above Willie's head on a plane of some thirty degrees relative to the ground, and so fast that Molly Chen heard the whirring sound it made. Then came a miniature whipcrack report, and in the same instant something seemed to happen to the man's face just below the peak of the jockey cap. His head jerked back as if struck by an invisible club. The gun fired once into the ground, then dropped from his hand, and he fell straight back like a tree going down before the axe, his head making an audible sound as it hit rock.

Willie said, "Stay put, Molly, there's a good girl," and ran to where the man lay. She watched, teeth chattering despite the sun's warmth, as he knelt by the limp figure. In the distance along the shore, the man in dark slacks and shirt lifted glasses to his eyes but made no other move. Thirty seconds later Willie Garvin walked back to her, a gun in one hand, a wallet and her bikini bottom in the other. He gave her the scrap of leather and said gently, "Thanks, Molly. Get dressed now." He turned, looked along the shore towards the man watching, and held the gun up high.

"Modesty always reckons that when it comes to handguns I couldn't 'it a barn if I was standing inside it," he said. "She's right, too, but *they* don't know that, and I don't think they fancy a shoot-out, even if there's one or two more we 'aven't seen. They must 'ave come round the point close in and under oars, or we'd 'ave seen or heard 'em."

She knotted the thong at her thigh with hands that trembled a little and said, "That one who had the gun, Willie . . .?"

"Probably wondering about 'is next incarnation," Willie said without noticeable regret. "He's certainly finished with this one. You keep an eye on that bloke who's watching us while I get our boat out."

"What about . . . the dead man?"

"Well, I don't want 'im. He's their problem. They're not the sort who enjoy 'aving inquiries made about their departed friends, so I

30

reckon they'll commit 'is body to the deep, as the saying is." Holding her arm, he had walked her to the small inlet as he spoke. Two minutes later she heard the engine start and he called from the boat, "Right, come aboard, love." Along the shore, the man with field glasses was still watching. Seized with sudden fury, she swung her bent arm with fist clenched in an uppercut, slapping her other hand against the bicep in the international sexual gesture of contemptuous insult, then she turned and slithered down the slope of rock to the boat.

Once clear of the shore, Willie turned east, away from where the other boat must lie and towards the little bay of Ghar Lapsi, where they had left the car. Beckoning Molly to take the tiller, he sat facing aft with the revolver in his hand, watching until they had rounded the point. "Sorry about all this, Molly," he said. "I don't usually take a pretty girl away for a couple of weeks in the sun and end up nearly getting 'er shot."

She said, "Who *are* they, Willie?"

He shrugged. "I've never seen the bloke in the jockey cap before. I'll go through 'is wallet later. Might find a name that rings a bell."

"Why would they want to shoot me?"

He gave her a half smile. "I expect it was me they were after, Molly, but it rubbed off on you. They couldn't leave you around to tell the tale."

"So why did they want to shoot *you*?"

"I've been trying to think." He gazed out across the sea. "It's 'appened once or twice before. With Modesty, too. We upset a few nasty people in *The Network* days, so it's not surprising if one of 'em fancies 'aving a go now and again."

'Will you tell the police?"

He put a hand on hers to steady the tiller, and leaned forward to kiss her cheek. "Malta's a very religious country, Molly. The Pope's Garden, they call it. But I don't think they'd take kindly to my replay of the David and Goliath bit, do you?"

She tossed her head with a grimace of self-annoyance. "I'm sorry, Willie, I wasn't thinking straight."

"I'm not surprised. It's been a nasty few minutes, even for a girl who 'ad Wei Lu for a grandfather."

She managed a shaky laugh. "He wasn't into the heavy stuff. I've never been shot at before." She gave him a startled glance. "My God, Willie, how did you manage that bikini trick? You *must* have done it before."

31

"Not with a bikini." He kept his hand on hers, knowing her question was no more than a way of preventing her mind reliving what she had just experienced. "Normally I use a proper sling," he said lightly, "in case I'm with a girl who won't take 'er bikini off as quick as you. It's surprising 'ow accurate you can be with a sling. I do pretty well on the clay pigeon range Modesty's got at 'er cottage down in Wiltshire. Slings are quite interesting, really. Go on, ask me about slings, Molly."

She managed a strained smile, knowing that he was trying to distract her until the immediacy of the shock had passed. "All right, Willie, tell me about slings."

"Well, they're old. As much as ten thousand years old, and blokes who ought to know reckon they were the first ever long range weapon, even before the bow and arrow. They've found manufactured sling missiles on digs in Iraq going back seven thousand years. Pebbles sheathed in baked clay, some small, some as big as your fist. I've seen a sculptured mural in Nineveh showing Assyrian soldiers going into battle, and the slingers are marching behind the archers, so it looks as if they 'ad a greater range. That was one of Sennacherib's campaigns, around seven 'undred B.C. Would you like to 'ear something funny, Molly?"

She nodded, thankful to feel the tension within her easing a little under the soothing of his conversational manner. "Yes, I would, Willie."

"Well, when you get to the Greeks and Romans, they went in for moulding projectiles of lead, and they often put inscriptions on them. Mostly they just carried the number of the legion, or something like that, but some 'ave been found with words scratched on, like 'A blow from Caesar' or 'Up yours, Pompey'."

A moment of laughter surprised her. They had rounded the point now, and when she looked back the long strip of shore was no longer in sight. Willie pressed her hand and said, "These old sculptures usually show slingers whirling their slings parallel to the body, but I reckon they were the 'eavy artillery, using long slings to drop big missiles on massed infantry two or three 'undred yards away. For accuracy I've found I do best with a shorter sling whirled round over the head at a bit of an angle to the ground. What did I just say?"

She gave a guilty start. "Oh . . . about 'Up yours, Pompey'. Wasn't it?"

"I thought so. You only remember the dirty bits."

She laughed again, gave him the tiller, and moved to sit close to him, slipping her arm through his. "Thank you, Willie. Do you think they might try again?"

"Not for a while. They'll be in shock from seeing their button-man chilled. That might put them off for good. Anyway, don't you worry, Molly."

They were coming into the little bay now, and she studied him as he steered for the slipway, thinking how at ease he seemed now, even after the close encounter with death only minutes ago, compared with the fear he had shown that day nine years before at the prospect of returning to Modesty Blaise empty handed. "Yes, all right, Willie," she said quietly. "I won't worry."

They were to fly home next day, and on this last evening of their holiday he took her to the casino to dine, and dance, and gamble a little before returning to the villa. This stood on the Dingli cliffs only a few miles from Ghar Lapsi, and was owned jointly by Modesty Blaise and Willie Garvin, as were half a dozen other occasional residences around the world. It was also protected by a sophisticated alarm system.

In the big bed, under the soft light of a bedside lamp, Molly Chen lay with her small body sprawled over Willie Garvin, gently moving her fingertips in the hair above his ears, and smiling into his eyes. "It's been a lovely break, Willie," she said. "I've enjoyed it so much."

"Me too, Molly. I don't usually go for skinny little Chinese girls, but – oooh!" She had cut him short by pinching his ears, and now she lowered her head to give his shoulder a gentle bite before settling down with her head pillowed on his chest.

"I bet I make you take that back before we go to sleep," she said.

He chuckled and lay gently stroking her back, thinking how lucky he was in every possible way, and what a pleasing companion Molly Chen was with her gentle hands, her warm little body, and her slow, unhurried approach to making love. After a while she said, "You're so different, it's hard to believe, Willie. I mean, different from the man who came to my grandfather's office that day, just after he'd been taken into Red China as a prisoner."

"Sure," said Willie, and patted her bottom. "I'm different all right."

She lifted her head to look down at him again, and ran a finger along his lower lip. "You were so scared that day. So scared of Modesty Blaise."

He smiled lazily. "I was scared spitless . . . but not *of* Modesty. Just scared I was going to blow the job she'd given me."

"But you didn't. And now you're someone else. I'm truly happy for you."

"You're definitely a nice girl, Molly."

"And not skinny?"

He felt her comprehensively and shook his head. "Whoever said that must be an idiot."

"Good. Now let's roll over."

"With me on top? That might not be a good idea. Either you get crushed or I get sore elbows."

She laughed, her dark eyes sparkling, and pulled herself higher on his chest to kiss him deeply. After a while she lifted her head and said, "I didn't *just* mean roll over, like that. I've thought of something new, and I bet you'll enjoy it."

Much later, lying with his arm about her and her head on his shoulder she said sleepily in the darkness. "You're lovely, Willie. I'm going to miss you so much when the circus moves on and you're not there to throw those axes at me any more."

* * * *

In one of the guest bedrooms of a rambling cottage near the village of Benildon, Dinah Collier prodded her husband in the ribs with an elbow. Professor Stephen Collier opened one reluctant eye and focused it on his Canadian wife, a girl with honey-coloured hair and gentle, sightless eyes.

With a heavy Middle-European accent he said, "Ze managements of zis establishments iss not permitting of womens to hit der spouses mit der elbows."

"All right, how about this?" She took him by the nose, drew his head towards her, and kissed him.

"Zat iss bedder," he said nasally, "but iss still leafing room for improvement."

"Time to get up, tiger. Modesty said breakfast at nine." She threw back the bed-clothes and sat up. "Half an hour for you to make your interminable toilet."

He reached out to put an arm round her waist from behind, and said,

"Modesty runs a relaxed establishment. She wouldn't mind if we didn't appear till noon."

She patted his hand. "You do that, honey. I'm hungry."

He said indignantly, "I'm not lying here *alone*. I didn't even bring my teddy, did I?"

"So on your feet, buster."

Collier grinned. "I know what it is. You just can't wait to get down there and sample another helping of Danny Chavasse, the world champion wooer."

"Danny's very nice, you said so yourself, but he's not trying to woo *me*, dopey. He's here with Modesty. And anyway he doesn't broadcast his attraction, you know that. She used him in the old days of *The Network* for handling women, but he has to switch it on."

"Ha! And suppose he switched it on for *you*, me proud beauty, would you go all rubbery-kneed and cross-eyed and heaving-bosomed as you threw yourself into his sinewy arms, casting old Collier aside like a worn glove?"

She giggled and twisted round, kneeling now, holding his hand. She wore no nightdress, her body was firm and shapely, and Collier thought with a familiar pang how he wished she could see his eyes and know how much he adored her. She said, "I'm not telling old Collier what might happen to my knees, eyes, and bosom, because I want to keep old Collier on his toes. Come on, get up now."

"Or you could get down?"

"Steve, I don't think – ah no, dammit, what kind of wife is that? You want me, here I am."

He laughed and patted her thigh. "Raincheck, sweetheart. Modesty's infinitely tolerant, but I agree with you, we mustn't be inconsiderate guests."

"Okay, raincheck." She cocked her head, listening. "I hear the sound of feet on that gravel path. Two pairs of feet. They must have been out for an early morning run."

Collier sighed and got out of bed. "I don't know how a nice girl like her can do things like that," he said.

In the big kitchen Modesty Blaise closed the back door, glanced at the clock, and said, "It's getting late, and the Colliers will be using the guest bathroom. You'd better join me for a quick shower, Danny."

He smiled. "There must be worse ways to start the day."

Twenty minutes later, when he had shaved, he came down to find her slicing bread, with eggs and bacon set out in readiness on the work surface beside the cooker. She wore a shirt, a pleated skirt, and sandals. Her legs were bare, her hair tied loosely back, and she wore no scrap of make-up. She gave him a smile and he began to set the table, watching her as she worked, remembering.

When she had recruited him in the early days of *The Network* he had been a little afraid of her. Most of her people were. It had never once occurred to him to attempt to use upon her the gift that was his, of making women want him. Two or three years later, when she had sent him on a routine mission to seduce a woman for information she required, there had come the moment of shock when he found, in the hotel on Lanzarote, that the name she had given him was false, and that the subject of his mission was herself.

In the days that followed he learned that two rapes in childhood had left her emotionally crippled. Behind the façade presented to the world of a feared and efficient creator of *The Network*, she was sexually afraid of men. His task was to make her whole, and in this he had succeeded, gently, patiently, with the genuine sympathy and affection he was able to command within himself, which was perhaps the core of his success with women.

It had been his last mission for her, and he knew it at the time, knew that she could not have him return to *The Network* once she had been his mistress. The parting had been affectionate and she had made generous provision for him. More than that, much more in Danny's opinion, she had become his friend. With a shiver he remembered Limbo, the bizarre plantation in the Guatemalan jungle where some of the wealthiest men and women in the world had been brought as captives and made to work as slaves. His own slavery had been a chance affair, but he had endured three years in Limbo before a freak of fate roused Modesty Blaise's suspicions. He remembered her coming, with Willie Garvin, and the fearful battle of the last day in Limbo.

Watching her now, relaxed and serene, he was immensely glad that he had contributed something to the making of her as she was today. Not everything, by any means. He had watched her create Willie Garvin as he was today, but that had not been a one-way affair, for Willie had given much in return. Danny Chavasse remembered that the first time he had seen her almost smile had been the day Willie came to her in Tangier after his extraordinary feat of bringing Wei Lu out of Red China. Later he had seen her truly smile, and even laugh. This was

Willie Garvin's gift to her, and over the years it had put tiny crow's feet at the corners of her eyes which, strangely, seemed to make her look younger.

The Limbo affair had come long after she had wound up *The Network* and retired; and following his rescue with the other slaves, Danny Chavasse had been an occasional visitor, either to her London penthouse or to the Wiltshire cottage where he had joined her three days ago. She had never regarded her debt to him for healing her female psyche as having been repaid, and he knew that he was always welcome to her home. By profession he was now a cruise director, a job for which he was ideally suited, and at the moment he was on a six week vacation.

With the table set, he sat down and said, "Are you worrying a little bit about Willie?"

She cut rind from a rasher and said thoughtfully, "Perhaps a tiny bit. We just can't afford to worry too much about each other. If we did we'd be old and grey by now."

"When he rang last night from Malta did he have any idea who was behind the attempt to kill him?"

"None at all, Danny. He gave me the whole story in a mixture of free cryptic and Arabic, but I had no ideas to offer. I don't think he expected me to. He phoned because if somebody's after him, they may be after me, too, and he wanted to warn me. Also, he knows Dinah's here, and we're both practically paranoid about her getting mixed up in any sort of trouble."

Danny said, "Yes. Steve told me how you've pulled her out of one or two real horror stories, but they didn't happen because of you, did they?"

"No, but they happened. How many eggs, Danny?"

"May I have two, please?" He pondered for a moment, then said, "What will you do? Explain to Dinah and ask Steve to take her home today?"

She broke eggs into the pan, then gave him a wry smile. "I know it sounds ridiculous, with Dinah being blind and weighing in at maybe eight stone, but she's sort of . . . protective towards me. If she thought trouble was brewing she'd stay around so she could sit up all night listening."

Danny nodded. It had not required his particular sensitivity to the female of the species to realise that the blind girl with the gentle face

37

and beautiful hair had a deep affection for Modesty Blaise. Not many women would like Modesty, he acknowledged candidly to himself. Perhaps that was at least partly why Dinah's affection was so clearly reciprocated.

"What will you do?" Danny repeated.

The toaster ejected four slices. She put them in a toast rack and fed in four more. "Just keep my eyes open," she said. "You might do the same."

"Sure." He made an apologetic gesture. "But I was never a combat man."

"I don't want you to be —"

She broke off as there came the sound of footsteps from the hall, and Stephen Collier's voice saying, "My darling, I would love to go running before breakfast, but I have this old war wound."

Dinah came in saying, "War wound? You were never in any war."

"At *The Treadmill* last year. My knee —"

"*That*? You tried to play a war game with Willie Garvin, you knelt on a lead soldier, and you promptly surrendered." She looked towards the cooker. "Hallo, honey." Then at the table. "Hi, Danny."

As salutations were exchanged, Collier clasped Modesty round the waist from behind and peered over her shoulder at the pan. "Who's that for?"

"Danny."

"What about mine, eh?"

"After I've done Danny's and then Dinah's."

Collier sighed and mooched to the table. "Why does *everybody* hate me? It's enough to give a chap a persecution complex."

Danny held a chair for Dinah to be seated and said, "Dinah, how did you know I was here when you came in, and where I was sitting?"

When she hesitated, Collier chuckled and said, "She smells you, laddie. No, I'm not being my usual offensive self. What does Danny smell like, sweetheart?"

"Sort of like . . . well, the way that Chopin Prélude sounds. I forget which one."

"She confuses the senses," Collier explained, taking a chair and reaching for the coffee pot. "Modesty smells like brandy tastes, and Willie like a muted trumpet sounds. Mind you," he slid a cup of coffee in front of his wife and guided her hand to it, "she doesn't always confuse the senses. An occasional exception is made."

Modesty gave a snuffle of laughter. Collier said, "Yes, I thought that would get a guffaw from our beloved hostess and renowned hooligan. Before our marriage Dinah indicated that I smell the way suede feels, an acceptable simile I think. However, she has now revised this, and asserts that I, her lord, smell like rice pudding."

Danny choked on a laugh, and said, "I'm sorry."

Dinah said, "I only asserted it once, lord, and anyway you know I love rice pudding. I really do."

"Be that as it may, I prefer to smell like the sound of temple bells, or the taste of caviar. My God, is that splendid dish really for Danny? Ah, well. While I'm waiting and starving, tell us what young Garvin is up to in Malta."

"He took a friend there for a little holiday," said Modesty.

"A girlfriend?"

"What else, dopey?" said Dinah. "Is she nice, Modesty?" Without waiting for a reply she turned her head, the sightless eyes gazing a little to one side of Danny. "I adore Willie, so I take an interest in his girls."

"Brazen hussy," remarked her husband.

Modesty said, "Yes, she's a nice girl. Her name's Molly Chen, and she comes from Hong Kong."

Danny looked surprised and said, "Not the Molly Chen who . . . ?"

"The same. Two eggs, Dinah?"

"Please, honey."

Collier said firmly, "Let's not digress, because I scent a story here. Right, Danny?"

"Well, yes. But it's up to Modesty whether or not she tells it."

"I shall hypnotise her into so doing," announced Collier. "I have these incredible powers, you see –"

Dinah sucked in her breath sharply and gave a shudder. Her husband broke off and gently took her hand. "Hey, did I say something, darling?" Modesty paused in the act of lifting eggs from the pan with a slice, head turned, concerned.

Dinah said, "No . . . no, I don't know what it was. Somebody just walked over my grave, I guess. Ugh! Jumped on it, by the size of the shiver. Don't worry, I'm fine now."

Danny saw Modesty and Collier exchange a worried look. He was aware that Professor Stephen Collier, a statistician by profession, had a considerable reputation as an investigator of psychic phenomena; also that his wife, Dinah, had some curious abilities in that field. She was a highly skilled diviner, and in the past had been employed by industrial companies to locate water, metals, and the run of underground gas-pipes and electrical conduits. Before her marriage she had been saved by Modesty and Willie from vicious men who had kidnapped her to aid their search for an immense treasure.

Danny Chavasse also knew that it was Dinah who had located him in the Limbo slave camp, using a map, a small brass pendulum, and his own very special Breguet gold watch as a contact. He wondered if, in the last few seconds, some word or thought had triggered a random psychic reaction in the girl. Once he had been a sceptic about such phenomena. Now, though by no means credulous in a broad sense, he quite simply believed that without Dinah's extra-sensory faculty he would have been long dead. Modesty had told him that Dinah would have wished her psychic faculties away if she could, for she found any exercise of them mentally punishing, and resented the capricious nature of her gift.

Dinah said abruptly, "Don't snow me, Modesty – is Willie okay? I mean, is he maybe caught up in some dangerous caper?"

Modesty brought Danny his breakfast and said, "When he rang last night he told me somebody had tried to kill him and Molly Chen. He doesn't know who or why. I wouldn't have told you, but you asked. He's quite all right though, and Molly too."

Collier rested his head in his hands and said in a taut, savage voice, "God, how I hate these *shits* who kill people at the drop of a hat – not because they're threatened in any way but simply for money, power, general greed, simple sadism –" He broke off and lifted his head to glare at Danny. "Do you know what two bastards of that ilk did to Dinah in Tenazabal, not long before she located you in that slave plantation?"

Dinah put an arm round him and said, "Yes, of course Danny knows. Please don't get worked up. It's all past now."

"Having someone try to kill you isn't that long past for Willie and his Chinese girl. And what about –" He stopped suddenly, relaxing a little. "Hey, was that graveyard shiver you had a reaction to what happened to Willie yesterday? A touch of retrocognition?"

"Could be, Steve, but I just can't tell. You know that." She turned her head in Modesty's direction. "What happened to whoever made the attempt, honey?"

Modesty said, "There were two or probably more men in a boat, and one came ashore on a quiet stretch of beach to do the killing with a gun. Willie found an answer and the man won't be doing it again. The others made off."

Collier said carefully, "Do I understand that the shit with the gun is now a dead shit?"

"Yes."

Collier exhaled loudly. "Well, that helps to ease my distress by a notch or two," he said with satisfaction. "The Garvin boy has a most amiable nature, but he tends to be rather terse with people who attempt harm towards his ladies. I may well buy him a small gin and tonic on his return. Now what's this Molly Chen story, please?"

"There's not a lot to it," said Modesty. "Soon after I first met Willie I gave him a trial run on a job in Hong Kong. It was to do with Molly Chen's grandfather, who was something of an entrepreneur there. Willie ran into some nasty snags, but managed to sort them out. That was . . . let me see, yes, nine years ago. Then last year Willie's circus was doing a Far East tour –"

Danny Chavasse looked up from his plate and said, "Excuse me, did you say *circus*?"

"Yes, didn't you know? Willie bought a half share in a travelling circus soon after we retired. It's mainly run by his partner, Georgi Gogol, but Willie usually spends a few weeks with it every year, sometimes here if it's touring Britain, sometimes abroad. I've done a few odd jobs there myself on occasion. It's truly fascinating."

Dinah said, "I once spent a whole day at the circus with Willie. It's a marvellous place for smells, Danny."

"Let us have no reminiscences concerning the mucking out of the elephants' washroom, please," said Collier. "I'm waiting to hear about W. Garvin Esq. and Molly Chen, and if there are any further interruptions I shall clear the court."

"Willie joined the circus for a while in Hong Kong," said Modesty, "and looked up Molly Chen. Her grandfather had died a few years ago. We don't know what happened to his money, but Molly didn't get it. She married, but her husband was killed in an accident just before Willie looked her up, and she was having a pretty thin time. She wanted to get out of Hong Kong, so Willie fixed her up with a job in the circus. It's doing a season in England just now, and Molly was due for a holiday, but it wouldn't have been much fun on her own, so Willie took her to Malta for a break."

Dinah said, "Is that the girl Willie was throwing knives at when you took me to the show near Guildford? You mentioned she was Chinese."

"That was Molly. She sells programmes, mends costumes, and does any job that comes to hand, but if Willie decides to do an act, then she plays target for him. He tells me she loves the life and has a burning ambition to become a clown."

Collier patted his wife's arm. "Now there's an example for you. If we got you a big red nose and some baggy pants–" He broke off sharply. "No, wait! That's not what I was going to say. What was I going to say? Ah, yes. Before that woman with the frying pan distracted me I was going to say that her rendition of the Molly Chen story is typical of the Blaise method of narration. She has a unique capacity for killing any story stone dead. I quote – *'first met Willie'* dee-dah dee-dah, *'job in Hong Kong'* dee-dah dee-dah, *'ran into some nasty snags'* dee-dah dee-dah, *'managed to sort them out'* dee-dah dee-dah."

Collier shook his head in a gesture of despair. "How does she do it? How does she bring the art of the anecdote to such abysmal depths? The questions are rhetorical, Danny boy, go on with your breakfast. What I want to know as I sit here starving is, *what* job was he supposed to do? *What* snags did he encounter? *How* did he sort them out? And how and why and when and where did they first meet under what conditions and what happened?"

Modesty said, "Mind the plate, Dinah, it's hot." She set Dinah's breakfast in front of her.

"Thanks, honey. Smells great. Would you feel utterly betrayed if I endorsed what Steve just said? You tell a lousy story."

Modesty laughed. "I know. Just let me see to his breakfast and I'll try again." The phone on the wall rang, and she veered away from the cooker to answer it. Collier began to butter some toast for his wife. Danny Chavasse poured more coffee for her. On the phone, Modesty said, "Yes, at Kingsbrook. I can be there in fifteen minutes." She was jotting on a pad beside the phone. "Pick up at Stansted and deliver to North Thursby. Yes, I'll look it up. You'll arrange for reception? Thank you. Goodbye."

She put down the phone and tore the sheet from the pad. "I'm so sorry, but I have to dash."

"Dash?" Collier echoed. "*Dash?* What about my breakfast?"

"I have to fly a transplant kidney up to an airfield near Hull. Would you mind taking over, Dinah? I'll be back this afternoon."

"Sure. You take care now."

"I will. Steve, get the car out for me, will you please? Keys on the rack there."

"Yours to command, my lovely." Collier went out of the back door as Modesty left the kitchen by way of the hall.

Danny Chavasse said, "For one crazy moment I thought I heard Modesty say she was going to fly a kidney to somewhere."

Dinah nodded. "That's right. She's one of the St. John Air Wing volunteers, and she's on call this week. They make emergency flights to take medical stuff from A to B when it's needed fast, like some rare blood group, or serum, or transplant organ. That must have been her co-ordinator on the phone."

"These are all pilots who have their own aircraft, like Modesty?"

"Yes, that's how it works. She brought her Piper Comanche down here to the airfield at Kingsbrook last week."

He watched Dinah pick up the last morsels of her eggs and bacon as deftly as if she had been sighted. "Does it happen often?" he asked. "I mean, being called out like this."

"Modesty's only been called out once before, and that was when she was down in the South of France. The scheme operates all over Europe, with kidney-matching centres linked by computer. This other time wasn't a kidney, though. She flew a patient from Nice to Stoke Mandeville for some emergency operation."

Collier returned to the kitchen. Dinah put on an apron and began to make breakfast for him, first sensing with a light touch of her slim fingers the utensils and food set out beside the cooker. Two minutes later Modesty came downstairs wearing slacks, sweater and headscarf, a jacket over her arm, a small overnight bag in one hand.

Dinah said, "If you want company, honey, you can borrow Steve. He'll complain all the way there and back, but you're used to that."

Danny said, "No, I'll go along."

Modesty shook her head. "We fly with a co-pilot, so I'll be picking one up at Stansted. Please all go riding this morning, as planned, or do whatever you'd like to do. There's all sorts available. Oh, and don't forget Dinah wants to go shopping in Marlborough some time today." She touched the blind girl's arm. "I expect Steve will try to wriggle out of it, but Danny's a dream-boat to go shopping with. Quite inspiring.

43

Goodbye all, and I'm sorry to be an absentee hostess."

At the door, Collier halted her for a moment to kiss her cheek. "Safe trip, darling," he said quietly, and went out with her to the car.

Dinah gave a little sigh and said, "We're always worrying about that girl."

Danny watched, fascinated, as she neatly turned over some rashers of bacon then listened with head cocked and nostrils flared a little as if judging the progress of the cooking by sound and smell. He said, "Modesty's a very competent pilot."

"Oh sure, but I didn't mean that exactly."

"Well . . . she survived long years of very real danger running *The Network*, which means she's highly competent in quite a few ways."

"Oh God, we know that, Danny. But she's always getting herself *involved*. She and Willie both. I mean, involved in situations where it's a surprise if you don't end up dead. She got involved in the Mus treasure thing because of me, and she got involved in Limbo because of you. That's how it goes on, so we're always wondering what's coming next."

Danny said, "I sometimes think that if somebody has a particular capacity to cope, it seems to attract the particular situations that he or she is fitted to cope with. Of course, that doesn't help you to stop worrying. You and Steve have a great rapport with Modesty and Willie, haven't you?"

"Yes, we're very close and we all understand one another. I guess that happens when you go through bad times together."

"Dinah, when you had that . . . that shiver a little while ago, was it a premonition of some kind?"

Before she could answer, Steve Collier returned. He was frowning, and went straight to his wife, resting his hands on her shoulders. "That was a real flash you had, wasn't it, darling?"

She nodded slowly. "Danny just asked me the same thing."

"I remember I'd just said I was going to hypnotise Modesty and that I had these incredible powers. Any trigger word there?"

"Could be. But if so I don't know which it was. Wish to God I did. It might give me some idea of . . . of the *shape* of what scared me." She scooped the contents of the frying pan on to a hot plate and turned off the hob. "Sit down and have your breakfast, Steve."

"In a second, sweetheart." He turned her gently towards him. "I felt that shock-fright hit you. Was it connected with any of us?"

She screwed up her eyes tightly as if trying to recapture an impression. "No . . . it wasn't specific. Oh God, you know how vague these things are, Steve, you've tried hundreds of experiments with me. I just get a – a *flash* in my head, and a couple of moments later it's hard to recall whether it was visual, aural, or just a *feeling*, nothing to do with the senses."

Danny said quietly, "Visual?"

Without turning his head Collier said, "Dinah didn't become blind until she was eleven. She has normal conception of form and colour." He touched his wife's brow with fingertips. "There's always some kind of content in a flash, Dinah. It's never been a complete void for you before. Does nothing come back to you now?"

She said in a strained voice. "Wait. I'm trying." Then, after a few seconds and very slowly: "There must be a connection . . . but I can't find it. There was just this . . . yes, this *face*. No, a head. I'm sorry, it's so difficult. A head with a halo round it? Well, like a halo. A saint?" She pressed the heels of her hands to her eyes and shook her head in despair. "No, that can't be right. Why would a flash image of a saint terrify me?"

Collier grimaced, patted her arm and said, "Sorry. I shouldn't have pressed you to verbalise the impression. I've probably distorted it now." He guided her to the table. "Just forget it, and listen to me eat my breakfast. You don't know any terrifying saints, do you, Danny?"

Danny Chavasse picked up Collier's attempt to lighten the mood and said, "Not personally, but maybe this was Saint Paul. His ideas on women were pretty terrifying."

Dinah rubbed her arms as if chilled, and managed a small smile. "The halo impression made him *look* like a saint. I hope to God it was a freaky false flash, Steve, because what he felt like was something dead inside . . . a zombie."

3

Thaddeus Pilgrim was a big man with a round face and fluffy white hair that stood up round his head like a halo. The monk's robe he wore was of coarse brown material. His feet were in strong sandals, his hands rested with fingers linked, relaxed. White eyebrows curved over large eyes whose watery gaze was courteous but kept wandering vaguely, as if the mind behind them was on other and higher matters. Seated at his desk in the austerely furnished study of the Hostel of Righteousness, he transferred his remote gaze from the jackdaw in a cage by the window and focused with a kindly smile on the reporter sitting opposite him.

"It is true that we seek no converts, Mr. Papadakis," he said gently. "In fact we discourage the notion, for we have no creed to which we seek to convert our fellow mortals." A glint of humour touched the mild blue eyes. "Also, we seek no funds for our work. You will find no evidence of our persuading gullible people to donate their wealth or work or time to us, I assure you."

Papadakis smiled deprecatingly as if he needed no such assurance, and wrote something in his notebook. He was a dark, well-built Greek in his middle thirties, speaking fluent English. "I understand there is a branch of your society in Macau, another in South Carolina, and another in England," he glanced at his notebook, "in the village of North Thursby, near Hull."

Thaddeus Pilgrim inclined his head. "We have a handful of followers at each of those branches, Mr. ah . . ." He paused to lean forward and study the card on his desk. "Yes . . . Mr. Papadakis, is it not? Perhaps I should not have referred to them as *followers*, since I do not, you understand, in any sense consider myself to be a *leader*. That might involve the sin of pride, might it not? I suppose it would be true to say, or at least it would not be *un*true to say, that I am – through no merit of my own I hasten to add – that I am perhaps the *centre* of our little group, since it was I who had the privilege, the very substantial

46

privilege, I assure you, of founding the Hostel of Righteousness here on Kalivari. I would not, of course, have you imagine, or cause the readers of your no doubt excellent newspaper to imagine, that what one might call my *position* here is in any sense superior to that of my colleagues, Mr. ah . . ." He leaned forward to look at the card again, the halo of white hair stirring a little with his movement. "Ah yes, Mr. Papadakis . . ."

Papadakis mentally tuned the longwinded ramblings to a background noise and concentrated on blocking out the story he would write. Not just write, but write and syndicate worldwide. It would be that kind of story. The weekly ferry, on which he purported to have arrived from Athens this morning, would pick him up this evening when it called after making its rounds of some of the nearer islands among the wide scattering called The Cyclades. By dawn it would be at Piraeus, and by noon he would be sitting at his desk in Athens with the whole story written.

The Hostel of Righteousness had once been a monastery, abandoned and decaying until the followers of Dr. Thaddeus Pilgrim had leased the small island of Kalivari from the Greek government and restored the building. There was no other habitation apart from The Hostel itself and the various outbuildings. The small fishing boat in which Papadakis had in fact come to Kalivari after dark the previous day had left at once after putting him ashore half a mile from the miniature harbour and quay. This morning it had not been difficult for him to hide near the quay and mingle with the few visitors and men handling supplies when the early ferry arrived.

Papadakis became aware that Thaddeus Pilgrim had actually droned to a halt. Making a meaningless scribble in his notebook he said with assumed interest, "May I ask what is the precise purpose of the Hostel of Righteousness, as opposed to the purposes of other and larger religious bodies, Dr. Pilgrim?"

"Oh, I am sorry to hear you use the word '*opposed*', Mr. ah . . . yes, Mr. Papadakis. We are not *opposed* to other religious bodies –"

"No, I didn't quite mean that –"

"Neither do we attempt to recruit from such brethren, I assure you. We of the Hostel of Righteousness are humble folk." Dr. Pilgrim beamed mistily upon the reporter, though his focus was disconcertingly a little to one side, as if he were addressing somebody behind Papadakis. "When I say *humble*, I hope you will not, indeed I pray you

47

will not, misconstrue this as mock humility, or would it be more accurate to say *false* humility? That is not our way, Mr. ah . . ., not our way at all. Ours is not a narrow religion, if indeed we may dare to call it by the name of religion. Our God is the Being who made all things, and we do not dare to define Him more specifically than that." Thaddeus Pilgrim's voice sank to a lower tone. "You will understand that I use the word 'Him' merely for convenience, and without in any way presuming to invest the Creative Being with – ah – with *gender*."

"And your particular purpose, Doctor?" Papadakis said quickly. "Can you sum it up in a few words?"

Dr. Pilgrim's gaze wandered about the reporter's head, then he spread his arms in a gesture of simplicity. "I can sum it up in a *single* word, Mr. Papadakis. A single word will suffice, if you will forgive what may seem, but I assure you is not, a somewhat extravagant boast, which would be entirely contrary to the nature of our little community, you understand."

He stopped abruptly, nodding rather shyly as if apologising for having made a point which might just possibly offend his hearer. After a moment or two Papadakis said, "What is the single word?"

Thaddeus Pilgrim started. "Oh, forgive me, Mr. ah . . . Yes, of course. I fear I did not complete the answer to your question. The word is . . . *prayer*. That is our sole purpose, dear friend. We follow no creed, no ritual, no formal procedures. We simply *pray*."

Papadakis jotted the words down verbatim, relishing them. Maintaining a sober air, he looked up and said, "What is it your people pray for, Dr. Pilgrim?"

"Oh, not *my* people, Mr. Papadakis." The white hair danced as Thaddeus Pilgrim shook his head. "We, that is to say our community here and elsewhere, pray for all the world. We pray for peace, for an end to poverty, an end to racial strife, an end to strife between – ah – male and female, in fact we pray quite simply for what is *good* to come about. We also pray, and quite specifically, for groups or for individuals who send requests for our prayers on their behalf, though I must ask you, in view of the nature of our community here, not to regard this function, if that is the correct word, as being in the context of *intercession*. That would be too – ah – too *doctrinal* in character for us. However, I believe that on both counts, that is to say both the general and the particular categories of our submissions to the Creative Being, we may claim, if that is not too assertive a word, that the Hostel of Righteousness is truly a *powerhouse* of prayer."

"I believe you have some thirty or forty people here," said Papadakis, "almost all male. Does this cause no problem?"

Thaddeus Pilgrim pursed his lips and looked like a man trying not to look reproachful. "None," he said in a low voice. "My colleagues are dedicated people, I assure you."

"Do you all do nothing but pray, Doctor?"

"Oh, no, no, my dear friend," said Dr. Pilgrim with a confiding smile in the direction of the jackdaw. "That is quite impossible. Positive prayer calls for considerable mental effort, though I hasten to say that we do not begrudge such effort, for we regard ourselves as labourers in God's vineyard, if you will forgive what may appear to be, though it is not meant as such, a somewhat sectarian phrase. No, we spend much time in meditation on the *subject* and *quality* of our prayers, and we also labour more practically, though not of course to better effect, on our little patch of crops and with our fishing lines. We are not self-sufficient, you will understand, but we try to keep our – ah – imports from the mainland to a minimum."

"On the subject of imports, Doctor, these must be paid for, which brings us back to the question of funds. I believe you said you seek no contributions from outside, and also that nobody becoming a member of the Hostel of Righteousness is allowed to bring money into the community, or to provide money for it in any way. So how do you exist?"

"Ah. Now, what you say is essentially correct, Mr. ah . . . essentially correct, but in the former part of the last sentence there is perhaps a degree of misunderstanding, which I have no doubt has arisen from my own failure to express myself clearly, and for this I hope you will accept my apology. It is true that we do not *seek* contributions to our work, but it is our firm belief that God will provide, and indeed He has done so – again I hope you will excuse the use of gender in this reference. We do not seek, but we do *receive*, because those groups and individuals for whom we pray, at their request, as I have explained, are invariably most generous in their recognition of our efforts, and indeed, if I may say so, of our achievements on their behalf. We do not lack for funds, my dear friend. What we need for our modest establishments, we spend. All surplus is passed on to those whom our meditations tell us are most in need of help. Oh, please excuse me."

The last words followed a tap on the door, which opened to admit a tall woman wearing a white robe with the hood thrown back, a handsome woman of about thirty. She was blonde, with her hair in ringlets, the eyes grey, the features strongly sculptured. Her body was hidden by the robe, but from the way she moved Papadakis had the impression that it might be a rather fine body to look at.

"Do excuse me, Dr. Pilgrim," she said in slightly accented English, "I thought you would wish to have a note of this evening's work before Mr. Papadakis leaves." She laid a piece of paper on the desk.

Thaddeus Pilgrim's erratic gaze wandered around and past her for several seconds before a beam of recognition lit his face. "My dear Sibyl, of course, of course," he said happily. "I believe you have not yet been introduced to our distinguished visitor from the Press. May I present Mr. – ah – Papadakis." He gestured with a large hand. "Mr. Papadakis, it gives me great pleasure, and I say this in all sincerity, to introduce a lady who is one of the stalwarts of our little community, Sibyl Pray."

Papadakis stood up and shook hands, trying not to let curiosity and speculation show in his face. "Delighted," he murmured.

Sibyl Pray studied him candidly and said with careful enunciation, "How do you do?"

Dr. Pilgrim had picked up the sheet of paper and might have been reading from it, but Papadakis doubted that, for the amiable voice was droning on again with its tortuous structure of clauses and sub-clauses. "You may well reflect Mr. Papadakis – indeed it would be surprising if you did not reflect, since the association of ideas, I would suggest, is manifest – that Sibyl's name is remarkably appropriate for that occupation which is the prime endeavour of our little community. I am of course referring to her surname, you understand, a fact which, in all probability, it is quite unnecessary for me to point out, and indeed I hope I have not in any way offended you by so doing, my dear friend."

Papadakis said politely, "You mean that your work here is to pray, and this lady's name is Pray?"

"Quite so, quite so, Mr. ah . . ." said Dr. Pilgrim, his head nodding in confirmation. "That is the nub of my remark. It may be of interest to you to know, since your journalistic vocation must demand – or so I have always thought – a wide variety of knowledge in matters both large and small, that the name Pray does not derive from the English word, as one might imagine, but from the paternal element of Sibyl's Anglo-Hungarian parentage." He lifted his eyes from the paper, placed it on his desk, smiled vaguely in the woman's general direction, and continued without pause, "Thank you, my dear, most kind of you to remind me that we have much to do this evening, and I hope, in fact I am sure we *all* hope, that Mr. Papadakis will consent to be our guest tonight, so that he may observe the nature of our prayerful submissions on behalf of those who have sought our help." He looked at the reporter, eyebrows arched in hopeful query.

"I'm sorry," said Papadakis with fairly convincing regret, "but I have to leave on this evening's ferry. Another time, perhaps."

"As you wish," said Thaddeus Pilgrim with a courteous inclination of his white head. "Thank you, Sibyl, I will not keep you longer from your duties, my dear. Perhaps you could spare me a few minutes when Mr. ah . . . our friend from the Press has left."

"Of course, Doctor." Sibyl Pray nodded briskly to Papadakis and went from the study.

Dr. Pilgrim said, "That is a greatly gifted lady. I much regret you are unable to stay and hear her lead us in one of our categories of prayer, but of course I must not dissuade you from your duty. Ah . . . have you obtained from me all you wished to obtain? Not that I have any desire to hurry you, of course, but . . ."

"If I might ask a few questions about your personal background, Doctor?"

"Well . . . I do not think that I, as a person, or my background, for that matter, is of any particular importance, but I will, if you so wish, answer a few questions to the best of my ability."

"Thank you, Doctor. Perhaps you would first confirm some facts provided by our London office. As a young man you held a commission in an infantry regiment of the British Army. You resigned to take holy orders, and in due course you were ordained as a minister in the United Reform Church." Papadakis flicked over a page of his notebook. "You were the incumbent of a church near North Thursby, in Yorkshire. There you married, and later two children were born, a boy and a girl. Some years later, with your family, you turned to missionary work and were sent to Africa, to Uganda." Papadakis looked up from his notebook and said quietly, "It was there that you suffered the appalling tragedy of your wife and children being murdered by terrorists, almost ten years ago now."

Thaddeus Pilgrim sat with his head turned to gaze out of the open window to the blue-green expanse of the Aegean. "Yes. All that is correct, my dear friend," he said absently. "Quite correct."

"We have no record of your work for some four years after that," said Papadakis. "Then you founded the Hostel of Righteousness. There was little publicity at the time, and has been little since. You are on record as saying that you seek neither publicity nor growth. Does that hold good today?"

"Oh, certainly, Mr. ah . . . Papadakis. We have been compelled to set up small branches of the Hostel by a mere handful of eager recruits who felt called to our particular work, but I shall be grateful, indeed we shall all be grateful, if you will be so kind as to make known to your readers that we would find further applications to join our number quite embarrassing."

"*Jesus, I bet you bloody would!*" thought Papadakis, nodding gravely. Aloud he said, "According to the information we received, you are now fifty-five, Doctor. May I ask if that is correct?"

"Ah, you hide your puzzlement both courteously and well, my dear friend." Thaddeus Pilgrim smiled mistily past the reporter's head. "My white hair gives the impression of a person substantially older, does it not? And indeed I am aware that my regrettable habit of – ah – circumlocution may tend to confirm that impression, but your information is quite correct."

Papadakis said slowly, "I don't wish to distress you, but I feel sure that the tragedy you suffered in Africa must have had a profound effect upon you, Doctor. Can you tell me how you spent the subsequent years before founding the Hostel of Righteousness?"

The man in the brown robe sat brooding deeply for a while, then looked up with a gentle smile. "I sought for a way to attain peace of mind once again," he said with a rather deprecating air. "To this end I withdrew from the world I had known, and travelled widely, going into retreat among wise and godly men of different religions and philosophies, both in the east and in the west. I hope, Mr. ah . . . I sincerely hope you will not think me guilty of self-importance when I say that after much seeking I felt called to do the work that I am now doing." He lifted his hands and gestured loosely about him. "A powerhouse of prayer."

Papadakis sat looking at the round, benign face, baffled, striving to penetrate what he knew must be the façade that concealed the real Dr. Thaddeus Pilgrim, but unable to detect the slightest flaw in it. After a moment or two he smiled, closed his notebook, and stood up. "I won't take up any more of your time, Doctor. Thank you for agreeing to this interview and for being so helpful."

"Not at all, not at all, my dear friend." Dr. Pilgrim got to his feet and accompanied the reporter to the door. "May I conduct you to the refectory? A few of my brothers and sisters in prayer will be enjoying a repast at this hour, and you are most welcome to join them, if you so wish, since the ferry is not due for another – let me see, how long would it be?" As they moved along a broad passage and out on to a terrace he drew a watch from under his robe, consulted it for some moments, then continued: "Fifty minutes, Mr. ah . . . that is assuming punctuality, of course. When I say that a *few* of us will be enjoying a repast, I should perhaps explain that we take turns at table, or perhaps, yes, perhaps *shifts* would be a more appropriate word, the reason being that there must always be *some* of us at prayer in order to maintain the – ah – the momentum or even the *dynamic*, if I may so call it, of our humble petitions."

When Papadakis was sure Thaddeus Pilgrim had finished speaking he said, "Thank you, but I won't intrude upon your community any further. It's a pleasant evening, and I shall be quite happy to sit on the quay and amplify my notes until the ferry arrives."

"As you please, dear friend, as you please. Then I shall bid you goodbye now. If you take these steps and turn to the right at the bottom, you will find yourself on the road leading down to the quay. Goodbye, Mr. ah . . . Mr. Papadakis. We shall remember you in our prayers."

Papadakis kept a straight face and said, "Thank you." The two men shook hands. Thaddeus Pilgrim watched the reporter go down the steps, waved a genial hand to him as he paused at the foot to look back, then turned and retraced his steps to the study. Sibyl Pray was already there, and with her now were two men in brown robes and another woman in white. One man was half a head taller than Sibyl Pray and about the same age, olive skinned and handsome, with black curly hair and wide-set dark eyes. His name was Kazim, he came from Anatolia, and he was standing curiously close to Sibyl Pray, his shoulder touching hers.

The other man looked the part of a monk, for he was plump and burly in the stamp of Friar Tuck, and though his head was not tonsured it was bald across the dome with thick hair on each side above the ears. The brown robe seemed well suited to him, as did the white robe to the second woman, for she was a Punjabi, small-boned, of indeterminate age, with hair drawn tightly back in a bun. She stood holding a clipboard and ballpoint pen, lips pursed disapprovingly, waiting with an air of suppressed impatience.

As Dr. Thaddeus Pilgrim entered the study and closed the door the Punjabi woman said briskly, "I am requiring immediate instruction, Doctor. Mr. Papadakis really must not be allowed to depart with his ill-gotten knowledge. It is my recommendation that Sister Pray and Brother Kazim be dispatched at once to break his cheeky neck damn quick."

"Patience, Mrs. Ram, patience," Thaddeus Pilgrim said soothingly, moving to take his chair. "Certainly our somewhat deceitful visitor must be – ah – divested of his cloak of clay before he can impart what you call, and rightly I feel, his ill-gotten knowledge, but it would be imprudent of us to cause him to disappear *here*, on Kalivari."

Mrs. Ram gave a sharp, affirmative tilt of her head. "Point taken, Doctor. At Piraeus, then? Our launch can leave after the ferry and still put executives ashore before Mr. Papadakis arrives."

"I would commend that suggestion," Dr. Pilgrim said cautiously, "but let us be double-banked, Mrs. Ram, double-banked. Far be it from me to intervene in your duties as our administrator, but if I may be permitted to think aloud for a moment or two, I feel you may well decide to have, say, our well-loved brother, Kazim, covering the newspaper offices, and our dear sister in prayer, Sibyl, suitably positioned in the hope of an immediate elimination at Piraeus, in the car park, perhaps. We were careful to obtain the registration of Mr. Papadakis's car, I believe?"

"Yes, that is most satisfactory." Mrs. Ram jotted busily on her clipboard in hieroglyphics, then looked at Sibyl Pray and Kazim. "Do you wish for any labourers to provide assistance, my dears?"

Their heads turned and they gazed into each other's eyes for several seconds, then the woman looked at Mrs. Ram and said, "No, we shall not find it necessary."

"Then I ask you to be ready to leave, and suitably dressed, in one hour from now, if you please." Mrs. Ram glanced sharply at the plump burly man. "Are you wishing to comment, Dr. Tyl?"

The man shook his head, smiling amiably in the way he had adopted to suit his friar-like persona. He was a Czech and his English was strongly accented. "No comment, Mrs. Ram," he said. As a psychiatrist and a psychologist, Dr. Janos Tyl's main duty was to assess the requests for prayer received by the Hostel of Righteousness, to consider information on the background of groups and individuals, and to suggest the action required in order that certain prayers be answered. As a doctor of medicine it was also his function to supply lethal drugs or subtle killing methods if required by executives of the community.

Dr. Tyl viewed with contempt such crude assassinations as were the speciality of the very physical Sibyl Pray and her tame satyr, Kazim, but he kept this feeling to himself. It would not have pleased Thaddeus Pilgrim, and Dr. Tyl was very much afraid of Dr. Pilgrim, for reasons quite beyond the reach of his own psychiatric skill to elucidate. Even Sibyl Pray and Kazim feared the white haired man with the wandering gaze. It must, thought Dr. Tyl, be something in the aura, which was absurd, for he did not believe in auras. He had long been aware that Mrs. Ram was unlike the others. She worshipped Thaddeus Pilgrim so intensely that there was no room left for the emotion of fear.

Dr. Pilgrim was studying the note Sibyl Pray had brought in earlier. "I do not think it would be wrong to declare that this was a considerable shock," he said, looking up. "No doubt Mrs. Ram can amplify the somewhat brief information herein contained, so I will not keep other colleagues from the pursuit of their duties. I am most grateful to you all for attending on me, and of course Sibyl and Kazim may rest assured that our prayers shall go with them in the matter of stiffing Mr. Papadakis."

He beamed upon the three of them as they left the study with polite murmurs. When the door had closed he said, "Perhaps you will summarise, Mrs. Ram."

She flicked back a sheet on her clipboard and said: "At nine-thirty a.m., before the arrival of the ferry, a member of Mr. Li Chang's security staff reported to him that a window in the private area of our establishment had been forced. Mr. Li Chang began prompt investigation, and later a brown robe was found hidden among rocks near the harbour. Assumption was made that an intruder had been put ashore by night, and had moved about by day in the guise of a male person of our order."

Thaddeus Pilgrim cleared his throat and said, "This was Mr. Papadakis?"

"Subsequent discoveries have so ascertained, Doctor. Careful but unobtrusive watch was kept on arrival of ferry boat, and Mr. Papadakis was observed to emerge from hiding to join persons from the ferry. Mr. Li Chang then advised me of his suspicions. It was my duty to greet Mr. Papadakis when he arrived for the interview as arranged, but I told him that you were deeply engaged in emergency prayer, and I insisted that he made a small tour of the island on foot with Dr. Tyl. To do so, he had to leave his case, for there was no point in carrying it, and he could not admit that it contained a camera since we had stipulated that there must be no photographs taken during his visit."

"Ah . . . and our good brother Freddie the Twirl contrived to unlock the case?"

"He said a child could have done it, Doctor."

"Freddie is, I am sure you will agree, too modest regarding his skills. But proceed, Mrs. Ram, proceed if you please."

"There was much film. I took it all to the Operations Room, and Mr. Carter made great haste to develop contact prints. These show that Mr. Papadakis contrived to penetrate certain of our private areas, though not the Operations Room or Records Section."

"Did he obtain sufficient photographic material to embarrass us, Mrs. Ram?"

"Oh, very much so, Doctor," she affirmed, nodding vigorously. "He penetrated to the armoury, also to the recreation room, where he took photographs of the bar and the what-do-you-call-them, pin up pictures, some of which are very dirty, and of course there would still be the fag-ends of grass that the Chinese fellows smoke, and the gambling paraphernalia. Furthermore, he contrived to take a sneaky photograph through a window of our Chapel of Ease. It shows two out of three resident whores in a state of déshabille, and still furthermore he was most fortuitously fortunate to have been within camera distance at a moment when Sibyl Pray and Kazim emerged from their morning swim and were having their first sexual connection of the day on the rocks, as is their custom."

"Their mutual affection is well-known and frequently demonstrated," said Thaddeus Pilgrim benevolently. "I take it the negatives have been destroyed, Mrs. Ram?"

"Oh, certainly, Doctor."

"Good . . . very good. And we can rely upon dear Sibyl and Kazim to, as it were, tidy up the loose ends. We must also, I think, review our security system once this matter has been dealt with." Thaddeus

Pilgrim leaned back in his chair and gazed at the jackdaw for a few moments, frowning slightly as if trying to collect his thoughts. "Ah, yes," he said at last, "I knew there was a matter about which I wished to ask you, Mrs. Ram. Has there been a satisfactory outcome of the project to eliminate that young Chinese woman? Ah, Molly Chen, I believe her name was. I must confess I had expected to have heard by now."

Mrs. Ram looked unhappy. "I regret I cannot give a good report on that, Doctor. I received deciphered radio communication this morning, while dealing with the matter of Mr. Papadakis, and was constrained to treat the latter subject as the more important. As you know, we subcontracted for the killing of Miss Chen, and unfortunately the contractors failed. It appears that Miss Chen was in the company of a male person in Malta at the time, and this male person dispatched the contractor's executive in what is claimed to be a remarkable fashion. It has now been ascertained that the person's name is William Garvin, more familiarly known as Willie Garvin. Our records show that he was chief lieutenant to Modesty Blaise when she ran *The Network*, and he is still associated with her. There is a related matter to report, Doctor."

His white eyebrows lifted. "A related matter?"

"Yes, Doctor." She turned the papers of her clipboard, darting a nervous glance at the man behind the desk. "We have had the weekly report from our undercover man at North Thursby. In general all goes well there. Being genuine cranks, the members of that Hostel have nothing to hide, and help very much to give us credibility in northern Europe, so we do not expect difficulties from that direction. But the report mentions that Modesty Blaise made a landing at the airfield near North Thursby in her private aircraft three days ago. Our man learned of this quite by chance and does not know if it is significant, but thought he should report it. May I ask if you wish me to give you a brief history of these two persons, Doctor?"

Thaddeus Pilgrim's gaze had become much less vague in the last minute or two. The mild blue eyes seemed almost alert as he said quietly, "No . . . I once studied the careers of Miss Blaise and Mr. Garvin in depth and with great interest, hoping they might become valuable members of our little community, but I discarded the notion, most reluctantly, on learning that they had retired. It does appear, however, that their retirement is somewhat a matter of – ah – definition. They are a most interesting pair, and I have no doubt that where one is involved the other will be involved also." He fingered his chin pensively. "The dispatch of Molly Chen was not of great importance, of course. Simply a matter of insuring against the small risk that she *might* know something and *might* talk about it. However, Garvin's appearance in the affair, together with Miss Blaise possibly showing an interest in our North Thursby hostel, must be given our close attention. It constitutes a potential danger that is quite unacceptable."

He was silent for a while, unmoving, unblinking, eyes not focused. Mrs. Ram watched him with breathless adoration. After a while he said, "If we send our own people to dispose of Molly Chen . . . that will set Willie Garvin seeking to discover who killed her and why. Then Modesty Blaise will certainly involve herself, which means we shall have potent enemies to distract us at the time of the Hallelujah Scenario, which is undesirable. So I think . . ." He hitched his chair forward, leaned folded arms on the desk, and looked at the Punjabi woman with a bright mischievous smile. "Yes, I think, Mrs. Ram, that we must give ourselves the exercise of devising a preventative operation against these two persons. But we must create a *suitable* scenario, do you do not agree? Our task is to perform acts of *purposeful* creation in a world of *blind* creation, is it not?"

Mrs. Ram clutched her clipboard to her chest and breathed, "Oh yes, Doctor Pilgrim, yes."

"Excellent, excellent." Thaddeus Pilgrim took out his watch and studied it. "Now, I must not forget that you have to brief Sibyl Pray and Kazim, and to get them away on the little mission we have given them." He looked up, and suddenly his eyes were completely and horribly empty, like holes in a skull as he said, "Tell them they would be well advised not to fail, Mrs. Ram."

She shuddered deliciously and dipped her head in fervent agreement. "Of course, Doctor."

Humanity returned to the face, and his gaze became amiable again as a nebulous smile wandered over his features. "Once you are free," he said with a courtly inclination of his head, "I should be obliged if you would attend on me here with our dear friend Dr. Tyl, so that we may, as they say, put our heads together and work out a truly interesting scenario for, ah . . . Miss Blaise and Mr. Garvin."

*　　*　　*　　*

It was still dusk, with the sun not yet risen, when Papadakis came off the ferry and made his way to the car park. As he unlocked the door of his car a woman's voice behind him breathed, "Please, Mr. Papadakis, please, I must speak to you."

He turned, and for a moment or two did not recognise her, for she was dressed in trousers and a sweater, her hair tucked in a beret. Astonished, Papadakis said, "But you're . . . Sibyl Pray! How did you get here?"

She stared at him with eyes that seemed almost luminous; with fear, he thought. "I will explain, Mr. Papadakis," she whispered urgently, "but please may we get in the car? I must not be seen. I have something shocking to tell you."

"Really? I don't think you can surprise me with your revelations, Miss Pray, but I shall be intrigued to hear them." He jerked his head. "All right, get in."

One or two cars were being driven off by other ferry passengers as he seated himself at the wheel, put his case with camera and film in the back, and leaned across to open the nearside door. She climbed in quickly, closing the door after her. "I already know what the Hostel of Righteousness *isn't*," he said, taking out his cigarettes, "but I'm not sure what it is –"

He was dipping his head to light the cigarette when she hit him a carefully calculated blow with he edge of her hand to the base of the skull, a paralysing blow that left him barely conscious. As he sagged, she pulled him towards her so that his head was on her lap, pinched his nose firmly, and sealed his mouth with a handkerchief folded in her other hand. If he could have seen her eyes now he would have found them yet more luminous, and would have known that this was not from fear.

After perhaps thirty seconds there was a feeble attempt at movement, but she stilled it easily and sat holding him as before, gazing through the windscreen at the wall fifteen paces away, noting that the ground sloped down towards it, and deciding that this would suit her purpose very well. Five minutes later, when she was sure he was dead, she got out and went round to the offside to release the bonnet catch. The car park was silent now, with the handful of ferry passengers gone.

She propped the bonnet open, lifted Papadakis from the car, carried him to the front, and draped him face down over the radiator, his head and shoulders over the engine. Using a torch, she unclipped the

59

distributor cap, removed the rotor arm, and put this in Papadakis's pocket. Nearby was a holdall she had hidden under a van after following Papadakis when he left the dock. From quite a variety of contents she took a bottle of ouzo and a short lead cosh. Moving back to Papadakis's car, she opened his case of photographic equipment, removed a notebook, poured the ouzo in, made sure the cassettes of ruined film were thoroughly submerged, then smashed the bottle with the cosh and let the fragments fall into the sticky mess. She closed the case, dropped it to the ground in front of the offside wheel, and stood considering the situation.

The dead man's feet were trailing on the ground, and after judging what effect this might have she lifted each in turn to prop it on the front bumper, so that he was sprawled in a frog-like position. Satisfied, she checked that the gear lever was in neutral and took off the handbrake. As the wheels began to turn, she ran to the back and heaved with all the strength of her powerful and highly trained body to give the car speed down the slight slope. A wheel bumped over the case holding the films, and the car was probably travelling at no more than four or five miles an hour when it reached the wall, but its ton weight at that speed proved more than sufficient to crush a human body.

She stood back and studied the scene, not breathing hard from her efforts. It was what Dr. Thaddeus Pilgrim would call a delightful scenario, she decided. Papadakis had removed the rotor arm from the distributor to ensure that his car would not be stolen while he was away on Kalivari, but on his return he must inadvertently have taken off the handbrake, perhaps while operating the interior bonnet-release catch. Then, as he was about to replace the rotor arm, the car had run forward, carrying him with it and crushing him against the wall. It was most unlikely that anyone would question the cause of his death. Even more unlikely that anyone would imagine that his films of disciples of the Hostel of Righteousness at their selfless work had been destroyed other than by accident.

Sibyl Pray picked up her holdall and walked to the car park entrance. There was nobody about. She stripped off the surgical gloves she wore, put them in the bag with Papadakis's notebook, took out a small radio transceiver and pulled out the aerial. She pressed the call button, and a moment later the voice of Kazim sounded from the earpiece, thin and metallic. "What is the situation?" He was speaking from a doorway near the newspaper office in Athens, five miles away.

She said softly into the handset, "The matter is concluded. I will wait for you by the launch."

Kazim said, "I am unhappy to hear this. You know why." There was reproach in the tinny voice. Sibyl Pray smiled. Yes, she knew why. Kazim had very much wanted to kill Papadakis himself, because Papadakis was Greek, and Kazim was Turkish, two hereditary and virulent enemies.

She pressed the switch to transmit, and said, "I will make it up to you. I will make you forget your disappointment completely." Her voice shook as she was swept by a wave of lust. "As soon as we are on the launch. I will be marvellous for you . . ." she glanced across the car park to the car pinning the dead man against the wall, ". . . after this."

4

Willie Garvin got up from the bench and poured a scoop of water over the sauna bricks. A cloud of steam engulfed him as he turned away and sat down again beside Modesty Blaise, absently massaging his ribs where she had caught him with a foot-strike towards the end of their work-out in the combat room. This was part of the long, sound-proof and windowless building that stood near the river in the grounds of Willie's pub, *The Treadmill*.

They had devoted the whole afternoon to a training session, to target practice with handgun and knife, to quarterstaff combat, to techniques for sharpening reaction, and finally to a jam session of unarmed combat using a variety of disciplines from the martial arts. For the last ten minutes they had been in the sauna. Modesty wore a shower cap and was dabbing with a towel at the sweat trickling down between her breasts. As Willie took his seat beside her again she said, "It's a pity you found nothing in that gunman's wallet to identify him or give us some sort of lead. Do you think it's remotely possible they were after Molly Chen rather than you?"

He mopped his face and said doubtfully, "I wondered about that, but Molly couldn't think of any reason."

"Her grandfather was in the rackets, but that wouldn't put Molly on the spot unless she knew something or had offended a Triad. What about her late husband?"

"She won't say much about 'im, but I get the impression he wasn't a lot of good. A bit of a loser, and treated Molly pretty rough. He could've been in the rackets, but I doubt if he was important enough for anyone to put out a contract on 'is wife months after he was dead."

"You whisked her out of Hong Kong. Perhaps they took a long time finding her."

"Could be, but he still doesn't seem important enough, not from what Molly says." He looked at her curiously. "Is your instinct running, Princess?"

She half smiled and wiped a drip of sweat from the tip of her nose. "I don't think so, Willie love. I'm just wondering aloud." Suddenly the smile was full and sparkling, and her eyes danced with pleasure in the way that uplifted him, making him feel that this was the smile he would gladly cross the whole world to see. She said, "I told Danny and the others the bit about you using Molly's bikini bottom for a sling. Danny loved it. So did I. Our poor Dinah worries too much about us to enjoy the moments of light relief, I'm afraid, and I suppose Steve's the same, but he hides behind caustic comment. Said that in his view the Garvin boy's action showed lack of savoir faire. To put down a contract killer with a pre-warmed slingshot was over-courteous to the point of being ingratiating."

Willie chuckled. "I'll tell Molly. She'll like it. By the way, she's leaving the circus when they finish at Clapham Common next Saturday."

Modesty looked surprised. "I thought she loved it."

"Oh, she does. She'll be going back when they come out of winter quarters next year, but I managed to get 'er into the Barton Circus School in Surrey. She starts there the week after next, so I've fixed 'er up with a little apartment at Chobham. She's over the moon about it."

Modesty punched his shoulder gently. "You're pretty fond of Molly, aren't you?"

He grinned and ran fingers through his wet hair. "Yes, I like 'er, Princess, but I'm not into a heavy romance or anything like that. It's just I'm glad to do something for Molly because . . . well, she was there with the Seahound to pick me up with old Wei Lu all those years ago. I'll always owe 'er for that."

Modesty thought, "So will I," but did not speak. She and Willie were not given to nostalgic reminiscence of times gone by, or to reflecting on the changes wrought in them and between them over the passing years. She was profoundly aware that she was the touchstone of his life and likely always to remain so. She was equally aware of all that he meant to her and of the immeasurable contribution he had made to her own life. Long ago he had come to her as a grateful hireling. Now, by degrees, there had grown up between them an effortless intimacy deeper than that of lovers. But neither she nor he dwelt on such things; they were no more to be thought about and analysed than breathing or the heartbeat.

For a few minutes they sat in easy silence. Willie Garvin, mightily content, was pondering the merits and demerits of a small second-hand car he was considering buying for Molly when she left her caravan for the flat at Chobham. Modesty was trying to recall something she had meant to say a few minutes before, when they were talking about . . .

It came to her, and she said, "Willie, the morning after you rang from Malta to tell me what happened, Dinah had one of her weird flashes. She didn't know what it was about or what it was connected with, but Steve told me later that when he tried to probe for an image she came up with an impression of a man's head with a halo round it like a saint. But not saintly. Pretty frightening, Dinah said. She had the feeling of someone dead inside. A zombie. Does that strike any chord with you?"

He shook his head slowly, anxiety touching his eyes. "No . . . does Steve think it's linked with Dinah?"

"That was my first question, but it's all right. Steve says she never gets psychic impressions involving herself. If it was valid, the link could be with Danny or with me, because we were there, or with you because we were talking of you."

Willie relaxed. "I'd just been in a bit of danger. Maybe Dinah picked up a distortion on that."

"Could be. Outside the divining and locating, that's a pretty wild talent of hers." She stood up and wrapped the towel round her waist. "I must get back to the penthouse. Are you ready for a shower?"

"Sure."

Later, as they stood under needles of icy water in the two shower cubicles, he said, "Is Danny Chavasse still with you, Princess?"

"Yes, I think he's going to spend the rest of his vacation with me. He's out with Weng this afternoon, at that club where Weng makes a fortune playing bridge. Danny plays to a good standard, but I think the wily Weng fancies there's an excellent chance Danny will distract a particular woman opponent Weng's been gunning for. I've told him Danny's magic doesn't work like that, but he just smiled inscrutably."

Willie chuckled. Weng was Modesty's houseboy and chauffeur, and it was Willie's opinion that he could easily have been a captain of industry, but he much preferred to be employed by Modesty Blaise. When they had dressed, and Modesty stood fixing her hair in front of a mirror, she said, "Will you do me a favour, Willie?"

She saw his pained look reflected in the glass, and smiled. "Well, if it's convenient, will you come to dinner on Friday and stay through Saturday? Dinah and Steve will be joining us."

"That's a favour?"

"I haven't got to the sting yet. Georgi Gogol is at Clapham Common with the circus, which is very handy. Steve was at a business meeting when I took Dinah to the circus at Guildford, so he's never seen you do your knife-throwing act as El Cazador and he says it's his overwhelming ambition." She pulled a wry face in the glass. "What he actually said was that though he has unfortunately had occasion to observe your expertise with trenchant weapons, which is why he could easily pass for a geriatric, he has never yet had the pleasure of seeing you throw to *miss* a human target." She turned to face Willie. "Could you slip your act in on Saturday so we can all come and watch?"

He laughed and took her arm as they walked from the dressing room down through the long combat room to the double doors at the end with security locks. "I'd planned to do the El Cazador bit on Saturday anyway," he said. "It's Molly Chen's last chance to make an appearance as a living target until next season, and she doesn't want to miss it."

They walked along a brick path and through a back door that led into Willie's kitchen. Beyond lay a private sitting room and then the saloon bar of the pub. It had opened half an hour before, and there were already plenty of customers, some at the bar, some playing darts, one or two at the small oak tables or in the inglenook seats. Modesty acknowledged greetings from Hazel and Mr. Spurling behind the bar, and Willie held the door for her as they went out to the car park. Her Mercedes Coupé stood in a space marked "Reserved" which was for her alone.

As Willie took her keys to unlock the door for her, he rubbed an ear with his palm, frowning a little. She looked about her and said quietly, "Trouble, Willie?"

It was a matter of intense interest to Steve Collier that Willie's ears would sometimes prickle when there was danger about. It was equally a matter of regret to Collier that this phenomenon was not subject to controlled experiment, but he fully believed in the fact of it since he had been with Willie on one memorable occasion when this curious forewarning had proved astonishingly accurate.

It was Collier's belief that all humans were, if not psychic to some degree, then at least hypersensitive within certain individual limits, though often a lifetime could be lived without a person becoming aware of the faculty. Dinah was exceptional. Lucifer, the poor deranged young man who believed himself to be Satan, was also exceptional within the narrow limits of being able to foretell the imminent death of an individual, if provided with a suitable object to use for psychometric contact. It was Lucifer who, by sensing the Breguet watch belonging to Danny Chavasse when Danny was in the Limbo slave camp, had declared him to be alive somewhere in the world – or rather, as the Prince of Darkness saw it, declared that this was a subject of his who had not yet been transferred by death from the upper levels of Hell to the lower. Few had such exceptional powers as these, but Collier held that Willie's prickling ears were also a minor psychic phenomenon, as was Modesty's extraordinary faculty for anticipation in combat.

In the car park Willie opened the door and handed Modesty the keys. "I just got a bit of a tingle as we came through the bar," he said apologetically. "It's gone now. Must've been a false alarm."

She stood looking at him for a few seconds, holding the hand from which she had taken the keys. "It's never been a false alarm before, Willie."

"No." He frowned. "I'd better check the car."

Five minutes later he closed the bonnet and stepped back. "She's clean everywhere, Princess." He shrugged and gave her a grin. "Maybe it's my age, and I've started getting 'ot flushes."

"Maybe. But thanks anyway. And take care."

"You too." He stood watching as the car turned on to the road, and lifted his arm to wave as she reached the bend.

Seated at one of the small tables in the bar of *The Treadmill*, Kazim looked across at Sibyl Pray. "They seem to be soft people," he said. "No force, no *ki*."

She smiled at him over her glass of tonic water. "The same could be said of Dr. Pilgrim, by appearance."

"You think they have hidden force?"

"It must be there. How else would they have such reputation? You have read the file."

"Perhaps their force has gone."

She shrugged. "Perhaps. It will make no difference."

He drank some beer and said, "After the first part of the scenario, after Garvin has killed her, will there be the opportunity for me to take Garvin one-to-one?"

She said slowly, "I am hoping Dr. Pilgrim will choose me to do that."

His black eyes stared reproachfully. "But *you* had Mr. Papadakis. You could speak for me when it is Garvin's turn, Sibyl."

She reached out to put her hand over his. "Perhaps I will, Kazim. You are always most vigorous and exciting after you have made a good killing. I like that very much, my beautiful Turkish bull."

He turned his hand to grasp hers, and said in a low, urgent voice, "We have had sight of Blaise and Garvin, which is what we came for, so let us go back to the hotel now. Quickly."

She pretended to consider this, but her eyes glowed. "We have still to locate Molly Chen and to make careful plans to implement Dr. Pilgrim's scenario. The problems of transporting an unconscious person are quite complex."

He smiled. "We shall make better plans afterwards, Sibyl. After you have enjoyed your beautiful Turkish bull."

She drew in a long breath and dug her nails into his hand. "Yes, Kazim. Yes."

Behind the bar, Hazel watched them go to the door. Lucky people, she thought. The blonde woman was beautiful, the dark man was handsome, and you could see they were potty about each other by the way they held hands and kept looking at each other as they went out. It was ever so sweet to see a couple like that, thought Hazel. Ever so sweet, really.

*   *   *   *

Dr. Thaddeus Pilgrim sat at this desk. Mrs. Ram and Dr. Tyl were to attend upon him shortly, but it would have been inaccurate to say that he was waiting. The passage of time had to a great extent ceased to have meaning for him. On the desk was a plate with some cheese and dry biscuits, and a tray with a pot of tea. His eyes were open but he was not looking at anything, and it was unimportant to him that the tea was growing cold, for his senses had long been anaesthetised to the point of barely responding to most forms of stimulus.

If need be he could, at this moment, have conversed, discussed, argued, and in general have maintained the benign and bumbling façade he presented to the world, while his inner being suffered not the least distraction from the dark ugliness in which it dwelt.

Thaddeus Pilgrim had once been a devout man of God, a zealous missionary dedicating himself and his family to the task of spreading the gospel. Then came the day in Uganda when the natives for whom he had worked so hard and so lovingly took pangas in their hands and cut his wife and children to pieces. Some weeks later, when he emerged from shock, another being occupied the shell of flesh that had once been Thaddeus Pilgrim. Now, the man behind the grief-ravaged eyes hated with murderous venom the God who had betrayed him and in whom he no longer believed. The illogic of such hatred did nothing to diminish it.

For several years Thaddeus Pilgrim disappeared from the world of those who had known him. To the extent that he was remembered at all it was believed that he had withdrawn into retreat abroad. During those years he sought to take revenge on the God who did not exist by turning to the Devil. In Europe, in Asia, in North America, and in the West Indies he devoted himself with intense passion to the obscenities of black magic, worshipping the Lord of Evil in a variety of forms and in hideous ways. But in the end there was no satisfaction, for he found himself devoid of belief in either his God or his Devil, and so he passed on into a kind of vacuum, his spirit detached from his senses, his soul extinguished within him.

For a long time now, all that remained of motive in the husk of Thaddeus Pilgrim was an urge to ape his non-existent God and Devil, each as cruel as the other, by manipulating human puppets, causing the little creatures to perform at his whim. His perception of malevolent potential was acute, and had assisted him in recruiting the inner core members of the Hostel of Righteousness. His control over such people stemmed from a power within him that was indefinable but was a natural by-product both of *what* he had become and the *means* by which he had become what he now was.

Sibyl Pray and Kazim, either of whom could have crushed him physically like a paper bag, feared him with that kind of fear in which there is a strong element of pleasure, the frisson of alarm that draws people to horror films and grand guignol. Similarly, Mrs. Ram regarded him with shivering masochistic delight. Dr. Tyl feared him deeply without being able to define the reason in psychological terms, which was additionally disconcerting to one of his profession. Thaddeus Pilgrim was aware of the fear he inspired. It did not give him pleasure, for he was beyond pleasure. To him it was simply a useful and vaguely interesting phenomenon.

There came a tap on the study door. A slender far-stretched cord, connecting the essence of Thaddeus Pilgrim with the husk of flesh and blood and bone at the desk, drew his inner being back from the repellent limbo in which it had been wandering. His eyes focused, and he said, "Come in, come in, please."

He smiled upon Mrs. Ram and Dr. Tyl as they entered, waving them to chairs, then picking up his cup of cold tea and beginning to sip. "Well now, Mrs. Ram, this is the moment for us to review the progress of our various little scenarios, is it not? A moment to which, I must confess, I look forward each week with – ah – unfailing interest. Your reports are models of efficiency, dear lady, models of efficiency."

"Thank you, Dr. Pilgrim." Her dark eyes gazed at him worshipfully for a few moments, then she consulted the papers on her clipboard. "First item. No repercussions from death of Mr. Papadakis. His death officially assumed to be accidental. I feel Sibyl Pray is to be congratulated on her handling of this matter."

"Oh, yes indeed," said Dr. Pilgrim, nodding his head slowly and putting down his cup and saucer. "I shall commend her highly on her return from the United Kingdom, you may be sure of that." His ambulant gaze came to rest for a moment on the jackdaw by the window, then wandered up to a corner of the ceiling. "And should not such executive skill be *rewarded*, do you think? One must, I agree, acknowledge that it is far from easy to reward our dear young friend Sibyl, or indeed her colleague, Kazim, in an appropriate manner. They are charmingly free from greed for things material, and money is not of importance to them. In short, their needs are very simple: a sufficiency of – ah – victims to dispatch, and what to others may seem an inordinate amount of sexual congress one with another. Since these needs are widely available to them, it is, as I say, somewhat difficult to devise an appropriate reward for excellence of service."

The watery blue eyes drifted down from the ceiling to gaze almost in Dr. Tyl's direction. "Perhaps your psychiatric qualifications will enable you to suggest some particular form of pleasure suited to Sibyl's temperament, Dr. Tyl? I will leave the thought with you. Please continue, Mrs. Ram."

"Thank you, Dr. Pilgrim." She made a tick with her pencil. "Second item concerns progress in the proposed scenario for Modesty Blaise and Willie Garvin. Latest radio reports from executives in the field are satisfactory. Action expected within three days from now. All transportation arrangements have been made."

Thaddeus Pilgrim had just put a piece of cheese and a small dry biscuit in his mouth. When he had finished munching he said, "And you will be ready to receive our visitor, Dr. Tyl?"

The Czech nodded briskly. "Yes. I have devised a programme and given Mrs. Ram a list of my requirements. She advises me that all the necessary materials will be assembled by the end of the week."

"Capital, capital," said Dr. Pilgrim approvingly. "We have never before, to the best of my recollection, brought any persons as – ah – as *independent*, I might almost say *intractable*, as Miss Blaise and Mr. Garvin into one of our scenarios. It should be a most interesting experiment."

He sipped some more cold tea and looked invitingly at Mrs. Ram. She folded back a sheet of paper on her clipboard and said, "We now come to the bread-and-butter scenarios. At this moment we have several hundred requests for prayers from individuals and organisations worldwide. All have been acknowledged in appropriate terms. Most can be discarded at once as unsuitable for our purpose. Of the remainder, careful inquiry and analysis reveal six potentially fruitful prospects. That is to say, six applicants whose needs can be satisfied by covert action on the part of our executives. That is further to say, by assassination, sabotage, arson, intimidation, and similar activities."

Dr. Tyl said, "Our two chief executives are engaged at present."

Mrs. Ram frowned. "I am of course aware of that, Dr. Tyl," she said reprovingly, "but once they have brought to Kalivari the person who is to be the subject of your programme, they will be free for the three weeks that you have declared you will require for said programme. Also we have half a dozen other executives in our A.T.P. section, all well trained, who are perfectly capable of carrying out requisite operations."

"I am always happy," said Thaddeus Pilgrim cautiously, "to have our Answer to Prayer Section fully employed. May I ask, Mrs. Ram, if some or indeed any of the applicants are likely to be generous in showing their appreciation when their prayers are answered?"

She studied her notes, then said, "I conclude that four would certainly be so, Dr. Pilgrim. The first is a quite wealthy religious sect which a certain South American country is about to banish. They ask our prayerful support that this threat may be lifted. Analysis reveals that removal of a particular minister in the government of said country will have desired effect. Then there is request from president of island republic in Caribbean, who does not want to get heave-ho from political rivals. He would show much gratitude I am certain. May I interpolate here that subtle change in sources of requests for our prayers indicate that certain persons and organisations may have become aware that satisfactory answers to Hostel of Righteousness prayers may be brought about by natural rather than supernatural powers. Subject for discussion, I think. However, not to digress, the third application comes from the Far East, and –"

"If," said Thaddeus Pilgrim with an apologetic wave of his hand, "if I may be forgiven for interrupting you, Mrs. Ram, I think we need not at this moment have a *detailed* account of future orders from clients. Our bread-and-butter work is of an ongoing nature, and it would seem, if I may say so without appearing injudiciously optimistic, that we invariably have sufficient orders on hand to keep our executives fully occupied. Therefore I am content to leave the choice of clients in your very capable hands, dear lady, and indeed the – ah – *modus operandi* also, though I am always of course available for discussion if you should feel the need of advice as to ways and means."

Dr. Tyl recalled some of the ways and means Thaddeus Pilgrim had contrived over the past few years. There was no doubt, he decided, that the man was a genius. An evil genius if the adjective had any meaning, which Dr. Tyl doubted. He was not interested in conceptions of good and evil. His sole interest was the degree to which it was possible to control and direct another human mind, and it was his unethical and unacceptable experiments in this area which had caused him to be outlawed from his profession and had eventually brought him to Dr. Thaddeus Pilgrim, who supported and encouraged such experiments.

The activities of the Hostel of Righteousness provided rich opportunities for Dr. Tyl's work. Experts in hypnosis, for example, always asserted that a person under hypnosis could never be made to commit an act which on moral or ethical grounds he would never commit while in a normal mode of consciousness. This was probably true. You could not put a gun in the hand of a man under hypnosis and simply order him to kill another. But you could induce a belief or hallucination by hypnosis, or by narco-hypnosis in the case of a difficult subject, which would certainly cause a man or woman to kill.

You could, for example, induce a visual hallucination to make a woman see a particular man as a hideous nightmare monster, and you could make her believe that the monster was about to kill her child. That would by-pass any moral barrier, and if given the means she would kill without hesitation. It was all a question of finding the right psychological key, and Dr. Tyl had achieved this twice with great success. Two applicants to the Hostel of Righteousness had received positive answers to their petitions for prayer, not by the intervention of the Answer to Prayer Section, but by the hand of innocent victims of Dr. Tyl's mind-bending.

In the study, Mrs. Ram adjusted a fresh sheet on her clipboard and said, "I now refer to The Hallelujah Scenario. All elements of this operation are proceeding satisfactorily through cut-outs. You have a copy of the itinerary, Dr. Pilgrim, and all factors are proceeding in accordance with time schedules set out therein."

She looked up with an air of deferential admonition. "It is my duty to warn that finances must not be neglected," she said. "Our bread-and-butter missions are very much bread-and-butter. Sometimes our prayerful interventions receive no financial appreciation. If all over-heads are taken into account, it may be that we run the Answer to Prayer Section at slight loss."

Thaddeus Pilgrim gazed with a puzzled air at the remains of cheese and biscuit on his plate as if wondering how they came to be there. "But surely, Mrs. Ram," he said, "our operation in the Far East – ah – let me see, some two years ago now, The Hosanna Scenario we called it, if I am not mistaken . . . surely this brought us funds in the order of several millions of dollars at, if you will forgive a dubious metaphor, one fell swoop. I would have thought our financial position was still quite satisfactory."

"A substantial percentage of said revenue had to be expended on laundering same and prolific use of cut-outs, Doctor," said Mrs. Ram. "Nevertheless, I do not say we are *short* of funds at this moment. I say only that expenditure exceeds income and this must not continue indefinitely."

Thaddeus Pilgrim spread his hands slowly and smiled with paternal affection in the Hindu woman's direction, his gaze wandering around and beyond her. "Mrs. Ram, Mrs. Ram," he said gently, "surely you cannot think it is our purpose in life to become rich and to live off the fat of the land? That is too easy, and is not at all in accord with our philosophy, with yours and mine and that of our dear friends and colleagues. All we desire is to live a *satisfactory* life, each according to his individual preference. Or *her* individual preference – I would not have you think me chauvinistic. For myself, I find satisfaction in our little scenarios, and I think I am correct in suggesting that you, dear lady, find satisfaction in your work of administration for our group."

His eyes roamed for a second or two until they found Dr. Tyl, and he continued, "Satisfaction for our good Dr. Tyl comes from his freedom to experiment with patients in ways disallowed by orthodox medical practice. Our friends of the Answer To Prayer teams ask nothing more than to exercise their lethal skills, and, in the case of Sibyl and Kazim, to enjoy untrammelled use of each other in a sexual context. The remainder of our community, the hewers of wood and drawers of water, if I may so describe them, are of no importance and quite expendable. Indeed, they will all have to be expended once we have completed The Hallelujah Scenario. Then we shall recruit afresh, as we did after the Hosanna Scenario."

He leaned forward, peered hopefully into his cup, and drank the last of his tea. "And let us not forget," he said, "that our financial return on The Hallelujah Scenario will be in the order not of a few million dollars but of at least one hundred and twenty million dollars." He set his cup down in the saucer and leaned back in his chair. Chin on chest, white hair fluffed up like a halo about his head, he looked up from beneath white eyebrows and said with a diffident smile, "No, Mrs. Ram, no, I really do not think you have any cause to fear for the state of our finances."

5

The machete spun through the air for twenty paces to thud into the timber two inches from Modesty's cheek. She blinked at the impact, then curved her lips and showed her teeth in a brilliant smile.

The man gaudily dressed as a Mexican, with a sombrero tilted back on his head, seized another machete from the rack beside him, turned his back, stood with feet astride, looked over his shoulder, and threw between his legs with a downward swing of his arm. The blade drove into the three inch gap between Modesty's upper arm and her body.

With a great jingle of silver buttons from his costume, El Cazador flung his arms wide and gazed up at the well filled tiers of seats round the circus ring, inviting a storm of applause. Danny Chavasse sat with Professor Stephen Collier and his wife, Dinah, in a front row. An empty seat beside them had been occupied by Modesty Blaise until the interval, when Georgi Gogol had brought a message from Willie Garvin to say that Molly Chen had failed to report for the performance, and would Modesty please stand in for her. Georgi Gogol was a tall thin man with a waxed moustache, a heavy accent, and a voice husky from his bellowing as circus ringmaster. "Veelie say he can get other girl, Mees Blaise, but he theenk maybe you' frien's like that you be target for heem."

She said, "I don't doubt they would. But do you know what's kept Molly Chen? She wouldn't want to miss her last performance with you this season."

Georgi Gogol shrugged and pushed his top hat back on his head. "Maybe traffic jam, maybe her car break down. Veelie say she been working herself stupid to make her new flat look nize, so maybe she fall asleep on bed."

"I expect it's something like that. All right, Georgi."

Collier had returned carrying ice creams as she was about to leave. "You're lucky to get these," he said. "I was the only adult in the queue, and it's terrifying. Like falling in a river swarming with piranha fish. A big kid of ten nearly broke my ribs with his elbow."

Dinah said, "It's a good thing you're dauntless, tiger. And here's good news for you. Modesty's going to play target for Willie, so you can eat her ice cream as well."

A grin of sheer delight stole over Collier's face as he looked at Modesty. "My cup is full," he sighed happily, "but what about costume, darling? I mean, Molly Chen is a little Chinese slip of a thing, so I'm told, and you're a brawny great wench."

She laughed and patted his cheek. "Don't worry. There'll be a costume I've used before in Willie's caravan."

When she had gone, Danny Chavasse said, "I hope you don't place a shred of reliance on your husband's picture of Modesty as a brawny great wench, Dinah. As a longtime admirer, I have to spring to her defence."

Dinah licked her ice cream. "Steve uses insults as endearments," she said. "Don't worry, Danny. There've been a couple of fraught occasions when I've had to cling pretty tight to Modesty, and I have a very sharp picture of her."

Twenty minutes later, "El Cazador and Conchita" made their appearance through the bandsmen's arch over the entrance to the ring, and from that moment onwards Collier was unable to stop laughing. So ornate was Willie Garvin's costume that it only just stopped short of being a parody, and he was wearing a drooping moustache so long that it hung down below his chin on each side of his mouth. A black wig hid his fair hair, and he strutted like a peacock as he entered, flourishing his sombrero, flinging out his arms as if to embrace the whole audience, and hamming outrageously.

Beside him, frisking, curtsying, pirouetting, Modesty wore fishnet tights and a costume of green and gold with a microscopic skirt and a low-cut bodice.

It was a short, five minute act, interspersed with rolls on the drum and bawled announcements from Georgi Gogol as to what El Cazador would attempt next. Thrown knives pierced apples held on Modesty's palms, or cut the end from a cigarette held in her mouth. Between each feat there was much skipping and bowing and curtsying. Danny Chavasse watched entranced, trying to reconcile these two, this man and woman revelling in a *divertissement* for the entertainment of their friends, with Mam'selle and Willie Garvin of *The Network* days.

Glancing sideways, he saw Collier wiping tears from his eyes, holding his wife's hand and talking as fluently as his laughter would allow, painting a word picture for her of the scene in the ring.

A round target had been set up now and Modesty was standing against it, legs apart, arms straight and spread a little way from her sides. The big machetes glittered and flew, thumping into the target so that they outlined her body and limbs. Down in the ring, Modesty kept the smile fixed on her lips and tried not to blink. She would not have confessed it to anyone, but her nerves were always a little taut for this part of the act. It was not that she doubted Willie's skill. He was accurate to a quarter-inch and was throwing to a two-inch margin. What made her nerves tingle was the fact that she was looking straight at him but could not recognise Willie Garvin because of his disguise. The man with black hair, drooping moustache, and flamboyant costume was visually a stranger, and she had to keep telling herself that this was truly Willie Garvin throwing the great blades so close to her.

There came a fanfare. Modesty stepped clear of the machetes that framed her, and a circus hand pulled them free while El Cazador and Conchita strutted and pranced to the applause. Another fanfare for the finale, and Modesty grasped two straps at the top of the target, then slipped her ankles into two loops at the foot so that she was spread-eagled against the great timber disc. The circus hand began to turn it, slowly at first then with gathering speed, and Willie picked up the first of four battle-axes in the rack beside him.

At the ringside, Collier winced as the great blade drove into the target midway between Modesty's knees. He glanced at Danny and shook his head, no longer laughing. "I'm buggered if I'm going to watch this bit," he said, and closed his eyes. "They've got no sense of proportion, those two."

The last axe struck inches above her head, the band blared out the closing music of the act, the spinning disc was stopped, Modesty stepped down. El Cazador and Conchita took their bow and backed with flourishes and curtsies through the entrance as the run-in clowns came tumbling into the ring.

Walking through the mounting place beyond the arch, Willie said, "Thanks, Princess. D'you mind if I don't come back with you and the others? I want to slip down to Chobham and see if Molly's all right. She 'asn't got the phone on there yet."

She said, "Yes, of course. Give me a ring if there's any way I can help."

As they were dressing in the caravan Willie used, she saw on the table a flat steel quoit, the metal about an inch in width and the whole ring six or seven inches across. The outer circumference was sharpened to a fine edge. As she sat to pull on her tights she said, "What is it, Willie?"

"Called a *chakra* or *chakram*, Princess." He fastened his belt and picked up the steel ring. "I've never 'eard of anyone but the Sikhs using it, but I thought I'd get 'old of one and experiment a bit."

She took it from him gingerly and examined it. "A missile?"

"That's right. Going back a century or so, I reckon. Some say you whirl it round your finger to throw, but I can't see that. The natural way is a kind of skating throw, like with a frisbee, except the *chakra* isn't much affected by air pressure, so it flies on a flat trajectory."

She pulled on her dress and said, "What do you think of it as a weapon?"

"Well . . . if you're accurate it's damaging. Lethal up to thirty paces. But I can't see it's got any advantage over a knife, and it's a lot more difficult to carry around." He grinned. "I've read that the Sikhs used to carry around several of different sizes, stacked on a pointed turban, the *dastar bungga* they called it, but I thought people might notice if I did that."

She smiled and picked up her handbag. "I don't know. You feel such a fool these days if you're not ethnic. Thanks for missing me with the machetes, Willie love, and let me know about Molly."

"Sure, Princess. I'll be in touch."

         *   *   *   *

It was after ten-thirty when Willie Garvin drew up outside the little block of single-bedroom apartments on the outskirts of Chobham. Molly Chen's flat was on the ground floor at the back, next but one to the communal entrance, and when he came round the corner of the building he saw that there was light showing round the edges of her curtained bedroom window.

As he pressed the bellpush of her front door his ears prickled, and automatically he brought all his senses to a high pitch of alertness. Ten seconds later the door opened and he found himself facing a tall woman with blonde hair in ringlets, wearing a severe grey trouser suit. She looked questioningly at him and said politely, "Yes?"

He said, looking into the empty sitting room beyond her, "I've come to see Molly Chen."

"Ah!" There was relief in her grey eyes, and when she continued speaking he was aware of her accent. "You are Mr. Garvin? Molly said you might come. She is not at all well. I am a neighbour from along the passage. Please come in, Mr. Garvin."

Since he had last been here, Molly had furnished the small sitting room. The furniture was second hand but chosen with taste, and already there was warmth and personality to be felt. "What's wrong with Molly?" he asked as the woman closed the door. "Has she called a doctor?"

"I do not think it is a case for a doctor." The ringlets bounced as the woman shook her head. "She is anxious to see you, Mr. Garvin. Please come through." She led the way along a very short passage, opened the bedroom door and stood back for Willie to enter. He gestured politely for her to go ahead of him, and she tilted her head in acknowledgement. It was a small bedroom, and she took only two paces before stepping to one side and indicating the bed. "You see? There is something wrong with her neck, I think."

Molly Chen lay on the bed, dressed except for a blouse or shirt or whatever she had been about to put on when she died. Her body was limp, pathetically childlike in its smallness. Her eyes were closed. Her head was at an ugly angle, only possible because the neck was broken. An instant after the shock hit Willie, the tall blonde woman spun with perfect balance to face him, and he glimpsed the hand clenched in *ippon-ken*, the ninth form of fist-strike, with the knuckle of the middle finger protruding.

The combat instinct in him, faster than thought, appraised every nuance of body posture, movement, timing and speed, and told him that this was an attack by a master. The same instinct, fractionally slowed by shock, set his body twisting and his forearm sweeping up in a defensive move to divert the strike from his solar plexus. Such power discharged against that nerve centre would drop him unconscious for up to ten minutes. The deflection was small but sufficient. Even so, the hammerblow of the fist against his breastbone would have been almost paralysing if he had not partly ridden the blow. Turning, going back, he continued the movement, coming up on the ball of one foot and bringing the other leg round in a reverse roundhouse hook to strike with the heel, aiming for the vital point at the base of the spine, exposed by the turn of her body, but she had already begun evasive movement, and his strike caught her high on the buttock. For a moment she was off balance, shock and pain in the grey eyes as she saw him come into position for following up with a hand-strike, but in that moment Kazim stepped from behind the door and swung a *shuto* strike with the edge of his hand to the *medulla oblongata* nerve complex at the back of the neck.

Willie Garvin dropped limply to the floor and lay still. Sibyl Pray and Kazim stared at each other across his body. Kazim said, "We were wrong. He is not soft. He is very, very good."

She nodded, tight-lipped, breathing hard through her nose. "And I am a fool. I was lax because I was sure he would be easy." She rubbed her buttock slowly. "You must punish me for that, Kazim."

"I will."

She walked into the sitting room and returned a few moments later with a small wallet. Kazim had rolled Willie on his back and pushed up the sleeve of his shirt and jacket to expose his forearm. Sibyl Pray took a hypodermic and an ampoule from the wallet, checked the time on her wristwatch, filled the hypodermic, then knelt to make an injection in Willie's arm.

"This must be repeated at one a.m.," she said, "shortly before we leave for the airfield. You have double-checked that pilot and aircraft will be ready?"

"Yes. It will be Lafarge with his Cessna Chancellor."

"That is satisfactory." She rose and began to put the hypodermic away.

Kazim watched her with hot brown eyes. "So we have three hours to wait, Sibyl. Three hours."

She smiled at him and began to breathe deeply. "Yes, my beautiful Turkish bull."

"Shall I remove the Chinese girl from the bed?"

"We do not need a bed, Kazim. We will use the sitting room."

He followed her out, switching off the light and closing the bedroom door. In the sitting room she checked the curtains, then began to take off her clothes very quickly. Her body was beautiful, and every few moments a quivering shudder passed through it. "I am in great fear of your punishment, Kazim," she said in a husky whisper.

"It will be prolonged," he said.

In the dark bedroom, Molly Chen was sprawled lifeless on the bed, and Willie Garvin lay unconscious on the floor where they had left him. In the sitting room the light had been switched off now. The two who occupied it were aware that the walls were thin, but this did not mar their enjoyment. The hours of muted striving together, the gasping whispers and small wordless cries testified to their endless resource in adapting their pleasure to whatever constraints might be imposed.

✳   ✳   ✳   ✳

At eight o'clock next morning, in Modesty's bedroom, Danny Chavasse was awakened by a warm soft weight on his chest. He opened his eyes to find Modesty Blaise half lying upon him, looking down at him. She kissed him, contemplated him in silence for a few seconds, then said, "A fine romance this is. What do I have to do? Pay?"

He grinned sleepily and put his arms round her, enjoying the lovely tactile sensation. "You know . . . it's hard to remember how scared of you I used to be," he said.

She thought for a moment, then said, "Impressed. You never had cause to be scared, Danny. Impressed, yes. I had to be impressive to run that bunch of villains." She frowned menacingly. "But you'll have cause to be scared of me all right if you go on neglecting me. Hell hath no fury like a frustrated spinster."

He laughed, running his hands joyously over her body, remembering how happily she always made love, giving without reserve, ranging through a wide spectrum from aggression to submission, many different women in one. It was a matter of pride to him that he had been the man to free her from a psychological prison and make her a whole woman. He knew very well that this, his gift to her, had also been a gift to other men she had since known, but he did not begrudge them the pleasure they had taken in her.

Putting his thumbs to the outer corners of her eyes, he pulled gently so that they became almond shaped, and said in a sing-song voice, "Please demonstlate to ignolant Flench gentreman how Japanese girl do it."

"With gleat preasure. Plepare to be amazed, fliend."

Later, as he shaved while she lay in the sunken bath behind him, he said, "So what are we doing today? Any special plans?"

She squeezed a spongeful of water over her breasts and said, "Breakfast, then I must spend an hour with a language tape. After that I'll be going along to a rehearsal room to dance for a couple of hours. You'll have to amuse yourself this morning, Danny. Meet you at Manzi's for a fish lunch, one o'clock, your shout. Then . . . well, we could come back here for a little sex in the afternoon, Willie swears it prevents torticollis and weak ankles –"

He turned to look at her in surprise. "You and Willie?"

She gave him an amused look. "Of course not, dopey. That seems to cross everybody's mind but ours. It would change everything, and we don't want that."

"Sorry. Go on. What happens after lunch and sex in the afternoon?"

"Well, once I've reduced you to a mere husk we could go down to the squash courts so I can beat the daylights out of you there. Then a swim would be nice, and when we come up from the pool I must spend half an hour with Mr. Erdnase and another half hour practising on two new locks Willie left with me. As for the evening, we could go out for a pre-theatre dinner somewhere and afterwards take pot-luck at any theatre we fancy, my shout. How does that sound?"

"I've had worse days," he said solemnly.

She was still disciplined, thought Danny as he put away his razor. Fluent in six languages, close to fluent in another four, she rarely missed spending an hour a day with a language tape, either brushing up on one she knew or following a course in a new one. At the moment she was busy with Cantonese, which she could practise with Weng. The dancing, too, was a discipline for her body, keeping it magnificently tuned. Practice with locks kept one of her old criminal skills up to date, and so did the session with Mr. Erdnase, an American gambler long dead now, whose illustrated book *The Expert at the Card Table*, impossible to find these days, was the definitive work on the subtle art of card-sharping. Danny had once spent a fascinating half hour watching Modesty and Willie duel with each other at the card table as they practised to keep their skills in good repair.

At half past four that afternoon he was sitting opposite her in the big living room of the penthouse, a tray of tea at his elbow, a low table between them, watching her shuffle, stack and cut the cards, trying to detect the instant when she performed the two-handed shift to restore the cut.

"Did you do it that time?" he asked as she began to deal.

She nodded. "You didn't spot it?"

"Not a flicker."

"Good. Once more, then."

The internal answer-phone buzzed, and they heard Weng move to answer it. A moment later he came into the sitting room and said, "Inspector Brook is in the reception hall and asks to see you, Miss Blaise."

She looked mildly surprised but said, "Yes, have him come up, Weng."

Danny said, "Shall I disappear for a while?"

"Oh, no." She was stacking the cards and putting them away. "Brookie's an old opponent, but we've been friends for quite a while. I'm unbelievably virtuous these days, so I can't imagine this is official. Anyway, he's with Central Office at Scotland Yard now, more concerned with admin. than going round feeling people's collars. It's probably a social visit. He says Weng makes much better tea than they do at the Yard."

While she spoke she had made her way along the length of the room to where three steps led up to a large square foyer edged by a wrought iron balustrade. In one wall of the foyer was the private lift to the penthouse, and as the doors slid open Weng came forward ready to receive hat, coat, or umbrella, but the man who emerged was bare-headed and wore only a somewhat rumpled suit.

"Hallo, Weng," he said.

"Good afternoon, Inspector."

Chief Inspector Brook was a tall man in his middle forties with straight black hair, receding a little at the brow, and a large beaky nose. In his early contacts with Modesty Blaise he had been extremely wary, but this was no longer so. From time to time she had made it possible for him to remove several highly undesirable persons from circulation by arrest and later imprisonment, which pleased him greatly. There was something more. Inspector Brook was a widower with a daughter of nineteen. Only a handful of people knew that Modesty Blaise and Willie Garvin had saved them both from a particularly horrible revenge killing two years ago.

She was waiting for him as he came from the foyer into the living room. Danny Chavasse watched curiously as he took both her hands and bent to kiss her cheek. "Hallo, Modesty. I'm sorry to intrude."

"It's good to see you, Brookie. You're just in time for tea." She took his arm as they moved down the room, and Danny got to his feet. "I'd like you to meet Danny Chavasse, a very old friend. Danny, this is Chief Inspector Brook."

The two men shook hands and exchanged polite greetings, then Brook gestured a little awkwardly and said to Modesty, "I'm not sure about tea. There's something I have to tell you, and . . ." He glanced at Danny.

She said, "It's all right. Danny was a part of my murky past. Is this something official, Brookie?"

"Well, I'm not here officially."

"Then sit down and tell us all about it."

He sat with her on the chesterfield, turned towards her, and said, "Something came across my desk by way of general information an hour or so ago. The Yard hasn't been called in yet, and even if they are it won't be my case, but I thought I'd let you know right away. Does the name Molly Chen mean anything to you?"

"Yes, certainly," she replied, a little puzzled. "Willie brought her over from Hong Kong last year, and she's been working for Gogol's Wonder Circus. You probably didn't know Willie worked in a circus for a while in his youth, and he bought a half share in this one from Georgi Gogol quite a few years ago. What about Molly Chen?"

"I'm afraid she's dead," Brook said quietly. "Murdered. Cause of death, a broken neck. It happened at Chobham, early yesterday evening the doctor says. Wasn't discovered till around mid-day today, quite by chance. Something to do with delivery of a dressing table she'd ordered. Left her key with the woman next door in case she was out when the men came with it. They got no answer, knocked next door, the woman let them in and went through to the bedroom with them. Molly Chen was lying dead on the bed."

Modesty gazed distantly past him, her hands folded in her lap. "They tried to kill her in Malta," she said quietly, sadly. "We thought it was Willie they were after, but we were wrong. Could it have been a Triad killing –?" She stopped abruptly and stared at Brook. "Wait a minute. Molly was to be Willie's target in his knife-throwing act for the evening performance yesterday, but she didn't turn up. After the show

Willie drove down to Chobham to see if she was all right – but he hasn't phoned or been in touch."

Chief Inspector Brook said, "A car was parked outside that little block some time after ten p.m. last night. It was still there when the murder was discovered. The local CID checked the registration number with Swansea, and it's Willie Garvin's car. There's no sign of his having returned to *The Treadmill* last night, and he hasn't been there all day. His present whereabouts are unknown. The local CID are anxious to interview him."

Danny Chavasse felt the skin at the back of his neck creep. Watching Modesty, he said nothing. This was her affair. She sat quite still and her face held no expression, but there was an almost tangible difference in her from the woman he had made love with, laughed with, relaxed with, the woman who had played up to Willie Garvin's parody in the circus ring, and whose favourite company was gentle and harmless people like the Colliers. Now there was suddenly an emanation of danger about her, of martial potency backed by a relentless will. It was as if the years had been swept away and he was back in *The Network* headquarters in Tangier once again, watching her as she ordered and controlled the hard, dangerous men who were her lieutenants.

Yet he knew that when she spoke her voice would be mellow, and it was as he remembered. "Is Willie Garvin under suspicion?" she said.

"No." Brook let his relief sound in the word. "They've checked his movements that evening, and Molly Chen was dead before he left the circus to drive down there."

She stood up and paced slowly towards the wide, floor-to-ceiling window that looked out over Hyde Park, holding her elbows, dark blue eyes seeming a little darker than usual. "So they've taken Willie," she said after a while. "If they wanted to kill him they could have left him with Molly. They're high class professionals. They'd have to be to take Willie, even if he wasn't expecting trouble, and then to hold him for the best part of twenty-four hours. No clues, Brookie?"

He made a small gesture. "They'll still be examining the place. There's no suggestion as to motive in the report we've had so far. I'm inclined to agree with you that it's a Triad affair. Could the girl have been mixed up with them?"

"It's possible, but only by accident, I would think. The Triads don't recruit women. Maybe she came to know something by chance, or they thought she came to know it." Modesty turned away from the window. "Molly's dead and I'm sorry, but there's nothing I can do about that. All that concerns me is finding Willie."

"Yes." Chief Inspector Brook looked down at the floor. He had no suggestion to offer. "I'll let you know if anything significant comes to light. No . . . I'll let you know whatever comes to light, and you can judge whether it's significant."

She lifted an eyebrow at him. "Can you do that? I mean, without risking your job and your pension?"

"No, I can't." He got to his feet. "But nothing I tell you will harm the force, and if it wasn't for you and Willie I wouldn't have a job, a pension, a daughter, or a life. Where are you going to start, Modesty?"

"Everywhere." She came towards him, still with forearms crossed, hands holding her elbows. "I'll start probing through every contact I've got, trying to pick up a line to work on."

"That friend of yours, the intelligence boss-man, he might be able to help. There's quite an overlap between crime and intelligence these days."

"Yes. I'll be speaking to Tarrant. But my old criminal contacts are more likely to bear fruit."

"Do you think . . ." Brook hesitated. "Do you think Willie's alive?"

She said in a neutral voice, "I have to believe that, Brookie. But it makes sense, too. If it was a killing, they wouldn't take the body away."

Brook knew there could be feasible reasons for taking the body away. He knew that Willie Garvin might be alive and in the hands of people who wanted revenge, or wanted to extort some kind of information from him. There were many possibilities, but Modesty knew them all as well as he did, and there was nothing to be gained by voicing them. "I'll keep in touch," he said.

"Thanks for coming round, Brookie."

He took her by the shoulders, studying her, but did not kiss her cheek as he would have done at any other time. Her eyes were hard and black as polished obsidian, her lips tight, the nostrils slightly flared. This woman wanted no sympathy, no softness, no comfort. Her enemy was unseen and unknown, but already there was the chill, bracing aura of the professional warrior about her. A battle had been joined, Brook realised, and it would not end until she had found and destroyed the enemy. Or was herself destroyed.

He gave a small nod of understanding, then turned away and walked towards the foyer and the lift. Weng had remained there during the brief meeting, and as soon as Brook had gone the houseboy came down into the sitting room and said, "I heard, Miss Blaise. I will make inquiries among my oriental friends. There are one or two who may have contact with the Triads."

"Yes. Please do. But very carefully, Weng."

"I am a discreet person, Miss Blaise."

"I know." She turned to Danny Chavasse. "I won't be able to play hostess to you any longer, Danny. Sorry to spoil your vacation, but I'm going to be busy. You're welcome to use the cottage, or there's the villa in Tangier if you prefer."

He stood up. "Let me stay and help, please. If things get violent I won't be much good to you, but I won't be a hindrance in any way, and I might be useful." He gave her a small grave smile. "I've worked for you before, Mam'selle. Let it be as it was then."

She said soberly, "Thanks. I'll be glad of somebody who's used to working with me, even if it's only for communications." She looked at the tray of tea. "Pour some tea, Danny. I'm going to get a list of contacts from my cubby-hole, and then we'll spend the evening making calls. There are two lines, so we can split the work."

He said, "Will you confine it to this country?"

She shook her head. "No. We'll cover home contacts first, but I want to spread the net wider than that."

Her bedroom was of pale green, ivory and silver-grey. One of the wall panels could be opened by setting the dressing table drawers in a particular way. Beyond the panel was a tiny room, six feet square, containing a variety of weapons and other items. Along one side were shelves bearing scores of neatly labelled files. She switched on the light, ran her hand along one of the shelves, and took down a file. There was no tension in her now. By a controlled mental effort the stress of anxiety had been sealed away in a kind of limbo, detached from her consciousness.

She switched off the light, closed the panel, and went back to Danny Chavasse. "We'll have to tell Dinah and Steve," she said, sitting down beside him and taking the cup of tea he handed her.

"Do you think Dinah might help?" said Danny. "I mean, she located me, didn't she?"

"Yes, she did." Modesty held the tea on her lap, staring down at it. "But that was different, there was no emotional involvement. I doubt if she can help with Willie . . . but she'll try, Danny. She'll try."

*　　*　　*　　*

The jackdaw fluttered about its cage, then came to rest on the perch. Dr. Thaddeus Pilgrim cut a piece from the omelet which was now cold and leathery, and put it in his mouth. ". . . and of course it should not in any way be construed as a criticism of those whose tastes may differ from mine," he said dreamily, "when I express my inability to comprehend the – ah – the *relish* with which the non-vegetarian consumes corpses. I mean, naturally, the corpses of the lesser orders of creation." Somewhere in the dark reaches of his being where the inward man dwelt, he recalled fleetingly and with amusement the flesh he had ritually consumed in his pursuit of Satanism, a creed he had found as vacuous as any other. "However," he continued, "it is foolish of me to preach vegetarianism to the converted, Mrs. Ram. Let us to business, to business. How is our visitor settling down? It is three days since he arrived, is it not?"

Mrs. Ram consulted the papers on her clipboard. "Yes, Dr. Pilgrim. Just three days, and Dr. Tyl is satisfied with progress. The subject was under sedation on arrival, and so far Dr. Tyl has been using his narco-hypnotic system to induce temporary but complete amnesia. When Mr. Garvin was permitted to recover consciousness he was told his name, and that he had suffered severe concussion while trying desperately to frustrate an attempt on the life of Modesty Blaise. He has accepted this, since it is in accord with a possibility fully acceptable to his subconscious."

"You mean . . .? Ah, yes. It *could* have happened. Pray continue, Mrs. Ram."

"Mr. Garvin believes that the attempt succeeded and that Modesty Blaise was killed. Despite loss of memory, her name is of immense significance to him, and he is deeply distressed." She looked up from her notes. "Not only distressed, but exceedingly vengeful, which gives much satisfaction to Dr. Tyl in view of scenario contemplated."

"It is always a pleasure to me, indeed to us all, I am sure, to know that Dr. Tyl is happy in his work. May I ask if you know how Mr. Garvin . . . ah, shall we say, how he *perceives* his present situation?"

The Hindu woman watched admiringly as Dr. Pilgrim folded the last piece of omelet on his fork, and put it in his mouth. She said, "Only Dr. Tyl can give fully authoritative explanation of his patient's mental condition."

"No, no, dear lady." Thaddeus Pilgrim raised his hands in protest. "I am a simple man, readily confused by technicalities. Your own rendering of the good doctor's report is much to be preferred." He folded his hands and beamed at her fondly.

She lowered her eyes, flustered, wishing that in some way it could be possible for him to consume her as he had consumed the omelet, and thinking how gladly she would give herself up to the funeral fire of *suttee* if only she belonged to him, and if only the old customs had not long perished. "Well . . . as I understand it, Doctor, an historical basis has been used in respect of Mr. Garvin's present situation. He believes that *The Network* still operates. He believes that this island is the present headquarters, and that all of us here are members of *The Network*. It is a *misty* conception, Dr. Tyl says, but as real as a dream is to a dreamer, and again it accords with Mr. Garvin's subconscious."

Dr. Pilgrim drank some milk and began nibbling from a dish of raisins. "I am intrigued to know how Dr. Tyl now intends to continue," he said. "Not that I would think of interfering in his very specialised field, Mrs. Ram. I am simply . . . intrigued."

"I am not fully clear on that point myself, Dr. Pilgrim. He has called for certain photographic items, and these arrived from England this morning. He speaks of using Mr. Garvin's mind as a . . . palimpsest, but I confess this word is not familiar to me."

"Palimpsest . . ." Thaddeus Pilgrim echoed the syllables in a measured tone. "Without wishing to be pedantic – and I use the word pedantic in its true meaning, to describe an ostentatious display of knowledge – I feel sure that a palimpsest is a piece of material, such as paper or parchment, on which the original writing has been erased and replaced by *other* writing. Would such a definition assist your understanding of Dr. Tyl's intention, Mrs. Ram?"

Her delight was almost orgasmic. "Of course, Doctor, of course! I see now that he proposes to efface Mr. Garvin's mental image of Modesty Blaise, and replace it with a different image. Then he can proceed to use the original image for the purpose envisaged in your scenario."

"Ahh . . . fascinating, fascinating," said Thaddeus Pilgrim, and closed his eyes in contemplation. Bizarre images flickered in his mind.

For some time he had known that the black magical disciplines he had practised in order to kill the natural sensitivities of the human mind were having a continuing effect upon him. In a sense, he was now devoid of comprehensible motive, and his decisions were increasingly made from no rational basis but seemed to spring at random from some part of his mind quite detached from his consciousness. If he had not also been devoid of all belief whatsoever he might have wondered if some alien entity had possessed him. As it was, he simply assumed that he was passing into the fringes of what was generally called insanity, but since such a term had no meaning for him he was untroubled by the notion.

"An unusually interesting scenario, one hopes," he said, and opened his eyes. "Now there is a matter on which I should be glad, and indeed most grateful, to have your advice, Mrs. Ram. I am concerned that our dear friends Sibyl and Kazim are . . . shall we say, showing indications of behaviour which I would *like* to describe as merely injudicious, but which an objective observer might regard as *tending* towards indiscipline." He bowed his head and looked up at her with a sorrowful air, as if peering over the top of spectacles.

Mrs. Ram pursed her lips sternly. "You refer to disregard by these persons of briefing given to them inasmuch as they did not bring Mr. Garvin from Piraeus covertly to this island, as instructed, but on regular ferry."

The halo of white hair wavered as Thaddeus Pilgrim nodded several times with great solemnity. "It is true," he acknowledged, "that Mr. Garvin was in a wheelchair, under sedation, wearing a hat and a grey wig, but this was, in my view, an unwise procedure. I feel it indicates a measure of . . . of over-confidence, even of *assertiveness*, perhaps. I am concerned that such an example might well affect others of our little community, which would be greatly to the detriment of our work. We really cannot afford to have any of our members becoming too . . . too . . ."

He gazed over her head, eyes wandering from side to side, lips moving slightly as he considered and rejected a variety of possible words, ". . . too fucking *cocky*?" he finished tentatively.

She sucked in her breath ecstatically. "That is exactly true, Dr. Pilgrim. I am extremely fond of Sibyl and Kazim, and they are most important persons in our community, but I fear that continued success in their special line of work has induced attitudes above their station. I hope you will speak to them with emphasis on this matter."

"Oh, I have done so, Mrs. Ram. I have done so in firm but I hope kindly tones, and I trust they have taken my admonition to heart. However, it might improve the . . . the spiritual *attitude* of our little community if dear Sibyl and Kazim were not *quite* to succeed in one of their projects – although not, of course, to the detriment of our cause."

Mrs. Ram's splendid dark eyes widened with a blend of surprise, pleasure, and doubt. "That would be highly desirable," she said, "but to arrange same would also be highly difficult. Do you have something in mind, Doctor?"

Thaddeus Pilgrim flapped his hands slowly in a gesture of negation. "Nothing specific, dear lady . . . I am just, as it were, putting a thought into your head; indeed, into my own head also, to the intent that if a suitable opportunity should arise, then we shall be ready to seize upon it."

He closed his eyes briefly and stretched his mouth in a smile that showed none of his teeth but was simply an elliptical gap in the flesh of his face, so that for a long moment he looked like a death's-head.

6

When the lift stopped at the top floor of the office block in Birmingham, the two men lounging in the reception hall stared appreciatively at the dark-haired girl who stepped out. She wore a summer dress, brown gloves and shoes, and carried a handbag on her arm. As she moved, the shape of splendidly elegant legs showed through the material of the dress.

Both men were young, both broad shouldered and in suits of fashionable cut. One had a heavy jutting jaw and cropped hair, the other's face was round and might have seemed cherubic if it had not been for the eyes. The first man sat on an upright chair tilted back against the wall beside a door marked *Private*, a girlie magazine open in his hands. The second leaned against the wall beside a window that looked out over the city.

They were not of the type usually to be found in the reception area of a business organisation, but Modesty Blaise felt no surprise, for these were the offices of a firm called *Dave Goss and Associates*. The man by the window looked her up and down and said, "I like it, Terry, I like it." He pushed himself away from the wall and strolled towards Modesty.

The other man said, "Very tasty, Bruce," and grinned.

Modesty said, "Good morning. Will you tell Mr. Goss that Modesty Blaise would like to see him, please?"

Bruce stopped in front of her, thumbs hooked in his trouser pockets, pale eyes stripping her. "Can't do that, darling," he said insolently. "We never bother 'im with birds in office hours. Strict orders."

She said patiently, "If you'd just tell him I'm here."

"Nah." Bruce shook his head. "But I tell you what, darling, I'm free meself this afternoon, so . . ." He leaned forward and whispered a suggestion of filthy obscenity, watching her face with pleased anticipation. The reaction was quite different from anything he had expected. Her eyes were suddenly large and dark, then she moved, slightly but innocuously it seemed, yet somehow a touch of her hands brought him off balance, and he was grabbing at her, missing, being spun round, feeling a grip of momentary but startling power on his wrist and upper arm, finding himself swept up in a twisting and accelerating momentum that scattered his wits, then having the impression of somersaulting under his own power yet without his volition, somersaulting over a bent back and flying through the air upside down, to hit the wall back first, head down, beside the door marked *Private*.

Terry of the heavy jaw was already out of his chair and coming at her fast, a short leather cylinder filled with lead shot in his hand now. She twitched her skirt higher to give her legs unrestricted play, backing too fast for him to get his timing right, then stopping abruptly and stepping inside the swing of his arm, blocking with her elbow and turning to use a leg sweep that scythed his feet from under. He fell squarely from a height of three feet on to his back with an impact that drove the breath hissing from his lungs.

She stepped back and stood biting her lower lip in annoyance with herself for having allowed long pent-up anxiety to break free and be discharged in a flurry of angry action. The office door opened and a man emerged, no taller than Modesty, body and head shaped like a large egg with a smaller egg on top, fair thinning hair, in his middle fifties, expensively dressed, a cigar clipped between the fingers of one hand.

"What the 'ell's going on 'ere?" he demanded, then stopped short at sight of Modesty. A beam of pleasure touched his face, and ignoring the fallen men completely he came towards her with arms flung wide. "Modesty, love! 'Ow *are* yer, then?" His voice was steeped in the pinched and contorted vowel sound of the Birmingham accent. "It's great to see yer, girl. Come in, come in."

She said, "I'm sorry, Dave. Your bodyguard got fresh, and I . . . sort of over-reacted."

"Stupid pillocks!" he said angrily, and took her arm, steering her towards his office, delivering a painful kick in passing to the behind of Terry, who had rolled over and risen dazedly to his knees, but now yelped and fell on his face. "I'm sorry, darlin'," said Dave Goss. "You just can't get decent staff these days."

In an office furnished with surprisingly good taste he seated her in an armchair, offered a drink, which was declined, asked if she minded him smoking, then seated himself behind the big desk and said sympathetically, "You're looking for Willie Garvin?"

"Yes, Dave." A small automatic smile. "I thought maybe the biggest crook south of The Wash might have heard a whisper."

He waved a deprecating hand. "Biggest? Well, it's just luck, really. Why didn't you phone, Modesty girl?"

"I seem to spend my life on the phone recently, Dave, and you're only an hour's run from London. I'm glad to get out for a break."

"Sure." He tipped ash from his cigar into an ashtray. "I read it in the papers about ten days ago. The girl murdered and the police anxious to contact a Mr. William Garvin, though he wasn't under suspicion, so I guessed the mob who did it must've taken him. The story didn't make much space, and I 'aven't seen anything about it since."

"And heard no whispers?"

He shook his head slowly. "Not a breath. I got an idea this is some foreign lot involved. If they were 'ome-based villains I reckon I'd 've picked up a whisper by now. And I've put out feelers, Modesty love. I knew if Willie was gone missing you'd be proper upset, so I was 'oping to pick up a line for you, but there's nothing. I'd 've been in touch right away if I 'ad anything."

"Thanks, Dave." She thought for a moment. "Would you be likely to hear if the Triads were involved?"

He drew on his cigar thoughtfully. "It's 'ard to say, but I've got connections there on a sort of demarcation basis, and I think something would 've filtered through."

"Well . . ." She picked up her handbag. "I won't keep you any longer, but if you pick up the slightest whisper –"

" 'Ang on, darlin', 'ang on. I've just 'ad a thought." He sat frowning down at the desk top for a few moments, then gave a little nod. "Yes. I don't know if it means anything, but you might as well 'ave it. Look, you know I use freelance pilots for a bit of special import–export business now and again?"

"Yes, I know, Dave."

"Well, there's a pilot called Lafarge I wanted for a job just about the time that Chinese girl was killed. Might 'ave been the same night. He couldn't do the job for me because he'd got another flying job on, right? So a couple of days ago this bloke's 'aving a drink in a club with one of my London managers and he lets his lip get a bit unbuttoned. Tells about a couple of weirdo foreigners he flew out from some airfield in Surrey, a man and a woman, and they spent most of the flight

93

screwing away like rabbits be'ind 'im. He thought it might even be a three-hander because they'd brought another bloke with them, but when he took a quick look round there was just the two of them doing the acrobatics, very mobile with it, too. The second bloke was out cold, and Lafarge thought he was paralytic drunk when they first arrived at the airstrip, but he never woke up, so it looks like he was doped."

Dave Goss gave an apologetic shrugg. "It's only 'alf a story. Lafarge told it for laughs I suppose, because of these two screwing in the back, same as my manager told it to me. Didn't say what the second bloke looked like, as far as I know. Probably nothing to do with Willie going missing, but I just thought I'd mention it as a long shot. You know . . . sometimes an outsider comes up."

She sat with head turned a little, gazing out of the big window to her left, and after a while she said, "Lafarge?"

"That's right. Roger Lafarge. Sounds Frenchie, but he's English. Flies a Cessna Chancellor. Lives somewhere in west London. I can give you the address." He touched keys on a desk computer at his elbow, looked at the screen and began to write on a white card taken from a leather box next to the telephone.

Modesty said, "Your manager didn't know where Lafarge was taking these people?"

"No, I asked 'im that, not for any special reason, just because I like to know things, but Lafarge only told about the Kama Sutra bit in the back. I got the impression it was a longish flight, though."

"Will it embarrass you if I question Lafarge? And maybe shake a few answers out of him?"

Dave Goss grinned and shook his head. "Feel free, darlin'. Say who told you, if you like. If I need a bent pilot I can find plenty without going to Lafarge."

She turned her head to look at him now, and as she did so the quiet impassivity of her face melted and became a smile. She stood up, and he thought her voice was not quite steady as she said, "You've given me the first spark of hope in ten days, Dave. I'm so grateful."

"I just 'ope it leads somewhere, Modesty girl." He came round the desk, gave her the card, and watched her put it in her handbag. Hesitantly he said, "You reckon Willie's still . . . you know. Alive?"

"Yes, I do." She put a hand on his arm and leaned forward to touch her cheek to his. "I'll let you know what happens."

"You do that, love." He moved with her to the door. "And if you find you could do with a few lively lads for back-up, just call me. Right?"

She shook her head. "I won't involve you. This one falls to me. But thanks again, Dave."

"Any time."

He held the door open for her, escorted her to the lift, and said, "Keep in touch, darlin'," as the doors closed upon her. Terry now sat behind the small table facing the lift, a hangdog look on his heavy-jawed face. Bruce was slumped in the chair by the office door, leaning forward, a hand pressed to his back. He looked up as Dave Goss moved away from the lift, and said in a whining, defensive voice, "I'm 'urt, Dave, I'm 'urt. She bleedin' near broke me back."

Dave Goss halted in front of him, eyes angry. "Poor ol' Bruce," he said with mock sympathy. "Po-o-or ol' Brucey. Got 'imself duffed up, and just because he treated Modesty Blaise like a scrubber." His open hand smacked resoundingly across Bruce's cheek, rocking him back in the chair, and Dave Goss bent to glare into his face. "You got no discrimination, Brucey!" he blared. "No discrimination!"

✳   ✳   ✳   ✳

Dr. Thaddeus Pilgrim rarely left his study, and there was much nudging and speculation among the mixed nationalities who formed the commonalty of The Hostel of Righteousness when he was seen making his way across the courtyard and past the recreation room to the technical section of the complex.

Dr. Tyl received him in the section's small office, seated him in a comfortable chair, and expressed delight that he had come to see for himself how the preparations for the scenario were progressing. "Let me give you a résumé of the method adopted, Dr. Pilgrim," he said, picking up a file from his desk and opening it. "As you know, our London agent was able to meet my request for a selection of colour photographs of Modesty Blaise. Also of a woman who has been Garvin's local mistress for some time now. She is Lady Janet Gillam, a Scottish aristocrat who works a farm not far from Garvin's public house on the River Thames."

"Ah, yes," Thaddeus Pilgrim murmured absently. "Mrs. Ram did advise me of Garvin's connection with a titled lady. A most interesting sociological phenomenon, is it not?"

"Most," said Dr. Tyl with suppressed impatience. "Now, the first stage of my system was to induce general amnesia. The second was to ensure that Garvin's mental picture of Modesty Blaise was totally erased. These two stages were accomplished by narco-hypnotic suggestion, reinforced by tape-recorded suggestion during semi-normal sleep. It was most important, however, that he retained his awareness of the *name* Modesty Blaise, and of the immense significance to him of her persona."

Dr. Tyl looked up from the file he held, eyes twinkling happily so that he looked like a very large living teddy bear. "The third stage," he said, "has been to create a new and false visual picture of Modesty Blaise in his memory, a picture of *another woman*, but one for whom he also has great affection. His mistress, Lady Janet Gillam."

"Do I take it that you have achieved this stage, dear friend?"

"Certainly. It is necessary to keep reinforcing the delusion, since there would otherwise be a natural reversion to the actual, but this presents no difficulty."

"Admirable, admirable. And what is the fourth stage?"

"That is being established now, Dr. Pilgrim, and by substantially the same means. Garvin believes that Modesty Blaise is dead, and that she suffered a fiendishly cruel death at the hands of a vicious criminal, a female to whom we have given the name Delilah. He believes, because we have told him so, that both he and Modesty Blaise were captives of this woman, and that Modesty Blaise sacrificed herself to save him. He has no memory of this, and knows no details. He believes that he suffered severe concussion during his escape, which has caused amnesia."

"You have simply implanted, as it were, the . . . ah, the *essence* of the false memory in his mind?"

"That is so, Dr. Pilgrim. As anticipated, the effect on Garvin of her supposed death has been profound. He is depressed, sullen, and filled with a virulent hatred for the woman Delilah." Tyl laid down the file and leaned back in his chair with a genial chuckle. "In this fourth stage we are now using photographs, drugs, and hypnosis to establish a clear picture of Delilah in Garvin's mind, and we are emphasising that this highly dangerous woman is still seeking *his* death."

Thaddeus Pilgrim's wandering gaze came to rest for a moment on his colleague's face. "And the visual image of Delilah in Garvin's mind, the hated image, will in fact be that of Modesty Blaise?"

"That is precisely how I plan to implement your scenario, Dr. Pilgrim," said Tyl smugly. "You will recall that Garvin believes himself to be among his friends of *The Network* here. I was able to secure a key name from him under hypnosis, Garcia, the name of a man he worked closely with. He now believes *me* to be Garcia. In that role I have said he must rest, take plenty of exercise, and become fully fit so that he will be ready for the moment when Delilah strikes again."

Thaddeus Pilgrim smiled vaguely at the ceiling. "I must congratulate you, my dear colleague, on your achievements – I might say your remarkable achievements – as an adept in the art of human puppetry. To erase, and create, and remould memories and concepts in the mind of a person such as Garvin is truly a major feat."

Tyl gave a contented sigh. "It is most satisfying," he said deprecatingly, "but not essentially difficult. All men believe their dreams while they are dreaming them, however improbable, and Garvin is dreaming now, has been living a dream these two weeks past." He looked at his watch. "Would you care to see him? He will be at lunch in the refectory now."

"He will not be curious about my identity? I should not wish to give him cause for questioning the – ah – myth you have so carefully constructed about him."

"He will question nothing, Dr. Pilgrim. He shows no interest in any of our workforce. Before Sibyl Pray departed with Kazim on the latest Answer to Prayer mission, she attempted to seduce Garvin, with Kazim's consent of course, but was brusquely rejected. Except for myself, I think all our people are mere shadows in the background to him. His sole concern is that Modesty Blaise was brutally killed, and his sole purpose now is to destroy the woman who killed her, Delilah. He sees me as his friend, Rafael Garcia, and is prepared to talk to me, though not to any great extent. Come and see."

Two minutes later they entered the refectory. A dozen or so men and two women were at table, Willie Garvin sitting a little apart from the rest. He wore a dark shirt and slacks. The top three buttons of the shirt were unfastened, and beneath it, next to his skin, was strapped a slim leather harness carrying two sheathed knives in echelon against his left breast. Sibyl Pray had found the knives and harness in his car on the night Molly Chen was killed, much to Dr. Tyl's delight. It had been a convincing touch when he produced them as spares from *The Network* armoury.

Willie Garvin sat eating a light meal of cold meat and salad, ignoring his surroundings. There was a quietness about him, not of reflection but of grey moroseness touched with a threat of irascibility, all of which would have been familiar to those who had known him before Modesty Blaise came into his life. What would not have been familiar to them was the immense underlying grief that made the blue eyes lifeless and set a barrier about him.

Thaddeus Pilgrim halted a few paces away and let Tyl go forward. The psychiatrist said, "What's the afternoon programme, Willie?"

He glanced up. "Hallo, Rafa." The voice was flat; not unfriendly, but by no means warm. "Programme? Oh, rest for an hour. Swim. Run." The eyes became sullen. "I need some good work-outs. Combat practice in the gym."

Tyl said regretfully, "I fixed it, and you played too rough, Willie. With Sibyl and Kazim away, we haven't anyone left to make a decent sparring partner for you."

Willie frowned. "Who? Who's away?"

"Sibyl and Kazim. You saw them for a couple of days before they went off on that Greek job."

Willie Garvin continued eating, still frowning a little. "They been with us long?"

"Jesus, Willie. Four or five years at least. Don't you remember?"

He shrugged. "It's mostly a bloody great blank. I can 'hardly remember anything yet. Might not know who I was if you 'adn't told me."

"It'll come back, Willie," Tyl said soothingly. "The doc. says it'll gradually come back. Just don't worry. Look, you remember Modesty well enough, don't you?"

"I remember." The voice was a strained croak. He dropped knife and fork on his plate, folded his arms, still staring down, and said, "I remember all that. Any word on that bitch Delilah?"

"Not yet, Willie. When we locate her, you can go after her. That's if she doesn't come after you first."

He shrugged. The blue eyes gleamed savagely for a moment, and a hand moved to touch the hilt of a knife. "Either way," he said.

"See you, Willie." Tyl turned away, and Thaddeus Pilgrim followed him from the refectory. Walking along the corridor, Tyl said, "You see?"

"I do indeed, dear friend, and I am greatly impressed. Are you still able, at this stage, to impose hypnotic treatment upon Mr. Garvin?"

"No problem. He will rest after lunch. By post hypnotic suggestion, he will at once fall into hypnotic sleep. Then I shall spend a little time with him in the laboratory, reinforcing what has been established, using suggestion combined with photographs thrown on the screen. He will return to his room and wake up remembering nothing."

"Your control of his mind is remarkably potent, Doctor Tyl. Remarkably potent."

Tyl chuckled. "That is because the subconscious cannot resist a properly designed suggestion. No doubt Mr. Garvin's *conscious* mind would have done so from the beginning, but it has never had the opportunity, since he was brought to me under sedation."

Thaddeus Pilgrim paused by an arched window and looked out over the broad white sill to the sparsely wooded end of the island and the blue-green sea beyond. "What do you expect to happen when Mr. Garvin is confronted suddenly by Miss Blaise?" he said dreamily.

"He will instantly kill her, Dr. Pilgrim. That is the scenario you required, and that is what will happen. Even if Blaise is armed, the result will be the same. I understand she is very adept with firearms, but of course she will not be expecting death at Garvin's hands. It will be over before she realises what is happening."

"But surely, dear friend – and please do not construe this as a criticism – surely that is a somewhat *limited* finale? Delilah lies dead, but what of Garvin?"

Tyl grinned broadly, pleased with himself. "Ah, that should prove to be of great interest, Dr. Pilgrim. The death of Blaise, by his hand, is the key which I have designed to unlock Garvin's memory and wipe away all the false visual images and counterfeit recollections I have implanted. In short, Garvin will suddenly wake from the dream in which he is living at present, to find that in the real world he has killed Modesty Blaise. What his reaction will be, I cannot predict. It is possible he may destroy himself, or suffer catatonic withdrawal, or become schizophrenic – but I do not wish to speculate, Dr. Pilgrim. I wish to keep an open mind and simply observe the effect upon Garvin. It is a truly fascinating prospect."

"I look forward to it myself," said Thaddeus Pilgrim, and began walking slowly on. "Thank you for your delightfully interesting exposition of the – ah – the situation as it stands at the moment, but now, I fear, I must return to my major duties. Mrs. Ram is waiting to bring me up to date with the progress of our Hallelujah Scenario." He screwed up his watery eyes in thought. "I wonder . . . without undue expectation, of course . . . I wonder if it might be possible for a *schizophrenic* Mr. Garvin to partake in the somewhat extensive killing to be carried out on that occasion?"

＊　　＊　　＊　　＊

Danny Chavasse said, "How will you play it?"

She did not answer at once. Seated on a tall stool at one of the three benches in her lapidary workshop at the penthouse, she had an emerald in the rough cemented to her dopstick and was cutting the first facet on it with a slitting-saw. A few seconds later she sat back, switched off the spinning phosphor-bronze disc of the slitting-saw, screwed a jeweller's glass into her eye, and examined the emerald.

"I'll try to buy information from him," she said. "Lafarge is a mercenary, so he'll probably sell."

"He may not know very much, Modesty."

"He can describe the passionate friends who spent the flight screwing, and he can describe the second man, who may have been Willie. He also has to know where he landed his Cessna. At least it's a start, Danny."

He waited until she had made another cut on the rough gem, then said unhappily, "Suppose he won't sell?"

She took the glass from her eye. "Then it gets tricky. We've never gone in for thumbscrew techniques, but if I can't buy him or frighten him, I might break a few rules."

Roger Lafarge lived in a rather expensive block of apartments in west London. Six times in the last two days when she had rung his number a machine had answered. She had left a message asking him to ring her, and confirmed this by a written note that Weng had delivered by hand. The assumption was that he was away on a job, and there was nothing she could do now but wait. It took all her hard-won skill in control of emotion and dispersal of tensions to preserve mental balance and prevent anxiety wearing her nerves to shreds. Many hours of the past two days of waiting had been spent in the practice of yogic disciplines.

Watching her now, Danny Chavasse marvelled at the quiet serenity of her eyes as she studied the emerald. An hour ago she had cooked a simple but pleasant dinner for them, and they had eaten in the dining room with a bottle óf claret. Conversation had been easy and companionable. She had not spoken of Willie Garvin, and in this he had taken his cue from her. There was gravity in her, and underlying sorrow, but no tension.

Danny's own nerves had been well tempered by the long ordeal as a slave in Limbo, under constant threat of flogging or death, but he jumped a little when the telephone on the bench where she was working rang. She lifted it without a start and said, "Modesty Blaise."

Then: "Yes. Thank you for calling back, Mr. Lafarge." A pause. "I'd like to see you because I think you may have some information I would be prepared to buy. Dave Goss gave me your name." Another pause, and she looked at her wristwatch. "Yes, I could be with you at ten o'clock, or you could come here if you prefer." She listened. "Your place? Very well, Mr. Lafarge, I'll see you shortly."

She put the phone down, pressed the switch of an intercom device and spoke into it. "Weng?"

After a few seconds Weng's voice said, "Yes, Miss Blaise?"

"Get some money out of the safe, please. One packet of a thousand, two of two thousand. I shall be leaving to see Mr. Lafarge shortly, so you'll be on standby till I get back."

"Very good, Miss Blaise."

Danny followed her to the bedroom. She took off her working smock, opened the wardrobe and selected a shirtwaister dress. As she began to change, he said, "Would you like me to come along?"

"No, Danny. You hold the fort here in case a message comes through from any of our contacts. Weng is on standby if I need him, and he's briefed on what he has to do."

"Well . . . good luck, darling."

She gave him a small smile. "Keep your fingers crossed for me. Keep them crossed for Willie."

Fifteen minutes later she parked the car and walked up to the third floor of an apartment block in Maida Vale. Roger Lafarge proved to be a man in his late thirties, well built, light brown hair carefully styled, a square and rather florid face with wide-set eyes and a sensual mouth that smiled easily. He had a drink in his hand as he opened the door, and eyed her with open curiosity as he stepped back and gestured for her to enter.

"Well, hallo there, sweetheart." His voice held an old-fashioned upper class drawl. "Come along in and have a little drink. The name's Roger, by the way." She was aware of his eyes on her as he followed her into a softly lit sitting room where a hi-fi was playing very quietly a Sidney Bechet tape.

He waved her to a deep armchair and said, "Sit you down and tell me what you'd like to drink. Sorry I didn't call back before, but I've only just got in from a longish job. In fact, if it wasn't for the name Modesty Blaise on your note and on the answering machine I'd have gone straight to beddy-byes and called you tomorrow. What will it be?" He was by a sideboard with an array of drinks, indicating them with a wave of his hand.

"Just a tonic water, please. No ice."

He looked amused but made no comment and began to pour the drink. "When I got your message I thought you probably wanted me for a flying job, but on the phone just now you spoke of information. Can't imagine what it might be, but let's not rush into that. I've just had a hard three days, and relaxing with a drink and a beautiful girl is just what the doctor ordered."

He brought the drink to her, and she gave him a convincing smile of thanks. It was immaterial that already she disliked Roger Lafarge. What mattered was that he knew, or might know, something very important to her, and this was all that mattered. He lounged back with his drink on the big leather settee and looked at her with a speculative, rather challenging air.

"Cheers," he said, lifting his glass. "So this is the famous Modesty Blaise."

She gave a rueful shrug. "Infamous might be a better word." It would be a mistake to hurry this man, she sensed. He knew that he was in a position to call the tune, and would do so when he was ready. He did know just how strong his position was, but probably hoped that a little preliminary indifference might help to provide a clue.

"How do you know Dave Goss?" he asked.

She had inwardly withdrawn now, leaving only enough of herself to play the role required of her in bringing this man to tell her what he knew. "It goes back a few years," she said. "A consortium was planning to take over Dave's organisation, and I got wind of it. Part of the plan involved knocking Dave off, so I warned him."

Lafarge grinned. "And he's been grateful ever since. Good for you. I understand you're not in business yourself now?"

"No. Not for quite a while."

"But you keep yourself occupied, don't you? A Fleet Street mate of mine reckons you work part-time for British Intelligence."

She laughed. "You get all kinds of rumours."

For a while he kept up a leisurely flow of small talk and she responded in a similar vein, showing no haste. At last he said, "Well, time marches on, so you'd better tell me what this information is you think I can give you."

"It's fairly straightforward," she said casually. "Just under a fort-night ago, on the Saturday night, you flew two men and a woman out from an old Surrey airstrip. I'd like to know anything you can tell me about them, and where you took them."

He looked at her with interest, got up to pour himself a fresh drink, and sat down again. "You have to realise, Modesty sweetheart," he said, "that like a doctor or a priest, I have to respect the confidentiality of my clients. Who told you this?"

"Dave Goss. You told his London manager."

He nodded slowly. "A minor indiscretion. But now you're asking for a major one, and I have my reputation to consider."

"I'm not asking you to risk your reputation for nothing, Roger."

He set his drink down on a small table, leaned back with hands clasped behind his head, and gazed at her with smiling effrontery. "Well, times are hard, sweetheart, and it so happens that I read the papers, so I might not be far wrong in guessing that you could be trying to pick up a lead on Willie Garvin. According to my Fleet Street mate, you and Garvin are like that," he held up a hand with the first and second fingers intertwined. "So I reckon any information I can give you is worth . . . at least three grand."

She smiled and shook her head. "It might be worth damn all, Roger, but I'm willing to gamble a thousand on it."

"You're a rich lady, and money is only money. Make it two."

She considered, then gave a brief nod. "It's a rip-off, but all right then. Two."

"Cash?"

"Cash now." She opened the handbag, took out a packet, and laid it on the small table. "Two thousand in fifties." She smiled. "I was pretty damn sure you'd talk me up from one."

"Clever girl." He settled himself more comfortably on the settee and looked at her blandly. "But the answer is no."

She was taken aback. "What do you mean? I've met what you asked."

"Indeed you have, but as I just said, money is only money, and that applies to me as well as you. It's not everything."

She stared at him with narrowed eyes, puzzled. "I'm not with you. What's the bottom line, Roger?"

He sighed. "Well, to put it bluntly, *you* are, darling. Here I am, a lonely bachelor, returned from a hard three day's work, in dire need of long and enjoyable dalliance with a beautiful, biddable girl such as you might well be. And behold, you have appeared before me."

She considered him for a moment or two, then said, "You're serious?"

He grinned. "Oh, I mean it all right, sweetheart. I need to be taken out of myself, not to mention being put into the above-mentioned beautiful biddable girl." He lifted a hand as she made to speak. "No, don't offer more money, darling. What's filthy lucre compared to a luscious lady? Two grand is dandy, but I can always get money. What I'm pretty sure I can't get any other way is an action-packed night with Modesty Blaise."

There was no decision for her to make. That he would have whatever use he wanted to make of her body for a night was of no importance beside the need to grasp the smallest opportunity of discovering what had happened to Willie Garvin. She said, "And that's the whole deal? You tell me what you know in return for two thousand and me for the night?"

He nodded, a hint of surprise in his smile. 'That's the whole deal. If you don't like it, you can always pick up the money now and go."

She said quietly, "All right, Roger, it's a deal."

He eyed her shrewdly. "It's understood that I'm not interested in having an icicle in my bed?"

"It's understood. You'll have no cause to complain."

He threw back his head and laughed. "Well I'll be damned. This is quite an occasion."

"Yes. Now tell me about those three people, Roger. Full descriptions and their destination."

"Oh-ho, not so fast, lady. The way we do this, *if* we do it, is that you pay your dues, and *then* I risk my reputation by telling all. Tomorrow morning. By dawn's shady light. Pillow talk."

After a little silence she said, "I see. But how can I be sure you'll deliver once I've paid, Roger?"

He spread his hands. "You'll just have to trust me, won't you, darling?"

She sat with her handbag on her lap, looking absently at a print of Picasso's *Blue Nude* on the wall above the fireplace, trying to judge whether Lafarge could be relied upon to honour the deal, then putting the question aside as unanswerable. She could only wait and see, and consider what might be done if he welched. "All right," she said, and looked at him again. "I'll trust you, Roger. I have to call my houseboy to let him know I won't be home tonight, and I shall have to be away from here by seven a.m."

He gave her another slow grin. "I wake at six, and I'm not a breakfast person, so that sounds fine to me." He glanced towards a bureau to one side of the fireplace. "There's the phone, sweetheart."

In the penthouse, Danny Chavasse and Weng were playing back-gammon in the sitting room when the phone rang. Weng glanced at his watch and got up to answer it. "Residence of Modesty Blaise."

He listened, and Danny saw the usually cheerful face harden suddenly. "Yes, Miss Blaise. At seven a.m.? I will be there. Do you wish me to be equipped as per briefing? Very good, Miss Blaise."

Weng put down the phone and returned to his chair. "Miss Blaise will not be returning home tonight, Mr. Chavasse," he said. "I am to be at Mr. Lafarge's apartment at seven a.m. tomorrow to pick her up."

Danny sat very still for a moment, suddenly motionless in the act of rattling the dice in the cup. Then he said with quiet sorrow, "I hadn't thought of that possibility."

"No." Weng's mouth was tight, his hands clasped between his knees.

Danny said tiredly, "It's a lousy break, but she can cope, Weng. It was far worse for her in Limbo, but she can shed it."

"I know she can cope, Mr. Chavasse," said Weng in a taut voice, "but I do not wish her to have to cope with a degrading experience."

"Neither do I, but it's for Willie Garvin, so there's no limit as far as she's concerned. What was that about you being equipped as per briefing?"

Weng looked up, his face impassive now. "Nothing of importance, Mr. Chavasse," he said, and reached for the cup. "Let us play."

Less than two miles away Modesty picked up her handbag from

beside the phone and turned towards Lafarge. "At your convenience," she said.

He exhaled a long sigh of satisfaction. "The sooner we start, the longer the programme, darling, so how about now?" He half turned on the settee and gestured towards a door. "Bedroom through there, bathroom beyond. Perhaps you'd care to go and make ready while I tuck my wages away in a safe place." He nodded towards the packet on the table.

Her outward self, to whom she had delegated whatever she might be called on to do in the hours that lay ahead, gave Roger Lafarge a friendly smile. "I'll see you soon, then," she said.

The bedroom decor was expensive but flashy, the bed a king-sized bed. She went through to a dressing room adjoining a well equipped bathroom, stripped off her clothes and took a brief shower. Drying herself, she paused to look critically at her body in the full-length mirror and decided that it ought to do well enough for Roger Lafarge.

For a moment she thought of Willie Garvin, and felt a pain so intense that she had to close her eyes and brace herself against it. Then she relaxed, letting the pain wash through her like water flowing through a net, and in a little while it was gone.

"Hang in there, Willie love," she whispered. "I'm doing all I can." Then she turned from the mirror and walked through into the bedroom where Roger Lafarge was waiting.

7

" A s regards progress of Hallelujah Scenario," said Mrs. Ram, "the situation is as follows." She consulted her clipboard. "Our tanker *Marimba* loaded two hundred thousand tons of oil at Kuwait on the ninth inst. Certificate of End Use was signed, declaring that destination of cargo was Hamburg. Once on High Seas, the name *Marimba* was painted out and new name, *Rossland*, substituted."

Mrs. Ram looked up from her notes. "One tanker is much like another, Dr. Pilgrim, and there is a *Rossland* laid up in North America. Many tankers are laid up at this time, which is why our Swiss-based company was able to buy *Marimba* for only fourteen million dollars. She is insured by Lloyds for fourteen million, and the cargo for sixty million."

Thaddeus Pilgrim nodded cautious approval. He appeared to be giving her his close attention, but in fact the major part of his being was far away in a grey void, contemplating nightmare savageries and obscenities. "Quite so, dear lady," he said, "quite so. That would appear to be satisfactory in terms of finance. Oh, I hasten to say that you should not take my use of the conditional case in that last phrase as implying doubt or criticism."

Mrs. Ram devoted a few moments to an attempt to work out what he meant, but failed, and with a grateful smile pressed on. "Thank you, Doctor. Captain Valerius is now sailing *Rossland* to Beira on the coast of Mozambique, where he will discharge his cargo of oil. Payment for this has already been made by government of Mozambique to our company based in the Cayman Islands. It is suspected that eventual destination of oil will be Republic of South Africa, but that is irrelevant to our operation."

She turned a page on her clipboard, cleared her throat and continued. "On leaving Beira, tanks of *Rossland* will be filled with sea water so that she will give the appearance of being fully laden still.

This was at Captain Valerius's suggestion, which I consider highly commendable."

Thaddeus Pilgrim sighed. "Yes indeed, Mrs. Ram, highly commendable. But," he made a small helpless gesture, "I do not think there is much ... ah, much *point* in advising Captain Valerius of our gratitude, since he will shortly be ..." his eyes under the white eyebrows lifted heavenwards for a moment and his voice sank to a respectful whisper, "be called to higher service. Of course, if you feel that he would die *happier* in the knowledge of our approval ...?"

"No, Doctor, no. My comment was simply a point of detail, not a request for action."

"Ah ... then pray continue, dear lady."

"After tanker leaves Beira the name *Rossland* will be removed and replaced with original name, *Marimba*. Voyage will continue round Cape of Good Hope into Atlantic Ocean and up west coast of Africa. At specified position off Senegal, tanker will suffer violent explosion. The Captain and four of his eight officers plus two seamen of the thirty man crew are aware that this will happen. They believe that explosion and subsequent fire will be so arranged that all hands will be able to take to life-boats after Mayday signal has been sent out, and that said hands will be picked up at first light by small cargo vessel on legitimate business but manned by our people."

"This," said Thaddeus Pilgrim tentatively, "was virtually the system we employed for our Hosanna Scenario in the South China Seas, was it not?"

"Up to the point so far detailed, system was similar," agreed Mrs. Ram. "Ship was smaller, cargo was steel, not oil. Also ship was registered in Panama, not Liberia, and belonged to Hong Kong company we had set up to operate scam."

For a moment the wandering gaze came to rest with curious fixity on Mrs. Ram's neck. "I referred to the *system*, dear lady," Thaddeus Pilgrim said reproachfully. "It greatly distresses me that you choose to correct my *general* remark by reciting the minor *factual* differences you have just enumerated. It indicates a lack of ... of *humility*, Mrs. Ram, a quite temporary shortcoming, I am sure, but one which I should be remiss in failing to point out, since error unchecked may cause grievous ill-health." He stopped speaking abruptly, with his mouth still half open, and gazed with unalive eyes through her neck.

Mrs. Ram wriggled in ecstatic terror, and said, "I am filled with remorseful apology, Dr. Pilgrim. Please accept that apparent discourtesy was due to overmeticulous element in my nature, and not to lack of humility."

"Ah," said Thaddeus Pilgrim vaguely, and leaned back in his chair with half closed eyes. "You were saying, dear lady . . . ?"

"Well, let me see now. Ah, yes. It is when *Marimba* reaches specified position off Senegal," said Mrs. Ram warily, "that the system for Hallelujah Scenario begins to differ from that of Hosanna Scenario. In South China Seas operation, cargo was sold covertly, ship was then scuttled, and insurance on both ship and cargo was claimed, yielding approx. ten million dollars, much of which has been used to finance present Hallelujah Scenario. All hands from scuttled ship were rescued safely. Five persons were privy to fact that loss of ship etcetera was no accident, and these five were later eliminated, two by Sibyl and Kazim, three by other executives of our Answer to Prayer Section."

She looked up from her clipboard. "One of eliminatees was the Chinese seaman married to Molly Chen, and it was later feared that he had passed sensitive information to his wife. Decision to eliminate her was taken as safety measure. She had left Hong Kong, and much time was spent locating her by group to whom we subcontracted her elimination. In the event, their attempt failed due to intervention of Garvin, but successful killing was later achieved by Sibyl and Kazim."

"Thank you, Mrs. Ram," said Thaddeus Pilgrim amiably. "That is not of great relevance to our Hallelujah Scenario, perhaps, but I am grateful to be reminded of an incident which has provided the seed of a new and most interesting experiment. You were referring, before your welcome digression, to the point at which the *system* for our Hallelujah Scenario now diverges from our earlier procedure. Pray continue."

"Difference is wide but simple, Doctor. At planning stage, you pointed out that rescue of all hands following tanker explosion might create unworthy suspicion in underwriters who have insured tanker and cargo to total value of seventy-four million dollars. This being agreed, decision was taken to arrange for rescue ship with our task force to be at the rendezvous early, with full A.T.P. Section under command of Sibyl and Kazim. They will board *Marimba* and eliminate all persons thereon, without exception, before causing explosion."

Mrs. Ram turned another page on her clipboard. "In my draft of briefing for your approval," she resumed, "I have inserted instructions that a number of *Marimba's* crew be eliminated in such ways as to suggest mortal injuries from explosion and fire. If a handful of such bodies are later found in drifting lifeboats it will add verisimilitude to the scenario. All others will go down with ship, of course."

"Excellent, excellent," murmured Thaddeus Pilgrim with fragile enthusiasm, "and I hope you will not feel I am interfering with your administrative function if I venture a suggestion of my own, Mrs. Ram."

She gazed at him with adoring admiration. It was five years now since Thaddeus Pilgrim, as an Adept, had initiated her into a group of Satanists practising black magic. Both had since moved on to far more sophisticated and profitable forms of malevolence, but the psychological necessity of submission by Disciple to Adept remained unbreakable. "Yes, Doctor?" she breathed.

"A thought occurred to me many weeks ago," he said pensively, "and I gave instructions for a search to be made . . ." His voice trailed away as he slowly opened a drawer of his desk. Moments later, using both hands, he set a piece of thick jagged metal on the desk, about the size of Mrs. Ram's clipboard. "There," he said, staring at it with a puzzled air as if he had momentarily forgotten what he was doing. "Ah, yes. This item was located in a small museum on the south coast of the United Kingdom, I believe, which was subsequently damaged quite severely by a fire, for which we must give credit to one of our A.T.P. teams."

He looked at Mrs. Ram with twinkling eyes. "You see, dear lady, I feel it is important that there should be evidence of some *cause* for the explosion which is to occur in our tanker, and preferably some *external* cause. Now this . . ." he waved a limp hand towards the metal, "this is a souvenir of the Second World War. It is a fragment from one of the magnetic mines sewn by the Germans in the Western Approaches, and I am assured that it can readily be identified as such."

Thaddeus Pilgrim leaned back in his chair, almost closing his eyes. "Now let us imagine a scenario spanning some forty years," he said dreamily. "It begins when a passing ship causes the mine to become detached from its mooring and rise to float near the surface, but by good fortune the ship does not strike it. Neither do other ships as it floats to and fro', to and fro' . . ." he waved a flaccid hand backwards and forwards with the words, ". . . out into the great Atlantic Ocean, there to make a random journey through that vast expanse, carrying its deadly burden across thousands upon thousands of miles, perhaps, for year after year."

He opened his eyes to peer at her. "The explosive, I am assured, will remain active, and the structure of the device is such that it is unlikely to disintegrate even after so long a watery sojourn." He smiled vaguely and repeated, "Watery sojourn," as if pleased with the phrase.

"Now," he said, with what for him was almost briskness, "in the early years, the odds against a chance collision with a vessel are very large, but as time goes by they must surely grow smaller until one day, one day soon . . ." He threw up his hands in a kind of slow-motion and said, "*Pouf*! An unfortunate tanker strikes it off the coast of Senegal by night, and in the explosion a fragment of the casing falls into a lifeboat hanging on the . . . ah, *davits* I believe they are called." He beamed across the desk. "I am referring, of course, to one of those lifeboats in which, as you have so wisely arranged, there will also be found a few bodies of those poor men who will appear to have succumbed to dreadful injuries shortly after abandoning ship."

Mrs. Ram moved her head from side to side wonderingly. "It is . . . it is quite perfect, Doctor," she said, trembling. "I am so excited, so excited . . ."

"I will give instructions that you be granted the particular facilities you require for the abatement of such excitement, Mrs. Ram," he said kindly, "but first I must crave your indulgence for a few moments to give me a brief report on the progress of current missions by our Answer to Prayer Section."

"Yes, yes of course, Doctor." Mrs. Ram took off the bulldog clip, rearranged her papers, and clipped them to the board again. "We have three teams in action at present, each consisting of two persons. Schedules provide that all missions will be completed in time for all executives to concentrate on Hallelujah Scenario. First team consisting of Ritter and Bonsu is presently in West African state, code-name Sirius. Young girl, white drop-out, has received ten years sentence for being in possession of drugs and insulting a Government Minister."

Mrs. Ram looked up for a moment. "Bonsu is a native of neighbouring state, and advises that the insult would be regarded as the major offence. Prison is disgusting, no medical service available, and there are grounds for belief that Government Minister framed girl following her refusal to sleep with him. Orthodox organisations such as Red Cross etcetera have failed to secure her release. Father of said girl is American millionaire who asks our prayers for her safety and release. Ritter and Bonsu report that death of above-mentioned Minister will allow

111

inexpensive bribe of his successor – through a cut-out, of course. Mercy release of girl will quickly follow. Assassination of Minister is planned for two days hence by long rifle. Political opponents will be blamed. I anticipate thank-offering by father of girl at not less than one hundred thousand dollars to Hostel of Righteousness in gratitude for our most effective prayers."

"Such a sum would surely leave us with a net return of . . . ah, at least, I would think, eighty thousand dollars after expenses," said Thaddeus Pilgrim piously. "That is most acceptable. We ask for nothing, of course. We can only cast our bread upon the waters, if you will permit a somewhat sectarian reference, Mrs. Ram, and hope that those whom we strive to serve will be moved to generosity."

She nodded. "If they are not so moved, we now use them as targets for training new Answer to Prayer teams, as you suggested, Doctor. It is an excellent system."

"How kind of you to say so, dear lady. And now, as to the two other teams in action? Quite briefly, if you please."

"Number Two team is Dixon and Patel. We received request for prayers from well known philanthropist, code name Midas, who is also top executive of large drug manufacturing corporation presently being sued by rivals over a matter of patents. Vast sum involved. We are asked to pray for just and happy outcome. This can be achieved by destruction of certain files in offices of international lawyer in Zurich, and suitable plans for arson are now finalised."

Mrs. Ram paused for a moment, but when Dr. Pilgrim gazed absently past her left ear without comment she continued. "Number Three team is Ms. Johnson and Zanelli, presently carrying out domestic A.T.P. operation for a wealthy French gentleman who is greatly distressed. He has invalid wife and attractive mistress, the latter wishing him to leave the former, which gentleman's conscience will not allow. He asks us to pray that he receives guidance, and we have arranged that he will receive the particular guidance he wishes for. Ms. Johnson reports that they propose to eliminate invalid wife by end of this week."

"With . . . ah, with due regard to avoidance of all suspicion, I take it? The French gentleman must not be suspected."

Mrs. Ram smiled politely. "I have briefed Ms. Johnson to the effect that the accident by which invalid wife will die must also include death of not less than two others, preferably more. This will naturally divert

112

suspicion. It is, of course, the principle we are adopting for Hallelujah Scenario but on a small scale."

"Thank you, Mrs. Ram, thank you," said Thaddeus Pilgrim courteously, gazing speculatively at the caged jackdaw. "It is clear that our A.T.P. work is thriving under your administrative hand. It only remains for me to ask if you have any new matter to report concerning Mr. Garvin's colleague, whom I suppose to be still seeking information as to his disappearance. I refer to Miss . . . ah, Miss Modesty Blaise, of course."

Mrs. Ram rested her clipboard on her lap. "We have Modesty Blaise under surveillance by very reliable agency, employed through cutouts," she announced. "It is probable that a person of her experience would sense close surveillance, so the agency has been instructed accordingly. Long-distance surveillance has been sufficient for them to report general movements. Modesty Blaise has visited a number of persons in England, but has always returned to her penthouse. Her current lover is there with her. She appears to have made no progress in her search for information about Mr. Garvin."

"Ah. Then since the gentleman in question is now fully conditioned for our scenario, you are no doubt devising means by which to . . . to *draw* the lady to us, Mrs. Ram. A most interesting exercise. I wonder," mused Thaddeus Pilgrim, "if she has paid a further visit to . . . ah, what is the name of the place where we have our English branch of the Hostel? Ah, yes . . . North Thursby. I seem to recall that it was the fact of her landing by private aircraft at the airfield nearby which first caused us to feel that it would be prudent to devise a scenario for – ah – promoting Miss Blaise and Mr. Garvin to a higher plane of being."

"That is correct, Doctor," agreed Mrs. Ram, "but it is now evident that her flying visit was simple coincidence. We have ascertained that she was acting for some kind of Air Ambulance organisation, and has shown no interest whatever in the Hostel of Righteousness."

"Dear me, dear me, then how fortunate we are that you chose to mention the *possibility*, Mrs. Ram, for otherwise we would have taken no action, and would thereby have missed the opportunity of creating a most stimulating scenario. I am very pleased with you, very pleased indeed."

Mrs. Ram shuddered blissfully and closed her eyes. "Thank you, Doctor," she murmured.

"And are you still excessively excited, dear lady?"

"Oh yes, Doctor, *yes*."

He beamed on her fondly and picked up the internal telephone. "Then I will give instructions for one of the whores to be placed at your entire disposal. Enjoy yourself, Mrs. Ram, enjoy yourself."

* * * *

At six o'clock Modesty Blaise roused from what might have appeared to be normal sleep but was more a form of self-hypnosis. Gently she moved away from Roger Lafarge, eased the duvet aside, and sat up on the edge of the bed. Before she could stand, a hand came from behind and clasped her hip. Lafarge's voice said, "One more time, sweetheart. We haven't quite run the gamut."

When she turned, her face showed only friendly amusement. "You're remarkably athletic, Roger."

"With the right partner." He lay on his back grinning at her, one hand still clasping her hip, and she kept her mind tightly closed against all emotion, focusing her energy on the role she was playing. "How do you fancy a little bondage?" he said.

She shook her head, still smiling. "Not my scene, Roger."

"It's part of mine."

Patiently, "It wasn't in the deal."

"It wasn't excluded from the deal, darling. Are you saying all bets are off?"

She kept the fury from her eyes and studied him, thinking of Willie Garvin. After a moment she enacted a smiling shrug and said, "Well . . . bring on the fetters."

Thirty minutes later, when he cut the cords to release her, she got up stiffly, went through to the bathroom and took a hot shower followed by an icy cold one. In the bathroom cabinet she found a new toothbrush still in its cellophane packet. She cleaned her teeth, dried her body, put on her clothes, ran a comb through her hair, and went back into the bedroom carrying her shoes in one hand and her handbag under her arm. Lafarge had put on a shirt, trousers and monk sandles, and was standing by the window. He moved away from it as she entered, and stood facing her, smiling a little, hands relaxed and resting very lightly on the front of his hips, feet apart so that he was carefully balanced.

"You were right, darling," he said. "I have no complaints."

"Good. Then describe those three people and tell me where you flew them to, Roger."

"I have no complaints," he repeated, "but I *have* had a change of heart. I've decided I can't, after all, ruin my reputation by breaking a client's confidence, not even for a memorable night with Modesty Blaise."

She looked at him with expressionless eyes and said, "I'm sure you don't mean that, Roger."

He sighed. "Oh, but I do, indeed I do. It will help me to feel that I've repented my sin of being *almost* led astray by the lure of carnal delights." He surveyed her contentedly. "There's the added pleasure of being able to say that I've played the great Modesty Blaise herself for a sucker, and in a big, big way." He was still smiling, but his eyes were watchful and his body poised as he went on, "I understand from my Fleet Street mate that you're a handy little practitioner of one or two martial arts, so in case you're contemplating the idea of venting your female outrage by committing a touch of mayhem on me, I'll give you fair warning. I hold a third degree Black Belt in Kenpo Karate, and if you try anything on me you'll end up hurt. Understood?"

In her stockinged feet she stood several inches shorter than the man and was outweighed by fifty pounds. Looking up at him she said, "I don't have to try anything, Roger. This isn't just a personal matter. The Triads are backing me for their own good reasons. I told them I could buy what we wanted from you quickly and without fuss. If you go back on our deal, you'll soon have a visit from our almond-eyed friends."

He stared down at her with contempt. "That's just about the stupidest bluff I've ever heard, sweetheart. The Triads? Backing *you*? Don't make me laugh."

She shrugged and said, "Go ahead, laugh," then turned her back on him and bent to put on her shoes. He began to relax, and saw but failed to interpret the swift flutter of her skirt which preceded the stockinged foot being driven up at an angle by the long, shapely but immensely powerful leg in a mule-kick of blinding speed. Her head, almost touching the floor, was turned to sight along the length of her body and leg as she made the unorthodox strike.

Because he was a karate-ka, instinct enabled him marginally to ride the blow and to twist so that it landed a trifle off-centre of the solar plexus, but she had walked the Middle East and North Africa unshod throughout her childhood, and her feet were like teak. The strike exploded against his chest to send him reeling back, gasping for air, and in the same instant she was upon him again with speed beyond his comprehension, her eyes huge, glinting with black flame in a stony face as she brushed aside his feeble defences, using *shuto, ippon-ken* and *sokuto* strikes.

He felt a lower rib crack, and tried to scream as his back hit the wall, but a touch across the windpipe, a touch that would have killed if not perfectly judged, wiped all power from his vocal chords. Within him was awareness of all she had submitted to at his hands during the past hours, and with this awareness was combined the terrifying knowledge that he was utterly helpless now, that the huge outpouring of her *ki* had overwhelmed his entire self and spirit, just as her hands and feet and elbows had paralysed and subdued his body.

Roger Lafarge started to sag down the wall, senses fading even before she hit him one last time, and then there was nothing more. She stepped back, breathing deeply, gradually relaxing the particular muscular controls that made her hands like stone clubs or steel axe-blades. For a few moments she gazed down at the limp figure on the floor, taking the first mental steps towards erasing Roger Lafarge from any degree of emotional memory within her, then she turned away, looked at her watch, put on her shoes, picked up her handbag, walked through the living room and opened the front door of the apartment.

A man in denim overalls was waiting by the lift, a bag of tools in his hand. It was Weng. He glanced up and down the corridor, then moved quickly towards her. As she beckoned him in and closed the door, he said, "We are not leaving, Miss Blaise?"

"No." She led the way through to the bedroom and indicated the unconscious man. "He welched on the deal."

Weng held his breath for a moment, then let it out slowly and looked at her with bland eyes. "I am deeply sorry, Miss Blaise."

She shrugged. "Just forget it. He's been softened up, his confidence is smashed, and I've primed him regarding the Triads. You shouldn't have any trouble opening him up without further damage. Where do you want him?"

Weng glanced about the room, then moved into the dressing room. Here the light came from a single window, and a chaise longue stood near one wall. "On the chaise longue, if you please, Miss Blaise," he said.

Together they carried Lafarge through, then Weng fetched his tool-bag and set it down. "Thank you, Miss Blaise," he murmured politely. "I will report to you at the penthouse when this matter has been dealt with."

* * * *

Roger Lafarge came slowly and painfully back to consciousness, deeply afraid without at first being able to remember why. Then mists of oblivion parted, and he cringed at the confused and fragmented memory of those moments when she had abruptly become another person, taking on a terrifying aspect that seemed physically to shrink him into insignificance, brushing aside his feeble defences, crushing him as if he had been made of paper. There was pain in his side where she had broken a rib, pain in his knee, shoulder, neck, thigh. He tried to move, and found he could not. His sluggish senses told him that he was lying on something soft but not very wide, arms extended above his head, and wrists secured to something with what felt like cord. His legs were bent at the knees, feet resting on the floor and well separated, ankles secured by more cord. Perhaps, he thought, inwardly shuddering, the same cord he had used for Modesty Blaise. His mouth felt strange, and when he tried to open it he found he could not. It was firmly sealed with surgical plaster, and – *Oh Christ, he was naked*! Stark naked, spread-eagled, and horribly, horribly vulnerable! With a great effort he opened his eyes. He was in the dressing room, lying on the chaise longue, but low down on it so that his knees were bent over the end with ankles bound to the two stubby wooden legs. The room was in semi darkness, with the heavy curtains drawn, but there was a curious blue light coming from somewhere a little to his right.

Lafarge managed to lift his aching head a few inches from the chaise longue. He looked with bleary eyes down the length of his naked body, then turned his gaze towards the source of the light, to one side and level with his hips. For a moment he stared uncomprehendingly, then abruptly his whole body was seized in a spasm that locked it rigidly, and he would have screamed aloud if his mouth had not been sealed.

A low table had been placed beside the chaise longue. On it stood a small spirit lamp, its steady blue flame giving the light that had attracted his attention. Beside the lamp stood a rectangular tin box which had probably contained it. This was in use simply as a support for a carving fork laid horizontally across it with the two tines of the fork touching the flame. They were glowing red, and Lafarge had little doubt as to their intended use, in general if not specific terms. Every nerve in his body seemed to curl up and retract at the fearful prospect. His eyes darted about the darkened room, and he turned his head this way and that as far as possible in an attempt to see . . . to see whoever might be there.

Modesty Blaise? Jesus, she had not come prepared with the spirit lamp and carving fork! All she had brought with her was a small handbag! So who . . .? And how long had he been unconscious? When would . . . somebody appear? And then what would . . . happen?

He lay with head lifted in that rigid position and with muscles locked for a full minute, mesmerised by the blue flame of the lamp and the glowing red steel of the fork, then at last his head fell back and his whole body shook as if with malarial rigors. Time passed. Two minutes . . . five. He was alone in the room, and there was not the slightest sound of movement in the apartment.

He closed his eyes, listening, trying to think rationally, trying to get some measure of control over his chaotic and terror-ridden thoughts. Still no sound. The apartment could have been empty. He opened his eyes and again screamed inwardly, body convulsing with shock as he found himself staring into eyes half an arm's length from his own. The face was hidden, except for eyes and mouth, by a black balaclava. A narrow smile that was not really a smile showed something of very white teeth, and the dark eyes were undoubtedly almond-shaped.

Triad! Oh Christ, she had said the Triad, and he thought she was bluffing! He must have been mad to play Modesty Blaise for a sucker! Mad, mad, mad!

The figure moved, straightening up and turning to the low table. It was a man in overalls and wearing gloves, not tall. He picked up the fork and examined it. Lafarge writhed wildly, lifting his head, shaking it, making dreadful whinnying noises behind the plaster gag. The man in the balaclava apparently decided to test the fork's suitability for his purpose, touching the prongs to the table. Wisps of smoke arose, and there was a smell of burning wood. The hooded head nodded slowly in satisfaction, then the tines were held in the flame again to restore the full cherry-red glow.

Lafarge redoubled his efforts to communicate, grunting, wagging his head, jerking his limbs to the extent that his bonds allowed. The almond eyes studied him calmly, then the hooded head moved close to his and a sing-song voice spoke very softly. "We require information you agreed to give Miss Blaise. All information. Persuasion now about to begin. Please indicate when ready to talk by affirmative movement of head."

The mouth smiled, then the man straightened and began to move to a position between Lafarge's well-spread knees. The grunts became frantic, and the chaise longue creaked with the total effort that Lafarge put into repeatedly nodding his head. The man in overalls halted, then moved back and stood with the carving fork held a few inches from Lafarge's eyes. The sing-song voice spoke again, this time with a distinct note of disappointment: "You wish to speak before commencement of persuasion?"

More head nodding and desperate grunts. The man with the red hot carving fork used his free hand to grip the broad strip of plaster sealing Lafarge's mouth and said reluctantly, "When gag is removed, you will begin to speak. You will describe the three persons that we and Miss Blaise wish to know about. You will give their destination. You will give any other information you have concerning them. If we suspect that you are lying, or not telling all, or if you try to call out . . ." the glowing fork waved before Lafarge's eyes, "there will be no more women for you. It is understood?"

A prolonged grunting and frantic nodding of the head. The plaster was ripped away in a single movement, but Lafarge was beyond feeling the pain of it. He sucked in a great breath, eyes on the now fading tines of the fork, and he struggled to speak, breathless, panting, his voice a hoarse and throaty whisper. "I'll tell you . . . I'll tell you . . . don't do anything . . . please . . . just give me a second . . . those three people, two men and a woman . . . yes, I'll tell you . . ."

*   *   *   *

Forty minutes later Modesty sat with Danny Chavasse by the open patio window that gave on to the terrace of the penthouse, a small tape recorder on the table between them. She had changed into slacks and a long-sleeved blouse, and sat relaxed in her chair. Danny could still see on her wrists the faint marks of cords, but he had asked no questions, and was thankful that her eyes showed no sign of strain in the aftermath of whatever had been done to her.

Lafarge's whispering voice had been coming from the recorder for two or three minutes now, jerky and uneven, hoarse with fear. During that time Modesty had spoken only once, when Lafarge described the man on the aeroplane who was either drunk or drugged. Then she had looked at Danny and said quietly, "Willie."

Now the voice on the tape was saying, "That's all . . . I swear to God, all I know. *Everything*! I don't know *where* they were going from Athens! Christ, I'd *tell* you if I did. Look, the money she gave me – it's in the bureau, top drawer – take it, take it! Just don't do anything with that . . . that thing. Please –"

The voice became distorted, then wordless, and was followed only by heavy breathing that sounded nasal. Modesty frowned slightly. "I think Weng's gagged him again," she said. "He was just supposed to give Lafarge a small shot of phenobarbitone to knock him out for a few minutes – time enough for Weng to disappear."

Danny listened to the shaky breathing of the terrified man. "Maybe Weng's picking up the money first," he said.

"Maybe." She half smiled. "I'd forgotten all about the money. Oh God, Danny, I'm so thankful it was Willie. They wouldn't fly him out covertly to Athens and beyond just to kill him. I don't know who they are or what they want with him, but at least there's a good chance he's *alive*, and –"

She broke off as Weng's assumed voice came suddenly from the recorder. "I have the money, Mr. Lafarge. The other payment our friend Miss Blaise made to you cannot be recovered, so we must teach you that those who mistreat our friends will never escape punishment. *So*."

There was a chilling sound from the recorder, a sound that could not fail to be Lafarge screaming through the gag; silence followed except for the hiss of the tape, and complete silence as it was switched off. Modesty stared wide-eyed at Danny Chavasse, then lifted her voice. "Weng! Weng! Get in here *now*!"

He appeared from the kitchen wearing a striped butcher's apron and a look of polite reproach, drying his hands on a towel. "I am at a crucial point of a most complicated recipe, Miss Blaise —"

"Never mind that." She pointed to the recorder. "What did you do to Lafarge?"

He gazed at her with hurt innocence. "Only what you instructed, Miss Blaise."

"Once you'd scared him into talking you were supposed to give him a knockout jab and come home."

"The jab was not necessary, Miss Blaise," Weng said patiently. "I left Mr. Lafarge asleep on the chaise longue, completely free. I even put a blanket over him." Weng contrived to look still more deeply injured. "It was not *I* who damaged him. *I* did not crack his rib and hurt his knee and neck and —"

"Just shut up a minute, Weng." She ran the tape back a short way and replayed the end, with Lafarge's muffled but blood-chilling scream. "What the hell was that?" she demanded grimly.

Weng beamed as if with sudden understanding, "Oh, *that*, Miss Blaise? That was Mr. Lafarge's imagination. I hope you will understand that if a person such as Mr. Lafarge behaves discourteously to you, it reflects upon me as your houseboy, so there was a personal debt to be paid."

She said quietly, "What *exactly* did you do to him, Weng?"

He finished drying his hands and hung the towel over his arm. "When I went to get the money you had given him, Miss Blaise, I also went to the kitchen and took a piece of ice from the fridge." Weng smiled reminiscently. "When I returned, I advised Mr. Lafarge that the Triad must punish him for what he had done, I took the carving fork from the flame, and I rammed the piece of ice into . . ." Weng coughed apologetically, "into his crotch. I think the first impact of intense cold must have felt exactly like intense heat to him — aided by his imagination, of course. It seemed to me to be the kind of retribution Mr. Garvin himself would have devised."

She looked at Danny, then at Weng again, and said, "My God." Then, after a moment, "So he fainted with shock?"

"In seconds, Miss Blaise. I did not have to use the phenobarb."

She nodded slowly and stood up, gazing out over London for a moment or two, then turning to look at Weng once more. "Yes, you're quite right, it's exactly the sort of come-uppance Mr. Garvin would have laid on Lafarge." Her mouth twisted briefly with pain, but she recovered and gave a small smile. "I hope you'll be able to tell Mr.

Garvin about it yourself soon. You did a fine job getting the information, and I'm grateful. Put that two thousand you brought back in your piggy bank, Weng."

"Thank you, Miss Blaise." He turned to go, then paused. "I have *assumed* that Mr. Lafarge fainted from shock," he said reflectively, "but for all I know he may have had a fatal heart attack." Weng smiled broadly at the thought. "Well, I must return to my recipe," he said. "I hope you have not ruined it, Miss Blaise."

8

D r. Janos Tyl sat on one of the sun-warmed stone tiers that sloped
back in semicircles from the ancient flagstones forming the
stage of the small Greek theatre at the eastern end of Kalivari.
The theatre had been built more than two thousand years before by
Antigonus, one of the heirs to Alexander's empire, who had planned to
develop the island as a private retreat. Why he had begun with the
theatre was unknown; why the plan had ended with the theatre was
owed to the fact that he went to war against an alliance composed of
other heirs of Alexander, among whom was Seleucus, who had swapped
India for a troop of war elephants. These played a substantial part in
bringing about the defeat and death of Antigonus at the battle of Ipsus,
leaving the handful of peasants and goats on Kalivari with a theatre and
nothing else.

Some four centuries later the Roman emperor Hadrian restored the
theatre, mainly because building and restoring theatres was a hobby of
his. As far as was known, total performances given at the theatre on
Kalivari could probably be numbered on two hands. This number
would not have included the kind of performance now in progress,
neither would it have included any of the scenarios devised by Dr.
Thaddeus Pilgrim and his colleagues which had taken place here since
they had leased the island.

Scattered about the amphitheatre seats were a dozen men and two
women, all operatives of the Hostel of Righteousness. Dr. Tyl wore his
brown monk's robe because he found it comfortable. The others were
lightly dressed in casual summer wear or training clothes, but all had a
monk's robe to hand in accordance with the strict rules of the
community, ready to put on if a boat were sighted from the permanently manned lookout station.

Dr. Tyl glanced about him, studying faces, more interested in the
reactions of the spectators than in what they were watching. There
was little variation in those reactions. All eyes were intent and

professionally appraising, most faces held a look of respect touched by wonder, and the murmured exchanges held a note of admiration.

From the stage came the clangour of metal on metal and the swift shuffle of feet on the great flagstones. Sibyl Pray and Kazim were in combat there, but in a manner which rolled back twenty centuries. Each wore the helmet and body armour of a Roman gladiator; a bronze cuirass covering breast and back, buckled to a gorget protecting the neck and to several half hoops forming a pauldron to protect the right shoulder – the shoulder of the sword-arm. Each wore a knee-length skirt made from narrow plates of bronze linked internally by flexible leather. The left leg only (the advanced leg for a right-handed warrior) was armoured with greave and cuisse.

They were fighting with short, flat-bladed swords and round shields of bull hide edged with bronze, replicas of the standard equipment of the Roman gladiator. Dr. Tyl sat pondering the nature of the drive that gave these two so huge an obsession with combat and weaponry. Their skill was undoubtedly dazzling, for they were moving fast about the stage, blades whirling, cutting, thrusting; footwork impeccable, point and edge clanking noisily against shield or armour, so that the whole impression was one of mortal combat. Yet Dr. Tyl knew that the mind tutored in this field, unlike his own, could perceive that attacks and ripostes where blades struck armour were fully delivered; but where a stroke menaced any unguarded part of limb or body, that stroke was stopped short with less than an inch to spare. It was like karate practice, in which the blows or kicks stop fractionally before the point of contact, except that much finer judgement and faster reaction was called for here.

Tyl had watched Sibyl Pray and Kazim play similar roles in a variety of combat disciplines, many as pointless in his view as this revival of a battle style two thousand years old, though he grudgingly supposed that any practice in sharpening reactions and tuning muscles must be of some general benefit. He glanced at the man sitting beside him wearing a dark shirt and slacks. Willie Garvin was watching the workout with an abstracted air. The part of him that lived in the strange dream world he now inhabited was professionally interested in a remarkable demonstration of skills in which he was himself expert. The part of him that had died in the belief that Modesty Blaise was dead had no capacity for interest in anything, only a fixed and zombie-like purpose.

124

Dr. Tyl nodded towards the combatants on the stage below and said, "Pretty good, Willie, huh?"

He nodded. "They're better than good."

"You don't remember them? Sibyl Pray and Kazim?"

He shook his head slowly, frowning. "No. Can't say I took to 'em much when they turned up the other day."

Tyl smiled. "That's part of the amnesia, Willie. Your emotions get distorted. They're good friends of yours, Sibyl and Kazim."

Willie Garvin nodded indifferently. Then he said, "Have we located Delilah yet?"

"We're getting close, Willie. Be patient. We've infiltrated a man right inside her organisation, but he has to play the hand very carefully."

On the stage, Sibyl Pray and Kazim had stepped back by mutual consent and were saluting each other to signal the end of the workout. Willie said, "All you got to do is tell me where Delilah is."

"That's not the way Modesty would want you to play it," said Tyl positively. "Delilah's well protected, Willie. Go up against her on her own territory, and you could easily be dead before you get to her. We're going to have her come after you, so you'll meet eyeball to eyeball. Then it will be up to you."

Willie shrugged and said, "Okay."

Sibyl and Kazim came climbing the steps. They were sweating, breathing a little quickly, and looking at Willie with an interest that might have puzzled him if he had not been entirely indifferent towards them. The woman said, "Did you like it, Willie?"

"Sure. Great." His manner was barely civil. He stood up, frowning, then said, "What's *The Network* doing? What operations 'ave we got running?"

Kazim put a hand on his arm and said, "Forget it, Willie. We're taking care of all that. You just concentrate on Delilah."

"Yeah. I will when I get the chance." Willie turned away. "I'm going for a swim."

They watched him climb the deep steps of the amphitheatre and disappear along the path leading down to the small sandy bay. "I do not like that one," said Sibyl Pray. "It would be a great pleasure to kill him."

Kazim said, "That is my feeling also. Garvin has a way of ignoring other persons which is highly insulting." He looked a question at Tyl.

"Do you think he will bring Dr. Pilgrim's scenario to a satisfactory conclusion by killing the Blaise woman?"

Tyl smiled jovially. "Garvin is primed, and Blaise herself will be the detonator. If he is fast enough and accurate enough with those knives of his, then she will certainly die."

"We have watched him practise," said Sibyl resentfully, "and in that particular skill he is beyond belief. It is a great pity. If he failed to kill Blaise, then Kazim and I could have one each."

With a touch of awe, Tyl considered the muscularity of the thigh showing beneath her skirt as she stood with one foot raised to rest on a high step. "It would not disturb you to be up against a man whose skill you have just praised so highly?" he asked.

Sibyl's white teeth showed in a laugh. "My praise was restricted to his knife-throwing skill, Dr. Tyl. I would like to meet him in unarmed combat. We have watched him at exercise, and he is lethargic, lacking in dedication. I would guarantee to break two of his limbs within sixty seconds."

"Perhaps less," agreed Kazim.

Tyl shrugged. He suspected there were areas of Willie Garvin that even he had not plumbed, and he doubted that apparent lethargy and lack of dedication were true reflections of Garvin's capacity, but he did not voice this doubt. "Let us see how the scenario works out," he said, lifting his face to the afternoon sun. "Whatever happens, I am sure Dr. Pilgrim will have a further interesting suggestion to make. He is a truly creative man."

Down in the bay Willie Garvin lay floating with eyes closed, hands behind his head, trying to force his sluggish mind to work coherently. The thoughts that drifted through his head were nebulous, and he could not get them to come clear; they were scarcely thoughts at all, mostly just feelings. It had been much the same through all the years before Modesty Blaise had found him, but from that moment the very fabric of his being was changed and he had become a complete human being, a totally happy man. Now she was dead, and the grey mists had engulfed him again, blanketing his mind. He disliked, even hated, his old friends of *The Network* here on Kalivari, and there was nothing in the world that he wanted – except the one thing that was now the core of his life, to find and destroy Delilah. Even the hazy thought of her sent murderous rage spurting through his body so that his eyes jerked open and his muscles tensed for action.

The image of her took shape in his mind's eye, the image instilled by colour slides and Tyl's insistent murmuring. Black hair drawn up in a chignon, striking face, quiet eyes of midnight blue; strange to think that those eyes could hide such appalling cruelty. Without knowing how he knew, Willie Garvin recalled what this woman had done to Modesty Blaise before killing her, and a cry of anguish broke from him. He turned on his front and swam furiously for ten minutes to neutralise the massive injection of adrenalin that rage and hatred had released into his blood.

At last he floated again, striving for calm. Somewhere, at some time, in a desert somewhere, he thought muzzily, he had been taught the ways of achieving mental balance . . . and other strange abilities, too. She had sent him there. Where was it? And the man . . . very old . . . Indian . . . ?

Despite the sea, sweat broke out on his body as he struggled to remember, but at last he shook his head in despair. It was no use. Nothing would come back. For the moment that sudden surge of hatred was past, but he was left with a feeling of wrongness. Surely she . . . surely the Princess never went in for revenge, did she? Reckoned it was . . . harmful to you in some way. So why was he going to kill Delilah?

Perhaps he was remembering wrongly. But no. He must kill Delilah. Garcia had said Mam'selle would want that. He couldn't stop himself now, anyway. Even if he wished to. And he didn't. The rage flared briefly in him again. With an effort he conjured up a mental picture of the Princess, of Modesty Blaise, to keep his mind from Delilah.

Modesty Blaise . . . with the greenish-grey eyes and short curly chestnut hair, and . . .

A spasm of unease shook him, and again he had a sense of wrongness. How was it possible that he seemed to know, that his body seemed to know, he had made love many times to Modesty Blaise with the grey-green eyes and chestnut hair? A deeper knowledge told him that this could never have been so, because . . . because it was . . . because it would have changed a perfect pattern? The concept dissolved in his mind before he could examine it, and he pressed the heels of his hands to his eyes in confusion, whispering aloud, "Christ, I just can't think straight, Princess . . . don't know where I am . . ."

Again he turned on his front and began to swim at an easy pace towards the shore, trying to keep his mind blank now. Perhaps, he thought vaguely, Garcia was right, and everything would become clear once he had killed Delilah. That was what Garcia kept insisting.

*   *   *   *

Thaddeus Pilgrim stirred a spoonful of ground glass into the tray holding the jackdaw's birdseed, then carefully clipped the tray back inside the cage. He did not quite recall when and why he had decided to kill the bird in this fashion, and did not anticipate deriving any particular gratification from the event. It was simply a small scenario which had involuntarily presented itself to him, and he was now far beyond the point where he questioned such scenarios or pondered what motive might prompt them.

"How very interesting, Mrs. Ram," he said. "One might almost say how *extraordinarily* interesting. If Modesty Blaise is now in Athens, as you report, it would seem to indicate – though of course one must be wary of making too ready assumptions – it would, as I say, *seem* to indicate that she has traced our – ah, our guest, Mr. Garvin, thus far. Have you as yet formulated any . . ." he waved a hand as if groping for the word, and sank into his chair, "any theory as to how she may have encompassed this?"

"I have report from London that she visited and spent one night with the pilot, Lafarge," said Mrs. Ram briskly. "It is my opinion he disclosed to her the destination to which he brought Sibyl Pray, Kazim, and Mr. Garvin – the last under sedation."

"I can see no harm in our adopting that as a working theory," said Thaddeus Pilgrim cautiously, eyes fixed vacantly on the jackdaw. "And if, as you say – oh, you will understand that I am not doubting the *accuracy* of your report, Mrs. Ram, I am simply using the appropriate grammatical construction – if, as you say, she has been making enquiries in and around Athens for three days now, it would not be imprudent to assume that she knows no more than that Mr. Garvin and his escort terminated their flight there."

"That is my view, Dr. Pilgrim," agreed Mrs. Ram. "It renders unnecessary the proposal I intended to suggest for your approval as to method of attracting Modesty Blaise to this location. She is already in Athens, and since Dr. Tyl assures us that Mr. Garvin is fully primed for instant killing, we now have only to ensure arrival of Modesty Blaise

128

here at appropriate time and under such circumstances as will ensure first-class performance of scenario."

Thaddeus Pilgrim wagged his head gravely. "That may well tax your ingenuity, dear lady. It is required that she should come here alone, at a particular time of night, under no constraints, and without anybody at all knowing her intention. Exacting requirements, I fear." Even if Dr. Pilgrim had been psychologically capable of fear, he would not, despite his words, have feared that the requirements might be impossible to meet. Mrs. Ram was a superb administrator, skilled in assessing information and devising plans based on such assessment. Also she was showing no sign of unease, which meant she was fully confident that whatever she had devised was sound.

"Following study of detailed dossiers," she announced, "copies of which have been provided by Salamander Four organisation at cost of fifteen thousand dollars, Dr. Tyl has made positive statement that it is psychologically certain Miss Blaise will *knowingly* enter a trap in order to reach Mr. Garvin, relying on her abilities and experience to effect later extrication. Therefore scenario requires only that we present her with opportunity so to do."

"To . . . ah, to enter our trap, Mrs. Ram?"

"Precisely so, Dr. Pilgrim. Approach must be subtle, of course, but dossiers have provided data enabling us to feed information to Modesty Blaise via a source she will deem to be totally trustworthy." She referred to her clipboard. "There is a male person named Krolli, a Greek who was one of her chief lieutenants in the days of *The Network*. He is no longer engaged in crime, but retains many contacts. Modesty Blaise has been seeking him, but he has been away on a business trip to America and is due back this evening. It is certain she will ask him to secure news of Mr. Garvin, and I have arranged that appropriate news be fed to Krolli from a source under our control within forty-eight hours."

With the tendrils of his mind that were present in the study, Thaddeus Pilgrim reflected that in certain ways Mrs. Ram quite resembled the jackdaw, and with this thought floated the vague speculation, unsupported by intention, as to what effect a good dose of ground glass might have upon her. "From what you tell me," he said tentatively, "it appears that I would not be wrong, not even perhaps optimistic, were I to anticipate the completion of our little scenario within a few days now, dear lady."

Mrs. Ram smiled. "I was hoping to effect culmination on the sabbath," she said, and touched her thigh where long ago she had been branded as his acolyte. "Just for old times' sake, Doctor."

✵   ✵   ✵   ✵

Modesty Blaise sat by the window of her room in the small hotel amid the winding alleys and flower filled courtyards of Plaka, the old quarter of Athens. It was late evening, and she was making the second of her two daily calls to Danny Chavasse at her penthouse in London.

"I'm leaving in a few minutes to see Krolli again," she said. "He rang just now and he's got something for me but I don't know what. I'm to meet him in Piraeus, and I'm to be ready to go on from there, which I take to mean that I'm to be fully equipped. It's promising, Danny. You know Krolli. He wouldn't trigger me without good reason."

That was true, thought Danny, gazing down sombrely at his hopeless position in the game of chess he had been trying to play against Weng. Krolli had been with her from the beginning, had been with her in the smalltime Louche gang when she was in her teens, when the gang was almost destroyed and she had taken over its remnants, fought off take-overs by bigger gangs, and laid the foundations of *The Network*. In time she had made Krolli leader of the task force that protected the organisation, and despite his being a macho Greek he had served her faithfully in the style she demanded of her people.

Years later, when she wound up *The Network*, it was Krolli who had taken over the Aegean area of operations, with her permission but against her advice. It did not last. Krolli was betrayed by his second-in-command, Lascaris, who disapproved of Krolli's refusing a contract killing job, and as a result Krolli ended up as a prisoner in Yugoslavia, sentenced to ten years in a labour battalion.

By a remarkable operation, Modesty and Willie had brought him safely out – not for Krolli's sake, for there was no debt owed, but simply because he had information they badly needed at the time. The last Danny had heard through the grapevine was that Lascaris was dead by an unknown hand, and Krolli had set himself up in legitimate business exporting olive oil.

Yes, what she said was true as far as it went. Krolli was too well trained and too experienced to set Mam'selle off on an operation of this importance unless he was sure she was heading in the right direction. Even so . . .

"How did Krolli sound?" Danny said into the phone.

There was a hesitation, then a shrug in her voice as she said, "Uneasy. He doesn't like it, but I can't help that."

Danny felt sweat on his palms and said, "What doesn't he like?"

"He doesn't know, Danny. He's been given a contact who knows something but will only deal with me."

Danny said, "My God, I don't like it either. Look, I hate your being on your own. Why not stall till I get out there?"

"No." Her voice was sharp. "I need you there in London as a communications centre, Danny. We've got inquiries out everywhere, and I can't risk losing information from other sources if this doesn't work out. Besides, I can always call on Krolli if I need another pair of hands. I'm sure he'd help."

"I'm sure too," said Danny. He kept the wryness out of his voice. Krolli was a fighting man and he, Danny, was not, but she had not made that point. "Okay," he said. "I'll carry on here, but I'll expect calls twice daily from you. Nine a.m. and nine p.m. or as soon after as possible."

"Yes, don't worry, I'll keep reporting. Have you heard from Steve or Dinah?"

Danny gave a little sigh. "One or other of the Colliers phones about four times a day. Can I please tell them you may have a lead? They badly need a shot of hope, Modesty – even if it comes to nothing."

After a moment or two she said, "Yes, all right. Tell them, and give them my love. Is there anything else?"

It was Danny's turn to hesitate. He rubbed a damp palm on his trouser knee and said, "I think you may be going down some sort of pipeline after Willie. Suppose you . . . suppose you stop reporting, Modesty? What do you want me to do?"

In the small hotel under the shadow of the Acropolis she stood by the table in the black tunic, slacks and boots that were her combat rig, mentally checking the items laid out on the table. "If I go absent, Danny," she said, "there's nothing for you to do except keep sending good vibes." She glanced through the open window at the rising moon. "I have to go now. Don't forget to phone Steve, and help him all you can with Dinah. She's a great worrier. 'Bye now."

The line went dead. Danny put the phone down, grimaced, and said,

"She's got a lead, but it smells like a trap to me. And to her."

Weng nodded slowly. "If it offers the slightest hope of reaching Mr. Garvin," he said, "then Miss Blaise will spring it."

"That's right," Danny Chavasse said tiredly. "And the only thing I have to do now is convince Dinah Collier that it's all going to work out fine. But she knows our lady as well as we do, Weng, and she's not going to bloody well believe me."

*   *   *   *

Krolli said, "I urge you not to go, Mam'selle. I feel responsible."

He sat behind the wheel of his car, parked near his beach bungalow at Glyfada. Krolli was a dark haired, powerful man in his early forties. He held a pencil torch with the beam directed on a map Modesty Blaise was studying in the passenger seat beside him. She looked up and said, "The responsibility's all mine, Krolli. Just go over it again, please."

He sighed and clicked off the torch. "I put out feelers through my contacts, as you asked, Mam'selle. After not very long, something comes back to me, but not direct. It is third or fourth hand. If anybody wishes to know something about Willie Garvin, let that person come alone to a particular rendezvous at a particular time tonight." Krolli shrugged. "It may not be reliable, and if it is reliable then it is almost certainly a trap. Better that you let me keep the appointment, Mam'selle. I will deal with whoever comes to the rendezvous, and screw the truth out of them. Then we can —"

"No, Krolli, no. They'll use a cut-out, perhaps more than one, and it's no use you sticking your knife against somebody's throat and telling them to talk if they don't know anything. I have to play this straight."

After a moment or two he said reluctantly, "Well . . . yes. But let me play it for you, Mam'selle. I owe you a big one, and I am not over the hill."

She shook her head. "There was a time when you got in the way of a bullet meant for me, Krolli, and it was no accident. You owe me nothing, even if we were counting, so thanks for the offer but I have to play this myself, because if it *is* a trap then it's me they want, not you, so I'm the only one who can spring it."

He sighed again. "Okay, Mam'selle. In half an hour from now I will drop you at the rendezvous." He switched on the torch again and pointed with a finger. "It is here, a turn-off from the coast road a few miles before Vouliagmeni. The instructions are that the person must be left at the top of the hill alone, and will be picked up there. It is permitted that the person be armed," Krolli lifted his chin to indicate contempt, "in order to show that the other party has no bad intention towards the person. I don't have much faith in that, Mam'selle. They could be lying in wait with submachine-guns."

"I can't believe it's a straightforward killing they want," she said briskly, "and let's not be pessimistic, Krolli. It's always possible that somebody is ready to pass on information about Willie, but is too scared to do it except under close wraps."

Krolli wrinkled his nose and said, "But you have a gun, Mam'selle?"

"Yes." She tapped the hip holster, hidden by her tunic and bearing a Star PD .45 automatic. "I'm well equipped."

Krolli put away the torch and folded the map. "There is no way I can tail you from that rendezvous without being seen," he said worriedly. "If there was time we could hide a bug on you and set up directional aerials."

She said gently, "Krolli."

He bit his lip, angry with himself for saying something so pointless. In the old days she would have snapped his head off for it. Her *Network* people did not waste time and energy thinking of what might be done if only the situation was not as it was. He said, "I'm sorry, Mam'selle. Is there anything you want me to do after I've dropped you at the rendezvous?"

She thought for a while, then said, "If I haven't made contact with you by noon tomorrow, ring Danny Chavasse at my London home and put him in the picture. You have the number?"

"Sure I have it. Just tell Danny the score? No instructions?"

"No instructions. We all know I'm going down a hole after Willie, and there's nothing anyone else can do but wait and see if I come out with him. How long to get me to the rendezvous?"

"Twenty minutes, easy."

"Let's go, then. We can wait at the turn-off if we're early. And thanks for your help, Krolli."

He reached forward to switch on the engine. "I hope to God you tell me that again later, Mam'selle," he said fervently.

At noon next day, when Krolli phoned Danny Chavasse, she was on a fishing boat manned by two Greeks, heading southwest through the Cyclades at eight knots, using mental techniques to keep her mind empty and free from impatience.

Five minutes after Krolli had dropped her at the rendezvous, a small van had appeared, the driver beckoning her to take the seat beside him. When she asked where they were going he had shaken his head, and had remained silent during the hour's drive that followed, a drive which first took them inland, then wound back to the coast by small roads. Here was the first cut-out, a taxi waiting at a road junction. At a sign from the driver of the van she climbed out and got into the back of the taxi. Half an hour later it pulled off the road by a stand of trees. The driver signed for her to get out, and drove off when she had done so.

She waited in the dark, arms folded, listening. Soon a man appeared dressed in denim trousers and a jersey, smelling of salt water and fish. She spoke to him in Greek, but apart from telling her to follow him he made no response. At the bottom of a cliff path beyond the stand of trees was a small bay with a fishing boat lying close inshore. An inflatable dinghy lay beached. He rowed her out to the boat, another fisherman leaned down to help her scramble on to the deck, then the two men hauled the inflatable aboard. A minute later they were heading out of the bay under sail.

The younger of the two fishermen, who had brought her down from the cliff, said to the other, "She speaks Greek."

The older man looked at her and nodded. "We sail for twenty-four hours," he said in a gruff voice. "We cannot answer questions. There is a bed for you in the cabin. We have food. Cheese and olives, smoked fish, bread, fruit, wine, halva. You want to eat tonight?"

She shook her head. These were genuine fishermen, hired for the job as the other cut-outs had probably been. "Just some water, please," she said.

"Yes. There are bottles of natural mineral water in the cabin."

"Thank you."

He indicated himself and the younger man, who was at the wheel now. "Do not be afraid to sleep. We are respectable persons. We will remain on deck."

She nodded. "I won't be afraid to sleep. Goodnight."

In the tiny cabin she took off her tunic, gunbelt, and other accessories, removed the kongo from the club of hair tied at the nape of her neck, and stretched out on the bunk. There was no doubt in her mind but that the fishermen were indeed 'respectable persons' as claimed, simply hired through a cut-out for this job. The older man had said twenty-four hours, and she believed him. An island seemed the most likely destination; that made sense as a base for whoever had taken Willie Garvin, but she was baffled by this present set-up, and would have been troubled, if she had allowed herself to be, by her almost total lack of information.

She had no idea in the world as to who had taken Willie Garvin, or why, apart from Lafarge's description of a blonde woman and an olive-skinned man, both impressive sexual athletes. It was fairly certain that the same people who had ordered Willie's capture were responsible for feeding Krolli with the information that had brought her to the bay and the waiting fishing boat, but she could imagine no plausible reason for the method they were adopting. A straightforward snatch, as with Willie, was what she would have expected if they wanted her. Instead they had set an obvious trap, yet were allowing her to walk into it fully armed.

Whoever they were, they must have known about her *Network* connection with Krolli, known they could offer their bait through him, and known that if need be she would spring their trap to reach Willie. It was not encouraging to have no information at all about your opponents while they knew so much about yourself, and she had to quell a stirring of unease. Why the long delay, she wondered, between Willie's disappearance and this tempting bait dangled before her once she reached Athens? Why hadn't they dangled a lure before her days ago in England, if they wanted her here? What would they have done if she had not got as far as Athens by her own efforts?

She lay examining the many questions, deciding at last that further speculation was fruitless. Time alone would reveal the answers, or some of them, perhaps. The core of her hope was that in twenty-four hours she would see Willie Garvin, alive and unhurt. Certainly he would be a prisoner, and it was probable that she would become one also, since the opposition held all the initiative. But the important thing was to be with Willie Garvin. What happened next would depend quite simply upon how, together, they coped with whatever the opposition had in store for them.

So be it. She closed her eyes and began the breathing rhythm and mental process that would send her to sleep within minutes. Once during the night she woke and looked out from the doorway of the little cabin. The older man was at the wheel, the other asleep on a canvas mattress on the deck. It was a clear calm night, but the wind had moved and the boat was under power now, its engine throbbing slowly. She did not have to check the stars to know that their heading was south-east. It was her gift to possess a sense of location that worked both on the smallest and largest scale, so that she could pinpoint herself in the maze of an Arab *souk* or in terms of the planetary grid. Willie Garvin claimed that she could be put down blindfold in the Pacific or the Sahara, and after a few minutes of reflection could give a map reference for her location correct to within fifty miles.

By morning the boat had changed course slightly, but this was to take advantage of the wind. Throughout the day she sat on deck on a pile of nets, asking no questions, making an amiable comment from time to time, responding to similar advances from the fishermen, complimenting them on the food and wine offered, and going through a sequence of physical exercises for half an hour in every two.

At dusk she went to the cabin to sleep. The younger fisherman called her shortly before midnight and she dressed quickly, winding her hair into a club that concealed the kongo, and checking her gun and accessories. When she emerged on deck the boat was hove-to, lifting gently to small waves, and in the light of a lamp above the cabin housing the younger man was manoeuvring the inflatable dinghy over the side.

When it splashed into the sea he held it on a short line, beckoned Modesty, and pointed west, where a small green light showed intermittently at ten second intervals. At first the light seemed to be impossibly high, but then she picked up the loom of land rising from the sea, and realised that the signal came from a cliff top, little more than half a mile away.

The younger fisherman said, "You row towards the light. There is a small beach, and a path leading up. At the top you will find the man you wish to see." He spoke the words without expression, as if he had learned them by heart.

She said, "What island is it?"

He shrugged. "We cannot answer questions. You must go now, please."

"All right." A thought occurred to her as she was about to turn away, and she paused. "Take a word of advice. As soon as I've gone, put out your lights and head east for a good while before turning north for home. It's possible that the people who paid you may not want you to be able to tell anybody where you've taken me tonight."

The man looked uneasy in the light of the lamp, and glanced towards his companion. She said, "Don't waste time, just do it as a safety measure." Turning, she swung a leg over the low rail and slid down into the dinghy. As she unclipped the oars the fisherman released the line, and in seconds the two craft had drifted apart. By the time she had located the green light, turned the inflatable and begun to row, the fishing boat was lost in darkness.

* * * *

Willie Garvin moved along the path running from west to east on the spine of Kalivari. Garcia had woken him half an hour ago and was walking beside him, which made Willie uneasy. He and Garcia had once been close friends, but now it was different. Garcia himself seemed strangely different, even though in speech and manner he was almost effusively friendly. As they reached the upper rim of the amphitheatre and stood looking down the central aisle between the stone tiers, Willie noted that almost the whole population of the island seemed to be here, scattered around the seats. They were completely silent, and barely visible in the pale starlight, but their presence irritated him.

"Why's all this lot 'ere?" he said dourly.

"They want to see it, Willie." Now that the moment was near, Tyl found himself almost overcome with excitement at the knowledge that his most recent piece of work would shortly reach a climax. He had taken Garvin's mind and manipulated it as a potter moulds clay, re-shaping, wiping out memory, creating false memory, instilling and nourishing a huge hatred, and priming this man in readiness for the spark that would cause him to explode, to kill by instant reaction. "Delilah is coming, Willie," he said. "It's just the way we planned. And all these are *Network* people. They want to see you destroy the monster who tortured Modesty Blaise to death."

"All right." Willie's voice creaked with fury. "Just see they don't get in my way."

"You needn't worry," Tyl said soothingly, "she's all yours, Willie."

They passed the place where Dr. Pilgrim himself was sitting flanked by Sibyl and Kazim on one side, Mrs. Ram on the other. Of all the people there, only Thaddeus Pilgrim and Dr. Tyl wore their monk's robes, while Mrs. Ram wore the female white, as always. At the point where the stone tiers gave way to the flags of the stage, Tyl halted Willie with a touch on his arm. "This is the place," he said softly. "She'll be coming soon from that direction." He pointed to the rear of the stage, where steps led down to the backstage area and the cliff path. "Delilah will be coming in just a few minutes now, and we'll put the lights on so you can see her, Willie. Then you kill her, you understand? Then you kill her." His voice was rhythmic and monotonous. "When she comes the lights go on. You see her, you kill her. All you have to do now is wait a little while, just a little while . . ."

Tyl let his voice fade and drew back towards the tiers of seats, then turned and mounted the steps to join Thaddeus Pilgrim, taking the seat in front of him and leaning back to whisper, "The scenario is about to take place, Dr. Pilgrim."

"A splendid atmosphere, quite splendid," Thaddeus Pilgrim murmured benignly. "I look forward with keen interest to the outcome, as I am sure we all do. Allowing Miss – ah, Blaise to retain her gun adds a touch of suspense, I feel. It is always possible, I suppose, that in self defence she *may* react quickly enough to shoot Mr. Garvin . . . though there would, of course, be a profound inhibition *against* this, an inhibition not reflected in Mr. Garvin, naturally, from whom you have so skilfully removed it, and who will undoubtedly have the advantage of surprise. However, we shall see. We shall see . . ."

His murmuring voice faded. On the edge of the stage below, Willie Garvin stood facing away across the circle of flagstones, eyes almost closed. His shirt was unbuttoned to the waist, exposing the twin knives in their sheaths, strapped on his left breast. His right hand moved to touch the hilts, lifting gently to ensure that they would draw freely and smoothly, then he was still again.

After the long and complex indoctrination, the moment Tyl had worked for was about to come, and most of Willie Garvin's mind was inactive, asking no questions of itself, void of curiosity, focused on one purpose only, to see the hated face that had been burned into his memory, the face of Delilah, to see the black hair, midnight blue eyes, high cheekbones . . . and to send his knife driving into the long column of her throat.

9

She had not needed the flashlight at her belt to find the cliff path leading up from the beach. For the first two hundred feet of height it wound back and forth across the steep slope, but then the ground flattened into a gentle rise, and the path ran straight up through a scattering of low trees.

Twice she stopped to listen, but heard nothing beyond the natural sounds of the night. A little way ahead now she could make out a row of taller trees across what appeared to be the top of the path. No . . . the trunks were too much alike and too evenly spaced for trees. They were pillars, one broken off short, the remains of some Greek temple perhaps; there were plenty of such ruins to be found throughout the Aegean.

'*At the top you will find the man you wish to see,*' the fisherman had said, repeating without comprehension the words he had been told to speak. She paused and drew in a deep breath, repeating a mantra in her head to blanket her imagination and ease the tension building within her. Soon, she knew, the trap would be sprung, and she wanted to have no preconceived notion of its shape, for this would hamper her reaction. There was fear to be subdued, too, fear born of the thought that if she found Willie Garvin in the next few moments she might find him dead, or in a situation of horror . . . maimed, tortured, crucified, it was impossible to know what the unknown enemies had done or planned to do.

When she had wiped all such speculation from her mind she lifted the edge of her tunic to clear the butt of the Star .45 automatic and to ease it in the holster, then she moved steadily on up the path. All she knew, all she could possibly know, was that if and when she found Willie Garvin in the darkness ahead he would not be a free agent. Something else, something shapeless but hostile, must surely be waiting for her.

Thirty seconds later she passed slowly and warily up a few stone steps and between two pillars to find herself on a flat area. The light from the moon was now cut off by what appeared to be the rim of a very high wall some distance ahead. Again she halted, taking a moment to realise that this was no wall but a steep upward slope like . . . like an amphitheatre. Abruptly the whole scene was bathed in light from two lamps mounted high on either side of the ancient flagstone stage where she stood. The light was soft and diffused, as if the lamps might be screened by coarse mesh, and her eyes adjusted quickly.

Willie Garvin stood facing her, eight paces away, wearing a dark shirt and slacks, blue eyes fixed on her with a kind of recognition but with a searing enmity that was like a physical blow, and his hand was moving, flashing towards the hilt of one of the knives showing at his chest, and his lips were drawn back from his teeth in a rictus of bitter hatred.

In the moment that followed she had no time for reasoned thought; there was only a degree of knowing without understanding, instinctive and immediate. This was a set-up, long and carefully planned; Willie Garvin had suffered some form of mind-bending; Willie Garvin had been primed to kill her; these three things she knew as if they had been carved in stone, knew them simply by the half-second sight of him since the lights had come on. His arm had risen for the throw, the blade glinting, and it did not cross her mind to try to draw her gun, or throw herself to one side. She had seen Willie Garvin in action too often not to know that his aim would follow her movement.

Without conscious decision she stood quite still, extending her arms quickly to the spreadeagled pose familiar to him from his circus act, and as his hand flashed forward she said without urgency, "Willie love, it's me."

Such was the knife's speed that she glimpsed only a flicker of movement through the air, but she felt the wind of its passing, even felt the Gerber Armorhide hilt with its sharkskin-like texture graze the side of her neck as the blade passed within a quarter of an inch of the flesh; then from somewhere behind her came the clatter of steel as the knife struck one of the columns and fell.

Willie's second knife was already in his hand, but although he was crouched a little, poised to throw, his arm had not lifted and he was frozen in mid-movement. She said again, "Willie love, it's me, Modesty."

The knife slipped from his fingers, and slowly he lifted both hands to clutch at his head. A wordless sound broke from his throat, and he reeled as if from the impact of some soundless explosion, then he was stumbling slowly towards her, eyes wide with fear, horror, shock and confusion.

"Princess . . . ? Princess . . . ? Princess . . . ?" he muttered dazedly. "You? They said she killed you . . . Delilah . . . no, you . . . I mean . . . oh Christ, what's 'appening?"

She had started towards him as the knife fell from his hand, knowing there must be watchers beyond the lights, knowing that her gun was useless since she was surely outnumbered and out-gunned by whoever had organised this complex yet incomprehensible set-up, knowing that the first part at least of their plan had failed, and that as a result she and Willie might be cut down by bullets in the next second. But to this she had no power of response, and for the moment all that mattered, if she lived, was to help Willie Garvin through the horror of whatever had been done to him.

He was reaching out towards her, face twisted with the huge effort of fighting the panic that tore at him, his whole body juddering as he croaked, "I'm sorry, Princess . . . I nearly . . . oh, God . . . I thought . . . thought you were . . . they said . . ."

His legs gave way as she reached him, and she sank to her knees with him, one arm about his body, the other hand at the back of his head, holding him with his face pressed to her shoulder, his cheek against hers as she whispered to him, "It's all right, Willie love. I'm here now. I've got you. Don't think. Don't try to work it out yet. It's me holding you, Willie love. Just take it easy. Give yourself time. Willie, do you know it's me? Modesty?"

She felt his head nod against her. His body was rigid as iron, even the flesh seemed hard, and he was clinging to her so tightly in his desperation that it was difficult for her to draw breath, but she kept gently patting his back, kneading the back of his neck, and did not try to ease his grip as she whispered on, staring beyond him to where she could detect movement now on the tiers of the amphitheatre. People were stirring, a lot of people.

She had been in action with Willie Garvin many times, and knew his quality. She had twice seen him engaged against impossible odds, with certain death seemingly only seconds away, fighting without hope but without despair, every lightning move controlled and reasoned by a superb brain backed by a peerless instinct, with all fear and pain and

141

potential panic not only under total mental control, but transmuted into useful energy.

Yet now Willie Garvin knelt clinging to her like a frightened child, because this was different. These people had invaded his mind, the core of his being, which made him what he was, twisting and shaping it to their own ends; and nothing in the world could be more terrifying, more destructive. She stared towards the movements in the darkness, and as Willie's body shivered against her she was swept by a fury and loathing that burned through her like fire, and her hand twitched to begin moving towards the gun at her hip before reason stopped the movement almost before it had begun.

Then a light went on at the top of the amphitheatre and she saw thirty or forty people standing or moving amid the lower tiers on either side of the central aisle, two or three women among them, one woman in a white robe, two of the men in brown robes, like monks. Four of the men held submachine-guns trained on the stage where she knelt holding Willie, and instinctively she braced herself for the possibility that they might open fire. Then one of the brown-robed figures spoke in the polite and tentative manner of a vicar soliciting alms.

"Ah . . . good evening, Miss Blaise. We should be grateful, indeed most grateful, if you would refrain from considering any action which might be construed as hostile, if you take my meaning, and which might thereby induce responsive action on the part of my colleagues."

She made no move, gave no answer, but began whispering to Willie again as she held him close. "We're staying alive for the moment, Willie love. That's a good start. I know your poor old mind has taken a beating, but I'm here with you now and you'll soon be fine again. Don't struggle, don't think too hard. I'll take care of everything. I've got you now, Willie love. Don't be afraid . . ."

She was still whispering when the brown-robed figure spoke again. "Thank you, Miss Blaise. Now if you will kindly remain as you are, two experienced colleagues of ours will attend upon you at once."

As she watched, keeping up her whispered words of encouragement till the last moment, two people moved down the steps towards the stage. One was a tall and beautifully built blonde woman, the other was a big swarthy man, and both moved like strolling tigers.

*　　*　　*　　*

Half an hour had gone by. In Thaddeus Pilgrim's study, Dr. Tyl sat rigidly in his chair, hands clasped tightly in his lap as he said for the third time, though in different words, "It was impossible to predict such a remarkable rapport between them. Impossible to imagine that she could find a key to unlock his memory, or his instinct, perhaps, or sufficient of either, in that brief instant *before* he killed her, to divert his aim. The sight of her lying dead was the planned trigger for his memory, of course. Impossible to surmount such rapport, even if one could have predicted it. I have never encountered such a phenomenal –"

"Quite so, Dr. Tyl, quite so," Thaddeus Pilgrim broke in without looking up from the file he was studying in what appeared to be a desultory fashion. "You have, I feel, expatiated sufficiently upon the reasons for your – um – failure to ensure the promised conclusion to our little scenario." He looked up now with the death's-head smile that showed none of his teeth. "I expect you are tired, dear friend, and would be glad to retire." His uncertain gaze wandered to Mrs. Ram, sitting a little way from Tyl. "But perhaps you would be so kind as to stay for a few minutes, Mrs. Ram. There are matters I should be grateful to discuss with you. Goodnight, Dr. – ah – Tyl."

Tyl got uneasily to his feet and moved to the door. "Do you wish me to carry out further treatment on Garvin?" he asked. "Or have you a scenario in mind for Blaise?"

Thaddeus Pilgrim pursed his lips. "I hope I would not be so remiss as to fail to inform you if I required your further services in respect of these two persons, Dr. Tyl," he said. His eyes came to rest on the man with an empty, glassy stare, and after a moment Tyl fumbled the door open and went quickly out, sweat beading his brow.

The white-haloed head turned, and Thaddeus Pilgrim beamed benevolently at Mrs. Ram. He was not in the least disappointed by the way the scenario had turned out, and in fact had found it most intriguing, but it was satisfying to pretend otherwise and cause such manifest fear in Dr. Janos Tyl. He allowed his gaze to drift towards the cage where the jackdaw lay on its side, barely alive now, and it came into his mind that after allowing an hour or so for Tyl to get to sleep, he would send for him and ask his opinion on the jackdaw's condition.

Mrs. Ram cleared her throat and said, "Will you be requiring me to effect demise of Miss Blaise and Mr. Garvin in any particular way, Dr. Pilgrim?"

"Oh, no, no, no, dear lady," he said reproachfully. "We must not *waste* such excellent scenario material, must we? I am mindful – as I am sure you yourself would be, had you not been more busily engaged than I in practical matters concerning our guests – I am mindful, I say, of how disappointing it would be for our good friends, Sibyl and Kazim, if such interesting visitors were to – um – shuffle off this mortal coil in what they – I refer to Sibyl and Kazim, of course, not to our visitors – in what they would consider a dull and mundane fashion."

He returned to his study of the file he held, but continued to ramble on. "Indeed, Sibyl herself has suggested a most entertaining scenario which I am confident will prove highly stimulating to our little community. It is for this reason, dear lady, that I am concerned to have Mr. Garvin restored with all speed to his normal and no doubt extremely efficient self, which in turn is the reason I issued certain instructions to you regarding the manner in which he and Miss Blaise should be accommodated and attended for the next day or two."

When she was sure he had finished speaking Mrs. Ram said, "As instructed, Miss Blaise was subjected to intensive search of clothing and person which revealed several items of offensive, defensive, and burglarious nature. Mr. Garvin remained in semi-catatonic state, muttering single word 'Princess' at frequent intervals. All footwear and clothing were removed from both, each was provided with two blankets, and they were then incarcerated together in basement cell of north-east dormitory, above-mentioned cell being provided with separate ablution and lavatorial facilities but having single door, easily guarded, and window at ground level too narrow for egress of human body."

"Incarcerated . . . " murmured Thaddeus Pilgrim approvingly, closing his eyes for a moment as if to savour the word. "Yes. Excellent, Mrs. Ram. I am sure we are correct in our view that the – ah – um –" he lowered his voice with an air of apology, "the denuding of our visitors is a deterrent to any formulation of plans to escape, both in practical and in psychological terms, as I imagine Dr. Tyl would agree, had he been consulted." He tapped the file with a limp finger. "But these are resourceful persons, dear lady. I trust you have arranged for a second lock on the door, of the hasp and padlock type? Also for two men to be permanently on guard?"

"As instructed, Doctor," said Mrs. Ram, dipping her head. "Furthermore I have ensured that food and suitable beverages have been, and will continue to be, provided to our visitors. The cell has two bunks and mattresses, so incarceration will not involve physical hardship – again as per your instructions. Having observed recent colloquy between yourself and Dr. Tyl, I am assuming you do not wish him to exercise his professional skills in the matter of restoring Mr. Garvin to mental normality?"

"That is so," agreed Thaddeus Pilgrim amiably. "I am moved to feel that it will do no harm, and may indeed be beneficial to our community, if Dr. Tyl is allowed to – um – to perspire for a little while in the light of his failure to implement his undertaking in regard to the scenario planned for tonight. I am also of the opinion – a layman's opinion, of course, though that is not always to be despised – that in view of the rapport emphasised by the good doctor himself, it is probable that Mr. Garvin will be restored more *rapidly* under the ministrations of Miss Blaise than by any treatment Dr. Tyl might attempt."

Mrs. Ram nodded brisk approval and ticked something on her clipboard. "Next matter," she said. "I am now deducing from happy manner of Sibyl Pray and Kazim that there is to be a scenario involving combat between said persons and our two visitors."

"Yes, yes indeed," Thaddeus Pilgrim said absently, eyes on the file again as he turned a page. "It should be profoundly interesting, I think."

"Suppose . . ." Mrs. Ram hesitated, then went on, "it is barely possible, of course, but suppose by some mischance dear Sibyl and Kazim were defeated. Expunged from mortal life. This might prove serious threat to success of Hallelujah Scenario."

Dr. Pilgrim looked up, white hair waving with the movement, lips smiling, watery eyes empty. "Now there you echo my own thoughts, Mrs. Ram," he said. "We must always prepare for the most remote contingency, and it would assuredly be a great loss to our community if we were to be deprived of the – ah – valuable expertise of Sibyl and Kazim. But . . ." he rested his hand on the file and half closed his eyes with an air of intense deliberation, "but strangely enough we now have in our midst two persons of outstanding reputation who, if only they could be persuaded to assist our endeavours, might prove no less effective than Sibyl and Kazim. I believe we agreed – did we not? – that Sibyl and Kazim have become a little above themselves of late."

Mrs. Ram blinked. "With greatest respect, I find it hard to agree that

Miss Blaise and Mr. Garvin would prove suitable replacements, Doctor. They are not at all of our . . . our persuasion."

"Perfectly true, dear lady." A hint of reproach tinged the patient voice. "But is it not our duty to win converts to our ways? Not by such experiments as Dr. Tyl favours, perhaps, but slowly, step by step, *drawing* them in, as it were. You will naturally ask *how* may we hope to achieve the first step in the face of recalcitrance from such as Miss Blaise and Mr. Garvin? Well . . . I answer that we must have *faith*, Mrs. Ram, and I have complete faith in that invisible power which transcends all others, that power to which all must bow the knee. Do you not concur with me in this?"

He looked at her expectantly, mouth half open, and after a moment or two of unease, not knowing what he meant, she said, "Of course, Doctor. Of course."

"Ah, splendid," he said vaguely. "So let us apply this great power in which we both believe. The power of *leverage*. And here in this dossier – which is most admirably detailed and worth every penny we have paid to Salamander Four – here, as I say, are the lever and the fulcrum to ensure that our visitors will co-operate in whatever we may require. That is, of course, supposing that the unlikely contingency we spoke of does in fact occur, namely that our good friends Sibyl and Kazim get stiffed and have to be replaced."

Mrs. Ram's dark eyes shone with admiration. "That is magnificent alternative scenario, Doctor. So intriguing that it is difficult not to wish for —" She stopped and shook her head in a self-deprecating manner. "Please excuse me, I did not intend to digress from practical matters. I am delighted that study of the dossier has revealed to you a fulcrum upon which you can apply most intense leverage to Miss Blaise and Mr. Garvin, and I find myself extremely desirous to be advised of specific nature of said fulcrum, Doctor."

"Ah, now here I must give credit to Dr. Tyl for the way in which his analytical notations in the dossier have clarified and identified the – ah – the particular *flaw* in Miss Blaise and Mr. Garvin which makes them so highly vulnerable."

Thaddeus Pilgrim laid down the file on his desk and gazed at Mrs. Ram. His body began to shake, the halo of fine white hair quivering about his head, and after a moment or two a curious sound began to come from his parted lips. It was the sound of Thaddeus Pilgrim's laughter, and Mrs. Ram had heard it only once before, years ago in

Persia, after he had killed a child during a black magic ritual in a temple of Ahriman. The sound was unlike human laughter, and there was no accompanying mirth in the eyes and face beneath the crescent of white hair, only a kind of obscene delight which sent spurts of joyous terror darting through Mrs. Ram. The sound faded, though the shaking of the body by suppressed paroxysms caused the words emerging from the parted lips to come in distorted gasps as Thaddeus Pilgrim spoke at last, and the only human emotion that the strangely ventriloquial voice now held was that of towering, measureless contempt.

"The fulcrum? The unyielding base on which the lever turns? Oh . . . *friendship*, dear lady. Simple friendship! That unnatural loyalty to another person which is perhaps the most truly nauseating of all human attributes." He tapped the file with a limp finger. "But there can be no doubt that Miss Blaise and Mr. Garvin are slaves to it, and we are thereby presented with a perfect fulcrum."

Her shoulders shook and a giggle broke from her lips. The jackdaw died as the man and woman cackled together in a chilling duet, then Thaddeus Pilgrim sighed, looked soberly at the ceiling, and said in his normal rambling voice, "Ah . . . the fishing boat which brought her here, a crew of two, I believe? You have news of their dispatch, Mrs. Ram?"

She was immediately grave, and without glancing down at her clipboard she said, "I regret we have no news yet, Doctor. Our cruiser is searching and will destroy on sight, but the last radio message from Ms. Johnson and Zanelli, who are in charge for this elimination of said fishermen, stated that they have been unable to pick up boat because lights of same were put out shortly before arrival of Miss Blaise on Kalivari. Search continues, but boat appears to be making circuitous detour."

"I wonder," said Thaddeus Pilgrim, fingering his chin, "if Miss Blaise had the – ah – prevision to *warn* the fishermen of possible elimination? Certainly it is a matter to be pursued, Mrs. Ram. We do not want the sturdy mainland fisherfolk talking about a young lady conveyed in somewhat mysterious fashion to Kalivari."

"In the event they are not picked up, I will identify them via cut-outs through whom we employed them, and initiate appropriate action, Doctor." She made a note on her clipboard.

"Thank you, Mrs. Ram. That will be all, I think."

When she had gone, Thaddeus Pilgrim sat staring into space for an hour, his consciousness far away in a world of chaotic horror. At last he stirred, drew a pad towards him, and wrote on it the words *Salamander Four*.

* * * *

There was light in the cell from a low-wattage bulb hanging from a short flex, no doubt fed by a generator somewhere on the island. As yet she had made no attempt to examine the cell, the door, or the narrow horizontal window grille piercing the wall at ceiling level within and at ground level outside. There was no point in contemplating escape until she had found a way to free Willie Garvin from the mental and physical paralysis, induced by shock, that gripped him like an invisible strait-jacket.

He lay on his side on one of the broad bunks, naked, half covered by a blanket, knees drawn up in a semi-foetal position, fists clenched against his chest, eyes tightly closed, every muscle locked rigidly, his whole body shaken from time to time by rigors. He was conscious, she knew, but the only words he had spoken since she had helped him to the bunk and spread the blanket over him were, "Sorry, Princess . . . sorry, Princess . . ." uttered in a croaking, barely audible whisper.

She had torn a blanket in two, using one half to cover the grille and ensure privacy. The other half was wrapped round her body below the armpits, like a sarong. Now she knelt by the bunk where Willie lay, gently stroking his forehead, holding his wrist with her free hand, and using all her resources to defeat the panic that was trying to possess her. To see Willie Garvin in such a condition, his mind fragmented like a broken jigsaw, was horrifying to her beyond all words. She knew that they – whoever *they* were – must have subjected him to prolonged and subtle brainwashing aimed at conditioning him to kill her on sight. The how and why of it were unimportant for the moment. This was what they had done, and they had come very close to succeeding in their objective. The knife would have been in her throat if Willie had not marginally changed his aim in the final instant of release.

She knew that he must have been brought to them unconscious in the first instance. Given warning of any prospect of brainwashing he could have set up a resistance in depth, using mental techniques learned long ago from his sojourn with the mystic, Sivaji, in the Thar desert far to the north of Jodhpur. But there could have been no chance of that. He had been brought to them helpless, and then they had begun the demolition and remoulding of his mind.

It was the ultimate outrage, in some ways more vicious than murder. A sudden wave of coldly furious hatred brought adrenalin into her bloodstream and helped wipe away the last traces of panic. Looking down at Willie, seeing the sweat on his body despite the coolness of the cell, seeing the muscles even of his face rigid with tension, watching him breathe deeply, shakily, she set herself to think how best she should begin to heal and restore him, allowing no room for doubt that this could be done.

His mind and body were both locked in a monstrous cramp. If she could bring ease to either, it would be reflected in the other. Quieten the mind, and the body would relax; then, simply by being close to him perhaps, by talking, by recalling times past, by reassuring him, she could slowly help to reassemble the broken jigsaw of his mind. Or begin by coaxing his body to relax; then the mind would be eased and opened to her.

She knew that the major element in the shock he had suffered was the sudden knowledge that he had come within a hair's breadth of killing her. It was therefore important for him to know that she understood, and that it had cost him no scruple of her affection. She bit her lip uncertainly, watching him, aware of the immense tension that held him in its paralysing grip, knowing it was vital to break that tension somehow . . .

She eased up on to the bunk beside him and slipped an arm beneath his neck, pillowing his head on her shoulder and continuing to stroke his sweating brow. "Willie love," she whispered, "can you hear me? Do you know I'm Modesty?"

His head moved in a fractional nod. She kissed his temple gently and said, "Listen, Willie. I need your help badly, so we've got to start getting you unwound. Unwound. Do you understand?"

Again the affirmative movement of the head, and a slurred word or two muttered against her flesh. "Trying, Princess . . . trying . . ."

"I know you're trying, Willie. Look . . . I'm not sure what's best, but we have to get those knots untied. You usually relax with a nice warm hunk of girl, but I'm the only one available just now. Would that help, Willie? You only have to say. Would it help if I made love to you?"

His arm moved across her body to hold her tightly to him, and she felt the quick firm shake of his head on her shoulder as he croaked, "No . . ."

Involuntarily she gave a small laugh, hugged him, and said, "You old flatterer."

He made a wordless sound and she felt his body give a tiny jerk. It was a responsive twitch of laughter, or as near as he could come to it, and she felt her heart lift a little. He raised his head a fraction and mumbled, "No, I mean . . . just keep everything . . . us . . . same as always."

His head sank down again, and she said, "That's fine, Willie love. Whatever's best for you. Now listen . . . they've taken you apart, but I'm going to put you together again, so we'll start with a session of *katsu*." She eased her arm from under him, rolled off the bunk and pulled the blanket away. "Come on now, on your back, Willie. I'm going to start with the diaphragm."

She helped him turn, and began the specialised restorative techniques taught only in the highest echelons of karate and allied forms of combat, techniques to repair near-fatal strikes to the body's nerve centres. "Don't try to figure anything out yet, Willie love," she whispered as she worked. "Just let go. Leave your mind wide open for an image of the tokens old Sivaji used when he was teaching you how to focus. The pebble, the feather, the twig . . . no, don't make any effort, Willie. It doesn't matter if you can't understand what I'm saying. The tokens Sivaji used in training you are bound to be among the first things to come back to you, and then you'll be able to unlock the door to all the rest. Just relax and trust me, Willie. These goddam bastards took you apart a little, but there's nobody in the world could take you apart so badly that I couldn't put you together again."

After five minutes she threw off her blanket-sarong, sweating from the physical and mental effort she was putting into the *katsu* techniques, and for the next hour she worked her way steadily through the nerve centres of his body, thankful to feel the savagely cramped muscles gradually loosen under her ministrations. Her awareness was now closed against all circumstances outside the healing of Willie Garvin. For the moment it was unimportant that they were captives of unknown but viciously dangerous people whose intention was probably to kill them both. If this was so written, then it would happen; she and Willie had long been inured to that concept. But there was no question of lying down and letting it happen. Even with the gun an inch from your heart and a finger squeezing the trigger, you kept fighting. However hopeless the situation seemed, you fought as she was fighting now, assessing the priorities and then giving total concentration to each in turn. The first priority now was to get Willie Garvin back to at least a reasonable semblance of his normal self, his memory sufficiently restored, his mind clear enough to operate, his confidence and his rapport with her re-established.

At last he lay with muscles limp, face down on the bunk, relaxed, breathing evenly, eyes closed. She went through to the small annexe with the lavatory and wash-basin, sponged herself down, dried her body, then returned and did the same service for Willie. Her watch had been taken, but her internal clock never failed, and she knew it was a little after three a.m. when she said, "Shove over, Willie, I'm coming aboard."

He sighed and muttered sleepily as she lay down beside him and took him in her arms, pillowing his head on the soft slope between her shoulder and breast. "Hey, listen," she said softly. "Do you remember that first day I saw you at the Thai-fighting match? And after, when I gave you that Hong Kong job to do? Lordy, lordy, I don't think I've ever told you how you left us completely stunned, me and Danny and Garcia, that day you turned up in Tangier with an extra twenty grand for hauling Wei Lu out of China . . ."

It had never been their habit to indulge in reminiscence. Close friends like the Colliers, or Sir Gerald Tarrant, the intelligence chief, had often suffered much frustration at the unwillingness of Modesty Blaise and Willie Garvin to recount details of various exploits, but their distaste for reminiscence was no pose. Apart from any lessons to be drawn from memories of yesterday, they regarded the unknown prospects of tomorrow as far more important.

But now Willie Garvin's memory was in chaos, and she had set herself the task of helping him, very gently, to restore it to order. She had left the dim light switched on so that he could open his eyes and see her as well as having the tactile comfort of her body; and now, in a manner of idle recollection, she began to talk him through their years together, not dwelling on detail, but trying to present him with a verbal photograph album, browsing through the highlights with him to reactivate the benumbed memory cells.

He lay with an arm across her, holding her, and there were times when she thought he slept, others when she knew he was in some measure conscious, but all the time she talked softly on, unhurriedly, often allowing a little silence between one reminiscence and another. At five o'clock she marked a change in his breathing and a new slackness in his body that could only mean he had fallen into a deep sleep. She let her voice fade to silence and settled his head more comfortably on her shoulder, hoping fervently that this was a turning point, that she had cleared the ground and made a firm base on which his immense resilience and mental techniques would enable his subconscious to build as he slept.

She did not even now begin to consider their situation as captives, or to speculate in any way on future danger, for such thoughts in herself could well be reflected in him, and she wanted no disturbance of his peace. Resting a hand against his cheek she whispered, "I've got you, Willie love. Everything's all right now." Then she began the self-hypnotic process that would give her restful sleep for the next three hours.

10

"She asked no questions when we took fresh food and drink at o-nine-hundred hours this morning, Doctor," said Mrs. Ram. "Mr. Garvin was very comfortably asleep, to judge from appearance. Miss Blaise had made her toilet but had not eaten food or touched the wine or bottled water. Presumably she had drunk water from the tap."

"And she asked no questions?" mused Thaddeus Pilgrim. It was mid-morning, and they were strolling on the terrace outside his study. "Most interesting."

"Interesting but also disconcerting," Mrs. Ram said, frowning. "She behaved as if we did not exist. Noting that she had consumed no comestibles, nor touched the wine or water, I surmised she was taking precautions against possibility that drugs had been introduced into same, taking into account that Mr. Garvin had obviously been subjected to such."

"Ah," said Thaddeus Pilgrim vaguely.

"I therefore consumed a portion of said comestibles and beverages in her presence," Mrs. Ram continued, "giving verbal assurance that we were desirous to see both herself and Mr. Garvin in jolly good fettle with all speed."

"A most intelligent deduction on your part, dear lady. And pray how did Miss Blaise respond?"

Mrs. Ram pursed her lips disapprovingly. "It is hard to be sure that she heard me, Doctor. She was studying the two guards who accompanied me and the weapons they were carrying. There is something about her I find hard to describe. I think she may prove to be a very . . . formidable person."

Thaddeus Pilgrim trod slowly on a beetle, nodding his white head. "Capital," he said with a nebulous smile. "And what effect, in your opinion, dear lady, has she had upon Mr. Garvin?"

"It is very soon to judge, Doctor, but I can report an impression I received."

"I have complete faith in your intuition, Mrs. Ram. What did it tell you when you observed our visitors this morning?"

"I think she is mending him, Doctor. And perhaps more quickly than Dr. Tyl would believe possible."

"Well now, that is quite splendid," said Thaddeus Pilgrim, gazing vacantly out to sea. "Our dear colleagues, Sibyl and Kazim, will be truly delighted, as indeed shall we all. I feel we may look forward with every confidence to a quite fascinating scenario."

A stone's throw away, in the little washroom off the cell, Modesty was spreading soft cheese on a piece of fresh crusty bread with a plastic knife when she heard Willie Garvin stirring. She gave him a minute or two to collect himself, then went through the door into the cell. He was sitting on the edge of the bunk, a blanket draped about him like a toga. She went to him, smiling, and said, "Hallo, Willie. Like some breakfast?"

He looked at her with quiet eyes, reaching out to take her hands, and said, "Princess . . ."

"There's some good bread, cheese, olives, honey, cold meat, and milk, water or wine to drink. Give me a minute and I'll make up a plate for you. Oh, and it's safe. No drugs."

He kept holding her hands and said slowly, "I'm still confused, Princess. Don't know what's 'appened, except I was brainwashed. Last night was . . . like a dream. But I remember all of it. There's no way I can say proper thanks."

Relief flooded her. His speech and manner were slow, but he was coherent, and he was stable. She freed a hand, made a loose fist, and pushed it against his jaw in a mock punch. "Don't start getting all formal with *me*, Willie Garvin," she said. "Come on, what will you have for breakfast, milk or retsina?"

"Milk, please. I'll come with you." He stood beside her in the washroom while she made up a plate of food and poured a beaker of milk. Back in the cell, she sat beside him on the bunk while he ate in silence, using one hand, his other hand holding hers.

When he set his empty plate aside she passed him the beaker of milk and said, "How's the memory, Willie love?"

There came the shadow of his usual grin as he said wryly, "Patchy. There are vague bits and blank bits, but they're gradually beginning to get filled in."

She said, "Will it upset you if we talk about what's happened?"

154

He shook his head. "Blimey, no. The sooner I know where we stand, the better I'll feel. Look, I'll tell you all I remember, which isn't much, then you tell me your bit. All right?"

"Yes, fine. But stop if you find yourself getting the jitters."

He said quietly, "I won't now. Apart from everything else, you got ol' Sivaji's tokens working bright and clear for me last night, some-'ow." He sat thinking for a while, staring at the floor, and she saw a spasm of grief touch his eyes. "They killed Molly Chen," he said sadly. "That's the last thing I remember before the brainwashing. There was a big blonde woman, combat trained. She was all set to knock me cold. I'd 'ave taken her, but . . . there was someone else. A man, I think. Not sure."

She remembered the man and woman who had supervised the body search before she and Willie had been put in the cell. Strange creatures. Sibyl and . . . Kassim? Kazim? They fitted Lafarge's description of the passionate nymph and satyr who had flown out of England with Willie, and she did not doubt that it was these two who had killed Molly Chen.

"I think they kept me sedated for a long time," Willie said softly. "Neuroleptic drugs, maybe. Are we somewhere on a Greek island, Princess?"

"Yes. Somewhere in the Cyclades, but I don't know the name."

"It's Kali . . . wait a minute. Kalivari. Yes." He shook his head, frowning. "Now I've sort of got two memories running parallel. I thought this place was *The Network* 'eadquarters, and that everybody 'ere knew you'd been . . . been tortured and killed by Delilah." He stopped short, staring at her. "Delilah? But she . . . she doesn't exist, does she? Christ, they primed me to kill her – that's right. Only they keyed 'er name to visuals of *you*, Princess!"

He rubbed his brow. "Wait a minute, it's gone a bit fuzzy. No, Jan came into it." The image of Lady Janet Gillam came suddenly and clearly to his mind. "Ahh, the bastards! They keyed *your* name to visuals of Jan. Yes, that's right. And I remember it didn't quite gel because it seemed I'd got memories of making love with you, and I knew that wasn't right."

She said, "Visuals of me, visuals of Jan, murder, kidnapping and high class brainwashing – there are big people behind this, Willie. Who are they? If they set you up to kill me, it *has* to be a revenge motive, so we're bound to know them."

He thought for a while, then: "I suppose it seems weird, but I don't think we do know them, Princess. Not unless the principals are staying right off-stage. Now let's see . . . the bloke I saw most of was the one I thought was Garcia. That seems crazy now. He's a big teddy-bear sort of bloke, dressed like a monk, nothing like old Rafa. Oh, Jesus – *yes!*"

His hand gripped hers painfully, and she said, "Willie, not so hard."

"Eh? Oh God, I'm sorry, Princess. But . . . he's the brainwasher. I can hear 'im now, on and on and on while they kept flashing pictures on the screen." He bit his lip and closed his eyes in an effort of memory. "Can't remember 'is real name. Maybe I never heard it . . . but if that evil bastard ever comes close enough, he's dead."

"Hey, Willie. Relax, please. Please?" She rubbed his hand between her palms and saw him allow the tensions to drain away.

"Sure, Princess," he said softly. "I won't get wound up. I won't blow whatever chances we've got. But he mucked up my mind so I nearly killed you, that one I thought was Garcia did. So at the end of it all, if I'm alive, he won't be."

"Let's worry about that later, Willie. What strikes me is that these people knew about Garcia being joint top man with you in *The Network*. They must have a hell of a good dossier on us. Is this Garcia-substitute the kingpin here, do you think?"

Again he reflected before answering slowly, "No . . . there's someone I 'ardly saw anything of. Dressed monk-like, same as the Garcia-bloke. Not young. Big face, weird eyes, sort of vague but creepy." Willie moved a hand above his head with fingers splayed. "White hair sticking up all round, like a halo." He felt a tremor of shock touch Modesty, and turned to look at her. "You know 'im?"

She shook her head. "No, I don't. But it fits an impression Dinah got one day at the cottage, not long before they killed Molly and snatched you. Steve had just used the word 'hypnotise' . . . that must have been the trigger. It was one of those shivery walking-over-your-grave impressions. No gazing into the future stuff. Just this fleeting impression of a man with a halo like a saint."

There was a silence, then Willie said, "This one's no saint."

"I believe you. How many are there here, Willie, and who else stands out?"

He rasped a hand across his bristly chin. "I've been living in a sort of dream, Princess," he said apologetically. "Hardly took notice of anything except . . ." he shrugged, "training to kill Delilah. Still, I'd

156

reckon there's maybe thirty or forty 'ere, all told. Nobody else stands out much, but working on a kind of retrospective memory, I reckon they've got a fair bunch of professional killers among 'em." He half closed his eyes in thought. "I got an idea they work in pairs. Don't recall any names except Sibyl and Kazim. Ah yes, they're the top combat pair. I've watched 'em work out, and they're good – *wait a minute!*"

He sat up straight on the last words, staring at her with shocked eyes. "She's the same! I mean, the same woman who was waiting for me at Molly Chen's place!"

Modesty patted his hand gently. "Yes, I thought so. But stay loose, Willie. We've got quite a few problems to solve before we can do anything about your brainwashing Garcia-man or the people who killed Molly."

He drew in a long breath and exhaled. "I know, Princess. Look, there's not much more I can tell you, except I know the layout of the island and the buildings if we get a chance to break." He looked at her, sitting beside him with the half blanket wrapped about her sarong-style, and his rueful smile was less of a ghost this time. "Can't see us getting a break just now," he said, "so p'raps you could bring me up to date on your end of the caper. I don't even know what day it is, or 'ow long I've been 'ere." He lifted her hand and touched her knuckles to his cheek in the familiar salutation that was his alone, saying quietly, "I only know that 'owever long it's been I've thought you were dead all that time . . . so I'm glad I've woken up now, no matter what."

Her own story was soon told, for there was little to it. She said nothing of her experience with Roger Lafarge, but gave the impression that he had sold her the information she sought. "Krolli doesn't know where I am," she ended. "The only people who do are the two fishermen who brought me here. If they didn't take my warning, they'll be dead by now, that's for sure. If they did take it . . . well, there's little chance of anything they know getting back to Krolli. There were at least two cut-outs between them and him."

Willie nodded absently. She was glad to see more colour in his cheeks now, and to note that even in the brief half hour since he had woken from sleep his speech, memory and responses had improved rapidly. She stood up and began to pace slowly between the bunks of the little cell, arms folded across her middle, hands holding her elbows. "The big thing we don't know," she said, "is what these people are up to. They can't have set this whole thing up just to have you kill me. That *has* to be a side effect of some kind. So what's their racket?"

She stopped and looked down at Willie, who shook his head. "No idea, Princess. If they've bought or leased an island for 'eadquarters, then it's got to be something big. You were saying this Indian woman you saw this morning told you they wanted us both in good nick, so maybe they'll tell us what goes on, sooner or later."

She nodded agreement. "If we're alive now, it's only because they want us for some purpose. They had four submachine-guns on us last night and could have blown us to hell and gone. Any guesses, Willie?"

He thought for a while, then said, "None at all, Princess. Still, we've 'ad this sort of puzzle before, 'aven't we? The only thing I'm worried about is if they aim to get at me with the drugs and the brainwashing again. And at you."

"Yes. But you had no chance to set up any defence before, Willie. What we're going to do for the next hour or so is help each other build barriers. Can't stop narcosis, but we can stop them twisting our minds around when we're under. Specific barriers, built on Sivaji disciplines. Those symbols he implanted, yours and mine, are with us for ever and deeper than anyone else can ever reach, drugs or no drugs. Right?"

He studied her soberly for a few moments, then said, "Sit down a minute, Princess. There's something I've got to tell you. I've just remembered."

She sat on the edge of the other bunk, facing him, careful to show no sign of unease. "All right, Willie. Go on."

"This is something I've never told you before, Princess. I wanted to find the right moment, but I reckon now's as good a time as any." He glanced about him and lowered his voice. "We're not bugged?"

"No, I've checked."

"Well . . . here it is, Princess. I once knew a girl called Genevieve who suffered from arachibutyrophobia." He stopped, gazing at her anxiously, and now she was careful to maintain a serious expression, hiding the joyous relief expanding within her. This was Willie Garvin again, not fully recovered yet, but surely well on the way to it if he could remember and play the obscure-word game with which he had amused and challenged her from time to time over the years. The routine was that he would use an obscure word; she would pretend to understand, but take the first opportunity to research the meaning. If she could use the word to him in context within a couple of days, victory was hers. If not, she would acknowledge defeat.

She said gravely, "That arachi – what you said, it can be pretty distressing, so I'm told."

"Arachibutyrophobia."

"Ah, yes. That." She pondered for a moment, and decided that circumstances dictated a slight change of routine. *Arachi* . . . ? Spiders, surely? Well, it was worth a shot. She said, "Mind you, I quite like spiders myself."

He gave her a pained look. "Arachibutyrophobia isn't about being scared of spiders, Princess."

"No? Oh, I must have got it wrong." She gave an apologetic shrug. "You'll just have to tell me, Willie."

"It means an obsessive fear of peanut butter sticking to the roof of your mouth. I thought everybody knew that."

She clapped a hand to her lips to stifle an involuntary burst of laughter, staring at him wide-eyed, knowing it was not a word he had made up. Genevieve might or might not exist, but the word would be genuine. The unwritten rules of the game were rigid on that point. She said, "Oh, Willie! What an awful phobia!"

He nodded. "It was certainly tough on Genevieve. She loved peanut butter. As a matter of fact a lot of medical people discussed it at the annual Phobia Conference two or three years ago in San Francisco," – that would be true, too – "but they didn't come up with any answers." He looked at his nails with a modest air. "I cured Genevieve meself in the end."

She anticipated a pay-off involving sex, and tried to imagine what it might be, but failed. "Tell me, Willie," she said, "how did you cure her?"

"Well, when she'd spread the peanut butter on the bread, I got 'er to bite into it upside down. Made 'er very 'appy. Fat, but 'appy."

She shook her head, laughing, eyes moist, and reached out to take his hands. "That's lovely, Willie. Welcome back. Now let's start setting up some barriers."

An hour later, when Mrs. Ram accompanied by two armed men brought lunch to the cell, she found Modesty Blaise and Willie Garvin sitting cross-legged on the bare boards of one bunk, facing each other knee to knee, hands resting palm-up on knees, fingers touching each other's. Their breathing was so slow as to be almost imperceptible, perhaps two inhalations a minute. Their eyes were open, the pupils widely dilated. If they were aware of her presence, they gave no sign, and when she spoke they made no response.

Before Mrs. Ram could prevent it, one of the guards gave Modesty Blaise an angry shove, his hand against her shoulder, but only moved himself by reaction, for it was as if her body had the weight of a stone statue. Once out of the cell with the door double-locked again, Mrs. Ram berated the guard for what she called "unauthorised activity", threatened to report his name to Dr. Pilgrim if he repeated such an offence, and punched him hard in the testicles to mark the extent of her displeasure.

When she reported on the condition of the two visitors to Thaddeus Pilgrim he gazed with a chaotic smile at the white mouse in the small cage which now stood on his desk and said, "Excellent, excellent, dear lady. Miss Blaise is clearly a most competent young person. Now, may I ask if you have anything fresh to report in respect of the Hallelujah Scenario?"

"Only that as anticipated in radio report of yesterday's date, tanker *Marimba* has discharged cargo of oil clandestinely at Beira and is now on high seas with tanks full of sea-water, en route for rendezvous with our cargo boat off Senegal, precedent to destruction of tanker and crew by combined Answer to Prayer teams."

"She must not be allowed to – ah – to *linger* over her sinking," mused Thaddeus Pilgrim. "That would be most imprudent."

"Yes, Doctor. Briefing will be emphatic on that point."

He appeared to reflect for a while, eyeing the white mouse speculatively. "How long do we have before the rendezvous?" he said at last.

"Precise date is to be finalised when *Marimba* has crossed latitude ten degrees south, but provisional date is twenty-two days hence. Cargo boat will be at Dakar one week before, and flight arrangements are in hand for expeditious transfer of A.T.P. personnel to Dakar three days before rendezvous."

He nodded solemnly. "That appears to allow ample time for us to implement the new scenario, dear lady. How fascinating it is to meditate upon the alternatives which may, or may not, spring from it. Now, before you go, may I trespass upon your kindness by asking you, some time today, and at your entire convenience of course, to bring me a few items from our medical equipment?"

Her eyes widened in alarm. "You are not unwell, Doctor?"

"No, no, Mrs. Ram, I am in excellent health, thank you." He smiled

160

mistily, and reached out to run the tip of a flaccid finger along the bars of the little cage, causing the white mouse to sit up and watch curiously. "Be reassured," he said. "The – ah – medico-surgical items I require are not for me."

*   *   *   *

It was raining in Whitehall. Sir Gerald Tarrant, head of a most secret Foreign Office Intelligence department, looked down on the sea of bobbing umbrellas weaving patterns along the pavement, then turned from his office window and said, "She's only been missing for five days, Collier. That's not a long time for Modesty when she's ... working. She vanished for a month in Limbo, you'll remember."

"Only too well." There was a thread of anger in Professor Stephen Collier's voice. He looked pale, tired, and on edge as he sat on the far side of Tarrant's desk. Beside him, Danny Chavasse was sombre but controlled. "It's over twenty days since Willie was snatched," said Collier, "and they weren't 'working' as you call it. Out of the blue, somebody killed Molly Chen and grabbed Willie. It took Modesty two weeks to trace him as far as Athens. She went after him, and vanished herself. Surely to God in your position you can do something to help? How much skin and blood has she left around doing things for *you*?"

Tarrant said quietly, "More than I care to think about. There was a time when I made use of Modesty with as much or as little personal regard for her as my job demands I should have for my properly employed agents. That time is past. I have long had a deep personal attachment to Modesty, as both of you have, and I'm in debt to her for my life – again as both of you are." He paused, looking at Collier. "So for these reasons among others, please don't ever presume to think that Modesty's welfare and safety mean more to you than they do to me."

Collier rubbed his nose with finger and thumb. "I apologise," he said. "Put it down to jet-lag and being somewhat frayed round the edges. You're quite right of course, she doesn't need anyone to land her in trouble. She and Willie are magnets for it. They have this stupid habit of taking up the cudgels for other people." He opened his eyes and smiled wanly. "People like us."

Danny Chavasse said, "Can we get down to the specifics of what we know and what we can do? When Willie had been missing three days,

Modesty flew Concorde to America and back to visit Lucifer, who told her Willie was alive. Steve here has just made the same trip, and . . ." He left the sentence unfinished, nodding to Collier.

"I was the best one to go, because I worked for weeks with Lucifer when I was a prisoner with Modesty in the Philippines," said Collier. "The one thing that poor lunatic can do, believing he's Satan, is to predict imminent death with about eighty-three percent accuracy, and pronounce as to whether a given individual is alive or not with about ninety-one percent accuracy. He needs a personal object to sense, and I gave him a letter she'd written me. He just touched it and said something like, 'This is my most faithful servant, Modesty. She dwells on the upper levels still, preparing my forces for Armageddon.' Upper levels are here on earth – the upper levels of Hell, in Lucifer's terms." Collier shrugged. "He could be right."

Tarrant shook his head. "No man with a wife like Dinah can pretend this world is hell, Collier. What would Modesty say?"

Collier eyed him grimly. "You certainly know how to straighten a chap up," he said. "All right, once more I'm sorry. I won't let my pessimistic streak get the better of me again. Facts not comments. We know, or very strongly believe, that Modesty and Willie are alive. What else?"

Tarrant said diffidently, "I take it Dinah has tried to locate them by the pendulum and map system, the way she found Chavasse in Limbo?"

Collier looked away, trying to close his mind to the memory of his wife kneeling on one of the superb Isfahan rugs in Modesty's penthouse sitting room, a scattering of maps all about her, a pointed brass plumb-bob on a silk thread lying across her lap, head bowed and hands covering her face as she wept silently with grief and frustration.

"She tried," said Collier. "We went to the penthouse, and used those pearls of Modesty's as a psychometric contact, the ones Willie spent seven years diving for. An ideal link for both of them. But the locator wouldn't work for her this time." He stared down at his clenched hands. "I expect it would work if Modesty and Willie were strangers to Dinah and she had no emotional involvement with them. But you see we . . . well, we've all been through quite a lot together, and there's a fair amount of what you might call affection for one another. So Dinah can't be objective about trying to locate them, and psychic faculties simply don't seem to work where there's emotional interference. It's like bad static on radio."

Danny said, "Don't let her try any more, Steve. She looked ready to fall apart."

Collier nodded and sighed. "She knew it was useless, anyway, but I suppose we both hoped for a miracle." He looked at Tarrant. "So all we know about location is what Danny's been told by this ex-*Network* man of Modesty's reporting from Athens. He says she went off to meet somebody, but he doesn't know who, on the understanding that this somebody would take her to Willie Garvin. She knew it was a trap, and decided the only way to find Willie was to walk into it. So that's what she did, and nobody's heard of her since."

Tarrant said, speaking to Danny, "Is this man Krolli trying to trace her?"

"Yes. He's trying to work back through the cut-outs, but even finding them isn't easy." Danny gave a small shrug. "No luck so far."

"Does Krolli have good contacts and influence, and above all will he really be trying to trace her, not just making a few inquiries?"

Danny said quietly, "He'll be trying as hard as we are, Sir Gerald. He was with her from the beginning, one of her top lieutenants, a very hard and capable man. As you can imagine, Modesty didn't set out to win anyone's affection when she ran *The Network*, but it's hard to convey the . . . well, the enormous pride those lieutenants came to take in being her men. You can bank on Krolli doing everything he can think of to get a lead. What's more, if he gets one, or if *we* get one, and some sort of task force is needed, Krolli will raise it. But Steve and I feel we should be doing something more," he smiled apologetically, "or at least prodding somebody with the resources to do something more."

"Yes, I understand." Tarrant fingered his grey moustache. "Let me put you in the picture. As soon as Modesty knew Willie had been snatched she came to me. I put out immediate instructions to all Section Heads overseas and all agents-in-place to be on the alert for any relevant information or even rumours. That instruction is still in force. I've also alerted certain European colleagues of mine who have reason to be favourably disposed towards Modesty. The only response I've had so far is that in the last few days our Athens group reports that the Greek underworld is buzzing with the rumour that anyone with information about Modesty Blaise can make a quick fortune."

Tarrant inclined his head towards Danny. "I think this confirms that your friend Krolli is being very active. I'm afraid I have nothing more definite to tell you. But, like yourselves, I feel distressingly inadequate, so I've decided to send one of my best agents to Athens in the hope of picking up a lead, perhaps in liaison with Krolli, if he's agreeable." Tarrant leaned forward and pressed the switch of the intercom on his desk. "Come in now, please," he said. Then, to the two men, "This agent isn't a stranger to you – especially not to Chavasse."

The door opened and a girl came in. She wore a pale lemon shirtwaister in wild silk, simple but of manifest quality. Her hair was short, fair and curly, her eyes blue and round, but there was nothing of the dumb blonde about her. Both Tarrant's visitors stood up, and Danny moved towards her with a smile of pleasure. "Maude!" He glanced over his shoulder at Tarrant as he took her hand in both his own. "I'd better not kiss you hallo while you're on duty."

"Better not, Danny," she agreed with a polite but friendly smile. "Hallo, Mr. Collier."

"Hallo, Maude." Collier remembered her well, though he had seen her only briefly one busy and emotional day in Belize. It was Maude Tiller who had been Willie's companion throughout the brutal, month-long torment of cutting their way through the Petén jungle of Guatemala to the slave camp of Limbo, there to join Modesty and Danny at the crucial moment of the final battle. She looked and spoke like an averagely attractive girl in her late twenties from a good county family, which she was, but Collier knew she was also very much more than this. Both Modesty and Willie held her in high regard and had great respect for her abilities, which spoke volumes. And their opinion was shared by Danny Chavasse, with whom she had gone on holiday in the Caribbean when given leave after her Limbo mission.

Danny was saying to Tarrant, "Would it help if I went with Maude to Athens? Weng's holding the fort for possible radio communication at the penthouse, so I'm not really needed here."

Tarrant lifted an eyebrow at the girl. "Maude?"

She thought for a moment, then said, "Yes, sir. It would certainly help in liaising with Krolli, because they're old friends, and it's another pair of hands and feet."

Danny said wryly, "Only for fetching and carrying, I fear. I'm not combat trained, Maude, you know that."

She shook her head. "Not important, Danny. Missions rarely involve combat, and we'll be looking for information, not trouble."

She half smiled. "If there's a woman in the case you'll be more use than anyone else I can think of."

Collier said, "Count me in. I'm no warrior either, and I haven't Danny's useful talent, but I can fetch and carry, and I've been right through the middle of two bloody horrifying capers with Modesty and Willie, so I can claim experience."

Tarrant and Danny Chavasse both started to speak, Danny yielding with a nod of agreement to the older man. "You will *not* go to Athens," Tarrant said forcefully, "you will go home to your wife, Collier, and take good care of her. God Almighty, man, if —" he corrected himself, "when Modesty comes back I certainly wouldn't have the courage to face her if I permitted you to put yourself at risk. I fancy Chavasse feels the same."

"I do," said Danny fervently. "If something happened, and Dinah was left – oh, don't be bloody mad, Steve."

Collier subsided in his chair, starting to mutter a protest, but Tarrant ignored him and spoke to Maude. "You can draw on any facilities you want. Make your own arrangements with signals. You understand that this is not an official mission?"

"Yes, sir. I'm on leave. How long may I have?"

"As long as it takes. Any questions?"

"No, sir."

"Off you go, then. Better take Mr. Chavasse with you, so you can make whatever arrangements you decide on between you. I'll expect you to be in Athens by tonight."

"Yes, sir."

When they had gone, Tarrant rose and opened a cabinet. "You're depressed, worn out, and jet-lagged," he said to Collier. "I'm going to give you a drink, and then I'm going to take you home."

"I'll be glad of the drink, but I don't need an escort," Collier said tiredly.

"I know you don't. My purpose is to see Dinah, a pleasure at any time, and to talk to her. I'm perfectly well aware that you feel you ought to be doing something positive, and I suspect Dinah will also feel you should – as indeed you have been doing, the result of your session with Lucifer is very encouraging. But I want Dinah to hear from me that there's no more you can do now except wait and hope. For her sake you simply must not involve yourself any further. We won't say as much to Dinah, of course, but she is clearly your first consideration.

Certainly she would be first consideration for Modesty and Willie, you know that as well as I do."

Collier nodded, taking the proffered glass. "I know," he said bleakly. "But it doesn't make anything easier."

Less than two thousand miles away, seated at a desk bearing a cage containing a white mouse, a cup of completely cold coffee, and an open dossier he had been re-reading, Dr. Thaddeus Pilgrim drew a pad towards him. At the top of the page were written the words *Salamander Four*, and beneath them he now wrote *Professor and Mrs. Stephen Collier*.

11

Willie Garvin buckled the breastplate to the pauldron covering Modesty's shoulder and stepped back to look her over. The narrow bronze plates of her knee-length skirt, hanging like heavy pleats, made a dull metallic sound as she turned quickly and extended her right arm, testing the ease of movement. It was mid-morning of their sixth day in the cell, and both felt relief that something was at last to happen. During those days Willie had mended apace, and they had devoted many hours to physical and mental exercise. No shadow of a chance to escape had presented itself. The solid door was double-locked with double guards outside. The narrow window grille was made of close-set bars, and even if they could have prised it away the space it covered would barely have accepted a child.

The bunks were of wood, and no metal tool could be improvised for tunnelling or for use as a jemmy. There had been no opportunity for a surprise move. When food was brought, when the cell was cleaned, when any visit was made for any purpose, they were first covered by a submachine-gun through the grille and made to lie on their bunks throughout. Apart from guards and the Hindu woman, they had seen one other person, a man who had accompanied the woman on a single occasion only. They had addressed each other as Mrs. Ram and Dr. Tyl.

Dr. Tyl had spoken several words to Willie in a language Modesty thought was Czech. He seemed to expect or to hope that something would happen, and when there was no response he went away looking unhappy. Willie recognised him as the man he had been made to believe was Garcia, the man who had brainwashed him. They concluded that the Czech words were triggers, implanted under narco-hypnosis so that simply by uttering them at any time Dr. Tyl could immediately cause Willie Garvin to fall into a state of deep hypnosis.

When the man had gone and they were alone again, Willie said thoughtfully, "Pity I didn't catch on sooner to what he was up to,

Princess. I could've pretended to go under. Might 'ave been a chance to learn something or even do something."

She gave a shrug. "Maybe. But I'll gladly settle for the fact that the bastard's right out of your mind, Willie. I can hardly bear even to think about it."

Willie nodded. "Worst thing ever 'appened to me," he said without apparent heat. "I aim to kill that one before this is over, Princess." His voice was casual, but she caught a glimpse of his eyes before he closed them and lay back on the bunk, and she decided that even with circumstances as they were, Dr. Tyl's future was likely to be short.

His visit had taken place on their second day in the cell, and since then they had been given no indication as to what lay in prospect for them until less than an hour ago, when the swords, round shields, garments and armour as worn by Roman gladiators two thousand years before had been brought to the cell, one set of suitable size for each of them. They had not considered refusing to dress, for this would be fruitless. Better to move on towards whatever was planned for them, and hope for an opening. Nothing could offer less chance than the last six days of confinement in the cell.

Modesty rotated her right shoulder, then shook her head. "Take the pauldron off please, Willie. Assuming the lunatics here are expecting us to fight somebody, I prefer speed to armour. I'm not even sure about the cuirass and kilt."

Willie nodded agreement and began to unbuckle the pauldron. The Roman sword was designed more for cutting than thrusting, but she was a first class fencer and would use point rather than edge. On balance she would do better unhampered by the restrictions of armour. He had yet to decide his own preference. It depended on a number of elements at present unknown. What little he and Modesty had been able to deduce about the people on Kalivari left them puzzled. Clearly a highly skilled criminal organisation was operating here, yet it seemed mainly concerned with devising lethal and complex charades that seemed quite irrational, as witness the extraordinary concept of setting up Willie Garvin to kill Modesty Blaise, and now staging this role-playing gladiatorial project.

Willie laid the pauldron aside and they looked at each other, moving about as far as the cell allowed, getting the feel of the ancient uniforms, watching each other intently. In their eyes there was now no hint of mutual concern, no scintilla of warmth or affection. In each the entire being was utterly concentrated upon mental and physical preparation for what was to come.

Willie said, "Could they aim to 'ave us fight each other, Princess?"

Her eyes went blank for a moment as she considered. Then: "I don't see how they can make us, short of threatening to kill one of us, which defeats the whole object. But in case they do . . ." Her voice trailed away.

He said, "There'll be guards with submachine-guns."

"Yes. So we fight, and you press me, and I'll retreat as close as we can get to a couple of them . . ."

"We lock swords, I take over yours . . ."

"You throw both to drop the nearest guards, and if we can get their s.m.g.'s quick enough for us to take out any other guards . . ."

"Play it by ear from then on. Right, Princess." That contingency was now covered to the limited extent open to them, and they left it.

Willie picked up one of the shields, slipping his forearm under the brace to grasp the grip. Modesty was trying the weight and balance of her sword. "You're the weapons expert," she said. "Tell me about gladiators."

"The blokes who fought with this gear were called *secutors*," said Willie. "Dress and weapons much the same as the Roman legionaries used, except for the shield. These are round, theirs were oblong and in-curved. Nothing much on record about techniques. Nothing to help us, anyway. I've got a hunch we're going to be matched against that weird couple I kept seeing around, Sibyl and Kazim. I saw them in action as *secutors* and they're good. I think maybe they specialise in this gladiator stuff." He put down the shield and stood thinking. "With your style, Princess, I reckon you'd do best with no armour at all."

"So do I. Speed and flexibility come first. But I'll have that pauldron on again for now, because I want us to go on parade in helmets and full rig. There's a nut-case or cases behind this who want a show, and it could pay to please him or them by putting on a colourful act. Might offer a better chance, once this part's over."

"Might keep us for another charade?"

"Yes."

"I've got a feeling you're right, Princess. So do we sign off whoever we're matched against?"

"I can't see there's anything to be lost by signing them off." Her midnight blue eyes were very dark and remote. "It won't change whether *we're* to be kept alive afterwards. And trying to pussyfoot around against experts so we don't actually kill them is stupid. If it comes to a thumbs-up or thumbs-down situation, that's for somebody else to decide, I suppose. But otherwise, if these people want mortal combat let's give them just that."

There was no arrogance or over-confidence in her assumption of victory. It was simply part of their combat readiness to entertain no concept of defeat. Willie said, "But first we put on a bit of a razamataz performance for the Chief Nut-Case, 'oping he'll reckon we're too good to waste?"

"It might pay, so it's worth trying."

Willie nodded. He felt very steady now, and there was no apprehension in him. If the Chief Nut-Case disapproved of their performance they might both be dead within the hour, but that was no new contingency, and their dying was of no particular importance except to themselves. It would be a pity, of course, if this was destined to be the one they would lose, but if it was written that way then Willie Garvin felt he could have no complaints. He had been one of the luckiest and happiest men alive for the last ten years, and you could hardly do better than that.

He picked up his sword, spun it in the air, and caught it by the hilt, frowning slightly. "It's all right for me, Princess. They don't seem to realise that to me a sword is just a big knife. I can put this through Kazim or whoever at thirty paces. But you'll be in close combat with a weapon you've never used before."

She shrugged. "I'll manage. Anyway, they may have cooked up something for us that isn't what we expect, so let's not speculate. Wait till we know what the game is before we decide how to play it."

"Sure."

He sat down on his bunk, watching her. She closed her eyes and began to feel the sword she held, sensing its shape, textures, construction, running her fingers lightly over it, hilt and blade, establishing rapport with it as if it were a sentient thing.

Willie laid his own sword aside. For a few moments he eyed his bronze-rimmed shield of bull-hide, then he picked it up and began to contemplate its qualities, seeking gently to construct a relationship between this inanimate object and himself.

※　　※　　※　　※

170

The courtyard of the monastery was a large rectangle enclosed by buildings two storeys high with a recessed balcony running the length of each short side. There were several doors leading from the courtyard into the ground floor, all closed, and a number of small windows, all shuttered. At one end the wooden gates of a square arch, large enough to receive a wagon, stood open. A flagged path ran round the perimeter of the courtyard, enclosing an area of dusty, hardbaked earth.

Modesty Blaise and Willie Garvin, followed at a prudent distance by three men with submachine-guns, came through the arch, each wearing the helmet and body armour of a *secutor*, sword in hand, shield on arm. A number of people were on the balcony facing them from the far end, and at once Modesty noted the halo-like white hair of the man with the big heavy face above the brown robe he wore. He was seated in the middle of the long balcony with its low balustrade, Mrs. Ram on his right and a cluster of others on either side, one a woman with broad shoulders and short-cropped red hair. Apart from Sibyl and Kazim, Tyl and Mrs. Ram, Willie had been able to give only vague recollections of those he had encountered during his dream-period on Kalivari, but this woman was clearly the one known to all as Ms. Johnson.

With the exception of Mrs. Ram, the only person on the balcony Modesty had seen close-to before was Dr. Tyl, sitting a little apart from the others, towards the western end of the balcony. When she glanced back, still moving with Willie up to the centre of the courtyard, Modesty saw that two of the escort guards had moved to opposite corners of the archway end of the courtyard, the third remaining by the open gates. On the balcony above the arch, another dozen or so men were gathered.

Four large square pedestals of stone, each about four feet high, formed a much smaller rectangle centred in the courtyard. Perhaps they had once been intended to bear statues of Greek or Roman gods, or of saints to inspire the long departed monks, but if any had ever stood there they had long since been removed. Together Modesty and Willie moved on, passing between the first pair of pedestals, keeping in step. They knew that if they lived this would in retrospect seem a lunatic occasion, but here in the morning sun of Aegean, at this present moment, they also knew that now was a time to kill or be killed, and there was no more true lunacy in it than in the butcheries of a clown called Nero. There was only raw evil. As they reached the second pair of pedestals Mrs. Ram stood up and called sharply, "Halt!"

Thirty yards to the balcony . . . within range of Willie's sword. It was clear that nobody had grasped the fact that to Willie a missile was a missile, whether knife, axe, sword, anything.

"It has been decided," said Mrs. Ram, lifting her voice, "that you are to partake in a scenario featuring gladiatorial performance. Other dramatis personae have been provided by members of our community on voluntary basis. Refusal to perform will be deemed capital offence, penalty is death by lapidation. Questions?"

The two helmeted figures remained silent, but both swords were raised as one in a salute. A murmur of surprise ran along the balcony, and even Thaddeus Pilgrim's wandering gaze became fixed for a moment or two. Mrs. Ram said in an undertone, "They are extremely unusual couple, Doctor. Who would expect such immediate compliance without further emphatic threat? And no questions, you see? They are most enigmatical people."

"They have, I think, though of course I may be in error, the valuable gift of *acceptance*, dear lady," said Thaddeus Pilgrim. "Ideal material for inducing a change of – ah – attitude, I would suggest. It is almost, I say *almost*, to be regretted that we are so shortly to lose them, unless, of course . . ." his voice faded, then resumed. "However, we must not think of sacrificing such a splendid scenario to the – ah – mercenary cause of recruitment, Mrs. Ram. What are they doing now, I wonder?"

Down in the courtyard, Willie Garvin had laid aside his sword and shield, and was unbuckling Modesty's cuirass. She had already removed her helmet and was unfastening the protective kilt. Next to the skin she wore a white cotton shift extending from shoulders to thighs, and brief shorts of the same material. Willie had been supplied with similar under-garments.

Willie said, "Same for me, Princess," and as she began to help him strip off his armour two figures appeared in the archway, a tall blonde woman and a dark muscular man. Sibyl Pray wore sandals, a kind of loin-cloth, and a light bodice which covered her torso, leaving her midriff bare. Her head was also bare, the hair drawn tightly back so that it looked like a golden helmet. Beside her, Kazim wore only loin-cloth and sandals. Each held a trident in the left hand, and carried something draped over the right forearm. A weighted net.

As Modesty lifted away Willie's backplate she heard him draw in a quick breath. "*Secutor* against *retiarius*," he murmured. "Three to one in favour of the net-man, they always reckoned. You'll 'ave to be very careful."

172

"So will you." She threw the backplate aside with a clangour, speaking rapidly in a whisper. "No use your putting a sword through one of them right away. We're here to give a show, that sticks out a mile. Look, those pedestals are going to be useful. We'll play this criss-cross. And mark where I've chucked these bits of armour. Hazards for them, not for us if we keep a mental picture of where they lie. When it's time to finish, better let me give the cue because you're more flexible. If things look bad when we've put these two down we'll take the best option on offer according to how we're placed. Three s.m.g.'s in the courtyard. A few doors leading off that might give way to a flying kick. Or I can reach that balcony if you boost me with a stirrup throw. Sword at White Hair's throat? Maybe. We'll see."

Willie gazed about him, spreading some of the discarded armour with his foot, marking all external factors of the situation for possible use. There would be almost an embarrassment of options available if things looked bad once the battle was over. It did not trouble him greatly that the best would offer no more than a slender hope of success.

At the far end of the courtyard Sibyl Pray and Kazim had performed an elaborate salute to the balcony with their tridents and now stood watching with a baffled air. Sibyl was angry. She had asked that she and Kazim should play the part of *secutors* against *retiarii* so that the odds would be against them and their victory would show wide superiority over the renowned pair of Blaise and Garvin. But Thaddeus Pilgrim had decreed otherwise, benignly venturing to suggest – though not, of course, not for a moment underestimating the very real abilities, not to say the wide experience, of her goodself and Kazim – to suggest that it would perhaps be . . . yes, *prudent* was an acceptable word, he trusted – prudent to reverse the roles, and he felt sure that Sibyl and Kazim would be happy to oblige him in this small matter.

"They are mad," Sibyl said now to Kazim as their opponents finished stripping off all protective armour, Willie Garvin retaining his sandals, Modesty Blaise discarding hers. "They can know nothing about the techniques of *secutor versus retiarius*."

"It could be a bad disappointment for us," Kazim murmured with a shrug, "but let us remember that you misjudged Garvin's ability the day we killed Molly Chen. We must not underestimate these two."

Sibyl Pray's nostrils flared a little as she inhaled. "I will not do that," she said. "But let us finish this very quickly, so it will be a disappointing scenario for Dr. Pilgrim. Then perhaps he will not underestimate *us* another time."

Between the four pedestals, Modesty picked up her sword and shield, glancing at Willie. "So it was one of those two who broke Molly Chen's neck," she said.

He gave a brief nod, and she could almost feel the surge of adrenalin in him. This was a useful preliminary, but to steady the flow she touched his arm with her elbow and said, "Just one thing . . ."

"M'mm?"

"What the hell is lapidation?"

He glanced at her, relaxing, knowing her purpose. "It means stoning," he said.

"I just wondered." She looked down the courtyard at the two figures who had begun to advance slowly, shaking out their nets. "All right, Willie. Let's go." They moved apart, towards the long edges of the courtyard, and stood waiting. Sibyl Pray veered towards Modesty, and Kazim towards Willie, both moving smoothly but warily. Sibyl held her net at one end so that it trailed behind her, trident poised. Her defence lay in the length of the trident, which far outreached the sword. The edges of the net carried a number of little lead weights, and at a distance from which it could be used bunched, with a sweeping motion, to coil about a knee or ankle, Sibyl halted to study her opponent.

An inch or two shorter, a few pounds lighter, the dark-haired girl stood with bare left foot slightly advanced, shield held in front of her obliquely, one edge forward to present a surface that would deflect rather than take the full force of a strike by the trident. Her face was impassive, the eyes like black stones lit from within by a tiny cold flame, and abruptly Sibyl felt a tremor pass through her body. She knew it could not be apprehension, but there was something in the eyes . . .

This one would not die easily, as Molly Chen had died, and Papadakis, and all the others over the years. This one was different. Not a victim. Sibyl remembered the dossier. This one had faced expert killers before. And survived. And dealt out death in return.

Sibyl heard the sound of metal on metal, and knew that Kazim had begun an attack. She made a low sweep with the net, and Modesty Blaise just lifted her forward foot long enough for the net to pass beneath it. Sibyl jabbed quickly with the trident, aiming for the knee,

174

but the edge of the shield slid between two tines of the trident, and a powerful twist almost jerked the weapon from Sibyl's hands.

She jumped back, crushing a momentary spurt of alarm with cold professionalism. In that moment Modesty Blaise gave a sudden sharp whistle between her teeth. There came an answering whistle from somewhere on the far side of the courtyard, then Sibyl heard a swift patter of running feet and a startled cry of warning from Kazim.

She flicked a glance over her shoulder, and saw with heart-stopping shock that Willie Garvin had broken away from Kazim and was racing towards her, sword held extended like a sabre, only ten paces away now. Kazim was in frantic pursuit but far out of range for a thrust, and Modesty Blaise was poised to come in at her unprotected back if she turned to hold off Garvin. The chill of despair struck like a knife, then in desperation Kazim drew back his arm and launched the trident in a spear-throw at Garvin's back, but in the instant before it left his hand Modesty Blaise whistled again, and Garvin swerved, ducking, so that the trident flew past him and would have taken Sibyl in the leg if she had not fended it off with her own trident. But to do this she had swung away from Modesty Blaise, exposing her own back, and Kazim was unarmed now, and unbelievably they were beaten, death was seconds away —

Willie Garvin veered off past one of the pedestals at a walk, joining Modesty Blaise, who had made no attempt to take Sibyl from behind, and they were chatting together, smiling with amusement as they strolled up the centre of the courtyard for a little way, then turned to come back on the far side of the pedestals from where Sibyl now stood panting as if after a hard race, and Kazim was snatching up his fallen trident.

On the balcony Mrs. Ram let out a pent-up breath. "What absolutely top-hole curtain-raiser for your scenario, Doctor!" she breathed, dark eyes shining with delight. "Perhaps imprudent of our visitors not to take advantage of surprise, would you say? Sibyl and Kazim are forewarned of unorthodox stratagems now."

Thaddeus Pilgrim glanced along the balcony to where the couples of his A.T.P. teams stood watching. They were speaking in low tones with suppressed excitement, but not a head turned, not an eye was taken from the scene in the courtyard below. "I suspect," said Thaddeus Pilgrim, "that our interesting visitors are, to use common parlance, 'putting on an act' to assert their superiority. A dangerous ploy, dear lady, against persons as skilled as our dear Sibyl and Kazim. Let us see what eventuates before we either applaud or criticise the – ah – style of our visitors. But certainly the scenario promises to be all that we could have hoped for."

Below, Sibyl and Kazim were showing that they had courage to match their high skills, and both *retiarii* had moved to the attack again, this time with Modesty facing Kazim and Willie facing Sibyl. Suddenly Kazim made a very good cast with his net, the weighted edges spreading beautifully, but a sideways leap by Modesty, unhampered by armour, took her easily clear before the net could descend. A forward jump brought her down on the edge of the net with both feet as it fell to the ground, and with a cry of triumph Kazim seized on her error, jerking with all his strength to whip her legs from under her. But she was rising again even as he jerked, and with her weight gone he staggered back off balance.

She was after him instantly, and he had to let go of the net to fend her off with desperate parries and lunges of the trident. Then she was gone, the net scooped up on her sword, moving very fast round one of the pedestals and on to the next. There, Willie had contrived to get the broad block of stone between himself and Sibyl, and now stood gazing at her with polite interest over the flat top as she tried to decide how best to come at him.

Modesty said, "Up," and Willie dropped to one knee briefly so that she was able to take a leaping step up from his knee and shoulder to the top of the pedestal. As he rose and turned to take Kazim's lunge on his shield, she flicked the sword to toss the net at Sibyl. It was no proper cast, and the net only half opened, but it entangled Sibyl's trident in its fall, and as she struggled to free it Modesty was down again, moving fast to join Willie against Kazim, so that the *retiarius* was forced to break and run from the double threat.

There was no pursuit. As the man fled, Modesty and Willie relaxed and moved to the space within the four pedestals, talking quietly again and seemingly unaware of the bitter recriminations between their opponents as Sibyl and Kazim re-armed and prepared to renew the combat. The next five minutes followed the pattern already set, though with rapidly decreasing dominance by the *secutors* as the *retiarii*, strong, skilled, and combat-wise, learned to defend against the bewildering criss-cross moves of their opponents.

There were times, too, when Modesty and Willie stood their ground for a while and fought one-to-one without frills against net and trident. On the balcony the entity that Thaddeus Pilgrim had become, the corrupt spirit of the man and what remained of his soul, was more wholly present than usual as he watched with fascination the scenario being enacted in the courtyard below, listening with interest to the murmured comments of the A.T.P. teams.

"Making it to look easy, but not so, yes?"

"Certainly not so, Patel old thing. Bloody clever. Especially the way they know exactly where those bits of scattered armour are without looking." This was Patel's partner, Dixon, one of the most able killers Eton had ever produced.

"They are working to a margin of millimetres," said Ritter, the Belgian knife specialist.

"*And* milliseconds, Sugar. Hey, Sibyl nearly got him then, though." This was the formidable Ms. Johnson from Los Angeles.

Then Bonsu, from Guinea, who worked with Ritter: "Whassa good *nearly* got him? How the hell Garvin always knowing what Blaise want, and her knowing what *he* want? Goddam magic stuff."

"Male and female perhaps, old boy?"

"Hey, Zanelli." Bonsu again. "You 'an Miz Johnson know to work this magic stuff, huh? Man-woman like Dixon say?"

Zanelli said softly, "What for they play games like this, Blaise and Garvin? Very dangerous. They are not faster, not stronger, not better than our two lovebirds. Only edge they have is what Bonsu calls the magic."

Dixon said dryly, "They're also highly creative, wouldn't you say?"

Zanelli shrugged. "That, also. But is it enough to permit that they play stupid games?"

"That's what we're waiting to find out, old fruit. For myself I would never risk one teeny weeny aggressive move towards our resident Nymph and Satyr, much as I detest them. Easy killing is my vocation, and they're far too good. Blaise and Garvin are taking stupendous risks even in *pretending* to fool around."

In the courtyard, Sibyl and Kazim were as yet untouched because their opponents had let opportunities pass. Modesty's cotton shift was torn and bloodstained on one side from a small gash over her ribs, and Willie had a minor cut on his face where one of the lead weights on Sibyl's net had caught him. He was facing Kazim now, with Modesty and Sibyl almost fifty paces away near the archway gate, and there was a momentary pause in the action as the combatants shuffled and weaved, breathing hard and sweating now as they made ready for the next move of attack or defence.

It was then that Modesty stepped back, laid down her sword and shield, and straightened up to stand with hands on hips. There came a murmur of astonishment from the watchers. After a startled moment, Sibyl cast her net. Another murmur, louder, more excited, for Modesty was no longer there. She had not turned, had simply moved straight back, but with an ease and speed that the watching combat experts found hard to credit. Hearing that sound from the balconies at each end of the courtyard, Willie Garvin knew what was happening. It was Modesty's unique gift, acquired for survival during her childhood wanderings of the Middle East and North Africa, that she could move back under full control faster than most people could advance.

On the main balcony, Ms. Johnson said, "Jesus! Will you look at that!"

Two seconds had passed. The dark-haired girl was moving back along one side of the courtyard in long, rangy strides, never taking her eyes from the blonde girl pursuing her, yet avoiding the obstacles of breastplate, helmet, sandals, pauldrons strewn in her path, clearing them by inches. Sibyl Pray had abandoned her net, held the trident in both hands as she ran, and was angling out slightly to herd her now defenceless opponent into a corner of the courtyard.

Four seconds had passed. Sibyl's foot caught a discarded helmet, causing the slightest of stumbles, and in that moment Modesty Blaise halted as if stopped by an invisible wall. Sibyl Pray lunged, the sun glinting on her finely muscled body as it was committed with all its power and perfection to the long extension of the death-thrust, from back-reaching foot through the line of leg, hips and torso to shoulders, arms, hands, and finally to the trident shaft tipped with its three vicious tines. She had been caught fractionally off balance, but this had slowed her by only a few milliseconds.

A few milliseconds were enough. It seemed that Modesty's body undulated in a curiously boneless way so that the nearest tine of the trident missed by a finger's width, sliding past at waist height. Her arm clamped down behind the tines, locking the shaft under her armpit as she gripped it a little higher with her hands, and the flow of movement through her body seemed to continue without interruption the flow of her opponent's lunge, sweeping from the arm that locked the trident in a smooth flexure across the shoulders and through the body, rippling down the far leg to send the bare foot flashing up in a rising curve, a blur of movement that ended with the rock-hard ball of her foot exploding against the side of Sibyl's neck just behind the hinge of the jaw.

The foot had known no shoe until Modesty was in her teens, and even now she often walked miles across country unshod. The precisely delivered blow with that foot, enhanced in power by the fierce exhalation of a *ki-ya* cry bursting from her lungs at the moment of impact, had the effect of a long-handled mace striking home, and Sibyl Pray was dead before her suddenly limp body crumpled to the ground.

Willie Garvin heard the cry and lowered his shield and sword. Then, as Kazim stared, wondering, yet not daring to look away, Willie said, "This is for Molly Chen." His right arm seemed to flicker. There was no time to duck or dodge, no time for Kazim even to register what was happening before the short, broad-bladed sword, thrown underhand, flashed across the six or seven paces between the two men on a rising flight to drive up under the breastbone into the heart. The trident and net fell from suddenly impotent hands, and a wordless sound came from Kazim's mouth as he toppled sideways.

Willie turned away, slipping the shield from his left arm and glancing up at the main balcony as he walked slowly towards it to meet Modesty. From the balcony there was utter silence. As he had done in the cell, Willie weighed the shield in his hands, sensing its nature and quality, eyes flicking again to the balcony. Behind him the three guards at the archway end of the courtyard were moving forward uncertainly, s.m.g.'s held ready.

Modesty came towards him smiling, pushing a lock of hair from her face, and perhaps only Willie Garvin could have known how false was the smile, or have detected the strain that lay deep in her eyes. He said barely above his breath, "Can I take out Tyl? *Now*?"

Her eyes widened in puzzlement, but she asked no question and simply replied in an undertone. "Yes. We reckoned the better show we gave, the better our chances, and it looks as if Tyl's in disgrace, so there's nothing to lose."

"Right." Willie glanced once more towards the balcony some fifteen paces away. People were beginning to stir now, and all eyes had turned to the white haired man in the middle. At the end of the balcony Tyl had risen and was also looking towards Dr. Pilgrim. Willie Garvin's arm swept round as he flung his shield away, high in the air, then he turned to take Modesty's arm and start walking towards the archway at the far end of the courtyard.

Only Thaddeus Pilgrim was watching when Willie threw the shield, though others may have caught the movement from the corners of their eyes, but not a soul registered its import, and even Modesty herself found it hard to credit what she knew Willie must have intended. The tossing away of the shield had been done with a deceptively casual movement, but there was rare strength behind it, and the disc of bullhide and bronze was carried smoothly up by the function of aerodynamics, spinning as it rose higher than the balcony, to be lost for a moment against the sun before angling down sharply.

Dr. Janos Tyl had no inkling that he was about to die. He was standing by the balustrade looking towards Thaddeus Pilgrim when the great disc slid down the slope of air to strike his neck like a blunt axe, hurling him forward so that he crashed full length on the flags of the balcony. Dixon and Ritter were the first to reach him. As the Belgian knelt over the brown-robed form, Dixon picked up the shield and gazed at it incredulously, then looked down to where Modesty Blaise and Willie Garvin were still walking unhurriedly away down the courtyard.

Ritter said, "He's *dead!*"

Dixon nodded slowly. "You don't astonish me, mon vieux. This thing weighs eight pounds, and I *heard* it hit him."

Walking at a deliberately idle pace beside Willie, her arm through his, Modesty had taken her cue from him and resisted the temptation to watch the shield in flight or to look round. "Think you made it?" she murmured through unmoving lips.

"No question." He pressed her arm. "This was one time it was there before I threw it, Princess."

So Tyl was dead, and that was especially good for Willie she decided. The man who had carried out the sickening purpose of entering his mind and taking control of it no longer existed. The three guards had lined up across the archway now, s.m.g.'s cocked and ready. At six paces Modesty and Willie halted, gazing at the men placidly, still not turning their heads to look back, waiting to hear the order to kill or reprieve, inwardly making ready for the diving somersault, hoping it might take them in under the spray of bullets that would inevitably cause the gun-muzzles to ride up, with a chance of securing a weapon

180

each and at least making an effort of last resort, hopeless though it might be.

Modesty said quietly, "I forgot to tell you. Dinah sent her love."

He nodded. "Thanks."

There was silence for perhaps ten seconds, then Mrs. Ram's voice sounded clearly as she called from the balcony at the upper end of the courtyard. "Dr. Pilgrim requires that visitors be escorted to their quarters."

Modesty smiled absently at the guards. "When you're ready," she said.

Two minutes later, when the cell door had closed behind them, they let go and fell limply on their bunks, limbs not quite steady, their breathing deep and ragged with reaction. "Jesus," croaked Willie, "they were good, those two. Never seen faster."

"Strong, too." Her voice wavered a little. With the ordeal past, they could allow themselves to acknowledge the frightening capabilities of their opponents, and to know fear in retrospect. "Let's try not to get into anything as close-run as that again, Willie," she said, eyes closed, a hand on her gashed flank. "If their timing hadn't been a touch off . . . and if we weren't so sneaky . . ."

"M'mm."

For five minutes they lay relaxing, letting nerves and sinews ease back to normal, then Willie stood up. "Get that shift off, Princess," he said, moving towards the washroom, "I'll 'ave a look at your side."

When he returned with a damp towel she had taken off the shift and lay with arm raised, examining the cut. "Nothing much, Willie. It's almost stopped bleeding. What about your face?"

"More blood than damage." He grinned, gave a thump on the door with his fist and lifted his voice. "Oi! You outside! Let's 'ave some first aid gear, and don't 'ang about!"

Sitting on the edge of her bunk he began to clean the small wound. After a while he said, "I wonder what 'appens next, Princess."

She smiled up at him. "God knows, Willie . . . but we're a lot better off than we were six days ago."

He nodded. "Or even an hour."

181

12

"That is the scenario we have devised for our – ah – shipping scam, as I believe it is termed by the criminal fraternity, or perhaps I should say the *English speaking* criminal fraternity, though I have little doubt that the term is also used, quite informally, of course, by English speaking legal and law enforcement authorities."

Thaddeus Pilgrim paused, gazing benignly across his desk. Twenty-four hours had passed since the battle in the courtyard. Modesty Blaise and Willie Garvin sat against the wall facing the desk, bathed and groomed, their clothes freshly laundered and pressed. Zanelli, the tall and sinewy Italian, leaned against the wall at a prudent distance to one side of them, a Uzi submachine-gun resting in the crook of his elbow. His partner, Ms. Johnson, similarly armed, was positioned behind and to one side of Dr. Pilgrim. Mrs. Ram sat near the window, clipboard on her lap.

It was fifteen minutes since Modesty and Willie had been brought to the study. Thaddeus Pilgrim had first introduced himself in tortuous fashion, hoping they would understand that he was not, that was to say not in any significant sense, a *leader* of the little – ah – community here on Kalivari, but should be regarded by Miss Blaise and Mr. Garvin – whom he was happy, indeed more than happy, to welcome among them – regarded more as a *representative* of the Hostel of Righteousness, a representative not only of those members whose acquaintance Miss – ah . . . and her companion had already made, but of those others whose acquaintance they would, he sincerely trusted, be making very shortly in the pursuit of certain – ah – aims and ambitions common to all.

Leaning back in his swivel chair, hands limply folded across his stomach, eyes wandering vaguely about the room as he spoke, Thaddeus Pilgrim had then gone on to explain, with many laborious circumlocutions, the general operation and fund raising activities of the Answer To Prayer teams. He was now concluding a detailed account, carefully whitewashed with euphemisms, of the plan for scuttling the tanker *Marimba* and murdering her entire crew; the Hallelujah Scenario, as he reverently called it.

Modesty and Willie had not spoken since entering the study, neither had they been called upon to do so, for any questions that entered Thaddeus Pilgrim's rambling narrative were purely theoretical, buried in sub-clauses of endless sentences. They had both made a brief assessment of the likely outcome of taking action, and decided that this would be fatal. It had not been necessary to exchange so much as a look to know each other's thoughts on this.

Both wore expressions of polite if not very profound interest, but this concealed an unease and discomfort which had been growing within them ever since entering the study, and they were powerfully aware of it in each other. The feeling was not quite fear and not quite apprehension, though there were perhaps elements of both present. It was basically an ever-growing repugnance, an abhorrence, a queasiness that stemmed from being in the presence of the bulky, brown-robed figure with its pale fleshy face, watery and unfocused eyes, slack mouth, incongruous halo, and pious air when speaking horrors.

Thaddeus Pilgrim was smoothly shaven, clean and fresh, with soft hands neatly manicured, but he exuded an aura of corruption, a psychic smell of putrescence, of death and decay, of foul impurities and rancid matter. Only one thing in the study hinted at this, slyly but obscenely. A white mouse in a cage on his desk was busily gnawing its own leg off.

It had taken Modesty and Willie a little time to comprehend what the creature was doing, and then it was hard to keep the eye from being drawn to the horrible sight. They knew the mouse must be the victim of a heavy dose of one of the hallucinogenic drugs, perhaps LSD; probably a fatal dose, in which case the little animal might die before it killed itself. But this explained nothing of reason or purpose. In fact there could be no reason or purpose, except that of idle sadism.

Every now and again, as Thaddeus Pilgrim rambled on, he would let his woolly gaze rest on the mouse for a few moments, then look at Modesty and Willie with a lifted eyebrow and inviting smile, as if hoping they might join him in fleeting contemplation of the creature's torment while attending to the main purpose of the occasion.

"I fully realise," he was saying now, "that the – ah – methodology of the Hallelujah Scenario is by no means new to you, Miss Blaise, nor to your esteemed colleague, Mr. Garvin, since you may well claim to have been the *originator* of this type of scenario in years gone by." He stopped speaking, eyebrows lifted, and after a few moments Modesty realised that a response was expected at last.

She said in a neutral voice, "I'm not claiming copyright. But whenever I ran a shipping insurance scam nobody was ever killed."

Thaddeus Pilgrim gave her his version of a roguish smile, and her gorge rose. "We must move with the times, Miss – ah . . . we must move with the times. Constant innovation is essential for continued success, is it not? You are, I am sure we would all agree, a long-standing practitioner yourself of that excellent maxim, so I feel you cannot fail to appreciate that, however reluctantly, we must face the sad necessity of – ah . . ." his voice sank to a hushed and reverent tone, "of causing one or two sea-faring persons, no more than two dozen, I am assured, to be received into the arms of their chosen mistress, the ageless sea."

There was a silence. Modesty resisted the temptation to turn her head and look at Willie. He would be as baffled as she was, and showing it as little. With an effort she kept her eyes from straying to the white thing destroying itself in the cage, and said politely, "Why are you telling us all this?" It was the only question she had asked so far.

"Ah, now there we come to the nub of the matter," said Thaddeus Pilgrim dreamily. "We feel – and I know I speak for all my colleagues, Miss Blaise – we feel as it were, *drawn* towards you and Mr. – ah . . . here, as kindred spirits. We wish you to become a *part* of our happy band, marching on shoulder to shoulder in pursuit of . . . of . . . of fucking *millions*, Miss Blaise."

Again came the travesty of a roguish smile. Then: "But I am sure you will perceive the need of a binding and indeed an *enforceable* agreement between us. It is for this reason that I have entered into a contract with Salamander Four. Your wide experience will of course have made you cognisant of the services provided by, and the unfailing reliability of, that curiously named organisation?"

She decided there was no point in pretending not to know about Salamander Four, and said, "I've never used them, but I know them by reputation. They're a secret international consortium run by very powerful men who are also highly respected industrialists. They used to deal only in Industrial Espionage, but now they've diversified and they're contractors for any crime up to and including murder, providing it's not political. They use very experienced people, they charge high prices, and it's their claim that they never fail." She did not feel called upon to mention that the claim was not quite true. She had tangled with Salamander Four herself in the past, to their loss, but she retained a very healthy respect for their power.

Thaddeus Pilgrim said confidingly, "They do indeed set a high price on their services. I think you will be quite shocked to hear that they are charging us *fifty thousand pounds* for a simple contract to perform an obscene killing of, let me see now, yes, of Professor – ah – Stephen Collier and his charming wife. Fifty thousand! Mrs. Ram feels we should have sought other estimates, but . . ." he wagged his head with an indulgent smile. "What is mere money compared with the pleasure, the satisfaction, the simple *joy* of securing the glad co-operation of your goodself and your valued colleague?"

For a moment her mind was in turmoil from the shock of Thaddeus Pilgrim's words, but her expression did not change. Smoothly she moved a hand to rest it on her knee, fingers straight and pressed together, a signal to restrain Willie from any sudden action, for she sensed the wave of fury emanating from him. "You believe that killing the Colliers will secure our co-operation?" she said mildly.

"Oh, no, no, dear lady," protested Thaddeus Pilgrim with avuncular condescension. "It is by *not* so doing that I hope to cement a lasting friendship between us, and it is to this end that I am employing what I feel might correctly be described as a variation of the Dead Man's Handle device."

Mrs. Ram leaned forward. "That is method used for railway engines," she explained. "Driver must hold handle to make train go. If he becomes dead or unconscious and lets go of handle, the train stops."

Her eyes on Thaddeus Pilgrim, Modesty said, "A variation?"

The white head nodded amiably. "At noon and at midnight daily I repair to our radio room to receive a call from a Salamander Four station somewhere in Europe. By responding to this call with a certain codeword – a word known only to myself, I hasten to say – I ensure that Salamander Four executives will *not* kill Professor and Mrs. Collier by obscene methods, or indeed by any method, for the next twelve hours. Should I *fail* to respond . . ." the limp hands gestured vaguely, "fail for any reason whatsoever, you understand, then the – ah – aggravated dispatch of your friends will be automatic."

Thaddeus Pilgrim smiled gently, turning his head so that his gaze drifted from Zanelli to Ms. Johnson. "I feel sure you may dispense with the – um – firearms now, my dear colleagues," he said. "Our new friends will realise that the slightest inappropriate action on their part, whatever the result, must inevitably lead to the demise of certain persons to whom they are strongly attached."

It was true enough, thought Willie Garvin savagely, struggling to hide the rage that sought to consume him. In the next minute or next hour or next day it would surely be possible to kill this hideously evil bastard and several of his people in a burst of action, but that would be the end of it, for the odds were too great. He and Modesty would die. More important, so would Steve and Dinah. He heard Modesty clear her throat, and turned his head slightly to look directly at her for the first time since entering the study, knowing she had a message for him. Her hand was moving nervously, wiping sweat from her upper lip, resting on her breast for a moment, then dropping to the knee again, fingers drumming slightly.

"What do you want us to do?" she said to Thaddeus Pilgrim. Her voice was hard and resentful, but in it were the unmistakable beginnings of resigned acceptance, and Mrs. Ram's eyes rested with glowing admiration upon her master.

"We would like you to lead our combined A.T.P. force in the Hallelujah Scenario," said Thaddeus Pilgrim with the air of one suggesting a great treat. "After all," he went on with a whimsical smile, "you have deprived us of the services of dear Sibyl and Kazim in this regard."

"You're talking about going aboard your tanker – what is it? The *Marimba*? All right. Then killing all the crew, sinking the tanker, and arranging evidence to make it appear she hit a mine. Is that correct?"

"I feel you have summarised the matter accurately," said Thaddeus Pilgrim reflectively. "You would not, I may say, be required to carry out such personal killings as you might feel were distasteful to you, since you will have ample assistance in this respect. What I hope for, dear Miss Blaise, is your – ah – experienced leadership, your organisational skills, and your . . . your compelling *authority*."

There was a silence. She stared down at the floor, tugged gently at an ear-lobe, then turned her head to look questioningly at Willie. He said dourly, "Why should we care what 'appens to anyone on the *Marimba*?"

She gave a shrug and looked at Thaddeus Pilgrim again. "All right. I don't like being pushed around, but I know when I'm over a barrel.

You've got a deal, with one proviso. If I'm going to be in charge I'll want right of approval of whatever plan you've got – if you've got one. I mean a detailed plan. That means a scale plan of the tanker, nominal roll of the crew, precise details of arrangements for the rendezvous and ship-to-ship communication. I'll want to drill the boarding party and rehearse every move. I'll want to assess every man –" she flicked a glance at Ms. Johnson, "or woman taking part. I'll want to allot specific duties to each. I'll also want Willie Garvin to check that your explosives expert, whoever he is, knows exactly how to simulate the effect of the tanker striking a mine. So how long have we got for all this?"

Thaddeus Pilgrim wagged his head admiringly. "Oh, my dear Miss Blaise, I am sure we shall all get on quite famously together. Such a . . . such an *incisive* approach. I am always urging the virtues of incisiveness upon my colleagues." His eyes wandered to the Hindu woman. "Perhaps, Mrs. Ram, you would be so kind as to, ah . . . ?"

She consulted her clipboard and said briskly, "With reference to question posed by Miss Blaise, schedule provides for this event, namely sinking of tanker, to eventuate approx. fifteen days hence, with arrival of *Marimba* in rendezvous area."

Modesty sat with narrowed eyes, calculating. "Two days for the cargo boat to reach the area from Dakar," she murmured. Then, sharply, "How are you getting the A.T.P. task force to Dakar? Christ, it's around five thousand miles. You're already too late by sea."

Mrs. Ram stared at her from dark, hostile eyes. "We have efficient administration, Miss Blaise. Task force will make short sea journey to Smyrna, and then fly by private charter aircraft to Dakar. Total time, less than thirty-six hours, arriving Dakar three days before departure therefrom on cargo boat, to allow for contingencies."

Modesty nodded slowly. "So we've got a full week here for training. All right. That should be enough."

The mutilated white mouse was rolled in a ball in a corner of the cage now, squeaking faintly. Thaddeus Pilgrim eyed it reproachfully and said, "I feel we have had a most satisfactory meeting this morning. Most satisfactory. I feel sure we would all agree that Miss Blaise and Mr. Garvin may now be given whatever facilities they require for the tasks they have undertaken. As recruits to the Hostel of Righteousness they must of course be provided with suitable robes for – ah – emergency wear, and I feel that when the weekly ferry calls it would, perhaps, be prudent, and our mutual wish, that we should gather in the chapel for silent prayer and meditation until the ferry has departed."

His white eyebrows lifted as he looked askance from under them at Modesty and Willie with a playful smile. "And you will, I am sure, understand that it is really quite – ah – unhealthy for new recruits to cling together. We must mix, dear friends, we must mix so that we become . . . *absorbed* into the community. Ms. Johnson will therefore take *you* under her wing, Miss Blaise, while Signor Zanelli makes himself responsible for – what is it called, Mrs. Ram? Ah yes, for the *induction* of Mr. Garvin."

✳   ✳   ✳   ✳

Krolli looked across the table at Maude Tiller. Then he looked at Danny Chavasse and said, "But she's a girl."

Danny sighed. "Don't talk like a male Greek. You never complained that Mam'selle was a girl."

Krolli shrugged. "That was Mam'selle."

"Right. And when I was in Limbo and Mam'selle came for me, she had Willie move in through the most hellish jungle you can imagine. The kind where you make maybe two miles a day, cutting your way. And you know who Willie chose to go with him? To cut through that goddam jungle and fight when they reached us? Willie *chose* Maude Tiller, and that makes her very special."

Krolli stared at the fair girl. "Danny's not kidding?"

Maude shook her head. "No. I'm good enough for Willie Garvin."

Krolli nodded soberly. "Then you're good enough for me, lady. Sorry not to be polite."

"That's okay." She gave him a smile. "Most men take a lot longer to convince."

"I guess they don't know Willie Garvin."

Danny said, "Let's clear the decks on one thing that might help, Krolli. Whatever we may need, money's no object. I mean literally no object. I can get whatever we want by a phone call."

Maude looked at him and said, "Some of those billionaires you were with in Limbo?"

"Handfuls of them. But Stavros is right here in Athens."

Krolli's eyes widened. "The shipping line Stavros?"

"That's the one. He was a slave in Limbo for four years, and he's got whip scars on his back still. When it was all over he tried to give Modesty an ocean going yacht."

"Sweet Jesus!"

Maude said, "I was with him just for a little while when we were mopping up, and he sent *me* a Rolls Royce. How do you send a Rolls back? It's still in the garage at my parents' farm with about five hundred miles on the clock."

Krolli laughed briefly. "So we can call on Stavros if we need to. That's good. Not so much for the money, more because he's a big man with a lot of influence. But right now I don't see any way he can help."

Maude said, "What can you tell us?"

Krolli made a wry grimace and sipped his ouzo. "I hit a block trying to trace back through the cut-outs. They were damn smart, those people who took Mam'selle. I got contacts everywhere trying to turn up *any* kind of lead."

Danny said, "Nothing?"

Krolli hesitated. "Maybe a ghost of something. I don't know. There are two fishermen, Nikos and George Petrakis, father and son, with their own boat. They fish out of Piraeus all their lives. The day after Mam'selle goes missing, they also go missing. I think maybe they know something, and I think maybe they got scared."

Maude said, "Fishermen? Could they have been the last of the cut-outs?"

Krolli lifted his glass to her. "Smart lady. Think now, Danny. Suppose they take Mam'selle some place. God knows where. She also is one smart lady, and she thinks, *If somebody don't want these fishermen to talk later, somebody is going to knock them off, maybe*. So she warns them. That figures?"

Danny said, "It figures. But I don't quite see —"

Krolli silenced him with a gesture of exasperation. "No more do *I* quite see how and why and where. But take it from me, it is very strange that they suddenly disappear, these fishermen."

Maude said, "Maybe somebody did knock them off to make sure they couldn't talk."

Krolli shook his head. "I don't think so. I think they have gone away somewhere, to hide. If not, then George's sister would be going to the police to say they are missing. And listen. Only yesterday I hear somebody *else* is looking for them."

Maude drank some retsina and suppressed a grimace. "Could we get hold of this somebody else and find out who hired him to look for the fishermen?"

Krolli said, "It would mean trying to trace back through more cut-outs."

"Yes. Well, is there anybody at all who might know where the fishermen are hiding, Mr. Krolli?"

He touched her hand. "Just Krolli, please. Yes, George's sister might know. She is the only close relative now, a widow of about forty, Helen Kaltchas. She has been asked by us about them, very gently so as not to frighten her, but she says they have moved to another fishing ground, she doesn't know where. We have offered good money, but still she says she does not know. I think perhaps she lies because she is afraid for her father and brother."

Danny said, "If the somebody else who's looking for these fishermen gets to Helen Kaltchas, they could well rip it out of her."

Krolli nodded. "I thought of that, and this morning my people removed the somebody else. There were three of them, and they are now on a slow boat to Madagascar." He smiled briefly. "Because of the cut-outs, it will be a long time before whoever hired them learns that they are no longer around." The smile vanished. "But we cannot do what *they* would do with Helen Kaltchas."

Maude said softly, "She's a widow?"

"Yes."

"And she needs persuading. So what would Modesty have done in *The Network* days, Krolli?"

"Mam'selle? Well, of course she would have sent in Danny —" The Greek stopped short and struck his forehead with an open palm. "Holy Jesus, I have become *stupid*! It is Danny's gift from God to win the trust of any woman! Listen, I will somehow arrange an accidental meeting for you today, and you take it from there, Danny. Okay?"

"Well . . ." Danny Chavasse looked from Krolli to Maude. "I'll try, but it's going to take time. This may sound weird, but I'm no con artist with women."

Maude patted his arm and said to Krolli, "I'll vouch for that. Danny took me away after Limbo, so I know."

Krolli said, "All right, so maybe it takes time, but there's no other lead, Danny. You go woo Helen Kaltchas, and I will work with Miss Maude to see if we can pick up anything else."

"Just Maude, please," said Maude.

Danny drank and set down his glass. "Don't expect too much," he warned. "I'm not as young as I was."

Maude shook her head reminiscently. "You could have fooled me," she murmured.

＊　　　＊　　　＊　　　＊

Mrs. Ram said, "I must confess to having felt dubiety as to whether leverage of friendship would prove sufficient to control such persons as Miss Blaise and Mr. Garvin once their personal weapons had been restored, but it appears you were right, Doctor." She gazed at him adoringly. "In three days there has been no slightest move on their part to cause anxiety. They have established good working relationship with other A.T.P. teams and with ancillary personnel, and have organised meticulous training. Using plan of *Marimba*, Mr. Garvin has marked out most careful deck plan of same on north beach, which is proving invaluable for rehearsal purposes."

Thaddeus Pilgrim nodded judicially. "We must, however, in all the circumstances, as I am sure you will agree, dear lady, maintain a *cautious* attitude regarding our new friends. We do not, I am happy to say, need the late Dr. Tyl to tell us that they have an immature fixation in respect of – ah – loyalty to persons with whom they have formed friendly attachments. Nevertheless, they are strongly independent characters who would, I have little doubt, seize any opportunity to escape from the compulsion under which they find themselves, and it is therefore essential to maintain our precautions, by such means as keeping all motorised vessels immobilised except when in use, and preventing any degree of private consultation between our new re-cruits."

Thaddeus Pilgrim picked up a cup of cold coffee with a white film on the surface, and drank it absently. "Fortunately," he went on, "our friends are aware that any hostile move will result in the obscene deaths of Professor and Mrs. – ah – Collier, and that even to escape from Kalivari, if that were possible, could in no way prevent Salamander Four fulfilling their contract."

"And what situation do you envisage after Hallelujah Scenario has been completed, Doctor?" asked Mrs. Ram earnestly.

"Oh, they will have committed themselves, dear lady." Thaddeus Pilgrim beamed at her and spread his arms. "They will have become members of our flock. Once they have taken part in the execution of Captain Valerius and his jolly tars, there can be no turning back."

A stone's throw away, Modesty Blaise and Willie Garvin were at lunch in the refectory with most of the A.T.P. personnel. They were not sitting together, and except for a brief exchange concerning the afternoon's training session they had made no attempt to talk to each other. It was clear that they understood, and accepted without seeming resentment, the restriction of not being allowed any private conversation.

"What else would you expect?" Dixon, the Englishman, had asked. "They're realists."

Reaction to them by A.T.P. executives varied. Dixon was coolly admiring, Zanelli and Patel more enthusiastically so. Ritter and Bonsu were resentfully jealous, but then they had been even more resentfully jealous of Sibyl Pray and Kazim. What Ms. Johnson thought about them, or about anything, nobody ever knew. She was a fitness fanatic and a highly efficient killer who worked well with her partner, Zanelli, but although she always had warm words and a smile for everyone, addressing male and female alike as Sugar, including her victims, the warmth and the smile never reached her eyes, which were like slate. She appeared to have no sexual leanings, normal or abnormal. Dixon had once raised a laugh by putting it to her that she might be a necrophiliac, and urging that necrophilia was really a feasible practice only for men. Ms. Johnson had laughed with the others and said she just loved his crazy English humour, but something had stirred in the slate-like eyes to make Dixon wish he had held his peace.

In the three days just past, Modesty Blaise and Willie Garvin had worked hard and thoroughly at the task given them by Thaddeus Pilgrim. They had checked the equipment in the armoury and declared it more than sufficient for the operation. They had checked the radio communications equipment, had grudgingly approved Mrs. Ram's briefing and administration, and had spent an hour with Frayne, the explosives expert, going over his plan for the scuttling of the *Marimba*. Outside working hours their demeanour had been neither friendly nor unfriendly; a little withdrawn, perhaps, a little taciturn, but without being hostile.

Sitting at the table now, Willie was exchanging a word with Patel while watching Modesty without appearing to do so. She had just finished a dish of moussaka, and her right hand was resting on the table beside the china mug of coffee. Willie saw the index finger tap the table twice, then the hand curled into a loose fist, turned on its edge, opened, and rested palm down again. The little finger tapped once and the index finger twice. The thumb moved out and returned, then the first two fingers drummed idly on the table for a moment or two. Every movement was casually natural and with no apparent significance.

Willie lifted a hand and rubbed his right eye to acknowledge receipt of the message. So it was to be tonight, at twelve-thirty. Since their first briefing by Thaddeus Pilgrim their only means of private communication had been the system of unobtrusive hand and body signals of the kind used by mind-reading acts in cabaret or variety, a system worked out years ago and practised regularly against time of need.

Tonight at twelve-thirty. That would be after Thaddeus Pilgrim had responded to the Dead Man's Handle call from Salamander Four, thereby ensuring safety for Steve and Dinah Collier until the following noon. Willie hoped nobody would notice the dew of sweat on his brow as he moved away from the table. There was relief in him at the prospect of making a move, but there was also profound apprehension of a kind he had not known for many years. Willie Garvin was scared, for he knew he was not yet quite himself. This had not troubled him during the battle in the courtyard against Sibyl Pray and Kazim, for then he had been operating under the wing of Modesty Blaise and as a unity with her. Tonight he had a task to perform alone, and he knew he was not quite ready to go solo yet. She had put him together again in a way that was almost unbelievable after the damage wrought by Tyl, but he knew he had still to reach that degree of being so utterly in harmony, mentally and physically, with whatever task was required of him, as to be able to transcend himself and operate beyond the limits of his natural capacity, however great that might be.

Modesty would have understood, but there had been no point in trying to convey this to her by signals. The crunch had to come, he told himself grimly, and the longer he waited the more his loss of confidence would affect him. The last vestige of Tyl's manipulations, the small demon that still lurked in Willie Garvin's mind, could only be exorcised by defeating it.

Bonsu was at his shoulder as he walked across the courtyard to the armoury, ostensibly to arrange for a session of live ammunition practice that afternoon. There was always somebody at his shoulder, and at Modesty's. The plan she had conveyed to him by signals over the three days since they had been placed in charge of the Hallelujah Scenario meant that at twelve-thirty tonight he would have to put his cell-mate, Zanelli, out of action. He was then to make his way to the armoury, break in by picking the lock, select a number of items at his discretion, set fifteen-minute detonators in plastic explosive to destroy the armoury, then make his way to the radio room.

Modesty Blaise, meanwhile, would be otherwise occupied, first in dealing with her cell-mate, Ms. Johnson, and then carrying out a task of her own. When Willie joined her in the radio room they would make their way to the little harbour. The blowing up of the armoury would serve a double purpose. It would massively reduce the fire-power available to the A.T.P. teams and their ancillaries, and it would also create a diversion.

Modesty had not troubled to lay out any particular plan for when they reached the harbour. The situation there would be governed by circumstances. Moored at the jetty were three or four sailing dinghies, a motor sailer, a cruiser, and a small sportsboat. If the cruiser could be started there would be no further problems. Failing this, the sportsboat might be a good prospect, providing spare cans of fuel were available. Next choice would be the motor sailer, but probability was that all engines were immobilised nightly. In which case, thought Willie, the best bet would be to wreck the engines and take the fastest of the sailing dinghies.

Waiting with Bonsu for the armourer to unlock the door, Willie touched his pocket to reassure himself that the simple lockpick he had fashioned from a piece of wire broken from his bedsprings was there. Then, angry with himself for yielding to such needless anxiety, he switched his thoughts elsewhere.

There were two things he and Modesty knew that were not known by the loathsome creature with white hair who sat sluglike in his study emanating an aura of putrescence. One of those things offered no particular advantage but was interesting. The master of the tanker *Marimba* was called Valerius, so Thaddeus Pilgrim had said during his labyrinthine exposition of the Hallelujah Scenario. Almost certainly this would be Captain Axel Valerius, an engaging villain who had worked on two maritime insurance scams for Modesty during *The Network* days. If her plan for tonight worked, Captain Axel Valerius would have a great deal to thank her for, though he would never know it. If her plan failed, then Valerius and all his crew would surely die. The Hallelujah Scenario could easily run without Modesty Blaise and Willie Garvin. They were part of it only by virtue of Thaddeus Pilgrim's sick passion for what he called "an interesting scenario".

The second thing Thaddeus Pilgrim did not know was infinitely more important. He did not know that given reasonably good fortune Modesty Blaise had a ninety per cent chance of getting a message out of Kalivari.

13

The air was heavy with an impending storm. Making no attempt at silence, Modesty Blaise threw aside the blanket, sat up on the narrow bed, and reached for her shirt and trousers on the chair beside her. Across the small cell a lamp was switched on and Ms. Johnson propped herself on an elbow, lips smiling, slate-grey eyes watchful.

"Going some place, Sugar?" she asked.

"Just out for a breath of air." Modesty belted her trousers and sat down to pull on her boots. "It's like a steam room in here."

"Okay, I'll go along with you." Ms. Johnson pushed her blanket aside and stood up, half a head taller than Modesty, twenty pounds heavier, beautifully muscled, wearing dark grey boxer shorts. "Let's take a walk down to the small beach, Sugar," she said. "Not the harbour, huh?"

Modesty shrugged. "Small beach is fine."

Ms. Johnson put on her bra and rested hands on hips, watching the dark girl with wary puzzlement. There seemed no tension in Modesty Blaise, no hint of impending action. But . . .

"How's about picking up Dixon and Patel as we go," said Ms. Johnson. "I bet they could use a little air, too."

"Sure." Modesty nodded indifferently and stood up. Then her head jerked slightly and she looked up at the flaking whitewashed ceiling with a start of surprise. "What the hell is *that*?"

Ms. Johnson looked up, and in that instant Modesty's whole body pivoted sharply so that its weight and power were transferred to her moving right arm, bent at the elbow; and that power was transmitted through the arm to the stiffened fingers, clamped together for the *nukite* thrust.

It was as if a blunt spear-head had hit Ms. Johnson with great force precisely on that vital nerve centre, the solar plexus. Apart from a brief exhalation of air she made no sound, but after a moment of total rigidity the splendid body crumpled bonelessly. Modesty caught her, eased her down on the bed, and bound the unconscious woman's wrists and ankles to the four corners with strips torn from a blanket.

All A.T.P. personnel carried a small first-aid packet as standard equipment. Modesty took Ms. Johnson's kit from the thigh-pocket of her trousers, removed two strips of plaster, and used them to seal Ms. Johnson's mouth. Already she was feeling uneasy that she had not disposed of the woman permanently. Under all the circumstances it was highly dangerous to let an enemy live who might well have a chance to kill you later. Willie would shake his head in silent disapproval, and rightly so, but she doubted that he would kill Zanelli. You needed very particular qualities, or lack of them, to be able to kill in cold blood.

Two minutes later she left the cell wearing her holstered Star .45 automatic. Ms. Johnson was still unconscious, her breathing shallow, the diaphragm fluttering as it strove to regain its rhythm. If she was unlucky she might choke or suffocate, but Modesty had no qualms about that. It would simply mean that this was Ms. Johnson's day to die.

Thunder rumbled close at hand as Modesty made her way soft-footed along a broad corridor, up a flight of stairs, then along a narrow corridor to the end where the radio room was situated. Here it seemed even more airless than at ground level. She schooled her mind and body to relax, but the coming storm seemed to have created tension in the atmosphere itself, and she could feel sweat on her lip and brow. Carefully she wiped her hands dry on her trousers. The kongo had been restored to her with her clothes and handgun, and now she drew the little double-headed mushroom from the pocket of her tunic.

The door of the radio room stood ajar, light came from within, and she could hear a voice on the loudspeaker, not on high volume, but very clear except for an occasional sharp crackle as lightning over the Aegean blotted out all transmission for a few moments.

". . . making routine report," said the voice in good English but with an accent. "We are on schedule for rendezvous and our e.t.a. is approximately – *crackle-crackle* – as per programme. Please advise any variation of programme at your end. Sea-horse to Land-crab, over." An illegal transmission, she noted, for no call signs were being used, only code names. Not that either party had anything to fear, even if they were overheard, for the source could not be pinpointed. Mention of a rendezvous made it highly probable that this was a transmission from the *Marimba*, and Modesty felt sure the voice was familiar. As she stepped into the room, the operator was lifting his microphone to transmit. In the muggy heat, he wore only trousers and a singlet, and his shoulders gleamed with sweat.

"This is Land-crab," he said. "I have no instructions about any change —"

Modesty struck with the kongo to the back of the neck, caught the man as he slumped, and lowered him to the floor. Earphones with a length of flex lay on the radio bench. She pulled the man's wrists behind him, threw a clove hitch round them, doubled his feet back and threw another hitch about the ankles, then peeled more plasters from Ms. Johnson's first aid packet and sealed the man's mouth.

The radio was squawking a query, interspersed with more bursts of static. ". . . say again, please. We lost you, Land-crab. We – *crackle-crackle*. Over."

She picked up the vox-operated mike and spoke into it. "Listen very carefully. This is the lady who used to be Rosebud when *you* were Snowman, four years, five years ago. Remember? Just yes or no. I've no time to waste and it's your life on the line, Snowman. Over."

The delay was no more than five seconds before the voice from the *Marimba* said warily, "Name two ships, Rosebud."

"*Cressida* and *Kutaya Star*."

"Hallo, Rosebud. Go ahead please." Captain Axel Valerius was a cautious man, but in no way slow-witted.

She said, "Land-crab intends to eat Rosebud. If he fails, there will be *no* rendezvous for you. If he succeeds, and if you keep the rendezvous, you are *dead*, Snowman, you and all your men, to make the scam convincing. No time for more. This is all I can do for you. Out."

As the last word left her lips she was reaching for the dial to change frequency, turning it to the twenty metre band, then turning to fourteen one-o-three megs. Seconds later she began to speak in Cantonese.

* * * *

Weng was asleep on a camp bed in the lapidary workshop of Modesty's penthouse when the alarm on the radio was triggered by a transmission. The radio was set up at one end of the workshop, and since Modesty's last phone call from Athens the houseboy had never left the room for longer than five minutes at a time, living on take-away food brought up to him by George the porter. During that time the alarm had been triggered three times, but always by radio amateurs transmitting by chance on the frequency.

This time it was different. A female voice from the loudspeaker was using Cantonese, and the sweat of relief broke out on Weng's body as he lunged from the bed to the radio table. She had known he would be here, waiting, listening out on the agreed emergency frequency; known he would be here without fail, day and night, for weeks on end if need be.

"*White Jade calling Little Garnet –*" this would have identified her even if he had not recognised her voice, for these were their emergency code names, "*– come in fast, please. How copy?*" She repeated the words, speaking quickly, and the moment she finished Weng spoke in the same language.

"*Hallo White Jade, here is Little Garnet hearing you well. Instructions, please.*"

"*Most urgent. Blind lady and her husband will be in extreme danger from noon this day. Contract put out to Fiery Lizard plus three. Advise titled official they must be moved to safe house and guarded. Acknowledge. Over.*"

Weng's mind raced as he lifted the microphone. Fiery lizard? Fiery lizard plus three? A contract? *Salamander Four*! And the titled official must be Sir Gerald Tarrant. He said, "*Fully understood, White Jade. Further instructions?*"

He could sense the relief in her even over the air and despite the sing-song tonal voice she was using. "*Thank you, Little Garnet. Now stand by for situation report. I have found Big Jasper. Our location is –*"

A burst of static, ear-splitting but very short, wiped out her voice. Then came silence. After a few seconds Weng said, "*Lost you, White Jade. Come in, please.*"

There was no response, and he could not even hear the hum of the carrier wave to tell him that the transmitter was still on the air. For five long and anxious minutes he listened. Then he ran his tongue across dry lips, swore savagely in his own language, and reached for the telephone to call Sir Gerald Tarrant at his private number.

It was as Willie Garvin reached the top of the steps on his way to the radio room that a ferocious crash of thunder overhead and a vivid glare of lightning through the corridor window heralded the first huge spots of storm rain. He had left Zanelli unconscious, secured and gagged in the cell, and was wishing now that he had struck to kill. It was bad policy to leave enemies around when the odds were so bad. On his back he carried a pack containing several grenades, some plastic explosive, detonators, two Uzi submachine-guns, and six spare magazines, all wrapped in a blanket to muffle sound. His own knives were in place, sheathed on his chest, the shirt open for quick access.

The thunderclap made his nerves jump, and he paused for a moment, looking out of the corridor window on to the courtyard to see if lights were being put on by people roused by the storm. The corridor light had flickered for a moment, but that was all. Evidently the generator was running steadily. No lights appeared below, and by the time he turned from the window it was impossible to see for the teeming rain.

He moved on, treading softly, and froze on the threshold of the radio room, shock draining the colour from his face. The operator lay on the floor, face down, mouth plastered, hands behind his back and secured to his ankles with flex. Modesty Blaise lay crumpled by the radio table, her chair overturned as if she had been flung from it. The radio itself was smoking slightly, and some streaks of liquid metal had solidified on its facia. The aerial lead, running up through the ceiling, was showing copper wire through its half melted insulation.

A second and greater shock hit Willie Garvin like a hammerblow to the heart. *The lightning! Jesus Christ, the aerial had been struck while she was using the radio, and . . . and . . .* ! For one brief second that seemed like an hour he was swept by fear, panic, and a murderous rage against whatever malign gods had so cruelly struck her down at this of all moments. Then, quite suddenly, an immense calm descended upon him as he shrugged the pack from his shoulders and moved into the room, dropping to one knee, turning her on her back, feeling for the pulse in her neck, bending to detect her breathing.

There was no pulse. There was no respiration. And her face was like marble.

The operator rolled on his side and stared with bolting eyes. Willie

Garvin's hand moved. A knife flashed through the air to drive oblique-ly into the floor an inch from the man's face. "You move and I'll *gut* you," said Willie Garvin quietly. "Believe it."

He knew that she might already be dead, but knew also that even without heartbeat and breathing she might be not quite beyond saving. The lightning had struck less than thirty seconds ago, and lightning was infinitely freaky in its effects. She appeared to have taken a secondary impact because of her proximity to the radio, which had suffered the main charge, and there were no apparent burns on her. If he could only restore heartbeat within the next two minutes she could survive without lasting harm.

As he rested his hands on her chest and started the rhythmic thrusting to stimulate the heart by external massage, he recalled that in approximately twelve minutes now the armoury would blow up. If he and Modesty were not away within a minute of that explosion, they would both be as good as dead; Steve and Dinah Collier also, perhaps, for he could not be sure that Modesty had got through to Weng with the all-important message to have Tarrant give them full protection.

Pump . . . pump . . . pump. A pause. *Pump . . . pump . . .* Sweat running down his face. Whispering, "Please, Princess. Please . . ." *Pump . . . pump* – and suddenly it was there under his hand, feeble and erratic at first, but rapidly becoming firm and steady. Joy swept him as he knelt over her, prising her mouth open, tilting her head back, pinching her nose as he leaned down to cover her mouth with his own and gently breathe air into her lungs.

Again . . . again . . . again. Five steady exhalations to the minute, for two minutes, three . . . five . . . eight, breathing the life-sustaining oxygen into her lungs, into her blood, praying for her shock-paralysed diaphragm to take over, one hand resting lightly between her breasts, over her steadily beating heart. And suddenly her body was shaken by a small tremor, an incipient movement. Willie knelt upright and saw her chest lift, heard the sigh of air drawn into her lungs, once, twice, again . . . again – and he felt the floor tremble beneath him as the pounding roar of the storm outside was drowned in the greater bellow of the armoury being rent apart by an explosion.

Still calm, still marvelling that he should be so, he tipped the contents of his pack onto the floor. No way could he carry her unconscious body and all this. He took a Uzi and slung it across his chest. Two grenades, at his waist inside the shirt. Two spare magazines, one in each trouser pocket. The blanket . . . he would need that, but not sodden by rain. In the corner was a plastic sack half full of paper rubbish. He emptied it, wrapped the blanket round the .45 from her holster before slipping it into the sack, and bent to snatch his knife from the floor. The operator's eyes rolled in terror. Twenty seconds since the explosion. Willie picked up a pair of insulated pliers from the bench, gripped the lighting cable stapled to the wall, and squeezed hard. There came a flash from cable and pliers as the circuit was shorted, and the lights in half the monastery went out.

In the darkness he laid the blanket in its sack over his shoulder, adjusted the position of the gun inside, then bent to lift Modesty and drape her over the padded shoulder. Moving carefully out of the room, he felt his way along the corridor wall for a few seconds until his eyes had adjusted. Rain was hammering furiously on the corridor window as he passed it. Then he was on the steps leading down, and a figure appeared, coming up. Willie said in a nice imitation of Zanelli's voice, "Who is that? What the devil is happening?"

The man was starting to reply when Willie's foot took him in the throat, hurling him back down the steps. Thirty seconds later Willie emerged through the small door at the southwest corner of the monastery into blinding rain. The temptation to make for the harbour and the boats was immense, but he knew that to do so would surely be fatal. Within the next two minutes the hunt for Modesty Blaise and Willie Garvin would be on, and not all the weapons on Kalivari were in the armoury. Every A.T.P. executive kept his own weapon, mostly submachine-guns and automatic rifles, though Bonsu favoured a Colt Python revolver and was highly skilled with it. There was also a heavy machine-gun hidden in the boat-house by the harbour, so that even if nothing at all could be salvaged from the armoury there would be ample fire power for the hunt, which would instantly focus on the harbour since this offered the only way of escape from Kalivari.

Dixon, Patel, Ritter, Mrs. Ram and the others knew their trade. Already some of them would be on their way to secure the boats, and moving much faster than Willie with his unconscious burden. Once the harbour was sealed off they could wait for daylight and the passing of the storm before starting a carefully organised beat from one end of the island to the other.

Soaked and half blinded by rain that hammered down like falling stair-rods, Willie moved slowly up the path to the ridge, away from the harbour, his mind calling up images of all that he could remember of those early days on Kalivari, trying to think of a secure hiding place, a place where he could find shelter for Modesty, where they would be safe from discovery while she recovered her senses and her strength. How long that might take he did not try to guess.

Five minutes later he rested, setting her down and holding her propped up in his arms while he felt her heart and pressed his ear to her lips to catch her breathing. Summoning strength for a fresh effort, he looked back to the west and saw a red glow through the driving rain. That was the outbuilding which had been the armoury, and unfortunately the storm was helping to douse the fire. He wondered if the destruction of weapons and ammunition was total. The armoury had been in two sections, divided by a wall of stone with an arched doorway, and because he had been at less than his best he had found time only to set up an explosion in one section. But he was fervently thankful that he had not lingered. Another two minutes getting to Modesty, and he would have been too late to save her.

Holding her propped against one arm, pushing the wet hair back from her face, he made himself accept the truth. It was a fact, a grim and brutal fact, that nowhere on this small island offered any hope of sanctuary. It was a rocky, scrubby place, very thinly wooded at one end, with little substantial ground cover, certainly not enough to allow the remotest chance of lying low and passing through a line of beaters. Worse still, there was a radio on the cruiser, and it might be possible for Thaddeus Pilgrim to call his land-based contact and whistle up a helicopter some time tomorrow. That would make the hunt very short.

Come daylight, the monastery and outbuildings would be scoured, and every inch of the harbour. Then would begin an organised search of an island that offered no place to hide. "This one's a bugger, Princess," Willie said aloud, vainly wiping away the rain streaming down over her face; yet still there was a kind of joy in him, because whatever the future held she was alive at this moment, and he was once again in harmony with himself, unafraid to be alone.

He opened his mind to consider all possible external factors, and minutes later the spark of an idea was kindled as he recalled making a trip round the island in the sportsboat with Dr. Tyl, believing the man was Garcia and insisting on the trip because he hoped it might restore his memory if he studied what he had been told was *The Network* headquarters. Yes . . . there was sheer cliff on the south side, dropping to a stony beach no more than two or three paces wide, and . . . it might do. It would have to do. There was no other option.

"Wish us luck, Princess," he said, and touched his lips to her wet cheek. Then he picked up the plastic sack, gathered her in his arms, and began to move carefully down the southern slope of the ridge.

* * * *

"There is overt dissatisfaction among A.T.P. personnel, indeed among all personnel, Doctor," said Mrs. Ram.

It was two a.m. and she sat in the study with Thaddeus Pilgrim. He seemed quite unruffled, except that a corner of his mouth would twitch now and again in an involuntary tic. "We must be tolerant, Mrs. Ram," he said benevolently. "Not all our friends can appreciate the – ah – *excitement* of creating a scenario which, as it were, suddenly takes on a life of its own. The boats are securely guarded, I take it?"

"Oh, certainly, Doctor. But I think we must conclude that Miss Blaise conveyed message to some person or persons via the radio. Kypseli, the operator, witnessed this."

"She was speaking in a Chinese sounding language when Mr. Kypseli came to his senses, I understand," said Thaddeus Pilgrim musingly. "But one cannot say *Kalivari* in Chinese, can one? Did Mr. Kypseli hear this word?"

"I have questioned him and he says most positively not. He is an intelligent person and can be trusted in this, I think."

"Then we must assume that our location remains unknown." The corner of the fleshy mouth twitched. "I would suggest, dear lady, that Miss Blaise was *first* ensuring that her friends the – ah – the Colliers should be protected, and that she was most opportunely struck down by lightning, via the radio, if I may borrow your own phrase, before she could convey further information. Please be so kind as to advise all our members to that effect. I am sure it will help to disperse what I am quite sure are only *temporary* feelings of dismay. You say that some of the weaponry has been saved from the armoury?"

"More than was at first expected," said Mrs. Ram. "Quite sufficient for implementation of Hallelujah Scenario, if you intend to proceed."

The watery eyes widened. "But of course we shall proceed, dear lady. There is nothing difficult about the operation, since the crew of the tanker will be *expecting* a demolition team from the cargo ship to come aboard at the rendezvous. The reason we – ah – went to the trouble of enlisting Miss Blaise and Mr. Garvin was not that their skills, their very remarkable skills, one must acknowledge, were *necessary*. We simply wished to . . ." he spread his arms in an embracing gesture, "to make them a corporate part of our little community. To make lasting *friends* of them." His mouth twitched again. "And also to create a deeply interesting scenario, of course."

Mrs. Ram relaxed a little. "In regard to demolition," she said, "Frayne will need fresh supplies of plastic, but we have four days to arrange for same so that is no problem. There remains only the matter of prompt elimination of Miss Blaise and Mr. Garvin."

"Prompt but not precipitate," said Thaddeus Pilgrim, a little less vaguely than usual. "Until daylight, security of the boats is essential. There must be no attempt to seek out our – ah – erstwhile visitors before dawn."

"I have already briefed personnel to that effect, Doctor."

He beamed at her mistily. "You are reliable in all things, dear lady. I am sure that in daylight hours the search will not be exacting. Miss Blaise, we know, is incapacitated, if not dead, and in any event there is nowhere that they could long conceal themselves, so I feel we may anticipate an early renewal of acquaintance." For a moment the whole of his heavy face was twisted by a spasm into a bloodless mask of malevolence. It passed, leaving him to stare sightlessly into whatever horrors his inward self dwelt among. "Then we shall compose such a scenario . . . such a scenario," he whispered.

* * * *

The storm had lasted an hour before passing on. Willie Garvin lay beside some scrubby bushes by the cliff edge, soaked but not cold, for the air was still warm and muggy. His mind was focused on a symbol, a small beetle carved in silver, lying on a scrap of black cloth. This was the token Sivaji had given him for the emergency enhancement of strength and stamina, a summoning of the body's powers beyond the normal.

She lay beside him, still insensible, but her heart was strong and her breathing regular. It was Willie's belief that her subconscious had taken over now, and that she had passed from unconsciousness into a form of trance in which a steady restoration of her vital forces was taking place.

He opened his eyes and stood up, feeling very strong, carefully controlling the energy that filled him. A pale moon gave visibility of ten or fifteen yards now. Opening the plastic sack, he cut the thick hem from the blanket and also an oblong of material the size of a hand towel. He removed the primers from the grenades, wrapped both separately in the blanket together with the Uzi, the spare magazines and the Star .45, bundled the blanket back into the plastic sack, tied the neck, and dropped it over the cliff edge to the stony beach a hundred and fifty feet below. His knives he retained. Their weight would make little difference to the task ahead.

He lifted Modesty on to his back with her right arm over his shoulder, then went down on all fours. Cutting a piece from the length of blanket hem, he brought her left hand forward under his armpit and tied her wrists together so that her arms were about him like a bandolier. The small oblong of blanket he wrapped round her wrists and hands for protection, securing it with short lengths of the hem. Finally he wound the remainder of the thick hem round and round both their bodies before knotting it to secure her firmly to him at the waist.

"We're going to win this one, Princess," he murmured, then crawled to the cliff edge, turned, and began the awkward task of easing himself over with his burden.

The cliff was of limestone, well seamed by wind and weather. He had good visual recall, and his remembered impression was that the drop was not quite sheer in most places along the half mile length of the cliff. The slope was steeper than one in one, perhaps almost one in one-half on average, but that might be enough to make the descent with his burden just possible. Spread-eagled on the cliff face, groping for toe-holds and hand-holds, he focused his mind on the rhythmic beat of Modesty's heart against his back as she hung pressed close to him, then he began to edge his way down.

For the next ninety minutes he strove to keep his thoughts frozen, so that he would not be weakened either by hope or fear, but would be totally committed to an ordeal without end. Only the narrow beam of judgement guiding his hands and feet was left open to stimuli. Slowly, slowly, like a blind and crippled insect, he crept down the cliff face, resting whenever a ledge or crevice or easier angle of slope offered the opportunity. Once, after fifty minutes, he reached a point where the drop became sheer for a while, and he spent ten minutes making a laborious traverse before deciding that the sheer stretch might extend across the cliff face indefinitely. There followed five crucifying minutes for nerve and muscle as he found his way down with her full weight hanging upon him, then came the blessed relief of a fractional slope again to ease his burden.

When at last his feet touched the pebbles of the beach it was several seconds before he could force his fingers to release their hold on the rock face. He sank down and lay prone, blood on his hands, her limp body lying on top of him as he dragged air into his lungs and set his teeth against the sudden onset of cramp. But the pain meant nothing compared with the deep glow of triumph that spread slowly within him as he opened his mind once again.

"I did it, Princess," he said in a croaking whisper. "I bloody did it . . . and on me own."

A little while later he cut himself free from her, found the plastic sack with its contents, and began to look for one of the small caves he remembered seeing when he had made the sea-trip round Kalivari with Dr. Tyl.

14

Dinah Collier said in a shaky voice, "You mean she actually *spoke* to Weng? He's quite sure it was Modesty?"

"A hundred percent sure, my darling."

"But then she went off the air? Suddenly?"

"Well, yes," Collier acknowledged. "But that's not necessarily anything to be alarmed about, Tarrant said."

"How does *he* know?"

"Well, he doesn't. He's just trying to reassure us. But let's keep hoping. Jesus, at least we *know* she was alive a few hours ago, and we know Willie was alive and with her after all this time, and she got a message through, didn't she? And we know they are extremely bloody good at staying alive, given a ghost of a chance, don't we?"

It was three a.m. and they were in the main bedroom of their cottage in Sussex, each packing a suitcase, Collier with somewhat less efficiency than his blind wife. Dinah, in white underwear and with a suit laid out ready to be put on, rubbed tears from her cheeks and said, "I'm sorry, honey. I'm just so glad and so scared at the same time. I want to be told they're absolutely fine and safe, but nobody can tell me that." She folded a dress and laid it in the case. "Is Sir Gerald sure Weng got the message right? Go over it again for me, Steve. I mean, why should *we* be in danger, for God's sake? It doesn't make sense."

Collier looked at his watch and said gently, "I made exactly the same comment to Tarrant when he rang just now to say he'd be coming down personally with two men to take us to some hideaway his department has up in Yorkshire. I told him it didn't make sense, and Tarrant blasted me in a way I'll not soon forget. He pointed out that it might not *seem* to make sense, but that perhaps I could remember being involved with Modesty and Willie in other events which didn't seem to make sense until later. She had managed to get on the air for a few seconds, he said, and in that time she had made *us*, you and me, her top priority, instead of giving her location. Did I not trust her? Was she, in my opinion, a neurotic type? Did I think she might be given to foolish imaginings?"

Collier shook his head and sighed. "I felt like a crawling worm, Dinah, and I deserved it. I ought to have known better. Anyway, Tarrant then insisted that I phone Weng for his confirmation of what Modesty had said, and I did. You heard my end of it. The only new thing Weng told me was that we wouldn't begin to be at risk from this Salamander Four lot until noon today, so Modesty said. But evidently Tarrant's taking no chances, and he'll be here with his no doubt highly trained minions by four-thirty at the latest." Collier gave a brusque laugh. "I don't blame him. If Modesty came back to find he'd slipped up on this little jig, he'd have to run away and join the Foreign Legion."

Dinah nodded, closing her case, then stood with a finger to her lip, thinking. At last she said slowly, sadly, "I've got a hunch we've been a trouble to them again, Steve. I don't know how or why, and God knows we haven't *done* anything, but it looks like this is one more time they've had to get between us and bloody murder."

He moved round the bed and took her gently in his arms. "I know, sweetheart," he said. "But they won't mind. That's what they reckon old friends are for."

*　　*　　*　　*

When her senses returned, Modesty lay still with eyes closed, trying to recall what had happened and to identify her surroundings. The last thing she remembered was speaking to Weng on the radio. Then . . . nothing.

She consulted her internal clock and knew it was within half an hour of five a.m., probably of the same day, though this was not quite certain. She was naked, wrapped in a blanket, lying on what felt like sandy ground in an enclosed place very near to the sea, her head pillowed on . . . on the shoulder of somebody lying beside her.

She said, "Willie . . ." and reached up to rest a hand on his chest.

"Welcome back, Princess."

She lifted her head, slowly propped herself on an elbow, and stared around. They were in a cave, small in width and height, but running back some way from the opening, beyond which she could hear the lapping of the sea. A hint of grey in the darkness confirmed that dawn was near. Her wrists were sore as if from some kind of abrasion, but otherwise she seemed unhurt. Willie lay beside her, and his shirt felt a little damp to her hand. She groped to find his cheek in the gloom and said wonderingly, "What the hell happened, Willie? And where are we?"

"There was a bit of intervention from on high, Princess," he said. "Did you get the message to Weng about covering Steve and Dinah?"

She thought for a moment, then said, "Yes . . . yes, I got that out. Oh, first I warned Alex Valerius not to keep the rendezvous, because he happened to be on the air when I got there. Yes . . . then I raised Weng, and he acknowledged instructions to have Steve and Dinah guarded. But I don't remember any more. What did you mean by intervention from on high?"

"You got struck by lightning. Or rather the radio did, and you copped the side-effect."

"*Lightning*?"

"That's right. I found you on the floor 'alf a minute later, and you were a goner. But I got the ticker going okay, and the breathing, only that took longer. Then the armoury went up, and I 'ad to get us out of there a bit sharpish."

"My God . . ." she said slowly, and sank back with her head on his shoulder again. "And where are we now?"

"In a cave at the foot of those cliffs on the south side. There's 'ardly any beach, and no access, so they won't find us unless they come looking by boat."

"You *climbed* down? With me to carry?"

"I tied you on me back with strips from the blanket. We ought to be all right for a while, Princess. I don't suppose they'd reckon it possible for us to get down 'ere."

"I don't suppose they would," she said, and cupped her hand against his cheek. "Thanks, Willie love. Now tell me about it."

He briefly recounted the events of the night, giving his reasons for what he had done. The climb down the cliff got a bare mention, but she had no difficulty in visualising the immensity of the ordeal. "We've got your Star automatic, a Uzi with three magazines, and two grenades," he said. "That's all I could bring away with me. Once we were down, I found this cave pretty quick, stripped you off, rubbed you dry and wrapped you in the blanket . . . and that's about it. Oh, I didn't try to bring you round. I 'ad a feeling you were getting better in your own way, and doing all right. I was worried in case you picked up a few burns from the lightning, but I found a pencil torch in your pocket and checked you over. Wrists are a bit raw from being tied together, but I couldn't find anything else wrong."

She patted his cheek and said, "There isn't, Willie. I'm just a bit limp, but once we start to make a move the adrenalin will get going and I'll be fine." She thought for a few moments, assessing the situation. Then: "Have you worked anything out yet?"

"Nothing specific, Princess. Once I'd got you settled I walked about for a while to get me clothes dry, more or less. The air's still warm out there. Then I came in and slept for a couple of hours. Only woke up a few minutes before you did, and I didn't know 'ow long you were going to be out, so I couldn't plan anything definite. In general terms I suppose our best bet is to lie low 'ere all day, then climb up and try to grab a boat tonight."

After a while she said, "Yes . . . but let's think it through from their viewpoint. At first light they'll search the harbour and the outbuildings there. Then the monastery. Then they'll start beating across the island. When they haven't found us in any possible hiding place by noon or thereabouts, they'll maybe start looking in impossible places, like this."

Willie sighed. "I'm a bit slow this morning, Princess. Sorry."

"You had a heavy night. I've done nothing but sleep. Look, how far are we from the harbour now, Willie? I don't mean going up and over, I mean along the coast?"

After a few moments he laughed, rolled over to prop himself on his elbows, and grinned down at her in the semi-darkness. "Old Tarrant once told me he believed your most valuable gift was being able to think simple, Princess. From this cave I reckon we can move a quarter of a mile west along the foot of the cliffs. Then we'd 'ave to swim another quarter mile where the cliffs jut into the sea. But that would bring us to the southern arm of the harbour, which is just a big jumble of rock piled up in a mole for about a hundred yards. If we worked our way round the end of it, we could come at the boats *from seaward*, after Pilgrim's crowd 'ave finished the harbour search. And that's the last thing they'll expect, especially in daylight."

"Say . . . half an hour from here to the harbour?"

"Thereabouts. That part's a bit chancy, but not very. The main snag is, they may have immobilised all engines."

"They probably have. On the other hand, once they've searched the harbour they may feel it's secure, and restore mobility. We'll have to see. If not, we could fire the cruiser and the sportsboat, and take the motor sailer. They couldn't tackle us with the small dinghies."

After a minute's silence Willie said, "I can't think of anything better."

"All right, we'll make that the general idea, but we'll have to play it by ear as we go along. Where are my clothes, Willie?"

"Just be'ind us, Princess, spread out on dry sand. They'll still be damp when you put 'em on, though."

"I've known worse problems. Let's sleep for another hour now. Are you warm enough or do you want to share my blanket?"

"I'm fine."

"An hour, then." She felt him quiver to a silent chuckle. "What is it, Willie?"

"Just trying to imagine Steve's face when we tell 'im you were struck by lightning."

She giggled. "Oh, God. He'll start raving at me as if it was all my fault."

Two minutes later they were both asleep.

*   *   *   *

Shortly before the hour was up they were awakened by the sound of an engine. It was unmistakably the sportsboat engine, and they were instantly alert, turning to lie prone, heads low, staring towards the mouth of the cave and the light of a new day beyond. The sound grew louder, and moments later they saw the sportsboat some two hundred yards off-shore, moving fast, parallel to the coast. A man in a dark shirt and a blue break cap was at the wheel. Another, bare-headed, sat facing the cliffs with field glasses raised to his eyes, but he was looking up towards the cliff top. Both were Hostel of Righteousness ancillaries.

In seconds the boat had passed out of sight, and the sound of the engine dwindled. Modesty exhaled a sigh of relief and relaxed. Willie sat up, and she heard the metallic click of a magazine being detached from the Uzi. "What's your guess, Willie?" she said.

"I reckon they were sent out to do a quick trip round the island, trying to spot us. If we were anywhere on the coast but 'ere they might've struck lucky, and they'd be saving a lot of time."

"I think the same. And that's good news, because when they get back to the harbour they're hardly likely to immobilise the sportsboat."

He said wryly, "Now for the bad news, Princess. This Uzi's bust. A spring in the trigger group, I think. Must've fallen badly when I dropped it over the cliff, even though it was in the blanket. All we've got now is your pistol and the two grenades."

She turned on hands and knees to give him a smile. "Then we'll just have to make do. I'll get dressed now, and we'll move in half an hour."

The sun was up as they made their way along the narrow strip of beach between the cliff and the sea's edge, ready to drop flat and roll into the water at the first sound of an engine. At the point where the cliff thrust into the sea they waded in and began to swim, keeping close to the rock face. Willie carried the grenades and handgun wrapped in the plastic sack. Hampered as they were by being clothed and booted, they moved at a leisurely breast-stroke to conserve their strength.

Thirty-five minutes after leaving the cave they reached the point where a mass of broken rock had been piled in a long narrowing mole which curved away from them to form the southern arm of the harbour. Keeping low in the water they edged their way along the tumbled rock towards the end. If they had guessed rightly, the search of the harbour and the boats would be completed by now and the bulk of Thaddeus Pilgrim's people would be moving inland, leaving only two or three to guard the harbour from landward approach.

It was as they edged round the very end of the mole, heads barely above water, that Modesty touched Willie's arm and pointed with her eyes. He looked out to sea. A large luxury yacht, sleek and white, was bearing towards Kalivari and no more than a mile away. Even as they stared there came the sound of small-arms fire from within the harbour, the chatter of a submachine-gun mingling with the slower sound of an automatic rifle firing on single-shot.

Willie's head jerked round to look a question at her. She lifted her mouth clear of the water and whispered, "God knows, Willie, but it's a distraction. Keep going."

Hugging the rocks, they rounded the end of the mole and surveyed the harbour. The cruiser and the other boats were moored at the jetty, all except the sportsboat, which lay only twenty yards away, moored to a buoy in the harbour entrance. One man was in it now, the man in the dark shirt and blue break cap. He was holding field glasses to his eyes, and his whole attention was focused on what was happening on the shore beyond the jetty.

There were several outbuildings set back from the hard. A slipway ran up the slope to a concrete apron with a boat-house on one side of it; on the other side stood a repair shop, an oil store, a housing for the harbour generator, and a large two-storey stone building with a flat roof and a parapet, originally built a century before by monks for making wine from the grapes they planned to grow. It was now used for general storage.

At least half the population of Kalivari was spread out among the buildings, firing sporadically towards the roof of the large store. In the middle of the road leading up from the hard to the monastery, two figures lay sprawled and unmoving beside what appeared to be a heavy machine-gun on a tripod. Even as Modesty and Willie took in the scene they saw a figure in camouflage jacket and cap flit across the roof of the store and fire down with an automatic rifle at an unseen target before ducking behind the parapet again for cover.

Modesty put her mouth close to Willie's ear and whispered, "This is crazy, but whoever he is he's on our side, so —" She broke off sharply, for the man in the sportsboat had laid down his glasses and picked up a rifle. Rising to set one knee on the gunnel, he lifted the rifle to a general aim in readiness for the figure on the roof to reappear. Modesty said urgently, "Take him, Willie," and vanished under the surface, swimming towards the boat.

Willie drew a knife from one of the twin sheaths on his chest, gauged the distance, and threw, aware as he did so of a new outbreak of shooting on the shore. It was not, Willie had decided, a moment to practise indulgence. The knife drove into the back of the man's neck, and he was dead in the next second, toppling sideways on to a thwart, the rifle falling into the sea. Modesty surfaced and slithered over the opposite gunnel, on the blind side from the shore, then turned and beckoned. Willie submerged and began to swim.

Moments later, when he hauled himself into the boat and crouched down in the well, the man's body was gone and Modesty was wearing the blue break cap, her hair well tucked in. With her black tunic, and seen from a distance, she presented a figure not very different from that of the man. She handed Willie his knife with the blade wiped clean and said mildly, "We lost the goddam rifle. That's the third bad break today so maybe it's the last. Give me the forty-five, Willie."

He passed her the handgun and said, "Who the *hell* can that bloke on the roof be, Princess? Don't tell me Dixon or one of 'em suddenly repented and changed sides. And what about this bloody great yacht coming in? If Pilgrim's called up some heavy reinforcements, maybe we ought to get going."

With the glasses to her eyes she said, "Not till we know who —" She broke off abruptly as the figure on the roof appeared again and fired on a man who had run from cover, apparently trying to reach the heavy machine-gun. The man went down, but a bare instant later the figure in the camouflage jacket was flung back as if by an invisible hand, the cap falling from a head of fair hair as a shot from below struck home. Then nothing was visible above the parapet.

Modesty said, "*Oh my God, it's Maude! Maude Tiller! And she's hit! Cast off, Willie!*" Even as she spoke, her hand was on the starter and the engine of the sportsboat roared to life. Willie slashed the line. She spun the wheel and the little craft heeled steeply as it went flying out of the harbour. Lifting her voice above the sound of the engine she shouted, "She found us, Willie! And that has to be Krolli coming in on the yacht with a few friends. Great move except they don't know we've got the whole damn place stirred up and ready for trouble. We *have* to stop that machine-gun opening up!"

The sportsboat swung round in a wide curve, heading back into the harbour, gathering speed every second. Crouched low, peering over the bow, Willie pulled the pin from one of the grenades.

Maude? he was thinking painfully. Hit? Lovely little patriotic Maude, who came with me to fight in Limbo? Ah, no . . .

Modesty called sharply, "In your own time, Willie. And after the bang we go for broke."

He put Maude Tiller out of his mind and knelt up. The sportsboat was hurtling towards the hard, and he could see two men by the machine-gun now, starting to set it up. *We're going to be too late*, he told himself bleakly, then realised with a shock of relief that she was heading straight for the slipway and keeping the throttle wide open.

Christ! he thought, *Old Tarrant wasn't wrong about her thinking simple.*

Holding the gunnel with one hand he swung his arm in a long high throw an instant before the sportsboat hit the slipway, judging that the boat-house would be momentarily between them and the men with the machine-gun to offer protection for him and Modesty when the grenade exploded, hurling its shrapnel fifty yards and more. The small black pineapple of the Mills bomb soared over the boat-house, and the iron bellow of the explosion sounded as the sportsboat flashed up the slipway with a shrieking howl from the propeller as it was freed from the load of water resistance.

For a second or two they were airborne over the hard, then the boat came down with a jarring crash and went skidding on, starting to roll, starting to turn, and as it cleared the boat-house Modesty called, "Jump!"

They dived together, against the momentum of the boat, now down to ten miles an hour, and landed with rolling breakfalls but still losing skin and collecting bruises on the rough concrete. Willie came up with a knife in his hand and killed Ritter at ten paces as the man emerged from behind a corner of the oil store. From the ground Modesty snapped off a shot with the Star .45 to drop a man aiming a Uzi at point blank range. She came to her feet, snatched up the Uzi, and ran for where Dixon and three of the ancillaries lay dead near the machine-gun, horribly torn by the grenade. "Get to Maude!" she called.

Willie had Ritter's gun now, a Stoner 63 carbine, and he ran for the store, aware of a figure appearing on his flank but knowing Modesty was covering him, glimpsing the man going down at a sharp *rat-tat* from her gun. As he smashed open the door with his foot he glanced over his shoulder and saw two launches, both crowded with men, moving swiftly under power from the yacht to the harbour and now less than half a mile away.

At an open window on the upper floor he paused to look out and saw that Modesty was in a good position by the boat-house, covering the heavy machine-gun so that nobody could reach it. Surprisingly, the sportsboat had not caught fire but lay wrecked on the hard. A group of three had emerged from behind one of the smaller outbuildings and were circling to come up on Modesty's flank. Willie dropped his second grenade amongst them, then moved to the steps leading up to the roof. Bonsu lay dead at the foot, shot through the heart, still clutching his handgun. Willie stepped over him and went on up the steps, thinking of Maude again now, and feeling his heart grow heavy within him.

She lay sprawled on her back near the roof parapet, her rifle and camouflage cap lying nearby, short blonde hair tousled about her face. Willie flinched inwardly and set his teeth, then walked across the roof to kneel beside her, staring hopelessly at the neat bullet-hole in her jacket, just below the breast-bone. He swore as he rested two fingers on her neck, then blinked in surprise at the steady pulse he could feel there.

He put a hand on her chest, felt the stiffness beneath the fabric, and hurriedly unbuttoned the camouflage jacket and the shirt beneath, revealing a contoured piece of body armour in light plastic that he recognised as Armour-Hide. In the centre, a crater-like eruption surrounded a hole, and in the hole he could see the flat base of a bullet. "Jesus," he muttered prayerfully, and pulled her shirt wide open to reach the securing straps. When he lifted the feather-light armour away he found that the nose of the bullet had fractionally penetrated her skin, and there was a smear of blood on a small area of bruised flesh around the bra strap just below the cleavage of her breasts. He unsnapped the front-fastening bra and was wiping the blood away to check damage when she spoke in a feeble whisper.

"Stop groping my tits, Garvin . . ."

He sat back on his haunches, concealing the gladness that swept him, saying plaintively, "Ah, come on now, Maude, don't be a spoilsport. It's just my adolescent curiosity."

She laughed a little groggily, and slowly propped herself on her elbows to stare down at the bruising and smear of blood caused by the bullet. "Stavros nagged me into wearing this gubbins," she said slowly. "I must buy him a drink sometime." Alarm touched her eyes and she stiffened. "Willie! There's a machine-gun —"

"Relax," he said soothingly. "Modesty's down there taking care of it. 'Ang on a tick." He went to the parapet, saw that the launches from the yacht had almost reached the jetty, gave a shrill whistle, then cupped hands to his mouth and called, "Maude's okay, Princess." Below, Modesty touched fingers to her lips and flicked her hand to him. He turned back to Maude, noting the backpack and the small radio in one corner of the roof. She was sitting up now, leaning back against the parapet.

"Who's Stavros?" said Willie.

"One of Danny's and Modesty's billionaires from Limbo. Greek shipping tycoon. Remember?"

"Ah, that one. Yes." He sat down beside her. "What's been 'appening, Maude?"

Modesty heard the sound of the launches as they reached the jetty, then a rush of feet as a bunch of men came into view, pouring on to the hard, spreading out among the buildings under shouted instructions from Krolli in the lead. They were variously dressed and variously armed, but they looked like men of experience. From here and there a few random shots were fired, then she saw a handful of Hostel of Righteousness survivors scrambling away in flight over the rough ground flanking the road.

Ms. Johnson appeared from a shallow gully fifty yards away, a revolver dangling from one hand. Modesty aimed the Uzi and called, "Drop it!" Ms. Johnson made no move to lift the gun, but wagged a finger of her free hand from side to side in a gesture of polite negation, then turned her back and began to walk up the road towards the monastery, still carrying the revolver.

Modesty watched her for a moment, then shrugged and moved away from the boat-house. Curiously, there was hardly anybody to be seen at this moment, but a man in a beautifully tailored silk shirt and pale blue slacks, wearing a white yachting cap and carrying a pistol, was coming towards her. He was in his mid-forties, short, powerfully built, and with a grin of delight splitting his brown face.

"Stavros," she said. "What the hell are you doing here?"

He kissed her on both cheeks and nodded towards the splendid yacht standing off-shore. "Danny and Maude wanted a ship," he said. "I go with the yacht."

Krolli appeared from between two of the buildings, running, sweat trickling down his face, beaming at sight of her, calling, "Ah, Mam'-selle!" Danny Chavasse and two or three others were at his heels.

She said, "Hallo Krolli . . . Danny. It's good to see you. Look, don't let any of your boys get hurt winkling this mob out, Krolli. We'll just take away all the boats and leave the Greek authorities to sort things out. I expect Stavros knows who to talk to." She looked up towards the roof of the store with a vaguely puzzled air. "I saw Maude get hit, and it looked bad, but Willie just called down to say she's all right."

✻   ✻   ✻   ✻

With a considerable effort Thaddeus Pilgrim focused his concentration upon the real world, and upon Mrs. Ram clutching her clipboard. "It may indeed be advisable," he said, "for us to consider making an early departure on the cruiser, with one or two selected persons, of course, though I feel we should first ascertain *precisely* the cause of the – ah – outbreak of shooting we heard a few moments ago from the direction of the harbour. I note that it has ceased now, so – ah, here is Ms. Johnson. No doubt she can enlighten us as to recent events."

Ms. Johnson stood in the doorway. In one hand she held a bottle of whisky and a glass she had picked up on her way to the study, in the other a Colt .45 revolver. "Recent events?" she said amiably. "Let's not worry about recent events, Sugar. I've got a great new scenario for you." She stepped into the room. "It goes like this . . ."

Lifting the Colt, she shot Mrs. Ram through the heart, the heavy bullet passing through the clipboard and knocking her from her chair with its impact as it ploughed through her body. Ms. Johnson smiled warmly. "And like this . . ." she said.

With great care she shattered each of Thaddeus Pilgrim's shoulders in turn with a bullet, the first making him rear out of his chair, the second flinging him back till he struck the wall. He slid down to lie slumped against it, bleeding, eyes bolting, screaming thinly in a high-pitched voice, his inward self finally and totally united with his body in the real world.

"Not a bad scenario, eh, Sugar?" said Ms. Johnson. She set down bottle and glass on the desk, hooked a chair towards her with her foot, spun the revolver once on her finger, and shot Thaddeus Pilgrim in the stomach. Then she sat down, poured herself half a tumbler of whisky, and began to sip it, watching him die.

*　　*　　*　　*

On the roof, Maude Tiller pushed back hair from her grubby face and said, "Well . . . in a nutshell, Tarrant gave me leave and I came out with Danny to join Krolli in Athens. It seems Modesty warned two fishermen who brought her out here that they might be silenced. They got scared and disappeared – up to Salonika as it turned out. The only person who knew where they were was a woman relative, so we pointed Danny Chavasse at her and she melted in two days. Krolli got to the fishermen yesterday, and they said they'd taken you to Kalivari. Have you got a cigarette, Willie?"

"Sorry, I 'aven't, Maude."

"Good. I've given up anyway. Well, Krolli could raise plenty of men, but we needed ample transport and a bit of quick financial muscle, so Danny called Stavros, who raised hell because we hadn't called him earlier. We didn't know what was happening here, so Stavros laid on an aeroplane and I dropped in by parachute last night, just before that storm, to recce the situation. Landed about half a mile east of the monastery and humped my gear down here to the harbour. Found this store place and settled in just below, on the upper floor."

He whistled softly. "Blimey, you were lucky nobody spotted you getting 'ere."

She turned her head to scowl at him. "What do you mean, *lucky*?"

"Did I say that? I didn't mean lucky at all, Maude. I meant clever, 'ighly skilled, brilliant."

"And lucky, too, because I got here just before some bloody great explosion up by the monastery. *That's got to be Willie Garvin*, I thought. Right?"

"That was me, Maude. A child at 'eart. I love bangs."

"Well, after that there were all kinds of people charging about the harbour in that pelting rain, checking boats and shouting orders. A bit later some of them came in on the ground floor here out of the rain and I heard them talking. They knew you and Modesty had got away somehow, but they seemed to think she was hurt or dead, and didn't reckon they'd have much trouble knocking you off this morning. As soon as the rain stopped they went off – back to bed I suppose – leaving a guard on the boats. So I slipped up to the roof and got on the radio to Krolli and Stavros, telling them to come in at dawn with plenty of fire-power."

Willie said, "They'd have been sitting ducks for that heavy machine-gun."

Maude nodded. "I know. I had to open fire to stop this mob getting it set up, but I was scared I wouldn't hold them long enough."

"It worked out all right. Modesty saw you get hit, so she took over."

"Thank God for that. When I was listening to those people talking, they were on about something called a Hallelujah Scenario, and a pilgrim, and the best way to kill off a whole tanker crew – what the hell kind of monastery is this, Willie?"

He shrugged. "It's a long story, Maude. I'll tell you later, and you won't believe it."

"All right." Again she scowled at him. "Look, why are you and Modesty free and unharmed?" She massaged her bruised chest gently with the heel of her hand. "Christ, does that mean we've all been wasting our time?"

"Of course it doesn't. You came just in the nick of it, Maude. Can I do that for you?"

"Rub my chest? Ha! Who was going to take me to the Virgin Islands after that Limbo caper for a couple of weeks of ungovernable lust, and didn't?"

"And who went off with Danny Chavasse instead?"

"I did." She sighed reminiscently. "It's quite true about Danny and women, Willie. You can't imagine . . ."

"I'm not going to try. Don't undermine an old flame, Maude."

She laughed, fastening her bra and buttoning her shirt. As he got to his feet and extended his hands to her she said, "I've got a month's regular leave coming up in October, so book us for somewhere exotic."

"That's a promise." He drew her to her feet and held her by her small waist, looking down at her. "Maude?"

"What?"

"Thanks."

"Ah, shut up."

*　　*　　*　　*

Five minutes later Modesty and Stavros met them on the road up to the monastery. Modesty said, "Thanks for everything Maude." She looked at Willie. "Pilgrim's dead. Ms. Johnson killed him."

Willie bit his lip. "Sod it. That means the Salamander Four contract starts running at noon and there's no way to cancel it now."

"I doubt if there ever was, Willie. We don't know the code-word, the radio's bust, and even if it wasn't we don't know what frequency Salamander Four call on. What's more, I doubt that they'll cancel even when they know their client's dead. They've been paid, so they'll meet their obligation."

Maude said, "It's for a killing?"

221

"An obscene killing. Of Steve and Dinah Collier."

The fair girl stared. "Oh God, no."

Modesty said, "I got a message to Weng, and Tarrant will be guarding them for the time being, but they can't stay hidden indefinitely." She turned to Stavros. "How quickly can you get me to London?"

He glanced out at the yacht, riding at anchor beyond the harbour now. "Pretty damn quick. There's a little Hughes 300 helicopter on the ship, and my Learjet at Athens Airport, with pilot. Help yourself."

"God bless you, Stavros. Do you mind if I leave you to sort things out here with Maude and Willie?"

Stavros smiled a hard grim smile. "My dear," he said, "I am just the man for it, believe me."

15

Weng brought the Rolls Camargue to a gentle halt on the broad patch of greensward beside the stream. He switched off, got out, and opened the rear door for Professor Stephen Collier and his wife to alight. It was two hours before sunset and they were in Cumbria, amid the mountains of the Lake District. Three weeks had passed since Modesty and Willie had returned to England, and the Colliers had spent most of that time luxuriating on holiday at Pendragon, Modesty's villa near Tangier.

Standing beside the Rolls, Collier gazed wonderingly about him at the steep and rugged slopes of the fells. "Running?" he said incredulously. Then on a higher note, "Running? I mean, *running*?"

Dinah said, sniffing the air happily, "You're doing this multiple-echo thing again, honey. It's not good for you. Those high notes strain certain parts of the body."

"Eh? What multiple-echo?"

"Like when it emerged that Modesty had been struck by lightning, and you kept saying, 'Lightning? *Lightning*? LIGHTNING?' It was like shouting for echoes down the Grand Canyon."

"Ah, yes," said Collier, "but I didn't just *say* it, sweetheart, I kept waving my arms about, and glaring, and abusing her."

"That's right, and then both she and Willie fell about laughing because that's what they'd predicted."

Weng was lifting a picnic basket and a cold-box out of the boot. Collier said, "I'm afraid they have a coarse sense of humour, deficient in proper respect. Anyway, I'm bound to tell you that we are surrounded by peaks and ridges and fells and whatnot that only a very courageous fly would try to crawl up, so it's hardly surprising that I go into a multiple-echo on running when Weng makes the ridiculous allegation that Modesty and Willie have been navigating and *running* a thirty mile course through these fells today, and propose to complete another twenty tomorrow."

"There is nothing ridiculous about it, Mr. Collier," Weng said mildly. "Many people enter these events."

"Events?"

"This one is the Saunders Lakeland Mountain Marathon, and there are many entrants from all parts of the country, Mr. Collier. Not only men, but what you would call slips of girls also. There are different distances and different classes, some just for walkers, but the Scafell Class is for top fell-running navigators, which means people who have completed similar events to prove their ability."

"But . . . running?" said Collier, staring about him again.

"The pace is according to terrain, and of course they have to carry specified clothing and camping necessities in a backpack. Would you care to take the picnic basket, Mr. Collier? I will carry the cold-box and the car rug."

"Where have we got to carry them to?" Collier demanded suspiciously.

"Only to the overnight camp site, Mr. Collier. About half a mile up this footpath."

"Half a mile?" said Collier on a rising note, and winked at Weng. "Half a *mile*? Half a —"

"You're doing it again, tiger," said his wife. "Come on, be brave, grit your teeth, never say die. I'll hold your hand."

"Well, in that case . . ." Collier picked up the picnic basket, took his wife's hand, and began to walk up the footpath with Weng at his elbow. "So this is the surprise, my inscrutable young oriental?" he said. "We drop in unexpectedly on Miss Blaise and Mr. Garvin, with a magnificent repast from Fortnums and some nicely chilled bottles of champers, so that we can drink to their coming victory in this . . . this lunatic enterprise?"

"Not to their victory," said Weng. "They are not concerned to win, Mr. Collier. They save that for more urgent occasions."

"We can drink to there being no more urgent occasions," said Dinah, treading carefully, sensitive to her husband's guiding hand. "I don't want white hair just yet."

"Unanimous," said Collier. "I shall speak to them firmly on that point, giving them one of my steely looks. However, may I say, Weng lad, that we've greatly enjoyed the run up here and are vastly obliged to you for inviting us along on this jaunt, also for booking us into The Royal Oak tonight. But you've given us to understand that Miss Blaise doesn't know of her impending good fortune in having us call upon her, and we're somewhat puzzled by the slightly unfathomable expression you've been wearing. In short, we feel you're up to something, don't we Dinah?"

She nodded. "You're giving out vibes, Weng. Sort of excited vibes."

"It is only that I have brought with me a letter for Miss Blaise, delivered to the penthouse this morning, Mrs. Collier," said Weng meekly. "I felt she ought to have it as soon as possible."

"How do you know it's that important?" asked Collier.

"Because I opened it, sir. Naturally."

"Naturally?"

"Oh, yes. When Miss Blaise is away from home I have that responsibility, Mr. Collier. I am happy to say that she places great trust in me."

"Of course," said Collier. "I'm sorry, Weng."

The houseboy smiled. "Not at all, sir."

Dinah said, "It's not a bad-news letter, I hope?"

"Oh no, Mrs. Collier. It is very amusing, and I am sure Miss Blaise will wish to share it with you."

"I'm getting all agog," said Collier. "How much farther?"

"Only a couple of hundred yards, sir. Just over that ridge."

"If I don't make it, put up a plaque where I fall. Something touching, about my dauntlessness."

"Certainly, Mr. Collier."

Minutes later they crested the ridge and looked down a gentle slope to a flat grassy area where a colony of small lightweight tents had been set up near a higher reach of the same stream where Weng had left the Rolls. Around the tents men and women were occupied in various ways, mostly in pairs, studying maps, lighting spirit stoves, cooking, checking footwear, tending feet, gossiping by a large refreshment tent or simply resting. The atmosphere was extraordinarily pleasant.

Weng said, "Over there. The Jetpacker tent in the corner." Collier felt uneasily out of place as they made their way round the perimeter with the picnic basket and cold-box, but they received nothing but amiable greetings and the occasional pleasantry from those they passed. As they drew near to the corner, Collier laughed suddenly.

Dinah said, "What's funny?"

"The scene, my darling. There's this little bluey-green tent, and lying on the grass outside is none other than Willie Garvin, Esquire, on his back, head pillowed on hands, eyes closed, one bare foot resting in the lap of his team-mate, Miss Blaise, who kneels at his feet doing something to one of his heels by the look of it.''

"Well, I expect he's got a blister or something."

"I'm not surprised. But what about the nursing care? I'm green with envy. When did you ever do anything for a blister of mine?"

"You never walked far enough to get one, honey."

"Nonsense! What about the time you took me to a supermarket?"

Modesty lifted her head and saw them. For a moment she stared in surprise, then her face lit up. "Dinah! Steve! Well, this is a lovely surprise. What on earth made you think of it?"

"Weng insisted," said Collier, halting and bending to kiss her. "Practically kidnapped us."

As the two women touched cheeks Willie opened his eyes and said, "Weng? What's that little yellow peril up to now?" Dinah pinpointed him by his voice, moved to kneel at his shoulder, and bent to kiss him.

Collier said incredulously, "What is this man? A sultan? A pasha? A three-button mandarin? There he lies with one girl cosseting his repellent feet and another licking his ill-favoured face. I demand to be informed of his secret!"

Dinah said, "I'm not licking his face, I'm whispering in his ear."

"Oh, that's fine. That's dandy. Never mind about upsetting poor old Collier's stomach with these revolting carryings-on."

"No, I won't mind. Modesty, would you be a true angel and take poor old Collier walkabout for a couple of minutes so I can talk to Willie without a background of static?"

Modesty laughed and stood up. "You go ahead. I'll take poor old Collier over to the refreshment place and buy him a sticky bun."

Weng said firmly, "No bun, please, Miss Blaise. I do not wish his appetite spoiled for my picnic."

"No bun," she agreed gravely. "Instead I'll take him to see a small plant we found coming in. We think it's a Frog Orchid."

"The picnic will be ready in ten minutes, Miss Blaise."

"We won't be late, Weng."

She strolled away with Collier, and as soon as they were alone he said soberly, "I'm glad of the chance to have a quiet word, Modesty. Do you mind if I ask you something?"

"*Mind*? As between you and me? Oh, come on now."

"Well, it's just a bit awkward. Look, when you got back from

Kalivari you saw to it that Dinah and I were packed off to your place in Morocco more or less straight from that safe house of Tarrant's where you came to see us. We had a lovely time at Pendragon, thank you kindly, and Moulay looked after us as if we were royalty, but I noticed that we were unobtrusively but very thoroughly guarded all the time. Danny Chavasse came to see us, once he'd sorted out things with Stavros and made sure there wouldn't be any annoying publicity, and Danny told us a whole lot about what happened to you and Willie on Kalivari. Things you and Willie didn't mention."

"There wasn't time. We only saw you for an hour or so before you went off to Tangier."

"It could have been fifty hours and you wouldn't have told us a damn thing worth knowing. You never do, either of you."

"That's because you get all angry and pettish, Steve. How does Danny Chavasse know about what happened on Kalivari, anyway? He wasn't there until right at the end."

"No, ducky, but a certain Ms. Johnson was, a somewhat gruesome wench by all accounts, and she spilled the whole can of beans to Danny and Maude Tiller, and Danny spilled them to me."

"And you spilled them to Dinah?"

"Oh God, darling, what chance do I stand against Dinah? Besides, I felt she ought to know what had been done to Willie, and how you put him together again, and then did that crazy Roman gladiator bit when the two of you clobbered those bastards who killed Molly Chen."

"All right, so where's the problem?"

"Well . . . Danny also explained about Salamander Four, and this Dead Man's Handle contract Pilgrim took out as a means of forcing you to do what he wanted. I didn't comment at the time, and I know this simply wouldn't have occurred to Dinah, but it seems to me that the contract must still be running. As I understand it, the fee was paid, and Salamander Four never renegue on a contract. That's what Tarrant said when he rousted us out in the middle of the night."

Collier hesitated, then went on a little awkwardly, "The thing is, I worry terribly about Dinah. I realise you can't keep us guarded all day every day for ever, but I just felt I had to know if she's at risk."

They were walking by the stream now, and Modesty slipped her arm through his. "Steve, surely you know neither Willie nor I would let a situation remain that left Dinah at risk?"

"Well, yes, I do sort of know that. But I've kept thinking about it and I'm damned if I can see that there's anything you can actually do to *stop* Salamander Four. Is there?"

Modesty halted, looking down at a small flower by a dry-stone wall, recalling the moment only fourteen hours after she had driven the sportsboat up the slipway on Kalivari. Stavros's private jet had flown her to London, and at nine o'clock that same evening she was sitting with Sir Gerald Tarrant in the smaller lounge of Rand's Club, in Whitehall, where for the past three years now members had been allowed to bring female guests. She wore a grey skirt and a thin black sweater with a superb necklace of pearls. Her nails were chipped and there were signs of abrasion on her hands, wrists, and one cheek, but the sweater hid grazes on her arms, and her hair was neatly groomed.

"His routine never varies from Monday to Friday," said Tarrant. "He'll dine alone, and between nine o'clock and five past he'll come out of the dining room, pass by where we're sitting, and go to that table in the far corner by the window. It's where he always sat before women were allowed in this lounge, and he won't change even though he hates seeing them here. A glass of port and a pot of coffee are already there waiting for him. He'll sit and read his newspaper for half an hour over the port and coffee, then he'll get up and go home in his chauffeur driven limousine to his Surrey mansion – ah, here he comes now."

Sir Angus McBeal, a director of fourteen thriving companies, emerged from the dining room. He was in his late fifties but looked older, a tall thin man with a long scrawny neck, wearing a dark suit and a wing collar, his grey hair sparse and carefully spread. He walked with his head tilted slightly back, pale brown eyes gazing expressionlessly over the heads of those he passed.

Tarrant stood up and said, "Hallo, McBeal. If you could spare a moment I'd be greatly obliged."

The man stopped, looked at Tarrant without interest, and said in a rather high impatient voice, "Evening, Tarrant. What is it?"

"I don't believe you've met my guest, Modesty Blaise."

Sir Angus McBeal lowered his gaze to look at her for the first time. "Good evening, madam," he said briefly.

Modesty said very softly, "I realise you know nothing about me, Sir Angus, but *if* you were one of the four principal directors of Salamander Four, which you also know nothing about of course, it would be rather different, because then you would know a great deal about me. You would also know that Salamander Four was recently paid fifty thousand pounds for a Dead Man's Handle contract on Professor Stephen Collier and his wife."

The pale brown eyes blinked once, and McBeal said coldly, "I've no idea what your guest is talking about, Tarrant."

"Perhaps not," said Tarrant quietly, "but do listen as if your life depended on it, McBeal – because it does."

McBeal blinked again.

Modesty said, "The contract on the Colliers was activated at noon today when Salamander Four's client failed to respond to their radio call. I was on Kalivari this morning, Sir Angus, and I can tell you that the reason the client let go of the handle is because he's a dead man. So are most of his colleagues, and the rest will be in Greek prisons shortly. His name was Thaddeus Pilgrim, and we can now forget that part of the business. But knowing Salamander Four's reputation, I'm aware that they may intend to implement the contract regardless of the client's death, so I want you to know this —"

She stopped speaking as a steward passed within a few paces, then went on conversationally as soon as he was out of earshot. "I want you to know that the Colliers are under my protection, and if anything happens to either of them I'll come after you and I'll kill you. That's a promise and I don't promise lightly. It's possible that Willie Garvin, whom you also know nothing about of course, will get to you first. Either way, you'll be dead."

Not a muscle of McBeal's face moved, but his eyes flickered and the long thin mouth opened as if to speak. Modesty lifted a hand and said, "There's not much more, so let me finish. Salamander Four might well think it a good move to try to dispose of me and Willie Garvin, but I don't think that would be sound policy for pragmatic businessmen like Salamander Four, and I'll tell you why. If any such attempt is made, and fails, then we'll come after you and we'll kill you, Sir Angus. Perhaps I should point out that we're very good indeed at *not* letting people kill us, because we've had many years of experience. You've had none."

She paused briefly, then added, "Neither have de Chardin, or Gesner, or Pereda, who are quite definitely three of the four principal directors of Salamander Four, though that can't be proved. However, any friend of theirs ought to tell them that they'll be on my hit list, too, if the Collier contract isn't cancelled. It seems to me bad business for Salamander Four's directors to take huge personal risks when they've got fifty thousand pounds for free and a dead client who can't complain – but that's up to them to decide, together with whoever is the fourth of the principal directors."

She stopped speaking and gazed at McBeal with one eyebrow lifted in query. He pursed his lips, nodding slowly, then said, "If I knew what you were talking about, Miss Blaise, I'd be inclined to say you had made your point."

"I'm glad to hear it, Sir Angus," she said politely. "But I shall want some very positive assurance."

He tilted his head back, looking down his nose at her frostily. "You'll hardly expect a written guarantee from these – what did you call them? – these Salamander people, whoever they may be."

"No." The eyes looking up at him seemed almost black, and in the blackness were pinpoints of icy flame. "But I'll want an unmistakable sign," she said. "They're very clever, these Salamander people, so it's up to them to think of something." She rested her hands flat on the table, palms down, in a curiously final gesture. "If I haven't had a sign in three weeks, I'll assume the Collier contract is still running and I'll take pre-emptive action. That's all."

Sir Angus McBeal sniffed. "I've never approved of the club allowing female guests, Tarrant," he said thinly. Then to Modesty: "If you'll excuse me now I'll wish you goodnight, Miss Blaise. I have some urgent calls to make."

With a curt nod he turned away. They watched him move across the lounge, but he did not go to the table where his port, coffee and newspaper were waiting. Instead he went straight out through the door leading to the cloakrooms and foyer.

Tarrant exhaled a sigh. "I rather fancy you made an impression on him," he murmured. "You certainly made one on me, by God."

*   *   *   *

Modesty went down on one knee and touched the little flower gently. "There. I'm sure it's a Frog Orchid."

"Or a very unusual hollyhock," said Collier.

She laughed and stood up, then took him by the lapels of his jacket and looked up at him soberly. "Forget about Salamander Four completely. Dinah's quite safe from them, so are you. I've been in contact with them, and only the other day I received absolute assurance that they've cancelled the contract."

"Eh? How did you make them do that?"

"That's my business. All you need know is that it didn't cost me anything."

"All right. But . . . what's this assurance?"

Mischief glinted in her eyes. "I'll show you when we're back in London. Oh, unless Weng's brought it with him. Yes, that's possible, even probable. He just couldn't wait, that's why he dragooned you into this jaunt."

"He said he was bringing an important letter for *you*."

"A minor bending of the truth, in Weng's view. Let's go back, Steve."

A hundred yards away, sitting by the tent, Dinah was saying, "You didn't mind my asking, Willie?"

"Course not. It was pretty dumb of Modesty and me not to realise you might be worried about Salamander Four. We should've told you it was all taken care of."

"I guess I should have known, but I just wanted to be sure. It would never occur to Steve, of course, he's so lovely and thick in some ways, but if anything happened to him . . . oh, golly."

"You're both safe, love. Modesty fixed it. And she's got a surprise for you when we're back 'ome."

Dinah said, "You're grinning." She reached out and ran gentle fingertips over his mouth. "Yes, I thought so. What have you been up to?"

"Not a thing, honest. Here come Steve and Modesty."

"It isn't a Frog Orchid," Collier announced authoritatively. "It's a seedling from what we botanists call the *metatarsal prolapsis*. Picnic ready, Weng lad? Ah, what a splendid sight. I trust that her chewing of Mr. Garvin's ear hasn't spoiled my good lady's appetite."

As Modesty sat down by the spread car rug she said, "Let's have that item for Mr. Collier please, Weng. I'm sure you brought it with you."

"Certainly, Miss Blaise." Weng put down the bottle of Bollinger he had taken from the cold-box, produced a long white envelope from his inside pocket and passed it to Modesty, who handed it on to Collier.

"Received seven days ago," she said. "It's for you, Professor."

The envelope was addressed to Modesty at her penthouse, had been delivered by hand and was slit open. Wondering, Collier peered inside then gingerly drew out a piece of blue-grey printed paper. He stared for long moments, swallowed hard, and croaked, "Oh, dear God."

Dinah said, "What is it, honey?"

"It . . . well, you won't understand what it *means*, sweetheart," said Collier, stumbling over the words, "but what it is, well, it's a draft issued by a Cayman Islands bank for·. . . for fifty thousand pounds in favour of – oh, Jesus – of Stephen Collier. And attached to it is a slip of plain paper which says, *Contract cancelled – fee returned herewith*. No signature. Just *S4* underneath."

Several seconds later Dinah let out her breath and said shakily, "Of course I know what it means, dopey. I didn't think *you* did. But we can't take it! I mean, it's for Modesty and Willie. It has to be."

Modesty said, "No chance, Dinah. Willie and I do light deliveries with a handcart at weekends, so we're loaded. Come on, let's eat."

Dinah said, "But —"

Weng broke in smoothly as he went on setting out his elegant picnic on a white linen cloth. "To save further argument, Miss Blaise, may I now give you a letter that arrived for you this morning?"

She looked at him in surprise. "You really did bring something for me?"

"Oh yes, Miss Blaise. As I told Mr. and Mrs. Collier." Weng took an airmail envelope from his pocket and passed it to her. She took out the letter, unfolded it and began to read. As she did so her dark eyebrows lifted steadily higher, and her mouth fell slightly open.

"The reaction," said Collier with profound interest, "matches that of Goofy in an animated cartoon, when he walks over a bridge and is halfway across before discovering the bridge isn't there."

Modesty lay slowly back on the grass and started to laugh, resting a forearm across her eyes. The laughter began with brief, unbelieving chuckles, but grew steadily more continuous until her whole body shook with it. Willie stared. Dinah said wonderingly, "What on earth . . . ?" Collier demanded with great indignation to be made privy to the contents of so remarkable an epistle; and Weng, with a smug air, began cutting up a long French loaf.

Modesty reached out, flapping the letter in Willie's direction with wordless exhortation. He took it, read soberly for thirty seconds, then keeled slowly over sideways to lie convulsed with almost silent laughter, trying feebly to pass the letter on to Collier, who drew back in alarm and said, "Oh no, I'm not reading that! It's a witch's spell, a cantrip producing instant insanity in all who gaze upon it. Better send for the men in white coats, Weng."

Dinah said, "Ah, for heaven's sake *read* it, Steve! You want me to die of curiosity?"

Weng said, "Permit me to explain, Mrs. Collier. The letter is from Captain Axel Valerius, recently master of the tanker *Marimba*. I think you know that Captain Valerius believed he and his crew were to be rescued when the tanker was illegally scuttled, but in fact Dr. Pilgrim had arranged for every soul to be murdered."

Dinah said, "Yes, Danny Chavasse told us about that, and about Miss Blaise getting a radio message to the captain, warning him."

"She did, and since Captain Valerius has been employed by Miss Blaise in the past, he took her warning seriously. Being a very intelligent gentleman, he therefore sailed the *Marimba* into a West African port, paid off the crew, and sold the tanker for twelve point five million dollars."

When Collier could speak he said, "*Sold* it? A whole tanker? But . . . but you can't do things like that!"

"On the contrary, Mr. Collier, such things are not difficult in the world of shipping. It would require a little simple forgery of documents, perhaps, but in an industry so complex and international as shipping, with its flags of convenience, it is never easy to begin satisfactory legal action, mainly because there are always several countries and several different legal systems involved." Weng set out glasses on a small tray. "I assure you it would be no problem for Captain Valerius to find a quick buyer for the *Marimba* at a bargain price. Also, he knew the legal owner was currently in terminal contention with Miss Blaise, and he may well have surmised that Dr. Pilgrim would never be in a position to seek redress."

"A wise surmise," said Collier, "and I like your phrase 'terminal contention' Weng. Very genteel." He shook his head as if the whole matter was beyond him. "Lest you should wonder, Dinah my darling, our two laughing friends have now subsided into limp, quivering heaps, and I still haven't fathomed the reason for such excessive merriment."

Dinah said, "Me neither. I mean, good for Captain Valerius, and it's kind of funny about him just sailing into port and selling off the whole shebang to become a multi-millionaire overnight. But it's not really

233

rolling-in-the-aisles funny, is it? Modesty? Willie? Or is it? Are we missing something?"

Willie steadied his breathing and said hoarsely, "What you're missing, Dinah is . . . no, you explain, Weng."

"Certainly, Mr. Garvin." Weng looked up from opening a carton of paté. "The excessive merriment, Mrs. Collier, arises from the fact that Captain Valerius is not only an intelligent gentleman but a very sporting gentleman. He much appreciates that Miss Blaise, by her activities on Kalivari, saved him from being murdered and also provided him with an immense fortune. He is therefore pleased to inform her that he has deposited ten percent of the proceeds of the *Marimba* sale to her credit at a Swiss bank by opening an account with them in her name. He begs that she will call there at her convenience to complete the necessary formalities of identity, specimen signature, etcetera."

After long seconds of utter silence Collier said blankly, "Ten percent? But that's . . . that's one and a quarter million dollars! One and a quarter *million*!"

Dinah said in a stunned voice, "You're . . . you're getting towards the multiple-echo again, tiger. Not that I blame you. I think I'm about to have hysterics."

Modesty sat up and wiped the wetness of tears from her cheeks. "A glass of champagne for Mrs. Collier's hysterics, Weng," she said. "Willie, I'll give you a cheque for your half, and we must have a word about Danny and Maude and Krolli, but that can wait." She inhaled deeply, and picked up the map-case lying beside her. "Some of us have got twenty miles of fell-running tomorrow, so we'd better get on with this picnic."

Collier sat cross-legged in a daze of pleasurable astonishment, looking slowly round at his companions. Weng was untwisting the wire on the cork of a bottle of champagne. Willie lay propped on an elbow, surveying the food set out on the cloth, still shaken by an occasional chuckle. Dinah sat beside him; sightless, she was absorbing every element of the scene, head cocked to the pop of the cork and gush of champagne, nostrils a little flared to the various scents of the food, blind eyes still wide with surprise, one hand resting on Willie's shoulder to gather the tactile impression of his relaxed amusement; and, Collier knew, to sense with deep gladness the full measure of Willie's recovery from what had been done to him.

Then there was Modesty, tousled and sweaty from the day's work but looking very good, a small frown of concentration touching her brow as she pored over the map on her knees, absently tucking the million dollar letter into her shirt pocket.

Peter O'Donnell
The Silver Mistress £1.95

To free Tarrant from the nightmare of Chateau Lancieux, Modesty and
Willie tangle with a hellish assortment of villains, including Mrs
McTurk, the genteel assassin, Anfel, with her wire garrotte, and Mr
Sexton, who claims to be the best combat-man in the world . . .

Sabre-Tooth £1.95

The second caper of Modesty and Willie Garvin takes them on an
exotic and danger-filled trail from London to Paris, Lisbon and Tangier,
bringing them to the mountains of Hindu Kush – home of a modern
Gengis Khan with an army of ruthless mercenaries.

'Fantastic adventure and compelling drama'
HALIFAX EVENING CHRONICLE

Peter O'Donnell
Modesty Blaise £1.95

The first assignment of Modesty and Willie Garvin for British
Intelligence was to destroy the unknowns who planned to hijack
diamonds worth ten million pounds. Their quest races from London to
the South of France, across the Mediterranean to Cairo ending in a
vicious battle on a tiny island as they fight alone against a private army
of killers.
Over one million copies of this series sold in Pan.

'Highly entertaining murderous fantasy' NEW YORKER

The Impossible Virgin £1.95

On a fast and furious caper to Central Africa, Modesty and Willie land
in the tightest of tight spots – facing professional killers, maddened
gorillas, savage warriors and the ferocious guardians of the Impossible
Virgin . . .

'Some terrifying scrapes' DAILY TELEGRAPH

Fiction

☐ **The Chains of Fate**	Pamela Belle	£2.95p
☐ **Options**	Freda Bright	£1.50p
☐ **The Thirty-nine Steps**	John Buchan	£1.50p
☐ **Secret of Blackoaks**	Ashley Carter	£1.50p
☐ **Lovers and Gamblers**	Jackie Collins	£2.50p
☐ **My Cousin Rachel**	Daphne du Maurier	£2.50p
☐ **Flashman and the Redskins**	George Macdonald Fraser	£1.95p
☐ **The Moneychangers**	Arthur Hailey	£2.95p
☐ **Secrets**	Unity Hall	£2.50p
☐ **The Eagle Has Landed**	Jack Higgins	£1.95p
☐ **Sins of the Fathers**	Susan Howatch	£3.50p
☐ **Smiley's People**	John le Carré	£2.50p
☐ **To Kill a Mockingbird**	Harper Lee	£1.95p
☐ **Ghosts**	Ed McBain	£1.75p
☐ **The Silent People**	Walter Macken	£2.50p
☐ **Gone with the Wind**	Margaret Mitchell	£3.95p
☐ **Wilt**	Tom Sharpe	£1.95p
☐ **Rage of Angels**	Sidney Sheldon	£2.50p
☐ **The Unborn**	David Shobin	£1.50p
☐ **A Town Like Alice**	Nevile Shute	£2.50p
☐ **Gorky Park**	Martin Cruz Smith	£2.50p
☐ **A Falcon Flies**	Wilbur Smith	£2.50p
☐ **The Grapes of Wrath**	John Steinbeck	£2.50p
☐ **The Deep Well at Noon**	Jessica Stirling	£2.95p
☐ **The Ironmaster**	Jean Stubbs	£1.75p
☐ **The Music Makers**	E. V. Thompson	£2.50p

Non-fiction

☐ **The First Christian**	Karen Armstrong	£2.50p
☐ **Pregnancy**	Gordon Bourne	£3.95p
☐ **The Law is an Ass**	Gyles Brandreth	£1.75p
☐ **The 35mm Photographer's Handbook**	Julian Calder and John Garrett	£6.50p
☐ **London at its Best**	Hunter Davies	£2.90p
☐ **Back from the Brink**	Michael Edwardes	£2.95p

☐	**Travellers' Britain**	⎫ Arthur Eperon	£2.95p
☐	**Travellers' Italy**	⎭	£2.95p
☐	**The Complete Calorie Counter**	Eileen Fowler	90p
☐	**The Diary of Anne Frank**	Anne Frank	£1.75p
☐	**And the Walls Came Tumbling Down**	Jack Fishman	£1.95p
☐	**Linda Goodman's Sun Signs**	Linda Goodman	£2.95p
☐	**The Last Place on Earth**	Roland Huntford	£3.95p
☐	**Victoria RI**	Elizabeth Longford	£4.95p
☐	**Book of Worries**	Robert Morley	£1.50p
☐	**Airport International**	Brian Moynahan	£1.95p
☐	**Pan Book of Card Games**	Hubert Phillips	£1.95p
☐	**Keep Taking the Tabloids**	Fritz Spiegl	£1.75p
☐	**An Unfinished History of the World**	Hugh Thomas	£3.95p
☐	**The Baby and Child Book**	Penny and Andrew Stanway	£4.95p
☐	**The Third Wave**	Alvin Toffler	£2.95p
☐	**Pauper's Paris**	Miles Turner	£2.50p
☐	**The Psychic Detectives**	Colin Wilson	£2.50p

All these books are available at your local bookshop or newsagent, or
can be ordered direct from the publisher. Indicate the number of copies
required and fill in the form below   12

....

Name_____
(Block letters please)

Address_____

_____

Send to CS Department, Pan Books Ltd, PO Box 40, Basingstoke, Hants
Please enclose remittance to the value of the cover price plus:
35p for the first book plus 15p per copy for each additional book ordered
to a maximum charge of £1.25 to cover postage and packing
Applicable only in the UK

While every effort is made to keep prices low, it is sometimes
necessary to increase prices at short notice. Pan Books reserve
the right to show on covers and charge new retail prices which
may differ from those advertised in the text or elsewhere